ONLY BELOVED

A SURVIVORS' CLUB NOVEL

Mary Balogh

A SIGNET BOOK

SIGNET

Published by New American Library,
an imprint of Penguin Random House LLC
375 Hudson Street, New York, New York 10014

This book is an original publication of New American Library.

First Printing, May 2016

For more information about Penguin Random House, visit penguin.com.

ISBN 978-0-451-47778-1

Printed in the United States of America
10 9 8 7 6 5 4 3 2 1

Penguin
Random
House

1

$\mathcal{G}$eorge Crabbe, Duke of Stanbrook, stood at the foot of the steps outside his London home on Grosvenor Square, his right hand still raised in farewell even though the carriage bearing his two cousins on their journey home to Cumberland was already out of sight. They had made an early start despite the fact that a few forgotten items, or items they feared they had forgotten, had twice delayed their departure while first a maid and then the housekeeper herself hurried upstairs to look in their vacated rooms just in case.

Margaret and Audrey were sisters and his second cousins, to be precise. They had come to London for the wedding of Imogen Hayes, Lady Barclay, to Percy, Earl of Hardford. Audrey was the bride's mother. Imogen had stayed at Stanbrook House too until her wedding two days ago, partly because she was a relative, but mainly because there was no one in the world George loved more. There were five others he loved equally well, it was true, though Imogen was the only woman and the only one related to him. The seven of them, himself included, were the members of the self-styled Survivors' Club.

A little over eight years ago George had made the decision to open Penderris Hall, his country seat in Cornwall, as a hospital and recovery center for military officers who had been severely wounded in the Napoleonic Wars and needed more intense and more extended care than could be provided by their families. He had hired a skilled physician and other staff members willing to act as nurses, and he had handpicked the patients from among those recommended to him. There had been more than two dozen in all, most of whom had survived and returned to their families or regiments after a few weeks or months. But six had remained for three years. Their injuries had varied widely. Not all had been physical. Hugo Emes, Lord Trentham, for example, had been brought there without a scratch on his body but out of his mind and with a straitjacket restraining him from doing violence to himself or others.

A deep bond had developed among the seven of them, an attachment too strong to be severed even after they left Penderris and returned to their separate lives. Those six people meant more to George than anyone else still living—though perhaps that was not quite accurate, for he was dearly fond too of his only nephew, Julian, and of Julian's wife, Philippa, and their infant daughter, Belinda. He saw them with fair frequency too and always with pleasure. They lived only a few miles from Penderris. Love, of course, did not move in hierarchies of preference. Love manifested itself in a thousand different ways, all of which were love in its entirety. A strange thing, that, if one stopped to think about it.

He lowered his hand, feeling suddenly foolish to be waving farewell to empty air, and turned back to the house. A footman hovered at the door, no doubt anxious to close it. He was probably shivering in his shoes. A brisk early-morning breeze was blowing across the square directly at him, though there was plenty of blue sky above along with some scudding clouds in promise of a lovely mid-May day.

He nodded to the young man and sent him to the kitchen to fetch coffee to the library.

The morning post had not arrived yet, he could see when he entered the room. The surface of the large oak desk before the window was bare except for a clean blotter and an inkpot and two quill pens. There would be the usual pile of invitations when the post did arrive, it being the height of the London Season. He would be required to choose among balls and soirees and concerts and theater groups and garden parties and Venetian breakfasts and private dinners and a host of other entertainments. Meanwhile his club offered congenial company and diversion, as did Tattersall's and the races and his tailor and boot maker. And if he did not wish to go out, he was surrounded in this very room by bookshelves that reached from floor to ceiling, interrupted only by doors and windows. If there was room for one more book on any of the shelves, he would be surprised. There were even a few books among them that he had not yet read but would doubtless enjoy.

It was a pleasant feeling to know that he might do whatever he wished with his time, even nothing at all if he so chose. The weeks leading up to Imogen's wedding and the few days since had been exceedingly busy ones and had allowed him very little time to himself. But he had enjoyed the busyness and had to admit that there was a certain flatness mingled with his pleasure this morning in the knowledge that yet again he was alone and free and beholden to no one. The house seemed very quiet, even though his cousins had not been noisy or demanding houseguests. He had enjoyed their company far more than he had expected. They were virtual strangers, after all. He had not seen either sister for a number of years before this past week.

Imogen herself was the closest of friends but could have caused some upheaval due to her impending nuptials. She had not. She was not a fussy bride in the least. One would hardly have known, in fact, that she was preparing for her wedding, except that there had been a new and unfamiliar glow about her that had warmed George's heart.

The wedding breakfast had been held at Stanbrook House. He had insisted upon it, though both Ralph and Flavian, their fellow Survivors, had offered to host it too. Half the *ton* had been present, filling the ballroom almost to overflowing and inevitably spilling out into other rooms in the hours following the meal and all the speeches. And *breakfast* was certainly a misnomer, since very few of the guests had left until late in the evening.

George had enjoyed every moment.

But now the festivities were all over, and after the

wedding Imogen had left with Percy for a honeymoon in Paris. Now Audrey and Margaret were gone too, although before leaving they had hugged him tightly, thanked him effusively for his hospitality, and begged him to come and stay with them in Cumberland sometime soon.

There was a strong sense of finality about this morning. There had been a flurry of weddings in the last two years, including those of all the Survivors and George's nephew, all the people most dear to him in the world. Imogen had been the last of them—with the exception of himself, of course. But he hardly counted. He was forty-eight years old and, after eighteen years of marriage, he had been a widower for more than twelve years.

He was glad to see that the fire in the library had been lit. He had got chilled standing outside. He took the chair to one side of the fireplace and held out his hands to the blaze. The footman brought the tray a few minutes later, poured his coffee, and set the cup and saucer on the small table beside him along with a plate of sweet biscuits that smelled of butter and nutmeg.

"Thank you." George added milk and a little sugar to the dark brew and remembered for no apparent reason how it had always irritated his wife that he acknowledged even the slightest service paid him by a servant. Doing so would only lower him in their esteem, she had always explained to him.

It seemed almost incredible that all six of his fellow Survivors had married within the past two years. It was as if they had needed the three years after leaving Penderris to adjust to the outside world again after the sheltered safety the house had provided during their recovery, but had then rushed joyfully back into full and fruitful lives. Perhaps, having hovered for so long close to death and insanity, they had needed to celebrate life itself. He was quite certain too that they had all made happy marriages. Hugo and Vincent each had a child already, and there was another on the way for Vincent and Sophia. Ralph and Flavian were also in expectation of fatherhood. Even Ben, another of their number, had whispered two days ago that Samantha had been feeling queasy for the past few mornings and was hopeful that it was in a good cause.

It was all thoroughly heartwarming to the man who had opened his home and his heart to men—and one woman—who had been broken by war and might have remained forever on the fringes of their own lives if he had not done so. If they had survived at all, that was.

George looked speculatively at the biscuits but did not take one. He picked up his coffee cup, however, and warmed his hands about it, ignoring the handle.

Was it downright contrary of him to be feeling ever so slightly depressed this morning? Imogen's wedding had been a splendidly festive and happy occasion. George loved to see her glow, and, despite some early misgivings, he liked Percy too and thought it probable he was the perfect husband for her. George was very fond of the wives of the other Survivors too. In many ways he felt like a smugly proud father who had married off his brood to so many happily-ever-afters.

Perhaps that was the trouble, though. For he was not their father, was he? Or anyone else's for that matter. He frowned into his coffee, considered adding more sugar, decided against doing so, and took another sip. His only son had died at the age of seventeen during the early years of the Peninsular Wars, and his wife—Miriam—had taken her own life just a few months later.

He was, George thought as he gazed sightlessly into his cup, very much alone—though no more so now than he had been before Imogen's wedding and all the others. Julian was his late brother's son, not his own, and his six fellow Survivors had all left Penderris Hall five years ago. Although the bonds of friendship had remained strong and they all gathered for three weeks every year, usually at Penderris, they were not literally family. Even Imogen was only his second cousin once removed.

They had moved on with their lives, those six, and left him behind. And what a blasted pathetic, self-pitying thought *that* was.

George drained his cup, set it down none too gently on the saucer, put both on the tray, and got restlessly to his feet. He moved behind the desk and stood looking out through the window onto the square. It was still early enough that there was very little activity out there. The clouds were sparser than they had been earlier, the sky a more uniform blue. It was the sort of day designed to lift the human spirit.

He was lonely, damn it. To the marrow of his bones and the depths of his soul.

He almost always had been.

His adult life had begun brutally early. He had taken up a military commission with great excitement at the age of seventeen, having convinced his father that a career in the army was what he wanted more than anything else in life. But just four months later he had been summoned back home when his father had learned that he was dying. Before he turned eighteen, George had sold out his cornetcy, married Miriam, lost his father, and succeeded him to the title Duke of Stanbrook himself. Brendan had been born before he was nineteen.

It seemed to George, looking back, that all his adult life he had never been anything but lonely, with the exception of that brilliant flaring of exuberant joy he had experienced all too briefly when he was with his regiment. And there had been a few years with Brendan . . .

He clasped his hands behind his back and remembered too late that he had told Ralph and Ben yesterday that he would join them for a ride in Hyde Park this morning if his cousins made the early departure they had planned. All the Survivors had come to London for Imogen's wedding, and all were still here, except Vincent and Sophia, who had left for Gloucestershire yesterday. They preferred being at home, for Vincent was blind and felt more comfortable in the familiar surroundings of Middlebury Park. And the bride and groom, of course, were on their way to Paris.

There was no reason for George to feel lonely and there would be none even after the other four had left London and returned home. There were other friends here, both male and female. And in the country there were neighbors he considered friends. And there were Julian and Philippa.

But he *was* lonely, damn it. And the thing was that he had only recently admitted it to himself—only during the past week, in fact, amid all the happy bustle of preparations for the final Survivor wedding. He had even asked himself in some alarm if he resented Percy for winning Imogen's heart and hand, for being able to make her laugh again and glow. He had asked himself if perhaps he loved her himself. Well, yes, he did, he had concluded after some frank consideration. There was absolutely no doubt about it—just as there was no doubt that his love for her was not *that* kind of love. He loved her exactly as he loved Vincent and Hugo and the rest of them—deeply but purely platonically.

During the last few days he had toyed with the idea of hiring a mistress again. He had done so occasionally down the years. A few times he had even indulged in discreet affairs with ladies of his own class—all widows for whom he had felt nothing but liking and respect.

He did not want a mistress.

Last night he had lain awake, staring up at the shadowed canopy above his bed, unable to coax his mind to relax and his body to sleep. It had been one of those nights during which, for no discernible reason, sleep eluded him, and the notion had popped into his head, seemingly from nowhere, that perhaps he ought to marry. Not for love or issue—he was too old for either romance or fatherhood. Not that he was physically too old for the latter, but he did not want a child, or children, at Penderris again. Besides, he would have to marry a young woman if he wanted to populate his nursery, and the thought of marrying someone half his age held no appeal. It might for many men, but he was not one of them. He could admire the young beauties who crowded fashionable ballrooms during the

Season each spring, but he felt not the slightest desire to bed any of them.

What had occurred to his mind last night was that marriage might bring him companionship, possibly a real friendship. Perhaps even someone in the nature of a soul mate. And, yes, someone to lie beside him in bed at night to soothe his loneliness and provide the regular pleasures of sex.

He had been celibate a little too long for comfort.

Two horses were clopping along the other side of the square, he could see, led by a groom on horseback. Both horses bore sidesaddles. The door of the Rees-Parry house directly opposite opened, and the two young daughters of the house stepped out and were helped into the saddle by the groom. Both girls wore smart riding habits. The faint sounds of feminine laughter and high spirits carried across the square and through the closed window of the library. They rode off in evident high spirits, the groom following a respectful distance behind them.

Youth could be delightful to behold, but he felt no yearning to be a part of it.

The idea that had come to him last night had not been purely hypothetical. It had come complete with the image of a particular woman, though why her he could not explain to himself. He scarcely knew her, after all, and had not seen her for more than a year. But there she had been, quite vivid in his mind's eye while he had been thinking that maybe he ought to consider marrying again. Marrying *her*. It had seemed to him that she would be the perfect—the *only*—choice.

He had dozed off eventually and woken early to take

breakfast with his cousins before seeing them on their way. Only now had he remembered those bizarre night-time yearnings. Surely he must have been at least half asleep and half dreaming. It would be madness to tie himself down with a wife again, especially one who was a virtual stranger. What if she did not suit him after all? What if he did not suit her? An unhappy marriage would be worse than the loneliness and emptiness that some-times conspired to drag down his spirits.

But now the same thoughts were back. Why the devil had he not gone riding? Or to White's Club? He could have had his coffee there and occupied himself with the congenial conversation of male acquaintants or dis-tracted himself with a perusal of the morning papers.

Would she have him if he asked? Was it conceited of him to believe that she would indeed? Why, after all, would she refuse him unless perhaps she was deterred by the fact that she did not love him? But she was no longer a young woman, her head stuffed with romantic dreams. She was probably as indifferent to romance as he was himself. He had much to offer any woman, even apart from the obvious inducements of a lofty title and fortune. He had a steady character to offer as well as friendship and . . . Well, he had *marriage* to offer. She had never been married.

Would he merely be making an idiot of himself, though, if he married again now when he was well into middle age? But why? Men his age and older were mar-rying all the time. And it was not as though he had his sights fixed upon some sweet young thing fresh out of the schoolroom. That *would* be pathetic. He would be seeking comfort with a mature woman who would perhaps welcome a similar comfort into her own life.

It was absurd to think that he was too old. Or that she was. Surely everyone was entitled to some companionship, some contentment in life even when youth was a thing of the past. He was not seriously considering doing it, though, was he?

A tap on the library door preceded the appearance in the room of a youngish man carrying a bundle of letters.

"Ethan." George nodded to his secretary. "Anything of burning interest or vast moment?"

"No more than the usual, Your Grace," Ethan Briggs said as he divided the pile in two and set each down on the desk. "Business and social." He indicated each pile in turn, as he usually did.

"Bills?" George jutted his chin in the direction of the business pile.

"One from Hoby's for a pair of riding boots," his secretary said, "and various wedding expenses."

"And they need my inspection?" George looked pained. "Pay them, Ethan."

His secretary scooped up the first pile.

"Take the others away too," George said, "and send polite refusals."

"To all of them, Your Grace?" Briggs raised his eyebrows. "The Marchioness of—"

"All," George said. "And everything that comes for the next several days until you receive further instructions from me. I am leaving town."

"Leaving?" Again the raised eyebrows.

Briggs was an efficient, thoroughly reliable secretary.

He had been with the Duke of Stanbrook for almost six years. But no one is perfect, George mused. The man had a habit of repeating certain words his employer addressed to him as though he could not quite believe he had heard correctly.

"But there is your speech in the House of Lords the day after tomorrow, Your Grace," he said.

"It will keep." George waved a dismissive hand. "I will be leaving tomorrow."

"For Cornwall, Your Grace?" Briggs asked. "Do you wish me to write to inform the housekeeper—"

"Not for Penderris Hall," George said. "I will be back . . . well, when I return. In the meantime, pay my bills and refuse my invitations and do whatever else I keep you busy doing."

His secretary picked up the remaining pile from the desk, acknowledged his employer with a respectful bow, and left the room.

So he was going, was he? George asked himself. To propose marriage to a lady he scarcely knew and had not even seen in a longish while?

How did one propose marriage? The last time he had been seventeen years old and it had been a mere formality, both their fathers having agreed upon the match, come to terms, and signed the contract. A mere son's and daughter's wishes and sensibilities had not been taken into consideration or even consulted, especially when one of the fathers already had a foot in the grave and was in some hurry to see his son settled. At least this time George knew the lady a little better than he had known Miriam. He knew what she *looked* like at least and what her voice sounded like. The first time he had set eyes upon Miriam had been on the occasion of his proposal, conducted with stammering formality under the stern gaze of her father and his own.

Was he really going to do this?

What the devil would she think?

What would she *say*?

2

One might almost be lulled into believing that spring was turning to summer even though it was still only May. The sky was a clear deep blue, the sun was shining, and the warmth in the air made her shawl not only unnecessary but actually quite burdensome, Dora Debbins thought as she let herself in through the front door and called to let Mrs. Henry, her housekeeper, know that she was home.

Home was a modest cottage in the village of Inglebrook in Gloucestershire, where she had lived for the past nine years. She had been born in Lancashire, and after her mother ran away when she was seventeen, she had done her best to manage her father's large home and be a mother to her younger sister, Agnes. When she was thirty, their father had married a widow who had long been a friend of the family. Agnes, who was then eighteen, had married a neighbor who had once paid his addresses to Dora, though Agnes did not know that. Within one year Dora had realized she was no longer needed by anyone and indeed did not belong anywhere.

Her father's new wife had begun to hint that Dora ought to consider other options than remaining at home. Dora had considered seeking employment as a governess or a companion or even a housekeeper, but none of the three had really appealed to her.

Then one day by happy chance she had seen a notice in her father's morning paper, inviting a respectable gentleman or lady to come and teach music to a number of pupils on a variety of different instruments in and about the village of Inglebrook in Gloucestershire. It was not a salaried position. Indeed, it was not a real position at all. There was no employer, no guarantee of work or income, only the prospect of setting up a busy and independent business that would almost certainly supply the teacher concerned with an adequate income. The notice had also made mention of a cottage in the village that was for sale at a reasonable price. Dora had had the necessary qualifications, and her father had been willing to pay the cost of the house— more or less matching the amount of the dowry he had given Agnes when she married. He had looked almost openly relieved, in fact, at such a relatively easy solution to the problem of having his elder daughter and his new wife living together under his roof.

Dora had written to the agent named in the notice, had received a swift and favorable reply, and had moved, sight unseen, to her new home. She had lived here busily and happily ever since, never short of pupils and never without income. She was not wealthy—far from it. But what she earned from the lessons was quite adequate to provide for her needs with a little to spare for what she termed her rainy-day savings. She could even afford to have Mrs. Henry clean and cook and shop for her. The villagers had accepted her into their community, and while she had no really close friends here, she did have numerous friendly acquaintances.

She went directly upstairs to her room to remove her shawl and bonnet, to fluff up her flattened hair before the mirror, to wash her hands at the basin in her small dressing room, and to look out through the back window at the garden below. From up here it looked neat and colorful, but she knew she would be out there in the next day or two with her fork and trowel, waging war upon the ever-encroaching weeds. Actually she was fond of weeds, but not—please, please—in her garden. Let them bloom and thrive in all the surrounding hedgerows and meadows and she would admire them all day long.

Oh, she thought with a sudden pang, how she *still* missed Agnes. Her sister had lived with her here for a year after losing her husband. She had spent much of her time outdoors, painting the wildflowers. Agnes was wondrously skilled with watercolors. That had been such a happy year, for Agnes was like the daughter she had never had and never would. But Dora had known the interlude would not last. She had not allowed herself even to hope that it would. It had not, because Agnes had found love.

Dora was fond of Flavian, Viscount Ponsonby, Agnes's second husband. Very fond, actually, though initially she had had doubts about him, for he was handsome and charming and witty but had a mocking eyebrow she had distrusted. Upon closer acquaintance, however, she had been forced to admit that he was the ideal partner for her quiet, demure sister. When they married here in the village last year, it had been evident to Dora that it was, or soon would be, a love match. And indeed it had turned out to be just that. They were happy together, and there was to be a child in the autumn.

Dora turned away from the window when she realized that she was no longer really seeing the garden. They lived in faraway Sussex, Agnes and Flavian. But it was not the end of the world, was it? Already she had been to visit them a couple of times, at Christmas and again at Easter. She had stayed for two weeks each time, though Flavian had urged her to stay longer and Agnes had told her with obvious sincerity that she might live with them forever if she chose.

"Forever *and* a day," Flavian had added.

Dora did not so choose. Living alone by its very definition is a solitary business, but solitude was infinitely preferable to any alternative she had ever discovered. She was thirty-nine years old and a spinster. The alternatives for her were to be someone's governess or companion on the one hand or a dependent relative on the other, moving endlessly from her sister's home to her father's to her brother's. She was very, very thankful for her modest, pretty cottage and her independent employment and lonely existence. No, not lonely—solitary.

She could hear the clatter of china downstairs and knew that Mrs. Henry was deliberately hinting to her, without actually calling upstairs, that the tea had been brewed and carried into the sitting room, and that it would go cold if she did not come down soon.

She went down.

"I suppose you heard all about the big wedding in London when you went up to Middlebury, did you?" Mrs. Henry asked, hovering hopefully in the doorway while Dora poured herself a cup of tea and buttered a scone.

"From Lady Darleigh?" She smiled. "Yes, she told me it was a very grand and a very joyous occasion. They married at St. George's on Hanover Square, and the Duke of Stanbrook hosted a lavish wedding breakfast. I am very happy for Lady Barclay, though I suppose I must refer to her now as the Countess of Hardford. I thought her very charming when I met her last year, but very reserved too. Lady Darleigh says her new husband adores her. That is very romantic, is it not?"

How lovely it must be . . .

She took a bite of her scone. Sophia, Lady Darleigh, who had arrived back at Middlebury Park from London with her husband the day before yesterday, had said more about the wedding they had gone there to attend, but Dora was too tired to elaborate further now. She had squeezed an extra pianoforte lesson for the viscountess into what was already a full day of work and had had scarcely a moment to herself since breakfast.

"I will no doubt have a long letter from Agnes about it in the next day or two," she said when she saw Mrs. Henry's look of disappointment. "I will share with you what she has to say about the wedding."

Her housekeeper nodded and shut the door.

Dora took another bite from her scone, and found herself suddenly lost in memories of last year and a few of the happiest days of her life just before the excruciatingly painful one when Agnes drove off with her new husband and Dora, smiling, waved them on their way.

How pathetic that she relived those days so often. Viscount and Viscountess Darleigh, who lived at Middle-bury Park just beyond the village, had had houseguests—very illustrious ones, all of them titled. Dora and Agnes had been invited to the house more than once while they were there, and a few times various groupings of the guests had called at the cottage and even taken tea here. Agnes was a close friend of the viscountess, and Dora was comfortable with them herself as she gave music lessons to both the viscount and his wife. On the basis of this acquaintance, she and Agnes had been invited to dine one evening, and Dora had been asked to play for the company afterward.

All the guests had been incredibly kind. And flatter-ing. Dora had played the harp, and they had not wanted her to stop. And then she had played the pianoforte and they had urged her to keep on playing. She had been led up to the drawing room for tea afterward on the arm of no less a personage than the Duke of Stanbrook. Earlier, she had sat between him and Lord Darleigh at dinner. She would have been awed into speechlessness if she had not been long familiar with the viscount and if the duke had not made an effort to set her at her ease. He had seemed an almost frighteningly austere-looking noble-man until she looked into his eyes and saw nothing but kindness there.

She had been made to feel like a celebrity. Like a star. And for those few days she had felt wondrously alive. How sad—no, pathetic—that in all her life there were no other memories half so vivid with which to regale herself when she sat alone like this, a little too weary to read. Or at night, when she lay in bed unable to fall asleep, as she sometimes did.

They called themselves a club, the male guests who had stayed at Middlebury Park for three weeks—the Survivors' Club. They had survived both the wars against Napoleon Bonaparte and the dreadful injuries they had suffered during them. Lady Barclay was a member too—the lady who had just married. She had not been an officer herself, of course, but her first husband had, and she had witnessed his death from torture, poor lady, after he had been captured in Portugal. Viscount Darleigh himself had been blinded. Flavian, Lord Ponsonby, Agnes's husband, had suffered such severe head injuries that he could neither think nor speak nor understand what was said to him when he was brought back to England. Baron Trentham, Sir Benedict Harper, and the Earl of Berwick, the last of whom had inherited a dukedom since last year, had all suffered terribly as well. The Duke of Stanbrook years ago had gathered them all at his home in Cornwall and given them the time and space and care they needed to heal and recuperate. They were all now married, except the duke himself, who was an older man and a widower.

Dora wondered if they would ever again gather at Middlebury Park for one of their annual reunions. If they did, then perhaps she would be invited to join them again—maybe even to play for them. She was, after all, Agnes's sister, and Agnes was now married to one of them.

She picked up her cup and sipped her tea. But it had

grown tepid and she pulled a face. It was entirely her own fault, of course. But she hated tea that was not piping hot.

And then a knock sounded on the outer door. Dora sighed. She was just too weary to deal with any chance caller. Her last pupil for the day had been fourteen-year-old Miranda Corley, who was as reluctant to play the pianoforte as Dora was to teach her. She was utterly devoid of musical talent, poor girl, though her parents were convinced she was a prodigy. Those lessons were always a trial to them both.

Perhaps Mrs. Henry would deal with whoever was standing on her doorstep. Her housekeeper knew how tired she always was after a full day of giving lessons and guarded her privacy a bit like a mother hen. But this was not to be one of those occasions, it seemed. There was a tap on the sitting room door, and Mrs. Henry opened it and stood there for a moment, her eyes as wide as twin saucers.

"It is for you, Miss Debbins," she said before stepping to one side.

And, as though her memories of last year had summoned him right to her sitting room, in walked the Duke of Stanbrook.

He stopped just inside the door while Mrs. Henry closed it behind him.

"Miss Debbins." He bowed to her. "I trust I have not called at an inconvenient time?"

Any memory Dora had had of how kindly and approachable and really quite human the duke was fled without a trace, and she was every bit as smitten by awe as she had been when she met him for the first time in the drawing room at Middlebury Park. He was tall and distinguished looking, with dark hair silvered at the temples, and austere, chiseled features consisting of a straight nose, high cheekbones, and rather thin lips. He bore himself with a stiff, forbidding air she could not recall from last year. He was the quintessential fashionable, aloof aristocrat from head to toe, and he seemed to fill Dora's sitting room and deprive it of most of the breathable air.

She realized suddenly that she was still sitting and staring at him all agape, like a thunderstruck idiot. He had spoken to her in the form of a question and was regarding her with raised eyebrows in expectation of an answer. She scrambled belatedly to her feet and curtsied. She tried to remember what she was wearing and whether her garments included a cap.

"Your Grace," she said. "No, not at all. I have given my last music lesson for the day and have been having my tea. The tea will be cold in the pot by now. Let me ask Mrs. Henry—"

But he held up one elegant staying hand.

"Pray do not concern yourself," he said. "I have just finished taking refreshments with Vincent and Sophia."

With Viscount and Lady Darleigh.

"I was at Middlebury Park earlier today," she said, "giving Lady Darleigh a pianoforte lesson since she missed her regular one while she was in London for Lady Barclay's wedding. She did not mention that you had come back with them. Not that she was obliged to do so, of course." Her cheeks grew hot. "It was none of my business."

"I arrived an hour ago," he told her, "unexpected but

not quite uninvited. Every time I see Vincent and his lady, they urge me to visit anytime I wish. They always mean it, I'm sure, but I also know they never expect that I *will*. This time I did. I followed almost upon their heels from London, in fact, and, bless their hearts, I do believe they were happy to see me. Or not see, in Vincent's case. Sometimes one almost forgets that he cannot literally see."

Dora's cheeks grew hotter. For how long had she been keeping him standing there by the door? Whatever would he think of her rustic manners?

"But will you not have a seat, Your Grace?" She indicated the chair across the hearth from her own. "Did you walk from Middlebury? It is a lovely day for air and exercise, is it not?"

He had arrived from London *an hour ago*? He had taken tea with Viscount and Lady Darleigh and had stepped out immediately after to come . . . *here*? Perhaps he brought a message from Agnes?

"I will not sit," he said. "This is not really a social call."

"Agnes—?" Her hand crept to her throat. His stiff, formal manner was suddenly explained. There was something wrong with Agnes. She had miscarried.

"Your sister appeared to be glowing with good health when I saw her a few days ago," he said. "I am sorry if my sudden appearance has alarmed you. I have no dire news of any kind. Indeed, I came to ask a question."

Dora clasped both hands at her waist and waited for him to continue. A day or two after the dinner at Middlebury last year he had come to the cottage with a few of the others to thank her for playing and to express the hope that she would do so again before their visit came to an end. It had not happened. Was he going to ask now? For this evening, perhaps?

But that was not what happened.

"I wondered, Miss Debbins," he said, "if you might do me the great honor of marrying me."

Sometimes words were spoken and one heard them quite clearly, but as a series of separate, unconnected sounds rather than as phrases and sentences that conveyed meaning. One needed a little time in order to put the sounds together and understand what was being communicated.

Dora heard his words, but for a few moments she did not comprehend their meaning. She merely stared and gripped her hands and thought, with a strange, foolish sort of disappointment, that he did not after all want her to play the harp or the pianoforte this evening.

Only to marry her.

What?

He looked suddenly apologetic, and thereby resembled more the man she remembered from last year. "I have not made a marriage proposal since I was seventeen," he said, "more than thirty years ago. But even with that fact as an excuse, I realize that this was a very lame effort. I have had ample time since leaving London to compose a pretty speech but have failed to do so. I have not even brought flowers or gone down upon bended knee. What a sad figure of a suitor you will think me, Miss Debbins."

"You want me to marry you?" She indicated herself

with a hand over her heart, as though the room was full of single ladies and she was unsure that he meant her rather than any of the others.

He clasped his hands behind his back and sighed aloud. "You know about the wedding in London less than a week ago, of course," he said. "You doubtless heard about the Survivors' Club when we were all staying here at Middlebury Park last year. You would know about us from Flavian even if from no one else. We are very close friends. During the past two years all six of the others have married. After Imogen's wedding was over last week and the last of my guests left my London home a few days ago, it occurred to me that I had been left behind. It occurred to me that . . . I was perhaps just a touch lonely."

Dora felt half robbed of breath. One did not expect a nobleman with his . . . *presence* either to experience such a lack in his life or to admit to it if he did. It was the last thing she would have expected him to say.

"And it struck me," he continued when she did not fill the short silence that succeeded his words, "that I really do not want to be lonely. Yet I cannot expect my friends, no matter how dear they are, to fill the void or to satisfy the hunger that is at the very core of my being. I would not even wish them to try. I could, however, hope for such a thing, even perhaps expect it, from a wife."

"But—" She pressed her hand harder to her bosom. "But why *me*?"

"I thought that perhaps you are a little lonely too, Miss Debbins," he said, half smiling.

She wished suddenly that she were sitting. Was this the impression she gave the world—that she was a lonely, pathetic spinster, still holding out the faint hope that some gentleman would be desperate enough to take her? *Desperate,* however, was not a word that could possibly describe the Duke of Stanbrook. He must be some years older than she, but he was still eminently eligible in every imaginable way. He could have almost any single woman—or girl—he chose. His words, though, had wounded her, humiliated her.

"I live a *solitary* life, Your Grace," she said, choosing her words carefully. "By choice. Solitude and loneliness are not necessarily interchangeable words."

"I have offended you, Miss Debbins," he said. "I do apologize. I am being unusually gauche. May I accept your offer of a seat after all? I need to explain myself far more lucidly. I did *not,* I assure you, search my mind for the loneliest lady of my acquaintance, pick on you, and dash off to propose marriage to you. Forgive me if I have given that impression."

"It would be too absurd to believe that you need choose thus anyway," she said, indicating the chair opposite hers again and sinking gratefully back into her own. She was not sure how much longer her knees would have held her upright.

"It occurred to me after I had given the matter some thought," he said as he seated himself, "that what I most need and want is a companion and friend, someone with whom I can be comfortable, someone who would be content to be always at my side. Someone . . . all my own.

And someone to share my bed. Forgive me—but it ought to be mentioned. I wished—wish—for more than a platonic relationship."

Dora was looking at her hands. Her cheeks were hot again—well, of course they were. But she lifted her eyes to his now, and the reality of what was happening rushed at her. He was *the Duke of Stanbrook*. She had been flattered, made breathless, been ridiculously pleased by his courteous attentions last year. One afternoon he and Flavian had escorted Agnes and her all the way home from Middlebury, and he had drawn her arm through his and conversed amicably with her and set her quite at her ease while they outpaced the other two. She had relished every moment of that walk and had relived it over and over again in the days following, and, indeed, ever since. Now he was *here* in her sitting room. He had come to propose marriage to her.

"But why me?" she asked again. Her voice sounded shockingly normal.

"When I thought all these things," he said, "they came with the image of you. I cannot explain why. I do not believe I know why. But it was of you I thought. Only you. If you refuse me, I believe I will remain as I am."

He was looking directly into her face, and now she saw not just an austere aristocrat. She saw a man. It was a stupid thought, one she would not have been able to explain if she had been called upon to do so. She felt breathless again and a bit shivery and was glad she was sitting down.

And someone to share my bed.

"I am thirty-nine years old, Your Grace," she told him.

"Ah," he said and half smiled again. "I have the effrontery, then, to be asking you to marry an older man. I am nine years your senior."

"I would be unable to bear you children," she said. "At least—" She had not gone through the change of life yet, but it must surely happen soon.

"I have a nephew," he said, "a worthy young man of whom I am dearly fond. He is married and already father to a daughter. Sons will no doubt follow. I am not interested in having children in my nursery again, Miss Debbins."

She remembered that he had had a son who had been killed in Portugal or Spain during the wars. The duke must have been very young when that son was born. Then she recalled what he had said earlier about not having made a marriage proposal since he was seventeen.

"It is a companion I want," he repeated. "A friend. A *woman* friend. A wife, in fact. I do not have grand romance or romantic passion to offer, I am afraid. I am past the age of such flights of fancy. But though I do not know you well or you me, I believe we would deal well together. I admire your talent as a musician and the beauty of soul it suggests. I admire your modesty and dignity, your devotion to your sister. I like your appearance. I like the idea of looking at you every day for the rest of my life."

Dora gazed at him, startled. She had been pretty once upon a time, but youth and she had parted company long ago. The best she saw in her glass now was neatness and . . . ordinariness. She saw a staid spinster in her middle years. He, on the other hand, was . . . well, even with his forty-eight years and his silvering hair, he was gorgeous.

She bit her lower lip and gazed back at him. How could they possibly be *friends*?

"I would not have any idea how to be a duchess," she said.

She watched his eyes smile, and she smiled ruefully back at him and then actually laughed. So, incredibly, did he. And she was glad yet again that she was sitting. Was there a word more powerful than *gorgeous*?

"I grant," he said, "that if you were my wife you would also be my duchess. But—I hesitate to disappoint you—it does not mean wearing a tiara and an ermine-trimmed robe every day, you know. Or even every year. And it does not involve rubbing shoulders with the king and his court every week. On the other hand, there may be some amusement to be derived from being addressed as 'Your Grace' instead of just plain Miss Debbins."

"I am rather fond of Miss Debbins," she said. "She has been with me for almost forty years."

His smile faded and he looked austere again.

"Are you happy, Miss Debbins?" he asked. "I recognize that you may well be. You have a cozy home here and productive, independent employment doing something you love. You are much appreciated both at Middlebury and, I believe, in the village for your talent and for your good nature." He paused and met her gaze again. "Or is there a chance that you too would like a friend and companion all your own, that you too would like to belong exclusively to one other person and have him belong to you? Is there a chance that you would be willing to leave your life here and come to Cornwall and Penderris with me? Not just as my friend, but as my life's partner?" He paused once more for a moment. "*Will* you marry me?"

His eyes held hers. And all her defenses fell away, as did all the assurances she had given herself over the years that she was happy with the course her life had taken since she was seventeen, that she was contented at the very least, that she was not lonely. No, never that.

She did have a cozy home, a busy, productive life, neighbors and friends, an independent, adequate income, family members not too far away. But she had never had anyone of her very own that she would not have to relinquish at some time in the future. She had had her sister until Agnes married William Keeping, and she had had her again for a year before she married Flavian. But . . . there had been no one else and no one permanent to fill the void. No one who had ever vowed to cleave unto her alone until death did them part.

She had never allowed herself to dwell upon how different her life might have been if her mother had not run away from home so abruptly and unexpectedly when Dora was seventeen and Agnes was five. Her life had been as it had been, and she had made free choices every step of the way. But was it possible that now, after all . . . ?

She was thirty-nine years old.

But she was not *dead*.

She would not marry, though, just out of desperation. A poor marriage could—and would—be far worse than what she already had. But a marriage to the Duke of Stanbrook would not be from desperation, she knew without having to ponder the matter. She had dreamed of him for a whole year—fourteen months to be precise. Oh, not in *that* way, she would have protested even just an hour ago. But her defenses had come tumbling down, and now she could admit that, yes, she had dreamed of him in *that* way. Of course she had. She had walked beside him all the way from Middlebury on that most vividly wonderful of all the afternoons of her life, her hand through his arm as they talked easily to each other. He had smiled at her and she had smelled his cologne and sensed his masculinity. She had dared to dream of love and romance that day and ever since.

But only to *dream*.

Sometimes—oh, just sometimes—dreams could come true. Not the love and romance part, of course, but he had companionship and friendship to offer. And marriage. *Not* a platonic marriage.

She could know what it was like . . .

With him? Oh, goodness, with him. She could know . . .

And someone to share my bed.

She became aware that a longish silence had succeeded his proposal. Her eyes were still locked upon his.

"Thank you," she said. "Yes. I will."

3

George had been taken rather by surprise when he first stepped into the room and set eyes upon Miss Debbins once more. He had thought he remembered her clearly from last year, but she was a bit taller than he recalled her being, though she was not above average height. And he had thought her a little plumper, a little plainer, a little older. It was strange in light of his purpose in coming here that she was actually more attractive than he recalled her being. One might have expected it to be other way around.

She was a good-looking woman for her age despite the primness of the clothes she wore and the simple, almost severe style of her hair. She must have been very pretty as a girl. Her hair was still dark, with no discernible signs of gray, and she had a flawless complexion and fine, intelligent eyes. She also had an air of quiet dignity that she maintained despite the shock of his unexpected appearance and his sudden, abrupt question to her. Overall, she looked like a woman who had come to terms with her life and accepted it for what it was.

It was that air about her, he recalled, that had drawn his admiration last year. It had not been just her musical talent or her sensible conversation or her pleasant looks. He had told her a few moments ago that he did not know why his sudden idea of marrying and the image of her had come to him simultaneously, the one inextricably bound up with the other, neither one possible without the other. But he *did* know why. It was her air of serene dignity, which must not have come easily to her. There were doubtless some women who remained single purely from choice, but he did not believe Miss Debbins was of their number. Spinsterhood had been forced upon her by circumstances—he knew some of them from her sister. She had, however, made a rich and meaningful life for herself despite any disappointment she may have suffered.

Yes, he admired her.

Thank you. Yes. I will, she had said.

He got to his feet and reached out a hand for hers. She stood too, and he raised her hand to his lips. It was a soft, well-cared-for hand with long fingers and short nails. That at least he remembered accurately from last year. It was a musician's hand. It created music that could bring him to the verge of tears.

"Thank you," he said. "I will do my utmost to see that you never regret your decision. It is unfortunate that in almost any marriage it is the woman who must relinquish her home and friends and neighbors and all that is familiar and dear to her. Will it be very difficult for you to give up all this?"

Most people would think it an absurd question to ask when he had Penderris Hall in Cornwall to offer her and

Stanbrook House in London and wealth untold and the glamorous life of a duchess, not to mention marriage itself to replace her spinsterhood. But she did not rush her answer.

"Yes, it will," she said, her hand still in his. "I made a life for myself here nine years ago, and it has been good to me. Not many women have the privilege of knowing independence. The people here have been welcoming and amiable. When I leave, those of my pupils with the will to learn, a few of them with real talent, will be left without a teacher, at least for a while. I will regret doing that to them."

"Vincent?" he asked her, smiling. "Does he have talent?"

After he had been blinded and had clawed his way out of the fright and anger and despair of knowing that his sight would never return, young Vincent had challenged himself in a number of ways rather than sink into the despair of living half a life. One thing he had done was learn to play not only the pianoforte but the violin and, more recently, the harp. That last he had undertaken only because one of his sisters had suggested selling the harp that was already in the house when he inherited it because "obviously" he would never have any use for it. Vincent's fellow Survivors, who were never sentimental with one another, had teased him mercilessly about his proficiency on the violin, but he had persevered, and he was constantly improving. They did not tease him about the harp, which had caused him endless frustration and distress. Now that he was finally conquering its mysteries, however, he might expect the insults to start flying.

Again Miss Debbins did not rush into an answer, though she knew Vincent to be one of the duke's closest friends.

"Viscount Darleigh has *determination*," she said. "He works hard to be proficient and will never make an excuse of the fact that he cannot see the instrument he plays or the music he must learn by ear. He does extremely well and will get better. I am very proud of him."

"But there is no talent there?" Poor Vince. He did indeed have the determination not to see himself as handicapped.

"Talent is rare in any field," she said. "*Real* talent, I mean. But if we all avoided doing anything for which we are not exceptionally gifted, we would do almost nothing at all and would never discover what we can become. Instead we would waste much of the span of life allotted us in keeping to safe, confining activities. Lord Darleigh has a talent for perseverance, for stretching himself to the limits of his endurance despite what must be one of the most difficult of handicaps—or perhaps because of it. Not many people given his circumstances would achieve what he has. He has learned to give light to the darkness in which he must live out his life, and in so doing he has shed light upon those of us who think we can see."

Ah, and here was something else that reminded him why he felt such admiration and liking for her—this calm and thoughtful gravity with which she spoke upon topics most people would dismiss lightly. Many people would speak condescendingly of what Vincent had achieved despite the fact that he could not see. Not her. And yet she spoke honestly too. Vincent did indeed lack outstanding musical talent, even allowing for his blindness, but it did not matter. As she had just observed, he had the talent in superabundance for pushing the boundaries of his life beyond the limit of what might be expected of him.

"I am sorry that in marrying you I will be taking you away from this life, Miss Debbins," he said. "I hope Penderris and marriage to me will prove to be compensation enough."

She rested her eyes thoughtfully upon him. "When I came here nine years ago from my father's home in Lancashire," she said, "I knew no one. Everything was strange and a little depressing—living in a cottage that seemed incredibly small compared to what I was accustomed to, being alone, working for my living. But the adjustment to a new life was made, and I have been happy here. Now I have freely agreed to another complete change. You have not coerced me in any way. I will make the necessary adjustments. If you are quite sure, that is, now that you have seen me and spoken to me again."

He was still holding her hand, he realized. He squeezed it and raised it to his lips once more.

"I am," he said. "Quite sure."

He wondered what she would say or do if he dipped his head and kissed her lips. She could hardly object—she was now his affianced bride. The shock of that thought caused him to pause, and he wondered for a moment if he really *was* sure. It was suddenly difficult to picture himself kissing her, making love to her, becoming as familiar with her body as he was with his own. But he did know that he would have been horribly disappointed if she had said no. For it really was not just marriage itself that had come to his mind a few nights ago in London. It was Miss Dora Debbins and the strange, unexpected yearning to be married to her.

"When?" she asked him. "And where?" She bit her lower lip as though she feared she was displaying an inappropriate overeagerness.

He patted her hand and released it, and she sat down again. Rather than loom over her, he resumed his seat too. Idiot that he was, he had not thought much beyond the proposal itself. Or, at least, he had not thought of the actual process of wedding her. His mind had been focused more upon the imagined contentment of the years ahead. Yet he had just been caught up in all the frantic busyness of a wedding and knew it did not just happen without planning.

"Ought I to go to Lancashire," he asked her, "to speak to your father?" It had not occurred to him until now that perhaps he ought.

"I am thirty-nine," she reminded him. "My father lives his own life with the lady he married before I moved here. There is no estrangement between us, but he has little or nothing to do with my life and certainly no say in how I live it."

George wondered about that family situation. He knew some of the facts but not the full reason why she had left home and moved so far away. It was an unusual thing for an unmarried lady to do when there were male relatives to support her.

"We have none but our own wishes to consult, then,

it would seem," he said. "Shall we dispense with a lengthy betrothal? Will you marry me soon?"

"Soon?" She looked across at him with raised eyebrows. And then she lifted both hands and pressed her palms to her cheeks. "Oh, dear, what will everyone think? Agnes? The viscount and viscountess? Your other friends? The people in the village here? I am a *music* teacher. I am almost forty. Will I appear very . . . presumptuous?"

"I believe," he said, "indeed I know that my friends will be more than delighted to see me married. I am equally sure they will approve my choice and applaud your willingness to have me. Your sister will surely be happy for you. I am not a bad catch, after all, am I, even if I am nine years older than you? Julian and Philippa— my only nephew and his wife—will also be pleased. I am certain of it. Your father will surely be happy too, will he not? And I believe you have a brother?"

Her hands fell to her lap. "This is all so very sudden," she said. "Yes, Oliver is a clergyman in Shropshire." She worried her lower lip again. "We will marry soon, then?"

"In a month's time if we wait for banns to be read," he said, "or sooner if you would prefer to marry by special license. As to the where—the choices would seem to be here or in Lancashire or at Penderris or in London. Do you have a preference?"

Her sister and Flavian had married here at the village church last year by special license. The wedding breakfast had been held at Middlebury Park, and Sophia had insisted that the newly married couple spend their wedding night in the state apartments in the east wing there. It had all been lovely, perfect . . . but did she want to do exactly what her sister had done?

"London?" she said. "I have never been there. I was to go for a come-out Season when I was eighteen, but . . . Well, it never did happen."

He thought he knew the reason. Scandal had almost erupted last year after her sister went to London with Flavian following their wedding. A former fiancée of Flavian's, who had abandoned him when he was badly injured in order to marry his best friend, was now a widow and had hoped to marry Flavian after all. When she discovered that she had missed her chance, she had dug into Agnes's past and found dirt there. Agnes's mother—*and Miss Debbins's*—was still living, but her father had divorced her years ago upon the grounds of adultery. It was a spectacular scandal at the time, and even last year it had threatened malicious gossip and social ostracism for Agnes, the divorced woman's daughter. The *ton* would have eaten her alive if Flavian had not stepped in boldly and skillfully to handle the situation and avert disaster. That initial scandal would have been happening when Agnes was a child and Miss Debbins a young lady about to make her debut in society. It would have deprived her of all that excitement and, more important, of the respectable marriage she could have expected to result from a London Season, the annual grand marriage mart. She had stayed home instead to raise her sister.

Miss Debbins undoubtedly had a few ghosts to put

to rest as far as London and the beau monde were concerned. Perhaps now was the time.

"May I suggest London for our wedding, then?" he said. "As soon as the banns have been read? Before the end of the Season? With almost all the *ton* in attendance? If we are going to marry, we may as well do it in style. Would you not agree?"

"Would I?" She looked unconvinced.

"And, on the more practical side," he continued, "if we want friends and acquaintances around us, and I would suggest that we do, then London poses the least inconvenience to the largest number of people. I believe Ben and Samantha, Hugo and Gwen, Flavian and Agnes, and Ralph and Chloe are still there after Imogen's wedding. Percy and Imogen should be back from Paris. Vincent and Sophia will be happy to travel back to town, I believe, if the alternative is to miss our wedding. Perhaps your father and your brother can be persuaded to make the journey. I would guess Agnes and Flavian would be delighted to house them."

"London." She was looking a bit dazed.

"At St. George's on Hanover Square," he said, "where most society weddings are solemnized during the Season."

Her cheeks flushed as she gazed across at him, and her eyes were bright. It was only as she lowered her head that he realized the brightness was caused by tears.

"I am to be married after all, then?" Her voice was almost a whisper. He had the feeling she was not really talking to him.

"In London at St. George's one month from now," he told her, "with the very crème-de-la-crème of society filling the pews. And then a honeymoon if you wish in Paris or Rome or both. Or home to Cornwall and Penderris, if you would prefer. We may do whatever we wish— whatever *you* wish."

"I am to have a wedding with all world present." She still sounded a bit dazed. "Oh, my. What will Agnes say?"

He hesitated. "Miss Debbins," he asked softly, "would you like to invite your mother?"

Her head snapped back, her eyes widened, her mouth opened as though she was about to say something—and then it closed again as did her eyes.

"Oh." It was a quiet rush of breath more than a word.

"Have I distressed you?" he asked her. "I do beg your pardon if I have."

Her eyes opened, but there was a frown line between her brows as she looked at him. "I am feeling a bit . . . overwhelmed, Your Grace," she said. "I must excuse myself. I need . . . I would like to be alone, if you please."

"Of course." He got immediately to his feet. Damn him for a gauche fool. Perhaps she did not even know that her mother was alive. Perhaps Agnes had not told her about last year. "May I do myself the honor of calling again tomorrow?"

She nodded and looked down at the backs of her hands, her fingers spread on her lap. She clearly *was* overwhelmed, a fact that was hardly surprising when she had been given no warning of his coming.

He hesitated a moment before leaving the room, then closed the sitting room door quietly behind him.

The village street was empty as he strode along it in the direction of the entry to Middlebury Park, but he was not fooled. He did not doubt that word had already spread of his presence here and the call he had made upon Miss Debbins. He could almost feel curious eyes watching him from behind window curtains all along the street. He wondered how soon it would be before everyone knew why he had come and what answer he had received to his marriage proposal.

He wondered if he would say something to Vince and Sophia, and decided that he would not. Not yet. He had not asked her permission, and it was important to him not to appear high-handed. He was sensitive to the fact that he had a ducal title while she, though the daughter of a baronet, was now living as a spinster in a country village, teaching music.

The announcement could wait.

He wondered how the news would be received at Penderris and the neighborhood surrounding it. He wondered if he would be opening some sort of Pandora's box by taking a new bride home with him and setting about being a contented married man. He often found himself thinking of another saying, the one about leaving sleeping dogs lie, when he thought about his life at Penderris. There had been so much unpleasantness surrounding the death of Miriam even apart from the horror of the suicide itself. Although all the people whose opinion he valued had rallied around him and stayed staunchly with him ever since, there had been and still was an element of the population who had chosen to blame him.

Sleeping dogs had been allowed to lie until now. Apart from the weeks of each year the members of the Survivors' Club spent with him, he lived a pretty solitary life when he was in the country. Perhaps it was perceived as a lonely life, and perhaps the perception was accurate. Perhaps those people who had blamed him twelve years ago felt he deserved his loneliness at the very least.

What *would* it be like, taking Miss Debbins there as his duchess? There would be no unpleasantness toward her, surely? Or . . . worse. But what could be worse? All those events, about which he never spoke, not even to his fellow Survivors, had come to their dreadful conclusion many years ago.

Surely he was entitled not to forget—he could never do that—but to live again, to reach for companionship, contentment, perhaps even a little love?

He strode along the driveway within the park gates in the direction of the house and shook off the strange sense of foreboding that had struck him, seemingly from nowhere.

Predictably, Mrs. Henry bustled in no more than a minute or two after the duke had left, openly agog with curiosity.

"You could have knocked me down with a feather when I opened the door, Miss Debbins," she said as she bent to pick up the tea tray. "I had not heard that the viscount and his lady brought visitors back with them from London."

"They did not. His Grace arrived today," Dora said.

"And came to call so soon?" Mrs. Henry was re-arranging the dishes on the tray. "I hope he did not bring any bad news about Lady Ponsonby."

"Oh, no," Dora said. "He was able to assure me that Agnes is well."

"I did make a fresh pot of tea to bring in," Mrs. Henry said, "but you did not call for it and I did not like to disturb you."

"His Grace had tea at Middlebury Park," Dora explained.

Mrs. Henry decided that the sugar bowl was not positioned to her liking on the tray, but after moving it and glancing at Dora, who was obviously not going to volunteer any more information, she removed the tray and closed the door behind her.

Dora set two fingers of each hand to her temples and imagined how her housekeeper would have reacted if she had been told that the Duke of Stanbrook had come to Middlebury Park for the specific purpose of calling *here* to propose marriage to her mistress. But Dora's own mind could scarcely grapple with the reality of it. She was certainly not ready to share the news.

He knew about her mother. That was the first clear thought that formed in her mind. Agnes and Flavian must have told him. Or perhaps he had heard it from general drawing room gossip in London last year. He knew, yet he had still chosen to make her a marriage offer and wanted to wed her very publicly in London before the Season was over. He was even prepared to invite her mother to the wedding.

Did his status allow him to flout public opinion so?

For the whole of the evening and on into the night the fact that he would invite her mother if she wished churned about and about in Dora's mind along with everything else that had happened after he stepped into her living room. Even the next morning the unreality of it all continued to distract her while she tried to give her full attention to Michael Perlman. He was one of her favorite pupils, a bright little boy of five whose plump fingers always flew over the keyboard of his mother's harpsichord with amazing precision and musicality for one so young. His round little face always beamed with pleasure as he played, and he did so with such total absorption that he would start with surprise if she spoke. Michael Perlman was one she would miss.

Her mother had run away from their family with a younger man after Papa had accused them at a local assembly one evening of being lovers. In a dreadfully public scene that still had the power to haunt Dora's dreams, he had accused Mama of adultery and declared his intention to divorce her. He had been drinking too deeply, something his family always dreaded though it did not happen often. When it did happen, he was almost invariably in company, and he would say or do horribly embarrassing things he would not dream of saying or doing when he was sober. His behavior that evening had been worse than usual, the worst ever, in fact, and Mama had fled and never come back. The threat of divorce had been carried out amid lengthy and terrible publicity. Dora had neither seen nor heard from her mother since the evening of that assembly. Nor had she wanted to, for her mother had fled with her lover, surely confirming Papa's accusation. Dora's own life had changed catastrophically and forever.

Last year, when the old scandal had threatened to rear its head again, Flavian had discovered where her and Agnes's mother now lived and had called upon her. She had married the man with whom she had fled that night and they lived quite close to London. Agnes had chosen not to pursue the acquaintance, though she had told Dora about Flavian's meeting with her.

The duke's offer to invite her mother to their wedding had been the final straw for Dora when her mind had already been in a hopeless whirl. Good heavens, one minute she had been relaxing in her sitting room, too weary even to read, and thirty minutes later she was betrothed and discussing plans for her wedding in St. George's, Hanover Square in London—*with the Duke of Stanbrook*.

Had she really had the effrontery to ask him to leave her house? Perhaps today he would consider his offer null and void. There was a note awaiting her on the tray in the hall when she returned home after the lesson. Her name was written on the outside in a firm and confident hand that was unmistakably masculine.

"A servant from Middlebury brought it," Mrs. Henry said as she came out of the kitchen, wiping her hands on her apron. She hovered in the hall for a few moments, probably in the hope that Dora would open the note there and divulge its contents.

"You need not bring me coffee this morning, Mrs. Henry," Dora said. "Mrs. Perlman was kind enough to send some in to the music room."

She took the note into the sitting room and opened it without even sitting down or removing her bonnet and pelisse.

Her eyes moved first to the signature. *Stanbrook,* he had written in the same bold hand. She unconsciously held her breath as her eyes moved up the page. But he was not after all rescinding his offer—and how silly of her to fear that he might. The offer had been made and accepted, and no gentleman would withdraw from such a commitment. He had written that he understood she was to come to the house during the afternoon to give Vincent a lesson on the harp. He would do himself the honor, then, of coming to fetch her after luncheon. That was all. There was nothing of a personal nature.

But there did not need to be. He was her betrothed. They were engaged to be married. The truth of it struck her as though she were only now fully realizing it. She was going to be *married*. Soon. She was going to be a *duchess*.

She folded the note neatly and took it upstairs with her. She changed into older clothes, armed herself with her gardening tools and gloves, and strode out into the back garden to wage war on the weeds that had dared encroach upon her property. Gardening had always soothed the most turbulent of her emotions, and none were more turbulent than the ones that had raged within her yesterday and still did today.

The weeds did not stand a chance against her.

4

*D*ora was dressed neatly again and ready to go soon after luncheon since the duke had not stated exactly when he would come for her. Normally she would not leave for Middlebury for another hour and a half, but she did not want to be caught unprepared.

Today was worse than yesterday in some ways. Today she *expected* him. And today her stomach—and her brain—churned dizzyingly and quite out of her control, partly with excitement, partly with a fearful sort of awe. He was a *duke*. The only higher ranks were king and prince.

The gardening had soothed her for a while before luncheon, but she could not go back outside now. She seated herself at the pianoforte in the sitting room instead. It was a battered old instrument, which had been ancient even when she was a girl, long before she brought it with her to her cottage nine years ago. But she did not feel deprived for not having a worthier instrument. She loved the mellow tone of this one. She even loved the two tricky notes, one black, one white, which no amount of coaxing and fiddling with and adjusting by piano tuners could quite induce to behave as the other keys did. They felt a bit like old friends. This pianoforte had seen her through all the joys and sorrows, all the upheavals and tedium of several decades. In all that time it had never—or almost never—failed to bring her joy and to soothe away any trouble of her soul. She sometimes felt that she would not have survived without music and her pianoforte.

The Duke of Stanbrook must have knocked on the outer door. Mrs. Henry must have opened it and then tapped on the sitting room door before admitting him. He would scarcely have walked straight in as though he owned the cottage, even if he *was* betrothed to its owner. But the first indication Dora had of his arrival was an awareness of something large and dark at the edge of her vision where there had been no such object before. Her hands fell still on the keys and she turned her head slowly. He was standing just inside the door, where he had stood for a while yesterday.

"I beg your pardon," they said simultaneously.

He bowed. "I must say," he continued, "that it was extremely clever of me to choose a wife who can fill my home with music for the rest of my days."

He was doing what she remembered his doing last year when she was seated beside him at dinner prior to playing for the guests at Middlebury. He was smiling with his eyes and saying something that would set her at her ease. And she remembered the most vivid impression she had had of him that evening and during the subsequent days, that he had not only smiling eyes but also kind eyes. One did not expect kindness from a man of his lofty rank. One expected aloofness, even haughtiness of manner.

It was his eyes and what they suggested about him that had caused her to dream of him while he was still at Middlebury and after he left, though *dream* was the key word. In reality he had seemed universes beyond her reach. His was merely the kindness of condescension, she had told herself more than once.

He had the loveliest eyes of anyone she had ever known.

"I did not hear you arrive," she said, getting to her feet. "But I am ready. Are we walking?" But they must be. She surely could not have been so deeply absorbed in her playing that she had missed the sound of a carriage stopping outside her gate.

"Will you mind?" he asked her as she put on the bonnet she had set ready on a chair with her shawl. "The lovely weather is still holding, and it seems a pity to waste it."

"I do not mind," she assured him, draping the shawl about her shoulders. "I walk everywhere." She would have longer to spend with him if they walked. And she would have *the rest of her life* to spend with him after they married.

Oh, my. Oh, goodness. Suddenly she felt almost giddy with the pleasure of it all.

It occurred to Dora as they left the cottage and stepped out through her garden gate onto the village street that the arrival of the Duke of Stanbrook here yesterday would not have gone unnoticed. Word would surely have spread to every inhabitant before the day was over, as word of anything remotely unusual always did in a small community. She would be willing to bet that by now half the village knew he had returned today and that more than a few people fortunate enough to live or have their businesses on this street were watching discreetly from behind their window curtains for his emergence from her cottage. Now they were witness to the sight of Dora proceeding along the street in the direction of the gates into Middlebury Park, her hand drawn through the duke's arm.

She would not have been quite human if she had not felt a certain enjoyment at these realizations. Speculation would be rife for the rest of the day. Mrs. Jones, the vicar's wife, perhaps not purely by chance, was standing at her garden gate talking across it with Mrs. Henchley, the butcher's wife. They both turned and smiled and curtsied and commented on the lovely weather and looked significantly at Dora. The duke touched the brim of his tall hat with one hand, wished them a good afternoon, and agreed that yes, summer appeared to have come early this year. They would regale the rest of the village for what remained of the day with an embroidered account of the encounter, Dora guessed with an inward smile of fondness for her neighbors.

She and the duke turned between the gates into the private park about Middlebury but did not remain for long on the main driveway. Instead, the duke turned them to their left to walk among the trees that bordered the southern wall of the park, and there was an instant impression of peace and seclusion. The light of the sun was muted by the branches and the canopy of green leaves overhead. There were the lovely smells of earth and greenery, something Dora had never noticed in her many walks along the driveway.

It struck her suddenly, just as though one of the shafts of sunlight penetrating the trees had shone directly into her mind, that she was happy. It was a strange realization, perhaps, for she had lived most her life with the conscious determination to be contented with her life. She had never allowed herself to dwell upon any of the factors that might have made her *un*happy. But she knew in these moments, as they enjoyed their surroundings in a companionable silence, that she had never known true happiness until now.

She felt it with an inner bubbling of exuberant joy. All her dreams were suddenly, unexpectedly coming true, even if it was happening twenty years later than she had once hoped. That did not matter, though. Nothing mattered but the fact that it was happening at last. It was happening now. She wondered how the duke would react if she removed her hand from his arm and twirled about, her arms stretched to the sides, her face turned up to the distant sky, song and laughter on her lips. She smiled at the bizarre image of herself the thought provoked and lowered her chin so that he would not see beyond her bonnet brim.

But something needed to be addressed before they went any farther.

"I would rather we did not invite my mother to the wedding," she said abruptly.

"Then we will not." He set a hand over hers on his

arm and looked down at her. "You must provide me with a list of the people you *do* wish to invite, Miss Debbins, and I will put it into my secretary's capable hands with my own list the moment I return to London within the next couple of days."

So soon? The next couple of days?

"I wish to arrange for the first banns to be read next Sunday," he explained, "if, that is, I am not rushing you too much. But having conceived the idea of marrying, and having secured your consent to my offer, I am now all impatience to have the deed done."

Could he possibly know how sweet those words sounded to her ears?

"I will make a list when I return home," she said. "It will be a very short one, though."

"Then you must tell me," he said, "whether you wish my list to be equally short. I really do not care how small or how large our wedding is, provided only that you and I are there with the requisite number of witnesses to make all legal."

"Oh," she said, and was conscious of a certain disappointment.

Perhaps he saw it in her face.

"But if you have no strong preference either way," he continued, "may I reinforce a suggestion I made yesterday? You told me then that you could not possibly be a duchess. Until you said that, I had thought only of persuading you that perhaps you would care to marry *me*. I had forgotten that I must also convince you to marry that formidable being, the Duke of Stanbrook. I suppose I take him for granted because he has been with me for a long time. But though I hope we will spend most of our married life at Penderris, there will undoubtedly be times when I must be in London, and I most certainly would not wish to leave you behind in the country. You also told me yesterday that you have never been to London or mingled with the *ton*. Perhaps the best time to do both is now during the month leading up to our wedding and during the wedding itself— the grand wedding, that is. Will you come to London, if not with me during the next day or two, at least soon after? Your sister and Flavian are still there. So are most of the other Survivors, and I fully expect that Sophia and Vincent will return there too. Let them all introduce you about town. Let me do likewise as soon as our betrothal has been officially announced. Let me organize a betrothal party."

They had stopped walking and she had drawn her arm free of his. He stood looking down at her, his hands clasped at his back, kindness and concern in his eyes.

"Oh," she said again.

"But it is a mere suggestion," he said. "I am your servant, Miss Debbins. All will be as you wish."

Dora was strongly tempted to take the coward's way out and choose the quietest of weddings in London after all—or even perhaps a wedding here at the church where Agnes had married Flavian last year. But . . .

London?

During the *Season*?

As the betrothed of the Duke of Stanbrook and the sister-in-law of Viscount Ponsonby and the friend of the Earl of Berwick, who was now also a duke, and

Baron Trentham and Sir Benedict Harper and Viscount
Darleigh and the Countess of Hardford?

It was the stuff of which dreams were made. It was
the stuff of which fairy tales were made.

"There is no need to be frightened," he said.

"Oh, I am not frightened," she assured him. "A little
overwhelmed, perhaps—again. But you are quite right.
If I am to be your wife, then I needs must be your duchess too. Besides, I have always thought it must be lovely
to attend the theater in London, to stroll in Hyde Park,
to waltz at a real ball. Am I too old for that?"

His smile had turned to real amusement. "Do you
have the rheumatics in both knees, Miss Debbins?"

"No!" She was a little shocked at his open reference
to her knees.

"Neither do I," he said. "Perhaps we can contrive to
waltz together in some dark corner of some dark ballroom without making too much of a spectacle of
ourselves."

She beamed at him.

"Let us change course," he suggested, offering his
arm again, "or we will end up in the meadow on the far
side of the lake. We will stroll on this side instead and
then take the path up to the house. Vincent will be quite
wrathful if I keep you out beyond the time allotted for
his lesson."

"Is it possible?" she asked. "For Lord Darleigh to be
wrathful, that is?"

"I malign him," he admitted with a smile.

Dora had never walked by the lake, though she had
seen it from a distance. Nor had she walked on the railed

path from the house to the lake, which Lady Darleigh had had constructed after her marriage so that her blind husband could move more freely about the park without always having to be led. It was the viscountess too who had made inquiries about the possibility of training a sheepdog to guide him and give him even more freedom of movement. And she had had the wilderness walk in the hills behind the house reconstructed so that he could walk there in relative safely. She had had it planted with several aromatic trees and flowers to delight his other senses.

"Have you ever been across to the island?" Dora asked, nodding toward it as they strolled beside the lake. "Agnes told me that the little temple folly at its center is very beautiful inside. The stained glass windows make the light quite magical," she said.

"I have only ever admired it from the bank here," he admitted. "It is a delight we will experience together on our next visit to Middlebury—as man and wife."

Dora's stomach felt as if it had performed a complete somersault. She was not sure that even yet she was fully believing in this future to which she had agreed. She scarcely dared trust in such happiness.

"Penderris Hall is by the sea," he told her. "Did you know that? There are steep cliffs bordering the park on the south and golden sands below and an overall beauty that is quite wild in comparison with what you see around you here. I hope you will not find it bleak."

"I do not expect to do so," she said. "It will be home."

Home. Yet she had never seen it. She had never set foot in Cornwall or in Devonshire. Or in Wales, though she was not far from it here in Gloucestershire. And she remembered that his wife had died on those cliffs to which he had referred. Someone had told her, perhaps Agnes. The duchess had thrown herself over not long after losing her only son, their only son, during the wars.

What must it have been like for the duke, losing them both like that? How had he retained his sanity?

Dora was struck fully with the realization that she would be his second wife. He would be coming to her encumbered by years and years of memories of a family life with another woman and a child. He would be coming burdened by the memory of the terrible tragedies that had taken them both from him within a few months. Was it any wonder that he had no romantic love or passion to offer her? She could not possibly replace his first wife in his affections.

Well, of course she could not. She would not want to even if it were possible. Theirs would be a different type of relationship altogether. It was comfort and companionship he wanted from her. He had been quite honest about that, and she must not forget it. He wanted someone to help hold the loneliness at bay.

Well, and *so did she*. They could do that for each other. She could be his companion and friend, and he could be hers. She had music to offer too—in exchange for all the material goods and luxuries he would provide. She smiled when she recalled what he had said to her earlier about his cleverness in choosing a wife who could play for him.

She was not going to get depressed about what she could not have from her marriage. Gracious heaven, at this time yesterday she had fully expected that she would live out her life here at Inglebrook as a spinster. Yet now she was betrothed.

They turned onto the path up to the house.

"You are a peaceful companion, Miss Debbins," the duke said. "You do not seem to feel the need to fill every silent moment with words."

"Oh, dear," she said, "is that a polite way of saying that I have no conversation?"

"If it were," he said, "then I would be condemning myself too since I have been equally silent during much of our walk. I almost wish we had had time to keep going through the trees to stroll in the meadow and sit in the summerhouse. But I must, alas, behave responsibly and deliver you on time for your lesson."

"Do they know?" Dora asked. She could feel the fluttering of anxiety in her stomach.

"I did not feel I had the right to make any announcement," he told her. "It struck me as altogether possible that after thinking things over you would change your mind about facing the upheaval in your life that marrying me will bring. I did not want to embarrass you unduly if you had changed your mind. I was extremely anxious as I walked to your house earlier. I did not know what awaited me."

She glanced at him suspiciously, but he looked perfectly serious.

"It never once occurred to me to change my mind," she said. "I thought perhaps you would be the one changing yours after having seen me again yesterday afternoon. But I remembered that you are a gentleman and would not cry off, having made your offer."

He laughed softly. "I do assure you, Miss Debbins," he said, "that seeing you again yesterday only made me more eager to marry you."

Oh, dear, Dora thought. *Why?* But she felt warmed right through to the center of her heart anyway.

George was feeling anxious all over again. Vincent and Sophia, he could see, were outside, sitting in the formal gardens while Thomas, their son, toddled happily along the path near them. He stopped even as George spotted him to pluck the head off a flower and hold it out to his mama with a look of triumph.

"Oh, dear," Miss Debbins said, "they are outside, and Lady Darleigh has seen us. She will think it very presumptuous of me to be approaching the house from the direction of the lake and to be walking on your arm. I am their music teacher."

He smiled down at her and patted her hand. "I did inform them when Vince told me about his harp lesson that I would walk into the village and escort you back here," he told her. "Do I have your permission to tell them about our betrothal?"

"Oh," she said. "Yes, I suppose so. But whatever will they think?"

He was charmed by her primness, her modesty, her anxiety, for after all she was a lady, daughter of a baronet, and had probably expected to make a perfectly respectable marriage when she was a girl.

"I believe we are about to find out," he said. And yes, he was a bit nervous himself. His friends, he suspected, were going to be taken totally by surprise. He did not need their approval, but he certainly wanted it.

Vincent and Sophia were both smiling at them—she must have said something to him. Thomas was beginning to toddle in their direction, but Sophia scooped him up in her arms.

"I do believe, Miss Debbins," Sophia said when they were within earshot, "that George feared you would skip your lesson today on account of the lovely weather. He insisted upon going to fetch you here in person."

"I did indeed," George said. "If I had waited for her to come alone, I would have seen her for only a minute or two before she disappeared into the music room with Vince and the harp, and I would not have liked that at all."

Sophia looked speculatively at him as Vincent came up beside her, led by his dog, and Thomas changed his affections and held out his flower head to George.

"Miss Debbins has not let us down yet," Vincent said with a smile. "Good afternoon, ma'am. You will be cross with me, I fear. I have hardly had a chance to practice since my last lesson."

"That is quite understandable, Lord Darleigh," she said. "You have been to London."

"But before you whisk her away, Vince," George said, "I have something to say. You were mystified by my arrival yesterday, as well you might be since I had seen you in town just a few days before. I came for a particular purpose and accomplished it successfully after tea yesterday when I called upon Miss Debbins at her cottage."

Sophia looked from one to the other of them. Thomas offered his flower, slightly squashed from his grip, to Miss Debbins, who took it with a smile of thanks and raised it to her nose.

"Miss Debbins has done me the great honor of accepting my hand in marriage," George explained. "We plan to wed as soon as the banns have been read. I will then take her away from here and from you, I am afraid. I am also going to insist that you return to London within the month since we plan to marry with a great deal of pomp and circumstance at St. George's and we absolutely must have all our family and friends about us."

Miss Debbins was giving a great deal of attention to her flower. For a moment, Sophia and Vincent—yes, Vince too—gazed at them with arrested expressions while Thomas leaned out with both arms and nudged his father's shoulder.

"You are going to *marry*?" Sophia asked as Vincent took the child with his free arm. "*Each other?* But how absolutely . . . *perfect*!"

There was a great deal of noise and activity then and even some squealing as everyone hugged everyone else and hands were shaken and backs were slapped and cheeks were kissed and something was hilariously funny, for they were all laughing.

"I cannot decide for which of you I am more delighted," Vincent said as he beamed from one to the other of them for all the world as though he could actually see them. "I cannot think of anyone who deserves George more than you do, Miss Debbins, or of anyone who deserves you more than he does. But this is devilish sneaky of you, George. What are we expected to do now for a music teacher?"

"I would imagine, Vince," George said, slapping a hand on his shoulder, "all your household staff will offer up a prayer of thanks."

"Is that a reflection upon the quality of my instruction?" Miss Debbins asked severely.

"That will teach you to insult me, George," Vincent said with a grin. "Thomas, my lad, Papa's hair was not made to be pulled, you know. Those curls are attached to my head."

Sophia had linked an arm through Miss Debbins's and was drawing her in the direction of the house.

"I cannot tell you how excited I am," she said. "Are we the first to be told? How splendid. Come up to the drawing room for some tea and tell me about your plans. Every single one of them. Did you know George was coming? Did he write to tell you? Or did he just turn up on your doorstep unannounced? How very romantic that must have been."

"I cannot have any tea," Miss Debbins protested. "It is time for Lord Darleigh's lesson."

"Oh, but we would not dream—" Sophia began.

"I am not married yet, Lady Darleigh," Miss Debbins said briskly. "I still have work to do."

George took the child from his father's arm and grinned at Sophia.

"Off you go, Vince," he said.

5

$\mathcal{M}$iss Debbins's list, neatly written in a small, careful hand, was indeed very short. It consisted of her father and his wife—whom she did not call her stepmother, George noted—her brother and his wife, her sister and Flavian, her aunt and uncle from Harrogate, three couples from Inglebrook, and one from her former home in Lancashire.

George handed it to Ethan Briggs when he returned to Stanbrook House after being away for five days.

"Have I kept you very busy while I was away, Ethan?" he asked.

His secretary looked pained. "You know you have not, Your Grace," he said. "I have paid twenty-two bills and refused thirty-four invitations, some of which needed to be worded more tactfully than others. I have not done sufficient work to justify the very generous salary you pay me."

"Is it generous?" George asked. "That is good to know, for you will soon be earning it and more. Your time and energy will be taxed, Ethan, as they were during the weeks preceding Lady Barclay's wedding. Invitations are to go to everyone on this list. It is admittedly short, but Miss Debbins assured me she has included everyone of any importance to her. Ah, and there is this one too— my own list. It is lamentably long, I am afraid, but Miss Debbins did agree with me that if we are to do this thing properly, then we really ought to invite everyone who is anyone. There are certain expectations when one holds the lofty title of duke."

"Miss Debbins?" Briggs asked politely, taking both lists from his employer's hand.

"The lady who has been good enough to consent to marry me," George explained. "There are to be wedding invitations, Ethan. To St. George's, of course, at eleven o'clock in the morning four weeks from this coming Saturday if I am in time to have the first banns read this coming Sunday. As I daresay I will be."

His secretary, who had never before displayed anything approaching open astonishment, looked up at him with a slightly dropped jaw.

"I daresay it was that other nuptial service last week that aroused in me a distinct hankering to have a wedding of my own, Ethan," George said apologetically. "I am afraid your rest period is over. There will be a great deal more work for you to do even after you have written and sent the invitations. But at least you have had some practice."

His secretary had recovered his usual poise. "May I be permitted to wish you all the happiness in the world, Your Grace," he said.

"You may," George said.

"No one deserves it more," the usually impassive Briggs added.

"Well, that is remarkably handsome of you, Ethan." George nodded genially and left him to the arduous work ahead.

His own next task, not to be delayed one moment longer than necessary, was to make arrangements for the banns to be called. Not much longer than an hour after his arrival in town, however, he was back on Grosvenor Square, knocking on the door of Arnott House, which was on the opposite side of it from Stanbrook House. He was informed by Viscount Ponsonby's butler that my lord and my lady had returned from an afternoon outing not ten minutes before, and he was escorted up to the drawing room, where they joined him a few minutes later.

And no, George thought with a keener than usual glance at the viscountess, Miss Debbins did not much resemble her sister, who was taller, fairer haired, and more youthfully pretty.

"George." Flavian beamed at him and shook his hand before crossing to the sideboard to pour them each a drink. "We have not set eyes on you since Imogen's wedding. We were beginning to think you must have f-fled back to Penderris to recover from all the excitement."

"Do have a seat, George," Agnes said, indicating a chair and smiling her welcome. "You have probably been enjoying a well-deserved rest."

"I *have* been out of town," George admitted as he sat. "But not to Penderris. I have been at Middlebury Park."

They both looked at him in some surprise.

"You went with Sophia and Vince?" Flavian asked.

"Not with them, no," George said, taking the glass his friend offered him. "I went a few days after them. I had to wait until after my cousins left, though actually I had no intention of going anywhere myself until they had set out for Cumberland. Vince and Sophia were taken rather by surprise when I descended upon them without any warning."

"I am quite sure it was a happy surprise," Agnes said. "Did you by any chance see Dora while you were there?"

"I did indeed," he said. "Miss Debbins was, in fact, my reason for going."

They turned identical frowns of incomprehension upon him.

"I went," George explained, "to ask Miss Debbins if she would be obliging enough to marry me. And she was—obliging enough, that is."

"*What?*" Agnes laughed, but there was puzzlement in the sound. She was not sure if he was serious or making some sort of bizarre joke.

"I proposed marriage to Miss Debbins," George said, "and she accepted me. We are to marry at St. George's in one month's time. She will be following me up to town within the week. She has shopping to do, it seems, though she flatly refuses to allow me to foot any of the bills before she is married to me. Your sister is an independent, strong-minded lady, Agnes. Although she has never before been to London and is clearly somewhat awed, if not terrified, at the prospect of coming now in the middle of the social Season as the betrothed of a duke and of marrying him in grand style with all the fashionable world looking on, she still insists upon doing it at her own expense. She has agreed, though, that it is the sensible thing to do to come early so that she may meet the *ton* and allow the *ton* to meet her before the fateful day. She will not attend any formal entertainments, she assures me, but she has agreed to a betrothal party close to our wedding date. I am all admiration for her courage."

Agnes's hands had crept up to cover her cheeks. "It is really true, then?" she asked, doubtless rhetorically. "You are going to marry Dora?' Her eyes suddenly brightened with unshed tears.

"Why you sly dog, George." Flavian set down his glass, jumped to his feet, and crossed the distance between them in order to pump George's hand up and down in a hearty shake and then thump him on the back. "And to think that all of us in the club have been busy p-putting our heads together to think of a worthy lady who might t-tempt your fancy and take you off our hands. It is very lowering, let me tell you, for a man to be reduced to m-matchmaking, but you showed no sign of doing it for yourself. Yet all the time you had your sights upon my sister-in-law. I could not be happier, and Agnes is ecstatic. You can tell by the fact that she is w-weeping."

"Oh, I am not," she protested. "But . . . Oh, George, you cannot possibly know what this means to me. Dora gave up her life for my sake when I was a child. She stayed at home to raise me after our mother left when she ought to have been enjoying a come-out Season here in London. She might still have had that Season after the worst of the scandal died down if she had pressed the matter with Papa, but she never did. She would not even go to Harrogate when our Aunt Shaw would have taken her about and introduced her to some eligible gentlemen. She was quite adamant that she would stay with me, and she never once complained or made me feel that I was a nuisance and had blighted all her hopes. But now at last she is to have her happily-ever-after? With you of all men, George? And oh, dear, now I am weeping. Thank you." The thanks were for the large handkerchief Flavian had pressed upon her. He rubbed a hand over the back of her neck while she dried her eyes and blew her nose.

Happily-ever-after? The term made George a bit uneasy. He certainly did not have that to offer, but then Miss Debbins did not expect it. They were both old enough and experienced enough at life to understand that no marriage could offer unalloyed happiness. Not that he was a cynic. He was not, and neither, he was quite sure, was she. They were both realists. Of that he felt sure.

But . . . *Happily-ever-after?* For a moment that sense of foreboding threatened again.

The next ten minutes or so were taken up with answering all the questions they had for him. Finally, though, he got to his feet and withdrew a letter from an inside pocket.

"I have other calls to make," he said, "though I made this one the first for obvious reasons. I shall do my very best to make your sister happy, Agnes. She wrote to you while I was still in Gloucestershire so that I could bring the letter in person."

Agnes took it from him. "I am quite confident that you will make each other happy," she said.

Flavian shook hands with him again. "I hate to say anything to deter you, George," he said, "but has it occurred to you that we will be b-brothers-in-law?"

"A terrifying thought, is it not?" George said cheerfully.

He was still smiling as he left the house and made his way to Portman Square to see if Ralph and Chloe were at home. Wheels had been set in motion, and everyone of importance to him must be informed in person.

He was a bit surprised to discover that he was feeling something very like exuberance. If he was to regret his hasty decision to marry, it was certainly not happening yet.

He hoped it never would.

Dora left for London five days after her betrothed, having taken a hasty and, in some cases, a tearful farewell of her pupils, her neighbors and friends, and Mrs. Henry, who had decided to remain among her family and friends in the neighborhood of Inglebrook rather than accept the offer to accompany her employer into her new life in the capacity of personal maid. Dora traveled in opulent style, the duke having insisted upon sending his own carriage for her along with what seemed an extravagant complement of liveried footmen and burly outriders and even a maid. It was really almost embarrassing—and undeniably pleasurable. The deference shown her wherever they stopped along the road during the journey was something to which she must accustom herself, she supposed. Plain Miss Debbins, traveling post, as she had planned, would have been virtually ignored.

For the final hour before arriving at Arnott House on Grosvenor Square, she sat with her nose almost pressed to the window of the carriage, even though rain was drizzling down outside and the heavy gray sky added a pall of dreariness to everything below. It did not dampen Dora's spirits. This was London at last, and she could almost believe that the streets were indeed paved with gold. It was a good thing, she thought, that the maid was dozing against the opposite corner and therefore was not watching her quite unsophisticated delight in it all.

Her stomach was feeling more than a bit fluttery, however, by the time the carriage rocked slightly on its springs and drew to a halt. Here she was, twenty years late but about to carry off surely the greatest matrimonial prize the Season had to offer—even if he was forty-eight years old. She controlled her smile at the silly thought—the maid was waking up and setting her skirts and her cap and bonnet to rights.

What would Agnes say? And Flavian?

She was soon to find out. As one of the duke's liveried footmen set down the steps and reached up a white-gloved hand to help her down, the doors of the house opened and both Agnes and Flavian appeared in the doorway. Dora lost sight of them for a moment as the footman angled a large umbrella over her head and she hurried across the wet pavement and up the steps. And then she stepped inside and was enfolded in her sister's arms. Flavian stood to one side, beaming at her.

"But this is not a town house," Dora protested as she emerged from her sister's embrace. "It is a mansion." And Stanbrook House was somewhere on this square too. Then that must also be a mansion. There was no other type of edifice on the square. The enormity of what was about to happen in her life was beginning to dawn more fully on her—though, of course, the carriage in which she had traveled had been a harbinger.

"Dora, my love." Agnes was squeezing her hands almost painfully, her eyes sparkling with unshed tears. "Oh, how happy I am for you."

"Well." Dora, a bit embarrassed, spoke briskly. "I am rather elderly to be marrying for the first time, am I not? But better late than never, as the saying goes. I hope you are not annoyed with me, Flavian."

"Annoyed?" He tipped his head to one side and laughed softly. "Certainly I am. Let me show you how much."

And then she was enfolded in his arms and feeling considerably flustered.

"I recall one famous occasion last year," he said, "when George and I escorted you and Agnes home from M-Middlebury and I let him forge ahead with you because I w-wanted to propose to Agnes but did not want to be overheard—and a good thing too, as it turned out. I made a thorough m-mess of it and she let me know it. However, some good came of that afternoon, for what I was really doing, of course, was allowing George to become better acquainted with you. I foresaw this day though I do not suppose people would believe me if I said so, would they?"

"No." Agnes and Dora spoke together and Flavian raised that mocking eyebrow of his.

"In all seriousness I am happy for you, Dora," he

said, "and absolutely delighted for George. Come upstairs and have some tea. Agnes has been pacing from her chair to the window all afternoon, and just watching her has made me thirsty."

"You are well, are you, Agnes?" Dora asked as each of them took one of his arms.

"I am indeed." Agnes patted a hand over her abdomen, and Dora could see more of a swelling there than had been apparent at Easter. "Oh, Dora, we are going to have such a delightful time preparing for your wedding."

"I need to go shopping," Dora told her.

"Well, of course you do," Agnes agreed.

And shop they did during the coming days, though in a manner and on a scale far surpassing Dora's expectations. She had known, of course, that she would need new clothes, including an outfit suitable for her wedding to a duke in a fashionable church before half the fashionable world. She was soon made to understand, however, the naïveté of her expectation that one quick trip to the shops for the purchase of ready-made garments would suffice. The future Duchess of Stanbrook, it seemed, must first choose patterns and fabrics and trimmings and a fashionable dressmaker who would measure her and make them up exclusively for her. And all that, of course, meant many hours of browsing and many more hours of standing upon a pedestal in her shift while she was measured and pinned and poked. And then, when the garments were ready and she expected the ordeal to be at an end, she had to go through the whole process again while the dressmaker made note of all the minor alterations that needed to be made. Any feeble protestation Dora might make that a certain garment was "good enough" was soundly ignored. Only perfection would do for a dressmaker chosen to make the garments of the future Duchess of Stanbrook.

Dora was staggered by the number of new clothes of every description and for every imaginable occasion she needed—dresses for walking, for riding in the carriage, for morning wear, for afternoon tea, for riding, gowns for dinner, for formal evening wear, for balls. And each garment needed its own exclusive accessories—hats, gloves, reticules, shoes, slippers, fans, parasols, shawls, ribbons and bows, shifts and petticoats . . . the list went on.

There was an undeniable pleasure about seeing herself outfitted in such splendor, of course, but the expense! The modest savings she had acquired through hard work and careful management during the past nine years dwindled at an alarming rate. But she would not panic. If absolutely necessary, she would accept a loan from Flavian, though she had flatly refused a money gift from him when he had tried to press it upon her with the argument that she surely must have a birthday *some*time. Her funds would be replenished as soon as her cottage sold and she would be able to repay him. And after her marriage she would not need money of her own, though her carefully cultivated independence of spirit did not like the prospect of being wholly dependent upon a man, wealthy though he undoubtedly was. She would have to accustom herself to that aspect of marriage.

And then, just before Dora felt that she must indeed

apply to her brother-in-law for a loan, a letter of con-
gratulation from her father's wife brought with it a bank
draft from her father for a considerable sum to help her
with the wedding expenses. From him she would accept
a gift, she decided, with deep gratitude.

All the members of the Survivors' Club who were still
in town following Lady Barclay's wedding called at
Arnott House within a day or two of Dora's arrival to
express unqualified delight at the news of her betrothal.
She was begged to call them all by their first names since
she was soon to be one of their number. Soon she was
on terms of familiarity with all her betrothed's closest
friends—but not with him. It was an amusing fact, but
really she could not quite imagine herself ever calling
him George. It would seem far too presumptuous.

Each of the ladies of the group—Samantha, Lady
Harper; Chloe, Duchess of Worthingham, whom Dora
met now for the first time; and Gwen, Lady Trentham—
accompanied Dora and Agnes on at least one of their
shopping excursions, and each was free with advice and
opinions on her proposed purchases. Dora found herself enjoying their company immensely and realizing
that in all the years since her youth she had never really
had any close friends.

Her days were not taken up entirely with shopping,
however. Agnes and Flavian took her to the Tower of
London and to some art galleries. Ben and Samantha
took her to Kew Gardens, which quite took her breath
away, and then to Gunter's for ices, having noted her
remark that she had never tasted that particular delicacy.
Hugo and Gwen took her to see St. Paul's Cathedral and

Westminster Abbey, to climb to the Whispering Gallery in the former and to read all the inscriptions in Poets' Corner in the latter. Ralph and Chloe invited her with the duke and Agnes and Flavian to join them in their private box at the theater one evening, and Dora sat enthralled by a witty comedy of Oliver Goldsmith's.

The Duke of Stanbrook did not neglect her. On the day the announcement of their betrothal appeared in the morning papers he took her driving in Hyde Park at what Dora soon understood to be the fashionable hour of the afternoon. Large numbers of the beau monde moved about one small oval area of the park, less intent upon taking the air and exercise, it seemed, than upon greeting one another and exchanging news and gossip. It was instantly apparent that the two of them were the day's focus of attention. Dora was introduced to so many people that she felt rather as though her head must be spinning upon her shoulders by the time the duke's carriage left the park.

"I doubt I will remember a single face or name," she lamented. "And if I do, I will never recall which name goes with which face."

"It is understandable that you are feeling quite over-whelmed," he said, turning his head to look kindly upon her. "But one thing you will soon realize is that you will see the same people almost wherever you go. Soon you will begin to distinguish one person from another and even remember a few names. There is no need to be flustered until that happens. A smile and a regal nod will suffice for most people. And even if I am not always at your side, Agnes or Flavian will be or another of our friends."

"A regal nod," she said. "Does it differ from all other kinds of nods? I shall have to practice. I may have to indulge in the purchase of a bejeweled lorgnette." His eyes were crinkled at the corners, she could see, though he did not laugh aloud. "I have enjoyed the afternoon."

"Have you?" He turned his horses onto the busy street outside the park with consummate skill. "I have been afraid that you would regret not opting for a quieter wedding at Inglebrook."

"Oh, no," she said quite firmly. Despite moments of bewilderment, she had actually enjoyed every moment since arriving in London.

Her betrothed also organized a small party for a visit to Vauxhall Gardens one evening. It was somewhere Dora had long dreamed of going, and she was not disappointed. They approached the pleasure gardens by boat across the River Thames rather than by carriage over the new bridge, and the sight of the lights shivering across the water was quite enchanting. They listened to an orchestral recital, strolled along the wide avenues, illumined by colored lanterns strung from the trees that stretched on either side. They dined upon—among other delicacies—the wafer-thin slices of ham and succulent strawberries for which the Gardens were famous, and they watched a display of fireworks at midnight. Dora arrived home with the feeling that she had surely been robbed of breath all night. What a glorious wonderland Vauxhall was.

She felt as though she had grown backward a few years during the weeks since she had left Inglebrook. Even her looking glass lied to her and showed her a woman with the glow of youth apparently restored. She peered closely but . . . still not a single gray hair.

Sometimes she thought back to her days at Inglebrook and marveled that life could change so suddenly and so completely. Just one month ago—less—she had had no inkling that all this was in her future. Not that she wanted to stay in London indefinitely. She was longing to be married and to go to Penderris Hall, her new home. They were going to be happy, she and the duke, she dared to hope. There was going to be affection as well as friendship in their marriage. There surely already was.

The betrothal party the Duke of Stanbrook had promised while they were still in Gloucestershire was planned for two evenings before the wedding, and it was to be Dora's formal debut into the world of the *ton*. She had been seen at a number of public places since arriving in London but had chosen not to attend any private party or ball until she was properly outfitted and felt up to the ordeal. It seemed appropriate that she meet the beau monde at Stanbrook House just before she wed the duke. A number of people had been invited, he had informed her, though it was not to be a ball. He had explained by way of apology that there had not been sufficient time to organize such a grand event to his satisfaction.

By the day of the party Dora was very glad that it was not a grand ball she was facing, for panic was setting in. She had been introduced to a number of members of the *ton* in various places over the past three weeks, it was true, but she had not yet been called upon to mingle with them in large numbers, to make social conversation with them for a number of hours, to be on display as she surely would be as the Duke of Stanbrook's betrothed.

Panic was replaced by practicality and common sense, however, before she left for Stanbrook House. If her life had taken the course she had expected as a girl, by now she would be so accustomed to *ton* entertainments that she would approach a party like this evening's without a qualm of nervousness. She was, after all, the daughter of a baronet, and this life into which she was at last being drawn was her birthright. She had been brought up to expect it. Besides, she was perfectly familiar with a number of tonight's guests—her father and his wife; her brother, Oliver, and his wife, Louisa, who had arrived for the wedding and were staying at Arnott House; Aunt Millicent and Uncle Harold Shaw from Yorkshire; all six of the friends she had invited from Inglebrook and the one couple from Lancashire; and of course, the members of the Survivors' Club and their spouses.

The Earl and Countess of Hardford—Imogen, the former Lady Barclay—would be there too, having just returned from abroad. There had been some anxiety that they would not return soon enough for the duke's wedding, but they had arrived just in time. On the morning of the betrothal party they called first at Stanbrook House and then at Arnott House.

"I cannot tell you how very happy I am that George has decided to marry again," the countess said, squeezing both of Dora's hands in her own. "And I really cannot imagine a more suitable bride for him than you, Miss

Debbins." She turned to her husband. "Percy, when you hear Miss Debbins play the harp or the pianoforte, you will think yourself transported to heaven, I promise you."

Dora regarded the countess in some wonder. Could this warm, vibrant woman possibly be the same lady of rather marble demeanor she remembered from Middlebury Park last year? Her extremely handsome husband smiled warmly at her before shaking Dora's hand.

The evening of the party drew inevitably closer, and Dora found herself looking forward to it with real pleasure and distinct flutters of apprehension.

6

The betrothal party might not be a grand ball, Dora thought later in the evening, but when the duke had spoken of inviting a number of guests, he had actually meant a *large* number. She estimated that there were at least two hundred people, and His Grace presented her to all of them within the first half hour as they stood together in the receiving line. She recognized a few from Hyde Park and the theater and Vauxhall Gardens, but most were strangers. Would she ever be able to remember them all as well as their names?

She was wearing a gown of gold lace over blond satin that Gwen and Agnes had persuaded her into choosing.

"You are about to become a duchess, Dora," Gwen had reminded her, a twinkle in her eye. "Nothing is too grand for such an exalted personage. Besides, the colors and design suit you to perfection."

She had looked sincere while saying it. But of course she was sincere. They were friends, and she had come on the shopping trip specifically to offer her advice and opinion.

Agnes had insisted upon sending her own maid to Dora's room to style her hair in smooth coils high at the back of her head. They lent height and perhaps a little elegance to her appearance.

"I am the most fortunate of men, Miss Debbins," the duke had said upon her arrival at Stanbrook House, taking her gloved hand in his and raising it to his lips. "You are looking quite beautiful."

The compliment, though rather extravagant, had warmed Dora down to her toes. And he, incidentally, looked even more gorgeous than usual in his crisp black and white evening clothes, though she did not tell him so.

The rooms that were being used for the party were on the first floor and were really quite splendid, with a great deal of gilding on the friezes and hanging chandeliers and scenes from mythology painted on the coved ceilings and portraits and landscapes in ornate frames on the walls and Persian carpets underfoot. It was dizzying to realize that in a few days' time this would be her home—or one of her homes anyway.

All the rooms were filled with guests. There was conversation in the drawing room, music and conversation in the room adjoining it, cards in two smaller salons, refreshments in another. Dora did not spend a great deal of time with her betrothed after that first half hour. He was very properly mingling with all his guests and so was Dora, although she was not having to make any effort to do so. People came to her. They wanted to converse with her. Plain Miss Dora Debbins, music teacher in the small village of Inglebrook, had been transformed, it seemed, by the fact that the Duke of Stanbrook wished to marry her. It might have been a mildly disturbing realization if she had tried to hide in his shadow. She did not, however. She was a lady, daughter of a baronet. She belonged with these people. She smiled and conversed, and if anyone tried to monopolize her attention for too long, she smiled her excuses and moved on.

It was almost supper time when the Duke of Stanbrook approached her as she was stepping into the music room, having just moved away from a pleasant conversation with two elderly couples.

"I hired the services of Mr. Pierce for the evening," he explained, nodding in the direction of the pianist. "He makes a living from such events, I understand."

"He plays well," Dora said. She had noticed all evening the soft, soothing music, chosen with care to provide background melody without being in any way intrusive or making it difficult for people to converse. She felt just a little sorry for Mr. Pierce, however, for no one appeared to be taking any notice of him. She wondered if he had an artistic soul or if he was content just to make a living thus. Perhaps it was preferable to many other occupations. At least he probably did not have a Miranda Corley to teach. "I shall go and have a word with him."

"I will come with you." He smiled at her. "But before we do—" He looked consideringly at her. "I did think at first to ask you to favor my guests with a recital for a small portion of the evening. But I did not believe you would want the extra pressure on an evening that would surely already be making heavy demands upon you."

"Oh," she said, startled. She might have played for all these people?

"I ought to have consulted you," he said. "It should have been your decision."

"Oh . . . no, that is quite all right," she said. But she might have played, as she did at Middlebury Park last year, but on a far grander scale?

He moved his head a little closer to hers. "No, it is not all right," he said. "Forgive me, please. I have much to learn. I have been accustomed to command for so long that I do not even realize I am doing it. I made a decision for you on this occasion and hired someone with only a fraction of your talent."

"Not necessarily," she said. "Mr. Pierce is doing a job tonight and doing it well. How can he display talent in such circumstances? He is not here to draw attention to himself or even to the music."

"You are quite right," he said. "I am constantly reminded of why I like you so much. Will you play for our guests? Directly after supper, perhaps? I shall give Pierce a break and send him for supper belowstairs. Will you? Please?"

"I would be consumed by terror," she said. But oh, the yearning to say yes.

"Is that a no?" he asked. "But your eyes say yes. My motives are entirely selfish. I wish to share the talents of my affianced bride with those members of the *ton* gathered here and bask in your reflected glory. However, I will not press you. Tonight is probably a bit intimidating for you even as it is, though you show no outer sign of it."

"Just for a very short while?" she asked, and then wished she could recall the words.

"For as long or as short a time as you wish," he said.

She drew breath, let it out, and bit her lower lip.

"I do apologize—" he said.

"Very well," she said simultaneously.

He frowned in concern. Dora smiled. And he smiled too.

"You are sure?" he asked her.

"Absolutely not," she told him. "But I will do it."

"Thank you," he said. He offered his arm. "Shall we go and have a word with Pierce?"

Although it was not a ball and there would not normally have been a formal supper, there was to be one on this occasion, the duke had explained a day or two ago, because it was their betrothal party. Dora was seated beside him in the ballroom, which had been set up with enough tables to accommodate everyone. Candlelight from the chandeliers overhead glittered off fine china and crystal and jewels. There was a sumptuous feast. Dora could enjoy none of it. What had she agreed to? But she had no one to blame but herself.

The duke got to his feet after the guests had eaten their fill and waited for silence to fall. He welcomed those guests who had come to town specifically for his wedding to Miss Debbins, most notably his betrothed's father, Sir Walter Debbins, with Lady Debbins and her brother, the Reverend Oliver Debbins, with Mrs. Debbins. He proposed a toast to his betrothed, soon to be his wife.

Dora smiled at her father, at her brother and sister-in-law, at Agnes, at Chloe and Ralph, directly in her line of vision. Butterflies danced in her stomach.

"I have a special treat in store for you after supper," the duke said. "My betrothed is not only an accomplished musician, but an extraordinarily talented one too. I met her a little over a year ago when she dined at Middlebury Park and then played the harp and the pianoforte at the request of Lord and Lady Darleigh. Unfortunately, there is no harp here, but Miss Debbins has agreed to play the pianoforte for us directly after we have all returned to the drawing room. After you have heard her, you will understand why I did not forget her but went back a month ago to beg her to do me the honor of marrying me. Though I hasten to add that it was not *only* her musical talent that drew me."

He turned his head to smile down at Dora while laughter and applause rippled about the ballroom.

It was too late now to withdraw, she thought. But did she want to? She saw nothing but kindness and goodwill around her as she glanced about the room. She caught Flavian's eye and he winked.

The duke left the ballroom early. Dora followed with her brother and sister-in-law and Ben—Sir Benedict Harper—who was walking determinedly with the aid of two specially made canes.

"You are very brave, Dora," Louisa said, taking her arm. "But you are indeed talented. I am so very delighted for you. No one deserves happiness more."

"I was privileged enough to be present for that recital

last year," Ben said. "I was too dim-witted, however, to realize that a romance was brewing."

The drawing room had been transformed while they were having supper. Half the wall between it and the music room had been folded back, and chairs had been set up in both rooms, facing the opening, into which the pianoforte had been moved. The crowd looked much larger to Dora now than it had looked earlier. Almost everyone had taken a seat and looked expectantly toward the doorway, where the Duke of Stanbrook was awaiting her. He smiled and raised a hand for hers. He led her toward the instrument, and she seated herself and tried to compose her mind, her eyes upon the keyboard. Her hands felt clammy and a bit beset with pins and needles. The hush from both rooms seemed loud.

Then she set her hands on the keys and began to play a Beethoven sonata. For a few seconds her fingers did not seem willing to play the notes she knew so well, and her mind teemed with thoughts of everything except the music. And then she heard the melody and slipped inside it and created it anew through her fingers and hands. She did not lose touch with her surroundings. She knew she was at Stanbrook House, surrounded by a large number of people, some of whom were near and dear to her, most of whom had been strangers to her until tonight. She knew she was playing at the request of the Duke of Stanbrook. She knew she was doing something she had never done on such a scale before. But the person who was aware of those things seemed rather remote, someone she did not

have to worry about until later. For at the moment the
music claimed her.

She was startled at the volume of the applause after
she had finished, at the sound of voices, at the scraping
of chairs as her audience got collectively to its feet. She
looked up, bit her lip, saw the duke standing in the doorway of the drawing room, his face beaming with pride,
his hands clasped behind his back, and smiled.

"More," someone called, and it became a chant,
mingled with some laughter and one piercing whistle.

She played a Mozart sonata and, as a final encore when
the guests were not willing to let her go, the Welsh folk
song "Llwyn On," which she usually played on the harp.

This was, she thought as the applause died away and
she found herself surrounded by appreciative guests,
surely one of the happiest days of her life. And it was
only the beginning.

The day after tomorrow was her wedding day.

George did not often entertain on a grand scale, though
he had, of course, just hosted the wedding reception for
Imogen and Percy. This party, however, had been arranged
on his own account. He had wanted to introduce his
betrothed to the *ton* before their wedding so that that particular day would be less overwhelming for her. For by her
choice the betrothal party would be in the nature of a
social debut for her, more than twenty years after it ought
to have occurred.

He was more than pleased with the way the evening
had progressed. She was elegantly and fashionably
dressed, her hair becomingly styled. Yet she looked very

much herself too. She had made no attempt to look either younger or grander than she was. She wore no jewelry except for small gold earbobs. It was easy to see the disciplined, almost prim teacher in both her appearance and her demeanor. Yet she was poised and apparently at ease with all the attention that was being paid her. He had sensed as the evening went on that she was generally liked and approved of. He was certainly charmed by her.

Her musical recital, however, had lifted her above her role as his betrothed. It had established her as an interesting, accomplished person in her own right. The people who crowded around her after she had finished playing did so not because she had netted herself a duke for a husband, but because she was someone who had aroused their admiration.

He was more than pleased.

The next couple of days could not go fast enough for him. Not just so that he could have her in his bed—though there was that too—but so that he could have her permanently in his life. He half resented the fact that tonight she would return across the square to Arnott House with all her family, while he must remain here alone.

He smiled as he caught her eye across the room. And it occurred to him with something like surprise that he was happy. He often felt happiness, surely. He had felt it for all the officers who had left the hospital at Penderris healed, or at least on the road to healing. He had felt it for his nephew when he married Philippa and when Belinda was born. He had felt it in abundance for each of his fellow Survivors when they had married and had children. He felt happy for Dora Debbins tonight. But . . . when had he ever felt happiness for himself? Try as he would, he could not think of any occasion since he joined his regiment at the age of seventeen, when he had been happy for all too brief a time. Only recently had he begun to feel anything approaching it—when he went to Gloucestershire and made his offer and was accepted, a few times during the past month, and now this evening. Now at this moment.

He was a happy man, he thought, and this was only the beginning. Soon she would no longer be returning to Arnott House and leaving him alone here. Soon she would be his wife. They would remain together. He was almost shaken by the sheer pleasure of the thought.

And a moment later he was shaken again by the sudden lurching of fear low in his stomach lest something happen to destroy that happiness. Deuce take it, but he must learn to trust the present and the future, to put the past behind him once and for all.

Someone laid a hand upon his arm, and he turned to find his nephew standing beside him.

"You are being badly outshone by your own betrothed, Uncle George," Julian said with a grin. "My sympathies."

"Jackanapes," George said fondly. "I am standing here basking in her reflected glory."

"I would be obliged for a private word with you," Julian said, "if this is not too inconvenient a time."

"Not at all," George assured him. "I do not believe my presence will be missed for a little while. Come out onto the landing."

His nephew did not speak again until they were

leaning against the oak banister above the staircase and the hall below.

"Philippa and I have talked a great deal about your impending nuptials," he said, "and it has occurred to us that you may be feeling a bit concerned about us."

George raised his eyebrows and his nephew flushed.

"You made it very clear to me after . . . after Brendan's passing," he explained, "that you considered me your heir. You said at the time that you would never have another son of your own. No, don't say anything." He held up a hand as George drew breath to speak. "Let me finish. We are perfectly aware that Miss Debbins is not a . . . well, that she is not a very young lady and that you may well not be marrying her in order to set up your nursery again, but—"

"You are absolutely right," George said, firmly interrupting him. "I am marrying Miss Debbins because I have an affection for her. We have no wish whatsoever to populate the nursery at Penderris. Your status as my heir is not in peril."

Julian's flush had deepened. "I believe you, and I am sincerely happy for you," he said. "It has been abundantly clear this evening that you and Miss Debbins hold each other in deep regard. But the point is, Uncle George, that unexpected things do sometimes happen. I do not know if it is a possibility and, heaven help me, I do not want to know. But Philippa seems to think it is, and she may be right, she being a woman and all that. Anyway, we are in absolute agreement that we are perfectly happy with what we have and with who we are. I have rescued my own home and estate from the near ruin my father ran it into, and I have done a great deal more than that. It is thriving. I have much to leave my eldest son—if we have sons, that is—and adequate means with which to provide for Belinda and any other children with whom we may be blessed. We will not feel that we have been deprived of my birthright if you should have another son. After all, Papa was a younger son and never expected to succeed you, and I never expected it. There was always Brendan . . ." His voice trailed away and he frowned in apparent distress.

George was moved.

"Thank you, Julian," he said. "The unexpected, as you put it, will almost certainly not happen, but your assurances and the fact that you speak for Philippa too are a great comfort me. I could not ask for a better nephew—and niece."

He wondered for the first time if Miss Debbins really had dismissed from her mind all possibility of bearing a child—and if she would welcome such an outcome of their marriage so late in her life. Her childlessness might well have caused her some unhappiness in the past. As with all else, though, he guessed that she had dealt with any disappointment with the calm good sense that characterized her. Had his marriage offer revived some faint hope in her? He sincerely hoped not.

And then Julian spoke again.

"Did you know that Aunt Miriam's brother is in town?" he asked.

"Eastham?" George said, both startled and aghast to hear that his dead wife's brother was in London. Anthony

Meikle, Earl of Eastham, was actually Miriam's half brother. "But he has always been a near recluse. He lives in Derbyshire. He never comes to London."

"Well, he is here now," Julian said. "I saw him with my own eyes just yesterday outside Tattersall's. I even spoke to him. He told me he is here for a week or so on business. He did not seem particularly pleased to see me, however. He was certainly not inclined to settle into a lengthy chat. He was always a bit of a queer cove, was he not?"

"Don't take his unfriendliness personally," George said. "He would have been even less pleased to see me." A great deal less, in fact. George stretched the fingers of both hands to prevent himself from curling them into fists. His mouth was suddenly dry.

"I did think for a moment," Julian said, "that perhaps you had invited him to your wedding. But you would hardly have done that, would you? The two of you were never the best of friends."

"No," George said. "I did not invite him."

Julian frowned and looked as if he would have said more if he could have found the words. George patted him on the shoulder and pushed away from the rail.

"It is time I returned to my guests," he said briskly. "Thank you for your words, Julian. Thank Philippa for me, will you?"

He made his way back into the drawing room and saw that his betrothed, flushed and laughing, was still in the middle of a largish group. George smiled at the sight.

But the great welling of inner happiness he had felt

mere minutes ago had been replaced entirely by the creeping, surely baseless fear.

Eastham might have had any number of reasons to travel to London. His coming here now probably had nothing whatsoever to do with the fact that George was getting married the day after tomorrow. Why would it, after all? Coincidences happened all the time.

But what the devil *had* brought him?

7

$\mathcal{D}$ ora had discovered several times in the course of her life that time had the strange capacity of crawling and galloping along simultaneously. It seemed like far longer ago than one month since she had been at her cottage in Inglebrook, contented enough with her life and the set routine of her days, asking nothing more of the future than a continuation of the same. Indeed, it seemed almost like something that must have happened to someone else during a different lifetime. And yet . . . Well, she awoke on the morning of her wedding unable to believe that the month had already gone by. It seemed but yesterday that she had arrived in London with all the time in the world to adjust to the new reality of her existence.

She awoke with the panicked feeling that she had been rushed, that she was not nearly ready, that she was not even perfectly sure this was the right thing to be doing. There was a strange yearning to have the comfort and security of her old life back. This new one was far too vivid, too brilliantly . . . *happy* to last. The future yawned ahead, unknown and unknowable. Could she trust it? She was surprised she had slept, even resented the fact that she had. She had needed the night in which to ponder and consider.

But what was there to consider?

Was she afraid of happiness? Because it had let her down way back in her youth and she was wary of giving in to it again? She was about to marry a kind and wonderful man. She was even—she might as well be honest in the privacy of her own mind—a little in love with him. Perhaps a lot in love, though she would never admit to such foolishness outside the privacy of her own mind. In any case, she was going to marry him *today*. Before the morning was out, in fact. Nothing could or would stop that, for he was a man of honor. Besides, he wanted to marry her. He had come all the way to Inglebrook to propose to her, and there had been nothing in his manner since to suggest that he regretted having done so.

No, there really was nothing to ponder and nothing to fear. She threw back the bedcovers, got out of bed, and crossed the room to draw back the curtains from the window. It had rained on and off for the last four days, and the sky had been heavy with clouds the whole time. It had also been windy and chilly for June. But look! This morning the sky was blue with not a cloud in sight. The trees in the park at the center of the square below were still, not even a slight breeze rustling the leaves. Sunlight slanted through them from the east.

Oh, it was shaping up to be a perfect day. But of course it was. It would have been perfect even if it were bucketing down with rain and a gale was blowing.

It was still very early. Dora took her shawl from the chair beside her bed, wrapped it about her shoulders against the slight chill, and sat on the window seat. She drew her legs up before her and hugged her knees with both arms. She looked across the square toward Stanbrook House, but it was more than half hidden behind the trees. Was he awake yet? Was he looking across here? By tonight Stanbrook House would be her home. This time tomorrow she would be there with him. She could both feel and hear her heartbeat quicken and smiled ruefully. It was a bit embarrassing to be thirty-nine years old and a virgin while he, presumably, had years of experience behind him. Well, of course he did. He had been married for almost twenty years.

But she did not want to think of that. Certainly not today.

And suddenly, out of nowhere, came a great stabbing of longing for her mother. It took her breath away and made her stomach churn. She dipped her head until her forehead rested on her knees and swallowed against a lump in her throat.

Her mother had been vibrantly beautiful and full of smiles and laughter and love. She had doted upon her children and had never engaged a nurse to look after them. She had wept inconsolably when Oliver went away to school at the age of twelve, when Dora was ten. Dora had had her undivided attention for the next two years until Agnes was born. Mama had loved them equally after that. She had cuddled and played endlessly and happily with the baby, as had Dora, and she had talked with her elder daughter, dreamed with her about the future, promised her a dazzling come-out Season and a handsome, rich, loving husband at the end of it. They had laughed over how handsome he would be and how wealthy and how charming and loving. Mama had endlessly brushed and styled Dora's hair and made her pretty clothes and told her how lovely she was growing to be. She had taught Dora herself instead of hiring a governess, though she had insisted that Papa hire a good music teacher for her. She felt privileged and honored, she had once told Dora, to have been entrusted with such a musically gifted daughter. Her talent, Mama had often added, had certainly not come from her—or from Papa either.

When Dora turned seventeen, they had begun actively to plan the come-out Season she would have the following spring. Her music teacher was engaged for extra hours to give Dora dancing lessons, but the three of them had danced with one another between classes, Dora with her mother while one of them or both hummed the music until they were breathless and Agnes shrieked with laughter and clapped her hands. Then Mama, with Agnes's little feet balanced on her own, would sing and dance and Dora practiced the steps alone with an imaginary partner until they all collapsed in a heap of laughter and exhaustion.

Had those days, those years, really been as happy and carefree as Dora remembered them? Probably not. Memory tended to be selective. She remembered her childhood and early girlhood as endlessly sunny days of love and laughter perhaps because of the great contrast with what had followed.

Dora had been allowed to attend the infamous assembly because she had reached the magic age of seventeen. She had been not quite a young lady but no longer a girl. She had been over the moon with excitement, almost sick with it, in fact. Little Agnes had been excited too, she remembered, as she watched her sister get ready, her chin propped on her hands at one side of the dressing table. She had told Dora that she looked like a princess and wondered if a prince would ride in during the evening on a white steed. They had both giggled over that.

By the middle of the evening, Dora had been flushed with the pleasure and triumph of her local debut. She had danced every set, even if one of them had been with the vicar, who was as unlike a prince as it was possible for a man to be, and she had known all the steps of the dances even without having to think about them. And then Papa had enacted his terrible scene, his voice growing louder as he accused Mama of cuckolding him with the handsome and much younger Sir Everard Havell, who was on one of his extended visits to relatives in the neighborhood. Before Papa had been coaxed outside by two of their neighbors to "get some fresh air," he had informed the gathered assembly that he was going to turn Mama out and divorce her.

Dora had been so terribly mortified that she had hidden in a corner of the assembly rooms for the rest of the evening, resisting all attempts to coax her either into conversation or onto the dance floor. She had even told her best friend to go away and leave her alone. She had twisted her handkerchief so out of shape that even a heavy iron could never afterward make it look perfectly square. She would have died if she could have done so just by willing it. Her mother meanwhile had brazened it out, smiling and laughing and talking and dancing—and keeping her distance from Sir Everard—until the very end of the evening.

The whole ghastly situation might have blown over, hideously dreadful as it had been. Papa did not often drink to excess, but he was known for embarrassing himself and his family and neighbors when he did. Everyone would have pretended to forget, and life would have continued as usual.

But perhaps Mama had reached a breaking point that night. Perhaps she had been embarrassed and humiliated one time too many. Dora did not know. She had not attended any adult entertainments until that evening. Or perhaps the accusation was justified even if the public nature of Papa's accusation was not. However it was, Dora's mother had fled during the night, presumably with Sir Everard, since he too had disappeared by the following morning without taking leave of his relatives.

Mama had never come back, and she had never written to any of her children, even Oliver, who was at Oxford at the time. Papa had carried through with his threat even though the divorce had put a large dent in his own fortune and totally wiped out Mama's dowry, which was to have been divided in two to augment what Dora and Agnes could expect from their father as dowries when they married. Soon after the divorce bill was passed in the House of Lords, word had come to them that Mama had married Sir Everard Havell. Mrs. Brough, a neighbor and longtime family friend—and now Papa's wife—had brought the news. Mr. Brough had still been alive at the time, and he had received a letter from someone in London who had seen the notice in the morning papers.

Dora's life had changed as abruptly and as totally after the night of that assembly as it had changed a month ago in Inglebrook, though in a quite different way. There was no come-out Season for her in London when she turned eighteen. Even if it could have been arranged with someone else to sponsor her, there was the terrible scandal to deter her as well as Papa's comparative poverty. Besides, she would not have gone even if she could, just as she did not go to Harrogate a few years later when her aunt Shaw had urged her to come and promised to introduce her to society and some eligible gentlemen. She did not go because there was Agnes. Poor bewildered, unhappy little Agnes, who cried for her mother and could have only Dora instead.

Dora had stayed for Agnes.

It was as though the very thought summoned her sister. There was a light tap on the door of her bedchamber, and it opened slowly to reveal the anxious face of Agnes and then her full form, wrapped in a dressing gown.

"Oh, you are awake," she said, stepping into the room and closing the door behind her. "I thought you would be. What are you thinking about?"

Dora smiled and almost lied. They very rarely talked about the painful memories from the past. But she found herself telling the truth.

"Mama," she said, and she blinked as she realized her eyes had filled with hot tears.

"Oh, Dora!" Agnes hurried toward her, hands outstretched. "Do you miss her terribly? Even after all this time? I have thought about her occasionally since Flavian went to call on her last year. But I can scarcely remember her, you know. I daresay I would pass her on the street without knowing her, even if she still looked as she did all those years ago. I have only a few flashes of memory of her. But it is different for you. You were seventeen. She had been with you all through your childhood and girlhood."

"Yes," Dora said, squeezing Agnes's hands and then fumbling for her handkerchief.

"Does it make a difference to you, what she told Flavian last year?" Agnes asked.

"That she was innocent?" Dora said. "That she had done no more than flirt a little with that man before Papa said what he did? I can believe it. It was Papa who was the guilty one on that occasion, and I think I can understand why Mama fled. How would one face one's friends and neighbors again after such a humiliation? Perhaps I can even understand her leaving Papa. How could she forgive what he had done, even supposing that he asked for forgiveness? But she left *us,* Agnes. She left you. You were little more than a baby. She might have returned but did not. She might have written but did not. She used that horrible evening to do what she must have dreamed of doing for a long time. She ran away with that man. She married him. She put her own gratification before us—before you. No, what she told Flavian does not really make a difference."

"She would have been miserable if she had stayed," Agnes said. "Poor Mama."

"People often are miserable," Dora said. "They make the best of it. They make a meaningful life despite it. They make *happiness* despite it. Prolonged misery is often at least partially self-inflicted."

Agnes had pulled up a chair and sat beside her sister, one hand resting unconsciously over the slight swelling of her unborn child.

"You made happiness out of misery, Dora," she said softly. "You made me happy. Did you know that? And did you know that I adored you and still do? I am sorry . . . I am so sorry that you were obliged to give up your youth for me—or that you chose to give it up."

Dora turned her head and reached out one hand to grasp her sister's.

"There is no greater pleasure, Agnes," she said, "than making a child feel secure and happy when it is in one's power to do so. I know I was no substitute for Mama, but I loved you dearly. It was no sacrifice. Believe me it was not."

Agnes smiled, and there were tears in her eyes now too.

"I think," she said, "that after Flavian I love George more than any other man I know. They all do, you know—the Survivors, that is. They all adore him. He saved all their lives in more ways than just offering his home as a hospital. And he did it all with a quiet, stead-fast sort of kindness and love. Flavian says he had a gift for making each of them feel that he—or she in Imogen's case—had all his attention. He gave so much of himself that it is amazing he has anything left. But that is the mystery of love, is it not? The more one gives, the more one has. I am so happy that he is to have you, Dora. He deserves you. Not many men would. And you most certainly deserve him. Are you happy? You have not just . . . settled? Do you love him?"

"I am happy." Dora smiled. "I might have been felled with a feather, you know, when he appeared without any warning in my sitting room a month ago. I was actually cross when I heard his knock on the door. I had had a busy day and I was weary. And then he stepped into the room and asked if I would be obliging enough to marry him."

They both laughed and squeezed each other's hand.

"I am happy," Dora said again. "He is kindness itself."

"Just kindness?" Agnes asked. "Do you love him, Dora?"

"We have agreed," Dora said, "that we are too old for that nonsense."

Agnes shrieked and jumped to her feet.

"Shall I fetch a Bath chair to convey you to the wedding?" she asked. "Shall I have one sent to Stanbrook House to convey George?"

Dora swung her legs off the window seat, and they both dissolved into laughter again.

"I am fond of him," Dora conceded. "There. Are you satisfied? And I do believe he is fond of me."

"I am bowled over by the romance of it," Agnes said,

one hand over her heart. "But I do not believe you for a moment. At least, I do not believe it is just fondness you feel for each other. I was watching him while you played the pianoforte a couple of evenings ago, you know. He was positively beaming. And it was not just with pride. And I saw the way you looked at him after you had finished playing, before you were swamped with the attentions of the guests. Oh, Dora, this is your *wedding* day. I am so happy I could burst."

"Please don't," Dora said.

A tap on the door at that moment heralded the arrival of a maid with a breakfast tray for Dora, and Agnes took her leave, promising to be back within the hour to help her dress for the wedding. Dora looked at the buttered toast and the cup of chocolate without appetite, but it would be very embarrassing if her empty stomach began to protest during the nuptial service. She set about clearing the plate.

Yes, it was her wedding day. But Mama would not be there to witness it, though apparently she lived not far from here. Did she know? Was she aware that Dora was to marry the Duke of Stanbrook today? And would she care if she did? He had been willing to invite her, and for a moment Dora was quite illogically sorry she had said no.

"Mama." She murmured the name aloud and then shook her head to clear it. What an idiot she was being.

Soon Dora's wedding day began in earnest. Agnes returned as promised and was followed soon after by their sister-in-law, Louisa, and their father's wife—Dora never had been able to bring herself to call the former

Mrs. Brough her stepmother—and by Aunt Millicent. Agnes's own maid, with much advice and assistance from the ladies, arrayed Dora in her wedding outfit. She had chosen a midblue dress some people might judge to be too plain for the occasion, though Agnes and all the friends who were with her at the time had assured her that the expert cut and style made it not only smart but perfectly suited to her. She wore with it a small-brimmed, high-crowned straw bonnet trimmed with cornflowers, and straw-colored shoes and gloves. Agnes's maid styled her hair low at the neck to accommodate the bonnet, but prettily coiled and curled so that it did not look as prim as it usually did.

Everyone—except the maid—proceeded to hug her tightly when it was time for them to leave for the church, and all spoke at once, it seemed. There was a flurry of laughter.

And then, just when everything was quieting down with only Agnes left and Dora was composing herself for what lay ahead, there was a brisk knock on the door and Flavian poked his head about it, pronounced her decent—whatever would he have done if she had not been?—and opened the door wider to admit himself and Oliver and Uncle Harold. Flavian looked her over with lazy eyes and told her she looked as fine as fivepence—whatever that meant—and Oliver told her she looked as pretty as a picture and he was as proud as a peacock of her. Her brother had never been known for his originality with words. He then proceeded to fold her in his arms and attempt to crush every rib in her body while he assured her that if anyone deserved happiness at last, it was she. Uncle Harold merely looked sheepish and pecked her cheek after telling her she was looking fine.

Their father, Oliver informed her, was waiting downstairs to escort her to church.

Papa was neither an emotional man nor a demonstrative one—and that was a giant understatement—but he looked steadily up at Dora a few minutes later as she descended the stairs to the hallway.

"You look very pretty, Dora," he said. He hesitated before continuing. "I thank you for inviting Helen and me to your wedding and for asking me, moreover, to give you away. It was never our intention, you know, to make you feel obliged to leave home after our marriage."

Dora was not at all sure it had not been Mrs. Brough's intention. She had had what she had called a frank talk with her stepdaughter not long after Agnes's marriage to William Keeping and a year after her own marriage to Papa. She had explained that though Dora had had the running of the house since she was little more than a girl, she must not feel obliged to continue doing so now that it had a real mistress. Perhaps, she had suggested, Dora would care to visit her aunt in Harrogate for an indefinite period of time. Or perhaps she would like to make her home with Agnes and Mr. Keeping and allow her sister to look after her for a change. Dora had been hurt, since she had been trying very hard not to involve herself in the running of the home. At the same time, there had been a certain sense of relief in being set free to pursue her own future.

"I am very glad you both came, Papa," she assured

him quite truthfully. Her father had never gone out of his way to earn her affection, but he had never been unkind either, and Dora loved him.

He offered her his arm and led her out to the waiting carriage. The sun was still shining from a clear sky. The air was warm and welcoming. Numerous birds, hidden among the branches of the trees in the park, were singing their hearts out.

Oh, let it all be a good omen, Dora thought.

8

*A*t five minutes to eleven it was unlikely there was an empty space in any of the pews at St. George's Church on Hanover Square. Indeed, a few of the male guests were standing at the back and were even beginning to encroach upon the side aisles. Society weddings during the Season invariably drew a crowd of invited guests, but when the groom was a duke and the bride a virtual unknown, then the crowd was sure to be larger than usual. Even King George IV had explained that he would have been delighted to attend if a long-standing obligation did not oblige him to be out of town on the day in question.

The organist was playing quietly, muting the low hum of conversation.

George, seated at the front with his nephew, ought to have been feeling nervous. It was almost obligatory, was it not, for grooms to feel their neckcloths tighten about their throats and their palms grow clammy at this stage of the proceedings? But it was Julian who was showing signs of nerves as he patted one of his pockets to make sure the ring had not escaped its confines during the past five minutes.

George himself was feeling perfectly composed. No, actually he was feeling something more positive than that. He was aware of a boyish sort of eagerness as he awaited his bride. He was going to savor every word and every moment of the nuptial service with her at his side. The ceremony would usher them into the future they had chosen for themselves. It would be a perfect beginning to a marriage of perfect contentment—or so he firmly believed. He had hoped for it when he went into Gloucestershire to offer her marriage, but he had become convinced of it during the past month. She was the wife for whom he had unconsciously longed perhaps all his life, and he dared believe he was the husband she had dreamed of and been denied as a very young lady. Fate was a strange thing, though. He would not have been free for her at that time even if they had met.

"Is she late?" he murmured when it seemed to him that it must be at least eleven o' clock.

Julian pounced upon this small sign of weakness. "Aha!" he said, turning his head and grinning. "You *are* feeling it. But I very much doubt she is. Miss Debbins does not seem the sort who would ever keep someone waiting. But if she is late, she is certainly not going to be any later. I believe she has arrived."

Even as he spoke the bishop appeared at the front of the church, formally and gorgeously vested and flanked by two lesser mortals, mere clergymen. He signaled George to rise. The organ fell silent for a moment—and so did the congregation—and then began to play a solemn anthem. There was a rustling of heads turning to look back and a murmur of voices as the bride came into view and began to make her way along the nave on the arm of her father.

George's first strange thought as he turned and saw her was that she looked exactly like herself. Her blue dress, long-sleeved and round necked, simply designed and unadorned, suited her to perfection. Her straw bonnet was neat and small brimmed, and her hair beneath it was smoothly styled. She was wide-eyed and glanced neither to left nor to right as she approached, but she looked composed, even serene. Her eyes found him almost immediately and remained fixed upon him.

He felt a wave of warm affection for her and an utter certainty that everything was as it ought to be. He was going to be happy at last. So was she—he would see to that. He smiled, and she smiled back at him with a look of unguarded pleasure.

Then she was at his side, her father bowed and moved away to sit beside Lady Debbins in the front pew, and they turned together to be married. The congregation was forgotten, and George felt a sense of peace, of rightness. It was his wedding day, and within the next few minutes this woman beside him would be his wife. His own.

"Dearly beloved," the bishop said, and George gave his attention to the service. He wanted to remember every precious moment of it for the rest of his life.

". . . now come to be joined," the bishop was saying a few moments later in that distinctive voice of clergymen everywhere that carried to the farthest corner of the loftiest church. "If any of you can show just cause why they may not lawfully be married, speak now; or else for ever hold your peace."

He was addressing the congregation. Next he would ask the same question of the two of them, and then they would speak the vows that would bind them together for the rest of their lives. Despite himself, though, George felt the twinge of anxiety that all brides and grooms must experience during the beat of silence that followed the admonition. Someone coughed. The bishop drew breath to continue.

And the unthinkable happened.

A voice broke the silence from far back in the church before the bishop could resume—a male voice, distinct and loud and slightly trembling with emotion. It was a familiar voice, though George had not heard it for a number of years.

"*I* can show just cause."

And somehow it seemed to George that he had been expecting this, that it was inevitable.

There was a collective gasp of shock from the pews and a renewed rustle of silks and satins as the members of congregation, almost as one body, swung about in their seats to see who had spoken. George turned too, his eyes briefly meeting those of his bride as he did so. Even in that momentary glance he could see that she had turned suddenly pale. His blood felt as though it had turned to ice in his veins.

Anthony Meikle, Earl of Eastham, had made it easy for everyone to see him. He had stood and stepped out into the center of the nave. Or perhaps he had not been sitting down at all. Perhaps he had just arrived.

The bishop and the clergymen with him remained calm. The bishop held up a hand for silence and got it almost immediately.

"You will identify yourself, sir, and state the nature of the impediment," he said, still using his formal ecclesiastical voice.

Hugo, looking thunderous and menacing, was on his feet, George noticed almost dispassionately. So was Ralph a couple of places farther along the same pew, the slash of his facial scar making him look more fiercely piratical than usual.

In a dramatic gesture that looked too theatrical for any reputable stage, Eastham raised his right arm and pointed a slightly shaking finger at George.

"*That man*," he said, "*the Duke of Stanbrook*, is a murderer and a villain. He killed his first wife by pushing her off a high cliff on his estate in Cornwall to her death on the jagged rocks below. The Duchess of Stanbrook was my sister and would never under any circumstances have taken her own life. Stanbrook hated her, and he murdered her."

"Half sister," George heard someone murmur and realized it was himself.

There was a swell of sound from half the congregation, shushing sounds from the other half, and finally an expectant hush.

Anthony Meikle, now the Earl of Eastham, had made the same accusation immediately after Miriam's death twelve years ago to anyone who would listen— and a number of people did. He had made it despite the fact that he had been unable to offer anything by way of proof or even credible evidence. After the funeral he had vowed revenge. This, presumably, was it.

His rare appearance in London was explained. It struck George that he might have guessed that this or something like it would happen.

"You have evidence, sir, to prove this most serious of charges?" the bishop asked. "If you do, your proper course of action would be to take it to a magistrate or other law enforcement officer."

"*Law enforcement!*" Eastham exclaimed, his voice throbbing with contempt. "When he is a duke? He should hang by the neck until he is dead, and even that end would be too good for him. But of course it will not happen because he has the protection of his rank. I charge him with the truth nonetheless, and I charge you, my lord bishop, to do your duty and put an end to this farce of a marriage service. The Duke of Stanbrook must not be allowed to take a second wife when he murdered the first."

George turned his head to look at his bride again. She was as pale as chalk, and he wondered if she was about to faint. But she was looking steadily and apparently calmly at Eastham.

"I am afraid, sir," the bishop said, his voice stern, "that I must judge against your protest and continue with these proceedings. Your unsubstantiated accusation has failed to convince me that there is any valid impediment to the nuptials I am here to solemnize."

"There is none," George said. He made no attempt to raise his voice, though the silence was such that he did not doubt everyone could hear him. "I was the only witness to my wife's death, and I was too far away to save her."

"You are a filthy *liar,* Stanbrook," Eastham cried, and he took a few menacing steps forward. But Hugo and Ralph were already out in the nave and bearing down upon him, and Flavian was not far behind. Percy was pushing his way out of a pew on the other side of the aisle.

"Sir." The bishop's voice rang through the church with solemn authority. "Your objection to these proceedings has been heard and overruled. You will be seated now and hold your peace, or you will remove yourself from the church."

Eastham was not given the opportunity to choose. Hugo hooked an arm through one of his while Ralph did the like for the other, and between them they hurried him out backward, though he did not go quietly. Flavian and Percy followed after them. Percy did not reappear.

But George was only half aware of either what was happening or the renewed swell of sound from the pews. His eyes were fixed upon those of his bride, who had turned away from the spectacle to regard him.

"Do you wish to proceed?" he asked, his voice low. "We will postpone our wedding to another time if you prefer."

Or cancel it if she chose.

"I wish to proceed now." She did not hesitate, and her eyes remained steady on his. But her warm, radiant smile had gone. His own expression, he feared, was grim.

A heavy silence had fallen on the church, though it did not feel to George like a particularly hostile one. There was not a steady stream of guests making its outraged way to the doors, only the sound of boot heels on stone as his three friends made their way back to their places. But of course, almost everyone in the congregation would have heard that particular rumor long ago. It had caused a sensation in the neighborhood about Penderris Hall in the days and weeks following Miriam's death, and it was far too salacious a story not to have spread to other parts of the country, most notably London. There would always be those only too eager to cry murder after a violent death to which there had been only one witness, and that the woman's husband. The rumor had died with time and lack of either motive or evidence. It was doubtful that many people still believed it. Indeed, it was doubtful many people beyond the neighborhood of Penderris itself ever had.

The bishop proceeded with the service, picking up exactly where he had left off, and George tried to recapture his earlier mood and glanced at his bride to see if she had recaptured hers.

It was impossible, of course—and impossible to concentrate fully.

They spoke their vows with unfaltering voices, gazing directly at each other as they did so, and he fitted her wedding ring onto her finger while repeating the words the bishop read to him. Neither his own hand nor hers shook with even the slightest of tremors. Yet her hand was ice cold to his touch. He smiled at her and she smiled back. It took a conscious effort on his part, and doubtless on hers too. There was warmth in her smile but no radiance.

The bishop proclaimed them man and wife, and just like that, almost unnoticed, the moment he had anticipated with such boyish eagerness came and passed and they were married.

Had she known about those rumors surrounding his wife's death? George found himself wondering. Belatedly he thought that perhaps he ought to have raised the matter with her.

He drew her still ungloved hand through his arm when it came time to withdraw to the vestry for the signing of the register, and covered it with his own when he discovered that it was still cold. He curled his fingers about it to warm it, as though it were only her hand that needed comforting.

"I am so very sorry," he murmured.

"But it was not your fault," she said.

"I wanted our wedding to be perfect for you," he told her.

Her eyes looked fleetingly into his. "It was not your fault," she said again, "any more than it was mine."

But she had not assured him that it had been perfect.

They were both smiling when they came out of the vestry a few minutes later, the register having been signed and witnessed, the final seal placed on their marriage. A sea of smiling faces watched them from the pews, just as though nothing had happened to spoil the wedding and to set fashionable drawing rooms abuzz with gossip for days to come.

They walked slowly, nodding from side to side,

picking out particular friends and relatives—Agnes with her upper lip caught between her teeth and tears swimming in her eyes; Philippa with her clasped hands held to her mouth; Gwen smiling and nodding beside the flame-haired Chloe; Imogen, her eyes, luminous with tenderness, moving from one to the other of them; Vincent gazing so directly toward them that it was almost impossible to believe that he was blind; Oliver Debbins gazing with frowning concern at his sister, his wife smiling; Ben with . . . tears in his eyes? The other Survivors, George noticed—Hugo, Ralph, Flavian, and, of course, that Survivor-by-marriage, Percy—were conspicuous by their absence, and it did not take a genius to guess where they had gone and what they were up to. Not, at least, when one had been involved in five other Survivor weddings during the past two years, one of them only a little over a month ago.

They were waiting outside the church, along with a sizable crowd of curious onlookers, who set up a cheer when the bride and groom emerged. The four men, as George had fully expected, had armed themselves with great handfuls of flower petals, which were soon being flung into the air to rain down upon George's head and his bride's. He took her by the hand, and they both laughed and made a dash for the open carriage that awaited them. It had been decked with flowers before George left home. Without looking, though, he knew that by now it would have acquired a less pretty cargo of noisy, metallic things tied to the back, ready to set up a deafening rumpus as soon as the vehicle was in motion.

George handed his bride into the carriage and followed her in. Another shower of multicolored petals rained about their heads. The church bells were ringing out the joyful tidings of a new marriage. The members of the congregation were beginning to spill out through the doors.

The sun was shining.

A hand touched George on the shoulder and squeezed.

"Don't worry," Percy said for his ears only. "He is gone and will not be reappearing for a while."

And then the coachman gave the signal for the horses to start, and every other sound was drowned out by the unholy din of the unofficial carriage decorations.

George settled his shoulders across one corner of the seat and took one of his bride's hands in both his own.

"Well, my dear duchess," he said while she was forced to read his lips in order to hear.

She smiled and then grimaced and laughed at the noise.

He raised her hand to his lips and held it there while the carriage moved out of Hanover Square on its way to Portman Square, Chloe and Ralph having insisted upon hosting the wedding breakfast at Stockwood House.

George had intended to set his arm about her shoulders and kiss her on the lips for everyone outside the church to see. It was what his friends would expect. It would have been the perfect conclusion to a perfect wedding, the perfect start to a happy marriage.

He ought to have done it anyway. But it was too late now.

The day had been irrevocably spoiled.

*   *   *

The day had *not* been spoiled, Dora assured herself throughout the rest of it. What had happened in the church had been unfortunate—oh, what a massive understatement!—but it had been dealt with swiftly and firmly, the man had been removed, and the nuptial service had resumed just as if the unpleasant interruption had not happened at all.

Apart from those brief moments, the wedding service had been perfect. So had the weather. Sunshine and warmth had greeted them when they stepped outside the church, and there had been the delightful surprise of a cheering crowd and the merry, laughing faces of their friends as they showered them with rose petals, just as she remembered their doing at Agnes's wedding last year. Even the deafening noise of the pots and pans they dragged behind the carriage all the way to Stockwood House had been amusing. Her husband had held her hand in both of his all the way there and sat half sideways on the seat, gazing at her with smiling eyes.

Chloe and Ralph's house had been festively decorated for the occasion with ribbons and bows and urns of flowers. The ballroom had looked more like a lavish garden than an indoor room and had quite taken Dora's breath away when she stepped into it on the arm of the duke. It had soon been packed with guests, all of whom had bowed or curtsied and smiled and offered congratulations and best wishes as they passed along the receiving line. The food had been sumptuous, the speeches heartfelt and often laughter-provoking, and the wedding cake such a beautiful work of art that it had seemed a pity to cut it. And after the breakfast the guests had been in no hurry to leave but had moved into other rooms and out onto the terrace to linger and continue their conversations. But gradually the guests did begin to take their leave and finally only family and close friends remained.

Everything had been perfect.

No one had made any reference at all to what had happened during those five minutes in the church. It was almost as if Dora had imagined it.

At the end of the day what she remembered most were the smiles and laughter and unrelenting cheerfulness of so many people, all celebrating her nuptials. Why had it left her wanting to weep?

There had been those three or four minutes—definitely no longer than four—out of a long and eventful day that had been otherwise joyful and perfect. Like a worm at the heart of a perfect rose.

I can show just cause.

It was surely every bride's nightmare that someone would break that short silence in the nuptial service with just those words.

That man, the Duke of Stanbrook, is a murderer and a villain. He killed his first wife by pushing her off a high cliff on his estate in Cornwall to her death on the jagged rocks below. The Duchess of Stanbrook was my sister and would never under any circumstances have taken her own life. Stanbrook hated her, and he murdered her.

He should hang by the neck until he is dead. . . . The Duke of Stanbrook must not be allowed to take a second wife when he murdered the first.

It was almost incredible that the wedding and the breakfast had proceeded so normally, so merrily, so *perfectly* after those words had been spoken. How could they all have smiled the rest of the day away? How could he have smiled? How could she? Why had nothing been said?

It was unfair. It was so very unfair.

He was calling her "my dear," she noticed. She was calling him nothing. How could she continue to call him "Your Grace" when she was married to him? But how could she call him "George," when he had not invited her to do so? Did she need an invitation, though? He was her husband. And they were friends, were they not? A friendship had surely grown between them during the past month. But . . . did she know him? He had done forty-seven years of living before she even met him last year, more than half a lifetime. She really did not know him at all.

Well, of course she did not. They had spent only a month plus those few days last year together. She had felt she knew him, knew his spirit. But the truth was that she did not know him at all. Getting to know each other was what their marriage would be all about.

It was well into the evening when they arrived home. And even the homecoming should have felt perfect. The butler opened the double doors wide with something of a flourish, spilling light out onto the dusk-shaded steps, and bowed low. Behind him all the servants were gathered, standing formally in two lines extending along the hallway, the women on one side, the men on the other. Despite the lateness of the hour they were all smiling, their heads turned toward the doors. At what must have been a prearranged signal from someone, they all applauded as the Duke of Stanbrook led Dora over the threshold.

Someone must have dashed ahead from Stockwood House to warn the servants that they were on the way.

The butler had a speech to deliver, stiff but also endearing. The duke answered it and introduced Dora as his duchess. More applause followed and more smiles, and she thanked them for the welcome and promised to get to know them all by name in the next few days.

A tea tray was brought up to the drawing room and Dora seated herself to pour—her first duty as a wife in her new home. They sat on either side of the fire, which was welcome in the coolness that had come with the dusk. And they talked about the day, agreeing in effect that it had been perfect.

As it had been.

Except for those few minutes.

Several times Dora thought she would broach the subject but could not steel her nerve. Several times she thought the duke was going to make mention of it, but when he spoke it was of something else, some other fond memory of the day.

He did not stop smiling. Neither, she realized, did she.

"You are tired, my dear," he said at last. "It has been a long and busy day. A happy one, though, would you not agree?"

"Yes," she said. "Very happy."

Oh, dear God, what was the matter with them? How could they allow one deranged man to do this to them?

He was standing before her chair, extending a hand for hers. There was the wedding night to celebrate. Why was she feeling depressed? She set her hand in his, got to her feet, and allowed him to draw her arm through his. She did not even know, she thought, where her bed-chamber was, where her trunks were that had been brought here at some time during the day, where she would find what she needed, where she would undress, where . . .

He led her upstairs past wall sconces filled with candles, all cheerfully alight, and along a wide corridor before stopping outside a closed door.

"You are tired, my dear," he said again, his fingers curving about her hand on his other arm and raising it to his lips. "I will leave you to have a good night's rest and will look forward to seeing you at breakfast in the morning. Though you must not feel obliged to get up early if you wish to sleep on. Good night."

What?

But Dora had no time either to show or to express her shock. He opened the door to reveal a dressing room lit by candlelight and a maid curtsying and smiling at her. She recognized the fine linen nightgown she had chosen for her wedding night set out over a chair. She stepped inside, and the door closed behind her.

"I am Maisie, Your Grace," the maid said. "I will be your dresser for the time being until you choose some-one else, unless you decide to keep me, which I would like of all things."

Dora smiled.

Smiles. Perfection. What had happened in a few min-utes. It was how she would remember her wedding day as long as she lived, Dora thought as she gave herself up to the unfamiliar ministrations of her new maid.

Oh, and the absence of a wedding night.

You are tired, my dear.

My dear.

She did not want to be his dear. She wanted to be *Dora*.

9

George was standing at the window of his bedchamber, his knuckles braced on the sill, his shoulders hunched. He was gazing out into darkness, though he was scarcely aware that there was nothing to see. He was dressed for bed, his dark blue dressing gown belted over his nightshirt. Behind him the covers of the large canopied bed had been turned down for the night—on both sides.

He could hardly have made more of a mess of the day if he had tried. The appearance of Eastham inside the church and his dramatic pronouncement there had been totally unexpected, it was true, but life was full of the unexpected. In forty-eight years he ought to have learned better how to handle it. Actually, he believed that at the time he had behaved with the proper restraint and dignity, as had the bishop. He had even had the presence of mind to ask his bride if she wished to postpone the wedding.

It was the rest of the day that had been the disaster. And he was the one most to blame, he feared. Everyone else had taken their cue from him.

What he ought to have done was kiss his bride in the carriage, as he had planned to do, while everyone looked on. Then he ought to have spoken to her of what had happened with the promise that they would talk more fully later, when they were alone and not distracted by the din of the hardware they were dragging along. *Then* he ought to have raised the issue quite openly with his guests at the start of the wedding breakfast, explained again that there was absolutely no truth to the charges that the Earl of Eastham had made against him both this morning and immediately after Miriam's death, and invited everyone to put the unfortunate incident behind them if they could and celebrate his wedding day with him and his new duchess. Later, after most of the guests had left and only close family and friends remained, he should have raised the issue again and talked it out with them. And *then,* after returning home with his bride, he should have sat down with her and discussed the matter privately with her, talked the whole thing over with her yet again.

That was what he *ought* to have done. He had nothing to hide, after all, and nothing of which to be ashamed.

He had done none of those things.

Instead, after that brief apology to his bride in the church, he had said nothing at all to anyone, but had behaved just as though that shocking episode had not happened. And apart from Percy's quick word with him before the carriage moved off, everyone had followed his lead. All had been smiling, festive merriment for the rest of the day—the perfect wedding celebration with the perfectly happy couple.

Not a cloud in their sky. Only endless bliss ahead of them.

It had been one giant pretense. All day there had been a loud silence on the very topic that had surely been foremost in everyone's thoughts. Eastham would be delighted if he could know that he had ruined George's wedding day even though he had failed to put a stop to the proceedings.

George changed position to brace his hands on the side frames of the window just above the level of his head. A light was bobbing slowly and rhythmically about the square—the night watchman's lantern. His presence was unnecessary, however. Nothing disturbed the peace. Not out there, anyway.

And then there had been the greatest disaster of all. He had let his bride go to bed alone—on her wedding night. He had done it because she had looked tired and he had thought to do her a kindness.

Balderdash!

Why the devil had he done it, then? Because he could not quite bring himself to face her in the intimacy of the marriage bed? Because he feared that a part of her might believe what she had heard? Because retreating into his own inner world was second nature to him and he had needed to be alone?

On his wedding night?

He curled his hands into fists and pounded them lightly against the window frame. Was he going to allow Eastham to do this to him on top of everything else?

He felt suddenly and painfully like his seventeen-year-old self again, gauche and totally out of control of his own life and destiny. How could he have sent his bride to bed alone on their wedding night? He fairly squirmed with shame and embarrassment.

It was well after midnight, too late to go to her now. But was it? How likely was it that she was sleeping? Not very, at a guess. How could she be? He had so very much wanted their wedding day to be the happiest day of both their lives. Instead it had turned into perhaps the worst nightmare of a day either of them had ever lived through. Good God, she had been abandoned by her bridegroom on her wedding night—her forty-eight-year-old, oh-so-mature bridegroom, who had allowed himself to be completely overset by the spite of a man who had blighted a large portion of his adult life.

He did not take a candle with him into his dressing room or into hers beyond it. He did not want the light to wake her if by chance she was asleep. Or perhaps he did not want to illumine his own face if she was not. He tapped softly on the door of the duchess's bedchamber—in which he had not intended that the duchess ever sleep except perhaps for afternoon naps—and turned the knob quietly before opening the door and stepping inside.

The bed was untouched. He could see that much in the dim light from the window across which the curtains had not been drawn. For a moment he thought the room was empty. But there was a large, winged armchair beside the window, and he could see that she was curled up within it, her legs drawn up onto the seat and turned sideways, her arms hugging each other by the elbows beneath her bosom, her head against the chair back. She was very still and very quiet. Too still and too quiet to be sleeping.

He crossed the room to stand in front of her chair. She was indeed not sleeping. Her eyes were open and looking up at him.

"I am so sorry, my dear," he said. The same lame words he had used earlier in the day.

"Don't call me that." Her voice was quiet and toneless.

He felt a lurching of alarm.

"I have a name," she told him.

"Dora," he said softly. He had planned to call her that in the carriage before he kissed her outside the church, had deliberately not asked before their wedding day if he might have the privilege of using it sooner. He had looked forward to hearing her answer him with his own name. There was an intimacy in names, and he had wanted that intimacy within moments of their leaving the church as man and wife. Where the devil had "*my dear*" come from?

"I could not have mismanaged the day more than I have," he said.

"It was not your fault," she said, still in that dull monotone.

"Ah, but much of it was," he said. "A ghastly few minutes might have remained just that—a few minutes—if I had only spoken openly about the incident afterward to our guests, discussed it with our families and friends later, and explained fully to you when we were alone."

"You did not know it was going to happen," she said. "You had no chance to prepare an appropriate response. You behaved with dignity nevertheless."

He stooped down on his haunches before her. He would have taken her hands if she had made them available, but she continued to hug her elbows. She had not moved at all. She was deeply withdrawn into herself. If she could have disappeared into the chair, he believed she would have done so.

"Dora," he said, "there is no grain of truth in anything he said. I swear to you there is not."

"I did not even for a moment believe there was," she said. "No one did."

Perhaps not. But at the time there had been those who chose to believe, including a small clique of his neighbors at home who had indulged the deplorable human urge to convert a simple tragedy into a lurid sensation. Being accused of a heinous crime when one had no incontrovertible proof of one's innocence was surely one of the worst feelings in the world. One wanted to go about proclaiming one's innocence, but, knowing that to be futile, one retreated instead into the deepest, darkest core of oneself—and more or less stayed there forever after. That was what he had done, anyway, even though he was convinced that all the more sensible elements of society had long ago absolved him of all suspicion of guilt.

He reached out a hand and cupped it about her cheek. She neither flinched nor moved—even as far as to lean into his hand. He set one knee on the floor, the better to balance himself.

"I wanted our wedding day to be perfect for you," he said.

She said nothing. But what was there to say?

"Instead," he said, "it must have been one of worst days of your life."

He heard her draw breath as if to speak, but she said nothing to deny it.

"It is past midnight," he said. "A new day. Allow me to start afresh, if you will."

Did her head tilt a fraction closer to his hand?

"Let me take you to bed," he said. "To our marital bed in our room. Not here. This is to be your private bedchamber for daytime use. At least, I hope that is all it will be used for. Come to bed with me, Dora. Let me make love to you."

He could hear her inhaling very slowly. "I am your wife," she said, still in the same toneless voice.

He got abruptly to his feet and turned to the window. He braced his hands against the outer frames. The night watchman was long gone. There was nothing but darkness out there.

"Please don't," he said. "Don't make this a matter of duty. You owe me nothing out of duty. Nothing. I married you because I wanted a companion and a lover. I thought you wanted the same. If I was mistaken, or if you have changed your mind, then . . . so be it." There was a short silence. "Was I mistaken? Have you changed your mind?"

"Neither," she said.

"Forgive me for today," he said, "and particularly for this evening. I cannot explain even to myself why I said good night to you outside your dressing room. It was certainly not because I did not want you. Please believe that."

He felt a hand on his back then. He had not heard her getting to her feet.

"I am sorry too, Your Grace," she said. "We are both old enough to know better than to expect perfection of any day. How foolish we both were to expect it of our wedding day. And yet it was perfect except for those few minutes, which were neither your fault nor mine."

He swung around. "Your Grace?" He laughed. "Oh, no, please, Dora."

"George," she said. His name sounded a little prim on her tongue and altogether alluring.

He set one arm about her shoulders and the other about her waist and drew her against him. She was warm and shapely and womanly and clad in a predictably modest and unadorned nightgown of the finest linen. She smelled of that light floral fragrance he had noticed before. She set her hands against his shoulders and lifted her face. He could not see it clearly. Although she faced the window, she was in the shadow of his body.

He kissed her lips for the first time. She held them stiff and still, and it occurred to him with something of a shock that it was possible she had never been kissed before. Even if she had, it had probably been a long time ago. He drew his head a little way back from hers and turned them slightly so that the faint light of the outdoors was on her face.

"Smile for me," he murmured.

Perhaps it was surprise that caused her to do so.

He kissed her again, and her lips, still curved upward and slightly parted in a smile, were soft and yielding. He softened his own over them, moved them, touched his tongue to the seam of hers, pressed slightly between. She made a soft sound of alarm, but he had cupped her elbows with his hands and moved her arms so that they came over his shoulders and about his neck. He drew her against his body again and deepened the kiss without doing anything else that might shock her further.

He was surprised by the sensation of pure pleasure he felt from their almost chaste embrace. The pleasure had nothing to do with sexual desire, though there was that too. It had more to do with the fact that she was his woman, his wife, his companion, his *own* for the rest of their lives as long as they both lived. Some of the joy of the morning—of yesterday morning—returned.

Her head moved back from his then and he could see her face clearly enough to detect some anxiety there. "You do realize," she asked him, "that I am a virgin?"

He would be willing to wager that her cheeks were aflame.

He wanted to smile, even laugh, for she spoke in the voice she must use to the more careless of her music pupils, but it would have been the wrong thing to do. "I do realize it," he said gravely. "By the morning it will no longer be so. Come to bed, Dora."

Goodness, she must have been fathoms deep in sleep, Dora thought as she began to float upward to the surface. She was enveloped in warmth and comfort. The mattress had never felt so soft or the pillow so warm yet firm beneath her neck. She had never felt so totally relaxed or so filled to the brim with a sense of well-being. A clock was ticking steadily somewhere close by. She breathed in a pleasant but unfamiliar fragrance. As well as the rhythmic ticking of the clock, there was another sound, that of the deep, even breathing of someone asleep beside her. And—the only discordant detail—there was a soreness between her thighs and up inside her. Yet not really discordant after all, for paradoxically the soreness was the most deliciously comforting feeling of all and the origin of her utter contentment.

She had reached the very surface of sleep and broke through into consciousness, remembering. She was in an unfamiliar bed in an unfamiliar room. But the bed was . . . what had he called it? It was their marital bed. And this was their room, whenever they were in London, anyway. That other room where he had come for her was hers only for daytime use. But she had no wish to go back there.

He was lying beside her now, his arm beneath her head, and he was sleeping. He had made love to her before they slept. It had been a very one-sided activity, since she had been hopelessly ignorant and inadequate. But no, no, no, *no,* she would not think that. He had assured her she had not been. He had told her she had been wonderful and, oh, goodness, she had believed him because his voice had been low against her ear, and one of his hands had been stroking her hair, and his weight had been heavy on her, and he had still been . . . inside her. He had made her feel wonderful even though she had not had a clue of an idea what to do to make their love-making mutual. He had told her she did not need to do anything, only to *be* and to enjoy if she possibly could. He had apologized for the pain he knew he was causing her and had promised it would be better next time and better still after that.

He had not really understood, though she had tried to explain, that there was some pain that was not really pain at all even though it hurt. Well, it was no wonder he had not understood if she had described it that way. Had she really been so incoherent? But she could not put it properly into words even inside her own head. She had shed some tears because he was hurting her, but the tears had been less about the pain than about the sheer wonder of what was happening. How could one know all one's adult life the facts of what happened between a man and a woman and imagine what it would feel like, yet really have no idea how it would really be?

She had convinced herself over and over down the years that the absence of *it* from her life did not make her less happy or less fulfilled as a person or a woman. And of course she had been right. She would not have lived out her days as half a woman if he had never come to offer her marriage. But, oh, the delight of last night's discovery and the . . . the sheer *joy* of knowing that it would happen again and again in the future.

She was a married lady. In every sense—the wedding yesterday, the consummation last night.

It was not just the act itself that had been wonderful, though. He had been wonderful. He had been considerate and respectful of her awkward inexperience. He had extinguished the candles before joining her in bed, and he had not completely removed her nightgown but had only raised it to her waist and then lowered it after they were finished. He had removed his own nightshirt, but only after the room was in darkness. He was still naked beside her now. Along the side of her right arm she could feel the bareness of his chest, warm and lightly dusted with hair. He had also been patient. Ignorant as she was, she had sensed the restraint he had imposed upon himself as he prepared her with warm, skilled hands and a gentle, alluring mouth. And he had held the bulk of his weight above her while it was happening. He had eased his way slowly inside her. She was not sure he had thus saved her from any of the pain, but he had perhaps prevented some of the shock of the unfamiliar stretching and penetration *there*. Even after he had entered her fully, he had proceeded cautiously, she had sensed, until he was finished and she felt a liquid gush of heat deep inside.

Ah, yes, it had been both painful and shocking. It had also been—oh, by far—the most glorious experience of her life.

Despite herself her thoughts went back to their wedding, the day she had expected to be the happiest of her life. It had not been, of course, but upsetting as it had been for her, it must have been very much worse for him. That man—the Earl of Eastham—had been his brother-in-law and yet had accused him of murder. Why? And why so publicly and on just such an occasion? It had been somehow horribly reminiscent of another occasion when someone—her father—had spoken out with a public denunciation and changed her life forever. Was it pure spite on the earl's part because his sister's widower was marrying again?

She could not ask. Even though he had said last night

that he ought to have talked openly about the incident with his guests and friends during the day and discussed it fully with her when they were alone, he had not then proceeded to do just that. He had brought her to bed instead.

She was suddenly aware that she could no longer hear his breathing beside her. She turned her head to find herself being regarded with sleepy, smiling eyes.

"Dora," he murmured.

"George."

He chuckled after a few moments. "Well, that was a profound conversation."

"Yes," she agreed. She was only half joking. A name—a first name—was a powerful thing. Her heart had yearned toward him last night when he had called her by name for the first time. Calling him by his name seemed very personal and intimate when he was . . . the Duke of Stanbrook, whom she had thought of as some sort of remote, unattainable figure of nobility for well over a year. Yet now she was his wife. She was in bed with him. They had made love. He was George.

"I like waking to see you there." He closed his eyes and inhaled. "My bed has been very empty, Dora."

Since his first wife's death? But she did not want to be thinking that particular thought. And it did not matter. That was then. This was now.

"So has mine," she told him. Oh, she had not realized how very empty it had been.

He opened his eyes again. "Do you like waking up to me?"

"Yes."

"This conversation grows more profound by the moment," he said, and they smiled at each other and then laughed. It felt very good to laugh with him. She very much hoped there would be light and laughter in their marriage as well as the companionship and intimacy he had spoken of when he offered for her.

She wondered if he would talk to her today about yesterday and what might have provoked that incident. She knew nothing about his first marriage, about his first wife, about his son. She knew nothing about his heart. She would be going to Penderris Hall with him soon, where he had lived for almost twenty years with them. She had not thought of it that way before. Would she sense their residual presence? Would she be able to be all in all to him? Would he be able to be all in all to her?

Foolish, foolish questions. Their marriage would be what they made of it. They had agreed upon companionship, friendship, and intimacy, and those things had sounded very good indeed to her. They still did. She must not begin to yearn for all in all or happily-ever-after or those other romantic, fairy-tale things a girl might dream of.

His hand was resting lightly upon her abdomen, over her nightgown.

"You are undoubtedly sore," he said. "I will restrain myself for a night or two while you heal, but I want you here in this bed with me, Dora, tonight and every night. I hope it is what you wish too?"

"It is." She turned her head and rested a cheek

against his shoulder—oh, goodness, he smelled so masculine and so good. He nestled his head against the top of hers and Dora felt she could quite easily swoon with contentment.

Yes, it was enough. This was enough, this quiet happiness with the man she had married yesterday and slept with last night.

She nodded off to sleep again.

10

George escorted Dora across the square to her sister's house the following morning. They took the shortcut through the little park at the center of the square, but it turned into more of a long-cut since she had to stop several times to look at the flowers and comment appreciatively upon how they were arranged in their beds. She took particular note of the bed of roses and leaned over one dark red bud to cup it gently between her hands. She breathed in the scent of it and turned her head to glance up at him.

"Could anything in the whole universe be more beautiful or more perfect?" she asked him.

Actually he could think of one thing, and he was looking right at it—and he was not looking at the rosebud nestled within her slim, sensitive musician's fingers. She was wearing what he guessed was one of her new dresses, a somewhat smarter version of what she usually wore. The dusky pink color was a bit of a surprise, though. He suspected that Agnes or one of the other ladies had talked her into being a little more daring than usual. It shaved a few years off her age—or perhaps it would be more accurate to say that it lent some of the bloom of youth to her real age. She was clearly not trying to look like anyone she was not.

"Yes," he said. "Something could."

"Oh?" She straightened up and looked a bit indignant. "What?"

"Well," he said, "if I tell, then I will feel remarkably foolish, as though I had mistaken myself for a young sprig of a sighing lover with stars shining in his eyes."

He watched the indignation fade and give place to understanding. "Oh," she said, "how very silly."

"You see?" He gestured with one hand. "I am considered silly even when I do not tell. So I will. That little straw bonnet you are wearing is every bit as lovely as the rose."

She gazed at him for a moment longer and then burst into delighted laughter—and there went a few more years from her age.

"You, sir," she said, "have no powers of discrimination."

He suspected that he was grinning—unusual for him. "I would have to disagree with you, ma'am," he said, "most adamantly."

He offered his arm and they resumed their short walk to Arnott House. They did not speak again, but George felt warmed by the brief, foolish exchange. It was a huge relief to have got past that ghastly awkwardness of yesterday and to be relaxed and comfortable together today, as he had dreamed they would be from the start. This morning he was filled with hope again for the future. And it was a lovely morning again. There was warmth in the air and the whole of summer to look forward to.

He reveled in the thought that she was his wife, his lover as well as the woman to whom he was legally bound for the rest of their lives. The consummation had been sweet despite her awkwardness and the restraints he had imposed upon himself for her sake. It had been . . . perfection itself.

They were going to Arnott House so that Dora could take her leave of her father and Lady Debbins as well as of her brother and his wife, who were all setting out on their separate ways home. One carriage already stood outside the doors and two footmen were loading a trunk and numerous other packages and hatboxes onto it. There was a bustle of activity inside the house too as both couples prepared to leave, but everyone turned as one when George and Dora entered the hall unannounced. The men proceeded to look speculatively at George while the ladies hugged Dora. There was a great deal of sound and laughter.

"The drawing room is spilling over with l-ladies," Flavian told George with a theatrical look as he ran the tip of one forefinger beneath the high points of his shirt collar. "The Survivors have gone to Hugo's and are expecting me to bring you there if I can drag you away from your bride. We had better go. I have a strong suspicion that we will not be wanted here after the travelers have left. Mere men and all that."

George grinned at him.

"It is more a case," Agnes said, turning her attention

Mary Balogh

away from her family for a moment, "of us not being wanted there, Flavian. Hugo assured Gwen, of course, that she absolutely must not feel that she was being driven from her own home, but then Vincent arrived and informed her that he had just delivered Sophia to our door. It is the wives of the Survivors, among others, who are in the drawing room, Dora. Significantly, the husband of the only female member is not here, but I daresay that is a good thing for poor Percy."

Sir Walter and his wife were leaving, and attention focused upon them again. George shook his father-in-law by the hand and kissed the cheek of Lady Debbins. He watched as Dora also shook her father's hand until he covered hers with his free hand and said something to her that George could not hear. She set her hand on his shoulder then and kissed him on the cheek. It was not an effusive goodbye. Neither was it a cold one. She shook her stepmother's hand, and they exchanged smiles.

More than ten minutes passed before a second carriage bore the Reverend Oliver Debbins and his wife on the way back home to their children. Those goodbyes included prolonged hugs between brother and sister and sisters-in-law. Agnes too showed greater warmth toward them than she had toward her father and his wife.

That broken marriage so many years ago had caused much lasting pain, George thought.

"You will not mind if I go to Hugo's for an hour or so?" he asked when the carriage had departed. He had taken Dora's hand in his and was gazing into her eyes. There were tears there, though they had not spilled over onto her cheeks.

"Of course not," she said. "I would not subject you to a drawing room full of ladies, especially the morning after our wedding." She blushed.

"Quite so," he said.

Five minutes later Flavian's curricle drew up outside the doors and they drove away. The members of the Survivors' Club always spent time alone together whenever they could. They had done so almost daily during the three years when they were all living at Penderris Hall, and they had continued to do so most nights during their three-week annual reunions and whenever circumstances threw them together between times. They spoke openly and from the heart about the progress they had made, about their triumphs and setbacks, and about anything else that was of deep personal concern to one or other of them. They had become almost like seven segments of one soul while at Penderris, and they had remained closely bonded.

Nevertheless, George had always felt a little different from the others. For one thing, Penderris was his home. For another, he had suffered no personal injury in the wars. He had never been to the Peninsula or to Belgium, where the Battle of Waterloo had finally put an end to Napoleon Bonaparte's ambitions. He had shared less of himself than the others had. He had been better at listening. He had always seen it as his role to be the strong one, the comforter, the nurturer. He even thought he had been something of a father figure to Vincent and Ralph, who had been very young when they came to him.

Now, this morning, he suspected as he sat silently beside Flavian, he would be the focus of attention.

Yesterday must be accounted for. Sympathy, understanding, and aid would be his for the asking. He was
feeling remarkably uncomfortable. For what he had
never shared with these closest of friends could never
be shared. There were . . . secrets that were not his to
divulge.

Hugo lived at some distance from Grosvenor Square
in a house that had been his father's. The late Mr. Emes
had been a successful, prosperous businessman with no
pretensions to gentility. Hugo had been awarded his
title—Baron Trentham—after leading a particularly
vicious but successful forlorn hope in the Peninsula.
But then all forlorn hope attacks were vicious by their
very nature. They were always made up of volunteers
who knew that in all probability they would die.

George and Flavian were the last to arrive. The others were gathered in the sitting room, variously drinking
coffee and liquor. The only nonmember of the club was
Percy, Earl of Hardford, Imogen's husband, though he
got to his feet when George was ushered into the room.

"I do not belong here," he said. "I have no intention
of staying."

"You might as well sit while you are here," Hugo
said. "You are perfectly welcome to stay if you wish,
Percy, but you certainly need to be here for a while."

Percy sat again, and attention turned to George.

"We expected you a little earlier," Ben informed him
as George poured himself a cup of coffee and then took
a seat. "Up late this morning, were you, George? After
a late night, perhaps? And not too much sleep?"

"The duchess was looking remarkably r-rosy when

George brought her across to Arnott House, I could not help but notice," Flavian added. "Of course, the sun was shining, and some might say the walk across the square is a l-lengthy and somewhat strenuous one, but even so . . ."

George sipped his coffee with a steady hand. "Off limits, you two," he said. "Cut line."

"I think, Flave," Ben said, "it was almost definitely a late night and not too much sleep."

"One can but hope, Ben," Flavian said with a sigh as he sat down with a glass of something in his hand.

"About yesterday, George," Ralph said.

It was evident that he was referring not to the day in general, but to one specific segment of it.

George sighed and set his cup down. "I must thank you and Hugo," he said, "for removing Eastham with the minimum of fuss, Ralph. And you for keeping him removed, Percy. How did you do it?"

"I can be quite persuasive when I want to be," Percy said with a grin, "and very discreet too. There was no riot in Hanover Square when you emerged from the church, you may have noticed. No rotten tomatoes or eggs flying about your head or anyone else's. The man wanted to talk when I expressed some sympathy for his cause. I invited him to a tavern with whose reputation I am familiar. He did not have a chance to do much talking, however. It was most unfortunate, but we were caught up in a brawl no more than a couple of minutes after we arrived. It was quite unclear who started it. I escaped with my face and my wedding finery intact and hoofed it back to Hanover Square in time to accompany

Imogen to the wedding breakfast. Eastham, I understand, was not so fortunate. I believe his face and person suffered some slight damage."

"How did you know," George asked rather stiffly, "that his story would not have been worth listening to?"

"I do not doubt," Percy said, still grinning, "that it would have been *interesting* to listen to, George. But worthwhile? Hardly. Imogen would have me believe that you are on the side of the angels in all things and are perhaps even one of their number in human disguise. Murder does not seem quite in your style. However it is, I am done here. Alas, I promised the dog who adopted me the day I met Imogen and has been unwilling to *un*adopt me ever since a walk in Hyde Park, and if I fail to show up he will gaze reproachfully at me when I do with his bulging eyes and make me feel like the lowest, most heartless of mortals."

"Oh, Percy," Imogen said, "you know very well that you dote upon Hector."

"I think, Imogen," Vincent said, "Percy is trying to withdraw tactfully to leave us to ourselves."

"Oh, I understand that," she said, laughing.

"I am off, then," Percy said. "Thank you for the drink, Hugo."

And he sauntered from the room and closed the door behind him.

George cleared his throat.

"I assured my wife last night," he said, "that there was absolutely no truth in Eastham's accusation. I give you all that same assurance now."

"Well, that is a great relief, I must say, George,"

Ralph said. "We have known you for not quite a decade, so naturally when a stranger turned up in St. George's yesterday to accuse you of murder without a shred of evidence, we believed him without question and lost all faith in you."

"You did not really expect us to have any doubts, did you, George?" Imogen asked.

Vincent had leaned forward in his chair and was looking right at George in that uncanny way he had. "I believe you may have saved my life all those years ago at Penderris, George," he said. "I know you saved my sanity when I was still deaf as well as blind. I would not believe you guilty of murder or any violence against another person even if you were to stand up now and tell us you were. Not that you would. You are not a liar any more than you are a murderer. I would not believe anything ill of you. I would die for you if such a melo-dramatic thing were ever called for."

"Bravo, Vince," Hugo growled.

George felt absurdly close to tears and desperately hoped no one realized it.

He had not spoken much at all about his past—to anyone. His friends knew, of course, about the death of Brendan in Portugal and about Miriam's suicide soon after. They knew about his most persistently recurring nightmare, the one in which he ran toward the cliff upon which she stood, feeling as though he were moving through something thick and resistant rather than through air, trying to reach her in time to pull her back from the edge, trying to call out something that would persuade her to step back, and failing—and then thinking of just the right words a moment too late as his hand almost touched hers as she jumped.

"Eastham was Miriam's half brother," he said, "though he acquired the title after her death. They were very fond of each other. She used to go home quite frequently and stay for long periods—her father's health was poor for years before he died. Eastham—Meikle, as he was then—used to come to Penderris too until I . . . discouraged him. He came after Brendan's death to offer Miriam some comfort, though not to Penderris itself. After she . . . died, he accused me of killing her. He was beside himself, of course—as I was. But he did not retract the accusation in the days before the funeral, and he accused me to anyone who would listen. Many people did listen, of course, as you might expect, and a few who were predisposed to believe him did so. The gossip blew over in time, however, from lack of any evidence, and Meikle left Cornwall directly after the funeral, vowing revenge if it took him the rest of his life. I suppose yesterday was his revenge. I do not suppose he found it perfectly satisfactory, though he did ruin the day for Dora. Perhaps there will be more to come."

Deuce take it, perhaps there would be more. But what more could there be?

A lengthy silence followed his words. That was characteristic of their sessions. They never spoke merely for the sake of making sound or with any empty words of comfort or reassurance.

"You . . . *discouraged* him?" Ben asked at last.

"There was never any love lost between us," George said. "I was very young when I married—a mere seventeen. He was ten years older, a huge gap during the years when one is maturing. We had . . . reasons to dislike and resent each other. But finally he became too offensive to be borne, and he had caused great damage within my family. I informed him that he was no longer welcome at Penderris."

"Offensive?" Flavian said.

George looked at him and slowly shook his head. He would trust this group with his life. He loved them totally. But he could say no more.

"Offensive, yes," he said.

"I hope," Imogen said, "Percy did not do more harm than good yesterday, George. I hope he did not stir up more trouble for you by arranging to have that man put out of action for the rest of the day."

"Percy did his best to ensure that Dora's wedding day was not an utter disaster," George told her. "I will be forever grateful to him. If there is more trouble brewing, it is not because Percy embroiled him in a tavern brawl."

"What now?" Ralph asked. "What can we do for you, George?"

They all sat forward in their seats. They would go out and move mountains for him if he asked it of them, George knew. He forced himself to smile.

"Nothing at all," he said. "The worst of the trouble came years ago after Miriam died. It stirred to life again yesterday, and I do not doubt that it will be the main topic of conversation in clubs and drawing rooms for the next few days. I do not expect to find myself being shunned as a possible murderer, however, any more than I was then. Besides, I will be taking Dora home to

Cornwall within the next few days and that will be an end of the matter."

Except that he could not quite believe that.

"You do not expect him to follow you there?" Hugo asked.

"If he does," George assured him, his stomach lurching uncomfortably, "I cannot stop him, but he will stay somewhere other than Penderris Hall, and I shall ignore his presence. But I do not expect it. What would be the point?"

There was no point, was there, apart from dragging up old and stale resentments and embarrassing Dora.

"That old nightmare is not plaguing you?" Vincent asked.

"Not lately," George assured him. "I am confident that in time it will stop altogether. I have a new wife and a new marriage to give me hope and happiness."

There was silence again.

"It is just a pity," he added, "that some things can never be entirely forgotten just by trying. But we have all learned that lesson."

"Indeed," Imogen said.

Vincent would never forget that it was a foolish, naive move of his on the battlefield that had blinded him for life. Imogen would never forget that she had shot the bullet that killed her beloved first husband in the Peninsula when they were both in captivity. Hugo would never forget that he was one of the very few men to survive the forlorn hope attack he had led, or that he was the only one who had survived without even a scratch. Ralph would never forget that he had persuaded his three closest school friends to purchase commissions and join him in the Peninsula—and that soon after he had watched them blown to smithereens in a cavalry charge. They all had burdens they would carry for the rest of their lives even though they had learned to live with them and even to find happiness again.

He *would* be happy again, George thought, despite all the burdens of the past. He *was* happy. His heart lifted with gladness when he thought about Dora. He would see to it that she was happy too.

Flavian got to his feet and patted George's shoulder as he passed behind him to return his glass to the sideboard. "I had better take you b-back home, George," he said, "or my sister-in-law will stop speaking to me and then Agnes may stop too."

It was a signal for everyone else to leave, except Imogen, who would await Percy's return from his walk in the park. They would all be returning to their homes in the country within the next few days, and it was doubtful they would be together again until their annual reunion next spring. By then there would be a few new children to bring to Penderris—their core group of seven was rapidly expanding. They all hugged one another and wished one another a safe journey.

He had probably not been at Hugo's much longer than an hour, George thought as he sat beside Flavian in the curricle again. It seemed far longer than that. He smiled at the realization that he was missing his wife and could hardly wait to see her again. How old was he again? Forty-eight, soon to be nineteen?

"A penny for them, George," Flavian said.

"For my thoughts? Not even a pound, Flave." George grinned at his friend. "Not even twenty pounds."

They walked back to Stanbrook House about the square rather than across it through the park, Dora's hand drawn through George's arm. How lovely it was today, she thought, after all the pomp and excitement of yesterday, to be going home quietly with her husband.

"Oh, I must tell you," she said. "Someone has expressed an interest in moving to Inglebrook to teach music—a Mr. Madison. He is to call upon Viscount . . . upon Sophia and Vincent this afternoon. He is even interested in the fact that there is a cottage for sale in the village. He has been a member of a symphony orchestra for several years and has traveled all over Britain and Europe. But he has recently married and begun a family and wants a life that is quieter and more settled but still lucrative enough to provide him with a steady income."

"He will be a poor substitute for you," George said with a sidelong smile.

"Oh, what foolish flattery," she said. "But I thank you. I shall now be able to feel considerably less guilt about leaving so abruptly—provided Mr. Madison likes what he hears this afternoon, of course. Will you be going out again? To your club, maybe?"

"I had rather hoped to spend the rest of the day with my wife," he said. "Do you not have time for me?"

"Of course I do." She was absurdly pleased. "I thought all men spent their days at one of the clubs or in Parliament or at some other exclusively male preserve."

"Not this man," he told her as they climbed the steps to their house. "Not all the time, at least, and certainly not on the first full day of my marriage after I have been separated from my wife all morning. Did you enjoy yourself?"

"I did," she assured him, but did not add what a wonderful feeling it had given her to be a wife among wives, a friend among friends—or how lovely it had been to know that she had a husband coming back to her. She would have been ashamed to say such things aloud. She was a bit ashamed even to think them. What had happened to her pride in her independence, her ability to stand alone without any man?

They did not stay in for the rest of the day. Instead they went walking in Hyde Park, though not in the area where the fashionable world strolled and rode during the afternoon.

"People may feel obliged to stop and inform us what the weather is like if we go there," he said by way of explanation. "I do not want to be stopped and spoken to today. Do you?"

Dora laughed. "No," she said. "I have all the company I desire for today."

"Ah." He chuckled. "I have had my compliment and will now hold my peace."

She had had no idea that marriage would feel so . . . comfortable, that it would involve light banter and teasing remarks and laughter.

They walked along narrow paths that wound and climbed and descended among trees and sometimes presented stones or tree roots to trip them if they were unwary. The paths were quiet and secluded in the main, with occasional glimpses of lawns and small groups of people, both riders and pedestrians. Two children's nurses sat on one expanse of grass talking while their young charges dashed about at play. A small dog chased after a stick its master threw for it, its tail whipping up what must be a minor hurricane. George told her about Percy's dog, a former stray of indeterminate breed and unprepossessing looks, which had forced itself upon him until he had had no choice but to keep it and love it.

"I do like Percy," Dora said, laughing at the story. "He seems quite perfect for Imogen."

"He has made her glow," he said, "and for that I will always hold him in the deepest esteem."

She wondered if now, when they were alone together and away from home, he would talk about yesterday and about the death of his first wife.

"It was rather sad to bid farewell to your father and your brother this morning," he said. "You must have wished there could be more time with them."

"I was very glad they came," she assured him. "But Oliver has a busy life and Louisa does not like to leave their children for any longer than necessary. My father does not like to leave home at all."

"But he did so for your sake," he said. "I am pleased about that."

His head remained turned toward her, and she could feel unspoken questions in the silence.

"He was never an openly warmhearted man," she told him, "though he was not unkind or neglectful either—not to us, his children, at least. Mrs. Brough was one of my mother's friends. I liked her, and after Mama left she continued to call upon me with words of advice and encouragement. But after Mr. Brough died a number of years later, it was clear that her interest lay with my father more than with me. Their marriage came as no great surprise. But soon after their wedding she made it clear to Agnes that it was high time she considered marriage—and Agnes married William Keeping, something that ought never to have happened. Then she made sure I understood that there was no room for two mistresses in our home, though I had been trying very hard to efface myself. It was a great relief to all of us, I suppose, except perhaps Agnes, when I moved away to Inglebrook. I have never been able to think of Mrs. Brough by any other name, but since I can no longer call her that, I do not call her anything, I am afraid. It is a little awkward. As far as my father is concerned, we do not have a close relationship, but neither are we estranged. I am happy that he came here and gave me away. He was happy about that too."

"You resented his marrying again?" he asked.

She hesitated as he used his free hand to hold back a low branch that would have caught her across the face if he had not noticed it. "I tried not to," she said. "There was no reason he should not marry, and they seemed—still seem—fond enough of each other. It would have been reprehensible to resent his marriage purely for my own selfish reasons."

"Selfish?" he said. "But had you not given up your dreams in order to keep home for your father and raise your sister?"

"But not at his request," she protested. "It was my choice to stay. I can hardly blame anyone else for what I freely decided to do."

"I might argue that point, Dora," he said. "You did not blame your father for your mother's desertion? Ah, forgive me. That question was quite out of line. Ignore it if you will and we will admire the beauty of the park."

"Oh, I have blamed him," she said with a sigh, "especially after hearing what my mother told Flavian last year. I assume you have heard about that. And of course I have blamed her too. Initially the fault was entirely his. I was there when he accused her very publicly in the middle of an assembly and would not be hushed though a number of people urged him not to say what he would live to regret. But . . . she did not need to go away and never come back. Or perhaps she did. How can I know how intolerable their marriage had become to her? One never can really know such things from the outside, can one?"

"No," he agreed softly, "one cannot."

"But there was a child," she said. "There was Agnes. Surely—oh, I may be very wrong, but surely she ought to have put her child before any personal unhappiness with her marriage. Agnes was five years old."

"Her children, perhaps," he said. "There was you as well as Agnes. And your brother."

"I was old enough to look after myself," she said. "Goodness, you married when you were seventeen."

"I was a child and at the mercy of forces beyond myself," he said, "just as you were."

"Yes." She waited but he did not explain his words about himself. "Oh, I do try not to hate her, not to judge her, but I do not always succeed. We cannot know what another person's life is like, can we, unless we can live their lives from the inside, and that is impossible. I can judge my mother only from the pain she caused Agnes and me—and Oliver. And that is perhaps unfair especially when it was my father who started it all—or apparently started it."

They had left the trees behind them and were walking in sunshine. Dora lifted her chin so that she could feel the summerlike heat against her face beneath the brim of her bonnet. He stopped walking and turned them to face full into the sun.

"She had as much right to be with me yesterday as he had," she said, and realized too late that she had spoken aloud.

"You are sorry we did not invite her?" he asked.

"No." She closed her eyes briefly. "It would have been intolerable. You must have realized that after you made the suggestion a month ago."

"But possible," he said. "Most things are when one is a duke."

She looked at him. He was smiling in that gentle, kindly way of his.

"I found myself yesterday morning, you know, wondering if she knew about my wedding, wondering if she cared," she told him.

"You know, Dora," he said, and the kindness that shone from his eyes seemed to wrap itself about her like a warm blanket, "we do not have to set out for Cornwall tomorrow or even the next day."

They were planning to leave tomorrow. They were to go to Penderris, and she wanted with a passionate yearning to be on the way there with him. On the way home. She did not want to delay by even a day.

They stepped off the path to allow two young girls trailed by a maid to pass by. Dora waited until they were out of earshot.

"I cannot go to visit her," she said.

"As you wish." His smile warmed her even as the sun was obscured by a small cloud.

"I do not know where she lives," she said.

"Flavian does," he reminded her.

She moistened her lips with her tongue. "Do you think I ought to go?"

"I think," he said, "that I ought to allow you to decide that for yourself, Dora. But if you wish to stay another day or two, then we will. And if you wish to call upon your mother, I will accompany you—or not."

She tipped her head to one side and regarded him closely. "Now I know," she said, "what Flavian and Agnes mean when they speak of you."

He raised his eyebrows.

"That you are a gifted listener," she said. "That you give comfort and strength and support without in any way trying to impose your will upon anyone or attempting to control anyone's actions."

"It does not take a great deal of talent to listen," he said, "when one loves the speaker."

Loves?

"And you love everyone," she said.

"Ah," he said, "not so, Dora. You will not be able to make any sort of a saint of me, I am afraid."

"Your fellow Survivors do," she told him.

He laughed softly. "I was able to comfort them when they were at their lowest ebb," he said. "It was easy to be a hero when I was unhurt myself."

"Were you?" She frowned.

Something came down behind his eyes almost like a curtain.

"Shall we walk?" He gestured to the long stretch of grass before them, and they left the path and struck off in what Dora guessed to be the direction of the Serpentine. Perhaps he thought it was time for crowds again.

"You will come with me?" she asked after a silent minute or two.

"Yes."

"Tomorrow?"

"Yes."

But she did not want to go. Or did she? She was not looking for any kind of reconciliation. She never would be. She tried not to judge her mother's actions or hate her or blame her for the damage she had done to Agnes and herself—and probably to Oliver, but she could not . . . forgive her, just as could not really forgive her father. Yet she had invited him to her wedding—and to give her away. Ought her mother not to have equal consideration? The thought made her feel a bit light-headed.

"How strange!" she said. "If my mother had stayed, if

my life had proceeded according to plan, I would almost without any doubt not be walking here with you now. And I would have hated that. Though I would not have known what I was missing, would I?"

She turned her head toward him, and they both laughed.

"I would have hated it too," he told her.

11

The years during which Penderris Hall had been a hospital for wounded officers had saved George's sanity. He was convinced of that. And it was not just because the house had been full and life busy enough to keep his mind off himself. It was more that he had been needed. That fact had surprised him at first, for he had assumed that the success of his scheme would depend almost entirely upon the marvelous skills of Joseph Connor, the physician he had hired. All he would do, he had thought, was provide the space and the funding. He had found, however, that he had a function almost as important as Connor's, for he had discovered in himself a vast ability to empathize, to put himself in the place of the sufferer, to *listen,* to find just the right words to say in reply. He had discovered that he was a patient man, that he could spend as much time with each wounded man as was needed. He had spent many hours, for instance, simply holding Vincent during the ghastly months when the boy was both deaf and blind. During those years he had discovered in himself a capacity to love that reached out to anyone who needed it.

The reward of it all—ah, the biblical aptness of it!—was that in giving of himself he had also received in abundance. Every one of the officers who had been at Penderris and survived still wrote regularly to him. And the six who had formed the Survivors' Club with him loved him, he knew, as dearly as he loved them. It was a rich reward.

He could empathize with Dora. She had sacrificed her own prospects of a happy life as a young wife and mother so that her sister could grow up feeling secure and cherished. And then, when it had seemed that no one needed her any longer, she had made a new life for herself that had been admirable in its dignity and usefulness. But the wounds went deep—probably far deeper than she realized herself. She could forgive her father more easily than she could her mother because he had never been central to her life and because the bond of affection between them had always been lukewarm at best. But her mother had been all in all to her when she was a growing girl, and the woman's desertion and subsequent silence had devastated her. There was, he knew, a great black hole in his wife's life where her mother had been—no, worse than a hole. An empty hole did not feel pain. Pain had been pushed deep inside Dora, but it was there nonetheless, probably as raw as it had ever been.

He would do anything to put things right for her, though he knew from experience that no one could ever put someone else's life to rights. One could only listen and encourage and love. And *hold* when holding was appropriate.

He did not make love to his wife that night. He knew that he had caused her pain on their wedding night, though he knew too that she had welcomed it, that the physical side of their marriage would be important to her. Good Lord, what must half a lifetime lived in celibacy be like? And let no one try to tell him that women did not feel sexual yearnings and frustrations as men did. But now he would give her body a chance to heal. He would and did simply hold her. She had been quiet since their walk in the park, and he knew that her mind was on tomorrow and her decision to see her mother.

He slid an arm about her shoulders and snuggled her against him. With his other hand he cupped her chin and kissed her.

She was eminently kissable. She had a warm, soft, sweet mouth, and when he traced the line of her lips with his tongue she parted them and he was able to reach his tongue in to touch hers. There was heat and moisture there and a welcome. She turned onto her side to move closer to him and sighed deep in her throat.

There was something surprisingly lovely about cuddling a woman when one had no intention of having full sex with her. It was an entirely new experience for him, in fact. He kissed her forehead, her temple, her ear, her chin, her throat. And his hand moved over her, skimming the side of one breast, tracing the line of a hip, the flatness of her abdomen, circling the roundness of a buttock. She was warm and fragrant and sweet and . . . his.

That was the greatest marvel of all, the greatest miracle—that she was *his*. His wife, till death parted them. And not just his wife—ah, no, not just that. She was his companion, his bedfellow, his friend. And yes, they would be friends. They already were, though there was much still to know about each other and would doubtless be many adjustments to make. He liked her . . . oh, more than he liked anyone else in this world.

Her hand was light against his back.

"May we dispense with the nightgown?" he asked, his mouth against hers. "But only if you are comfortable with being skin to skin with me."

"I suppose it is what is done between married people, is it not?" she said, sounding so much like Miss Debbins of Inglebrook that he smiled in the darkness.

"We need do nothing that 'married people' do," he told her. "We will do only what we want to do."

"Very well," she said, and would have sat up if he had not held her in place with his arm about her shoulders.

He slid her nightgown slowly up her body, brushing the backs of his fingers over her thighs as he did so and then over her stomach.

"Raise your arms for me," he said at last, and removed the gown completely and dropped it over the side of the bed. "You are very, very beautiful, Dora."

"That is because the room is in darkness," she said.

"Ah, but my hands and fingers and mouth do not require light," he told her.

She did not feel like a girl, for which fact he was thankful. She had a woman's body, not voluptuous, but very feminine nonetheless. She was warm and soft-skinned and silky, and if he was not careful he was going to become more aroused than he wanted to be.

She was perfection.

He fondled her breasts with featherlight fingers and kissed her mouth and stroked the moist flesh within with his tongue.

"You may touch me too if you wish," he told her.

"I am touching—" she began, but he deepened his kiss.

"Wherever you wish," he said. "I am your husband. I am yours. I am for your pleasure as well as for everything else."

"Oh." She breathed softly into his mouth.

"I hope this will always be a pleasure for you as well as for me," he said.

"*Will* be?" She was Miss Debbins again. "Oh, George, it already is. You have no idea."

Yes. Yes, he did.

She moved her hands up his back to his shoulders and down to his waist. She slid them to the front and circled them over his chest, over his shoulders, down his arms to the elbows.

"You are very lovely," she said.

If he had been thinking in terms of romance, he might well have slid a little more in love with her at that moment. But he was thinking in terms of pleasure—hers more than his own. And in terms of holding her, protecting her, cherishing her, easing her burdens, especially the ones that she would face head-on tomorrow. He hoped he had done the right thing in nudging her in the direction of calling on her mother. He drew her close with both arms about her, trapping her hands between them, and kissed her softly.

"Sleep now," he said. "Tomorrow night we will make love again."

"Yes," she said, settling her neck on his arm and her head on his shoulder. "Yes, please," she added sleepily a few moments later.

George smiled and kissed the top of her head.

The following afternoon Dora, George, Agnes, and Flavian were together in the duke's carriage on their way to call upon Sir Everard and Lady Havell in Kensington. George had stepped around to Arnott House late yesterday to ask Flavian where the house was to be found and had returned a short while later with the news that Agnes was insisting that if Dora was going to visit their mother, then so was she.

Last year Agnes had refused to go. She was happy with what she had learned, she had protested when she told Dora of Flavian's visit, but she had no wish to become acquainted with the mother who had abandoned her when she was little more than a baby.

The sisters, seated side by side facing the horses, were gazing out through opposite windows while their husbands carried on what seemed like a strained conversation, though Dora did not try to follow what was being said. Instead, when Agnes's hand found hers on the seat between them, she clasped it and felt herself slip back to those years when she had been more of a mother than a sister to her younger sibling.

She would not be doing this, she was convinced, if George had not pressed her into it. Though that was grossly unfair. He had not exerted any pressure whatsoever. He had not even suggested she come. He had merely smiled kindly at her as she talked herself into doing what she had thought she would never do. He had listened while she explained to herself as much as to him that if she did not do it now, she probably never would and she might always regret it and continue to both hate and mourn the mother who had left her without a word. He had done nothing to persuade her before she decided or to dissuade her when her decision was made.

Yet she had a suspicion that he had somehow led her to it.

She caught his eye across the seats—their knees touched whenever the carriage swayed—and he smiled. Oh, that smile! It was a powerful thing. It suggested strength and support and kindness and approval. It was also a bit like a shield. How had he got her to talk about her family yesterday and about that most disturbing of events in their family history? She could not recall that he had asked any direct or intrusive questions. Yet talk she had. He had told her nothing of his own family, however, or of the terrible disaster that had put an end to it and left him alone and lonely. Would he ever tell her? She had the uneasy suspicion that he was not only unknown to her but also in many ways unknowable.

It was far too soon to draw that conclusion, though. They had been married for only two days. Soon, probably tomorrow, they would set out for Penderris. Once they were home he would surely open up his life to her as she had opened up hers.

She smiled back at him.

"Here," Flavian said at last as the carriage turned off the road. "It looks rather as though w-we are driving into unruly w-wilderness, but there is a pretty, well-kept garden about the house itself—at least, there was last year when I was here."

And indeed there still was. The house itself was a sturdy manor with an air of slight neglect though it was by no means derelict. Agnes's hand tightened convulsively about Dora's.

"Perhaps," she said hopefully, "they are not at home."

"I did not get the impression last year," Flavian said, leaning forward on his seat and possessing himself of her free hand, "that they are away from home often, Agnes."

"I doubt I will know her," she said. "I cannot really remember what she looked like—and I have not seen her for more than twenty years."

Dora merely gazed at George for courage. Neither of them spoke.

An elderly servant answered the door after George had rapped on it with the head of his cane. The man looked from one to the other of them before his eyes paused with recognition upon Flavian. He stood back from the door to admit them and took the calling card George handed him.

"The Duke and Duchess of Stanbrook and Viscount and Lady Ponsonby for Sir Everard and Lady Havell, if they are receiving," George said.

The man bobbed his head and made his way up the stairs to one side of the hall. He reappeared a minute or two later.

"My lord and my lady will receive you in the drawing room," he informed them, and turned to lead the way back up.

Dora would have loved to turn and flee, but she had

not come this far merely to play coward. She took George's offered arm and followed in the servant's wake. Agnes came behind with Flavian.

Sir Everard did not wait for them to be announced. He met them at the drawing room door, which stood open. He was smiling in welcome.

He had not aged particularly well, Dora thought, though he was easily recognizable as the once-handsome, once-dashing young blade she remembered from several lengthy visits he had made to relatives in their neighborhood during her girlhood. He had been much sighed over by the women. Several of the younger ones had set their cap for him. But in the years since then he had acquired a bit of a paunch, his fair hair had thinned and faded, and his face had grown rounder and ruddier. He was probably, she thought in some shock, no more than a few years older than George.

Her eyes assessed Sir Everard Havell's person because she did not wish to turn her attention upon the other occupant of the room, who was standing just beyond him.

"Welcome all," he said, his tone effusive and a little overhearty. "We have a previous acquaintance with Viscount Ponsonby, do we not, Rosamond? You, then, sir, must be the Duke of Stanbrook. And the ladies . . ."

Dora did not hear what he had to say about them. She had turned her gaze upon the woman he had called Rosamond.

She had aged quite noticeably. Well, of course she had. She was twenty-two years older. She had put on weight, though she bore herself well and the extra pounds were proportionately distributed and became her well enough. Her hair, formerly as dark as Dora's own, was a uniform silver-gray. Her face was lined, her jawline less defined, as was inevitable, though she still retained traces of her former beauty. Her eyes were still dark and unfaded.

She seemed like a stranger. For a few moments it was well nigh impossible to reconcile the appearance of this elderly woman with the memory of a vibrant, laughing, youthful Mama, dancing with each of her daughters in turn, giving the impression that for her the sun rose and set upon them and upon her absent son. But the unfamiliarity lasted for only those few moments before Dora saw in Lady Havell the mother she remembered.

Sir Everard was making an attempt to take Dora's hand and bow over it, but she ignored him. Indeed, she was virtually unaware of him.

"Dora?" Her mother's lips scarcely moved, and there was very little sound behind the word, but oh, dear God, she spoke with the remembered voice. "And . . . *Agnes*?"

"The duchess certainly inherited her mother's handsome looks," Sir Everard said, his voice still overhearty, "as I recall from the time she was a very young lady. Would you not agree, Stanbrook?"

Dora did not hear George's reply, if, indeed, he made one. She was experiencing the exact same problem she always had with the former Mrs. Brough. She did not know what to call this woman.

"Ma'am?" she said as she inclined her head. She was aware of Agnes making a slight, stiff curtsy beside her without saying a word.

"You came," their mother said, her hands clasping

each other very tightly at her waist—and, oh, she was wearing a silver ring that had always been on the little finger of her right hand. "We read the announcement of your coming nuptials in the morning papers, Dora. The wedding was the day before yesterday? I did not expect you to come, but I have dressed for visitors each day since I read the notice just on the slim chance . . . Oh, you have both done exceedingly well for yourselves. I am more pleased than I can say. But where have my manners gone begging? I have not even greeted the Duke of Stanbrook and Viscount Ponsonby." She dipped into a curtsy and looked at each of them in turn.

"Sit down, sit down," Sir Everard directed them. "Our man will be back here with the tea tray in a few moments."

It was all horribly, horribly painful, Dora found as Sir Everard talked and no one else had a word to say. It was an even worse ordeal than she had feared it would be. When she spoke at last, Sir Everard seemed almost to slump in relief, but she did not see his reaction to what she said.

"I have been haunted by your desertion since the night it happened," she said, addressing her mother with words she had not planned to speak—she had not really planned anything beyond the visit itself. "I have had enough of being haunted. I came here so that I could see for myself that a long time has passed and the woman I remember, the mother I remember, no longer exists. I have seen and now I am satisfied. You are Lady Havell, ma'am. You bear only a passing resemblance to my mother."

She listened to herself, appalled at her rudeness, yet glad she had found the courage to speak the truth. It would have been absurd if they had sipped tea and talked platitudes and then taken their leave.

Her mother looked back at her, her face without expression. But her hands were clasped, white-knuckled, in her lap.

"I do know," Dora continued, "that my father was as much to blame as you were—more so, in fact, on that night. Even if there had been truth in what he said, it was unpardonable of him to accuse you so publicly. I can understand that his words were an intolerable humiliation to you and that the prospect of living on as his wife seemed insupportable. I can even understand the lure of a younger man and a new love when your marriage was so obviously an unhappy one. But what I cannot understand—or at least what I cannot forgive— is your complete abandonment of *us* as well as of Papa. What had we done to you? You were our mother, our Mama, and we needed you. Agnes was a child. She could not even understand. She knew only that her mother was gone, that perhaps you had left because she was not lovable enough."

Her voice was shaking, she realized. So was she. She was also breathless. She had sat down upon a love seat, George beside her. He covered one of her hands with his own, though he did not clasp it or say anything.

"I suppose," Agnes said, "you loved Sir Everard. I can understand that sometimes a new romance might seem more enticing than the marriage one already has. But more enticing than the love of one's children?

Maybe I am being unjust to you, however, for perhaps, even probably, you would not have chosen Sir Everard over us if Papa had not pushed you into doing so. It was especially heinous of him to do so if indeed you were innocent, as you assured Flavian you were when he called here last year. Yet we speak to Papa and treat him with honor and respect. Perhaps it is wrong of us to have such a . . . double standard."

Their mother spoke at last.

"I did write to you, Dora," she said. "I sent you both gifts for your birthdays until the silence convinced me that your father must be withholding them from you. Besides, letters and gifts were no proper atonement for abandonment. I could not take you with me when I left. Your father would have pursued me and taken you back, and that would have been more distressing for you than my leaving you behind. Besides, at the time I had nowhere to go, nowhere to take you. Not that I even thought of it until later, I must confess. I ran away upon impulse, and when my heart began to ache for you with a terrible pain, I chose to stay away rather than return to you and your father too. But being forever separated from my children broke my heart in two. It has never quite mended."

"I do assure you, Dora, Agnes—" Sir Everard began.

Dora whipped her head about and looked incredulously at him. He faltered, and the color in his face deepened.

He started again. "I do assure you, Your Grace, my lady, that your mother had done nothing whatsoever to deserve the humiliation she suffered at your father's hand that night, any more than I had. A little flirtation . . . Well, everyone flirts, you know. It was entirely harmless. We had no more idea of eloping than . . . well, than of flying to the moon. But when your father said what he did, I was forced, as an honorable gentleman, to make one of two choices—either slap a glove in his face and call him out or take Rosamond away and wait patiently until I could offer her the protection of my name for the rest of her life."

"But as a chivalrous gentleman," Flavian said, his voice heavy with irony, "you were not honor-bound to consider Lady Debbins's ch-children." It was not a question.

The manservant chose that moment to bring in the tea tray, laden with drinks and dainties none of them wanted. Lady Havell made no move to pour or make any reference to the refreshments. By the time the servant left the room, the silence was loud and heavy.

"I beg your pardon for coming here uninvited to disturb your peace," Dora said, getting to her feet. "I did not intend to speak so harshly. I thought, I suppose, to extend some sort of olive branch. We all make choices in life and must then live with the consequences. And some choices are not easy to make. I have lived long enough to understand that as well as the fact that we can almost never go back if we regret a certain path we took. But thank you for your kindness in receiving us."

"I do not remember you," Agnes said, addressing their mother, "except for a few flashing images that are never complete episodes. But I do know that you did something very right. Dora was a wonderful mother to me during my growing years. She was warm and loving and nurturing. She could have learned to be that way only from you, for Papa was always a remote, humorless figure who saw to our material needs but never gave us much of either his attention or his love. It must have been difficult being married to him."

William Keeping had been another such man, Dora thought, though admittedly he had not been either a drinker or an openly jealous man.

The others had risen too. George had still not spoken a word. He did now, however. He reached out a hand to her mother, who was just getting to her feet.

"I am pleased to have made your acquaintance, ma'am," he said. "I promise you that I will cherish your daughter for the rest of my days."

Dora watched her mother bite her lip as her eyes grew suspiciously bright.

"I never wanted anything but her happiness," she said, "though my behavior suggested otherwise, I suppose. Thank you, Your Grace. I would say that Dora is a fortunate lady, but I do believe you are an equally fortunate man."

He smiled at her.

"Ma'am," Dora said before pausing and lowering her head to look at her hands. She began again. "Mother, perhaps you would care to start writing to me again at Penderris Hall in Cornwall. I will receive those letters, and I will reply."

"I will do that, Dora," her mother said.

"I am going to have a child in the autumn," Agnes blurted.

"Oh." Her mother turned wistful eyes upon her. "I am so glad, Agnes." It was probable, though, that she had already noticed.

"I shall . . . let you know," Agnes said.

"Thank you."

And then they were back in the carriage, less than half an hour after they had left it. Or was it an eternity? Dora and Agnes no longer sat together. Agnes had her back to the horses, Flavian's arm about her shoulders, her face hidden in the hollow between his shoulder and neck. Dora sat beside George, not quite touching him.

"I am sorry I brought you, my love," Flavian said.

That made Agnes's head come up. "You did no such thing," she informed him. "I told George I was coming and you said you would accompany me."

"I have always had a b-bit of d-difficulty with my m-memory," he said meekly, deliberately exaggerating his stammer.

"I am not sorry I came," she said, resting her head on his shoulder again. "I *will* write to her after my confinement. Why should I write to Papa, after all, and not to her?"

"Quite so," he said.

Dora ached to lean against George, to feel the reassurance of his warmth and strength. Perhaps he knew. He took her hand in his, laced their fingers, and raised it to his lips. He leaned slightly sideways until her head tipped very naturally against his shoulder.

"Bravo, Dora," he said softly.

She had to concentrate very hard upon not weeping.

How had she ever found comfort in her life, she wondered, before there was George's calm voice and kind eyes and firm shoulder and sheltering arms?

She might have been a little alarmed at the loss of her spirit of independence if she had spared it a thought.

Her heart ached for the mother she had lost twenty-two years ago and found again today and . . .

And *what*?

12

*A*gnes and Flavian set off for their home in Sussex, late as the hour was when they all arrived back on Grosvenor Square. Dora and George walked over to see them on their way.

"I am glad I went with you," Agnes said, "though I think I will be upset over it for a few days. She is a stranger, yet she is our *mother*. Oh, I do not know what to think. How are you feeling, Dora?"

"She is not a stranger to me," Dora told her, "and yet she is. If she writes to me, I will write back. Oh, it was so wicked of Papa, Agnes, to withhold her letters and gifts. Though perhaps he thought it was for the best. I am tired of blaming and resenting and hating."

They hugged each other, both with tears in their eyes.

"At least we have each other," Agnes said. "I love you more than I can ever say, Dora."

After they returned to Stanbrook House, Dora went upstairs to lie down in the duchess's bedchamber. She could not fall asleep, though, weary as she was. She kept remembering her mother's saying that she had dressed for visitors every day after seeing the announcement of Dora's upcoming wedding, and the memory made her throat ache with unshed tears. But how could she feel sorry for her mother? Agnes had waited day after day, week after week when she was a child. She used to prop up one of her dolls in her window each night when she went to bed herself, to keep watch while she slept, and every night she told the doll all she would have to show Mama when she came home. But sometimes she would shut the doll up inside a cupboard and hide beneath her bedcovers and refuse even to give Dora a good night kiss.

Oh, how one's heart ached sometimes, even with memories of events long past and best forgotten.

How happy she had been last week when Papa had come to London and agreed to give her away at her wedding. How his words on her wedding morning had warmed her heart. Yet Papa had driven her mother away and had then kept back her letters and gifts to her daughters. How could he have withheld gifts for a five-year-old?

Oh, but she really was tired, tired, *tired* of apportioning blame.

She must have dozed. She awoke when something warm covered her hand, which was outside the bedcovers. It was George's hand. He was sitting on the side of the bed, looking down at her with concern. Her cheeks were wet, she realized when with his other hand he dried them gently with a large linen handkerchief. She smiled at him and turned her hand beneath his to clasp it.

"You are so very good at that," she said.

"At . . . ?" He raised his eyebrows.

"At giving comfort," she said. "But who comforts you, George?"

She could have sworn for a moment that it was deep pain she saw in his eyes, but then they smiled with a kindness that was almost like a shield.

"I draw my comfort from giving it," he said.

She believed him. She had heard much about him from his friends and their wives and from Agnes, and she had experienced his kindness for herself. But the question remained. Who did comfort him? She was aware of a huge dark pool of loneliness in him. He had admitted it to her in Inglebrook when he had come to ask her to marry him, but at the time she had thought of it only as an absence of close friends, and the lack of a wife. She suspected now, though—more than suspected—that his loneliness went far deeper than that.

"Give comfort to me, then." She turned onto her back and opened her arms to him. But she had got beneath the covers when she came here. She drew them back with one hand and opened her arms to him again. "And let me comfort you."

He gazed back into her eyes for a moment and then about the room. "In the duchess's bedchamber?" he said.

"I am the duchess," she told him.

"Well," he said softly, "and so you are."

They were both fully clothed. He was even still wearing his Hessian boots. He pushed the covers back farther and climbed onto the bed without removing them or anything else, which might simply mean that he was weary and intended to lie down beside her and sleep.

He intended no such thing—or not yet, anyway. And

she had started it. Goodness, she had actually invited him into her own bed. In broad daylight. What sort of a hussy would he think her?

But there was no evidence that he was thinking at all, and very soon rational thought fled Dora's mind too. She had thought last night's embraces impossibly, wonderfully intimate after he had stripped off her nightgown and they were both naked. But today when they were both fully clothed . . . Well, today he fondled her with hard, seeking hands and a demanding, urgent mouth, and she explored him just as boldly despite the barrier of several layers of various garments. And today he lifted her skirts just high enough and knelt between her thighs after spreading them wide with his knees and unbuttoned the fall of his pantaloons at the waist and slid his hands beneath her buttocks and came plunging deep inside her—all within moments, it seemed, and all fully visible to them both.

Dora's breath caught in her throat, and her hands went to his fully clothed shoulders as he leaned over her, and her silk-stockinged legs twined about his and her feet came to rest on the warm, supple leather of his boots.

"Am I hurting you?" His eyes were heavy-lidded with desire.

"No."

And oh, my—*oh, my!*—he withdrew and plunged again and she tightened her hold on his legs and braced her feet and lifted her hips and they rode hard—there were no other words to describe what happened even if her mind had been searching for words. She did not know how long it lasted and would not have known even if there had been a clock within her line of vision, for there was no such thing as time. Her eyes were upon his and his upon hers, yet there was no embarrassment, not even any real awareness that they gazed into each other as they coupled. It might have gone on forever as far as Dora was concerned. But the wonderful, *wonderful* pleasure turned eventually to a need that was almost painful and yet more pleasurable than pleasure and finally so urgent that everything in her tightened and strained against him and his hands came beneath her again and held her hard while he drove inward and stayed there.

The universe broke apart—which was the silliest thought imaginable, Dora decided seconds or minutes later after she had felt deep within again that lovely gush of his release and he had uncoupled them and lain down beside her, his arm beneath her head. They were warm and rumpled and breathless and—oh, goodness me!—was this how married people behaved? Was this *normal*?

If it was not, she did not care. Oh, she *did not care.*

"Thank you, Dora," he murmured against her ear after a long time. "You are indeed an enormous comfort to me."

And sadness returned. For even giving herself to him as she had just done could not really comfort that pain she was sure she had seen in his eyes for one unguarded moment a little while ago. Perhaps, ah, perhaps he would share it when they went to Penderris. Perhaps he would tell her just exactly what the Earl of Eastham's appearance at the church during their wedding had been all about.

It meant more than it had appeared to mean, she was perfectly sure.

"We will go home tomorrow?" she asked him.

"I think I am at home now," he said. "Not here in Stanbrook House necessarily, but here with you in my arms."

For someone who had said there would be no romance in their marriage, he really was not doing badly at all.

"But yes," he said. "We will go home, Dora. Home to Cornwall. Tomorrow."

The journey between Penderris Hall and London was always a long one. The hours spent inside the carriage were tedious, and George had always found that it was almost impossible to read—the book moved too much in his hand despite the fact that his carriage was well sprung. And the passing scenery had ceased to charm a long time ago. Toll booths, the need to change horses, the need to eat and sleep at posting inns, the weather, sometimes in the form of torrential rain or, occasionally, even snow that made the roads impassable—all made the journey seem longer each time he made it.

But this time he did not find the return home either long or tedious. He saw everything through fresh eyes as Dora commented upon passing scenes and people. He enjoyed aspects of the journey that he had always taken for granted. It amused her, for example, that they were bowed and scraped to wherever they went, that there was always a private parlor available to them even when they stopped unexpectedly for a meal, that the best chambers were always ready for them and the best food was served in a timely fashion.

"I could grow accustomed to being a duchess," she said on the first evening as they finished their dinner.

"I hope you can," he said, "since you are stuck with being a duchess for the rest of your life."

She looked at him blankly for a moment and then dissolved into laughter.

He loved hearing her laugh.

She was not quite laughing one morning after they had been traveling for an hour or so in companionable silence. But she was smiling, and her eyes were bright with merriment.

"What is amusing you?" he asked.

"Oh," she said and looked mortified that he had noticed. "Perhaps it is just that I am happy."

"Happiness makes you smirk?" he asked. But he found that he was smiling now too.

She laughed outright then. "I was feeling dizzy at the realization that I am on my way home with my husband," she said. "I was thinking that perhaps I was dreaming, that I had fallen into a trance while trying not to listen to Miranda Corley plod her painful way through a set piece on the pianoforte and had concocted this lovely imaginary life for myself."

"Miranda Corley was not your star pupil?" he asked.

"Poor Miranda," she said. "I do not doubt she has a dozen sterling qualities. A musical talent is not among them."

"It was a lovely dream?" he asked.

"Well, consider it, George." She turned to look at him, every inch the Miss Debbins he had met last year. "Just a little over a month ago I was sitting in my humble cottage, taking tea and minding my own business, when along came a handsome, wealthy duke to beg for my hand in marriage. It was the stuff of fairy tales. But it does seem that it is real, for I am not waking up to Miranda's sorry efforts to produce music, am I?"

"Wealthy?" he asked her. "Are you sure?"

That gave her pause, and she blushed. "Are you?"

"I am." He took her hand in his and laced their fingers. "And *handsome,* Dora? The stuff of fairy tales?"

"Well, you are," she said, settling back in her seat. "And it is. Not to you, perhaps. But to me? Yes."

They lapsed into silence again while he thought about what she had said. He was Prince Charming to her Cinderella, was he? She could not know how close to a fairy tale their union seemed to him, though he had spoken of it before their marriage in practical, mundane terms. To have her beside him thus, his companion and lover, his wife, was lovely beyond words. He had said there would be no romance, but he had been thinking of the word in terms of hot, youthful passion. There was a romance of middle age too, he was discovering— quieter and less demonstrative, but nevertheless . . . well, romantic.

"George," she asked him, "why did you marry me? I mean, why *me*?"

He still did not know why and could speak only the truth.

"I don't know." He turned his head to look at her. Her eyes were on their clasped hands on the seat between them. He lifted their hands to his thigh. "I only know that when I thought of marrying as something I wanted to do, it was not marriage in the abstract of which I thought, but of marriage to you. It felt right when I thought it and it felt right when I saw you again. It felt right during the month in London, and it felt very right on our wedding day. It has felt right ever since."

She lifted her head to look into his eyes. She did not reply. She smiled instead. He loved her smile.

The weather was not good as they traveled across Devon and into Cornwall, the sea often in sight to their left. The sky was persistently gray with heavy clouds and the wind buffeted the carriage from the west. The sea, as a result, was rough and a gunmetal gray flecked with foam. At least the rain held off, but it must all look very dreary to someone who had not been there before. Like a boy, he had wanted everything to be perfect for his bride's homecoming.

"I wish I could have brought you here in sunshine," he told her on a late morning when they were within ten miles of home, "but I have no say in what the weather decides to do."

"Oh, but the sun will shine at some time," she said. She drew breath as though to say something else but did not do so. When she did speak, it was with a smile in her voice. "George, let us talk about our wedding day."

Instinctively he pressed farther back into his seat.

"Three or four minutes do not make a day," she told him. "Let us forget those minutes and remember all the rest. I want to remember it as the most wonderful day of my life."

Ah, Dora.

"And of mine," he agreed, settling his shoulder against hers. "What is your most precious memory?"

"Oh, that is difficult," she said. "I suppose the moment when the bishop told everyone gathered in the church that we were man and wife and no man—I suppose he meant no woman either—was to put us asunder. That was the most precious moment of my life. But there were many other memorable moments."

"Seeing you step into the nave on your father's arm," he said.

"Seeing you waiting for me," she said, "and knowing that you were my *bridegroom*."

"Sliding the ring onto your finger," he said, "and feeling how perfectly it fit."

"Hearing you vow to love and cherish me."

"Watching you sign the register, using your maiden name for the last time and knowing that the deed was officially done and you were my wife forever."

"Walking back along the nave and seeing so many smiling faces, some familiar, many not. Oh, and the music, George. That must be a magnificent organ."

"I shall take you to see it the next time we are in London," he promised her. "And to play it."

"Would it be allowed?" she asked, her eyes widening.

"All things are allowed a duchess," he said, and they smiled at each other—no, they grinned.

"The flower petals Flavian and your friends hurled at us when we left the church," she said.

"The metallic decorations attached to the carriage."

"The receiving line in the doorway of Chloe and

Ralph's ballroom," she said, "and all that goodwill directed just upon us."

"Hugging our family and friends," he said. "Seeing them happy for us."

"The food and the wedding cake."

"The wine and the toasts."

"My shiny wedding ring," she said. "I kept deliberately raising my hand just so that I could see it." She did it now.

"Our wedding night," he said softly, "though that happened on what was officially the day after our wedding. I am sorry that—"

"No," she said, cutting him off. "We are not to regret anything. Nothing is perfect, George, and our wedding day was no exception. But it was as nearly perfect as any day could be. Let us remember it happily. Let us stop trying to forget it merely because there was that merest flaw in it."

A *merest flaw. Ah, Dora.*

"A mere speck of dust," he said. "A mere grain of sand. It was the loveliest day of my life too."

"The . . . first time was not that?" she asked.

He drew a slow breath and released it. "No," he said. "Not the first time. Look, we are home."

The carriage had turned onto Penderris land, and the house was coming into sight on Dora's side. It could be seen as a forbidding sort of place, he supposed, especially in this weather. It was a massive mansion of gray stone set in cultivated gardens that at least displayed some color at this time of year even if the sun was not shining. Below the gardens at the front was wild coastland scenery of coarse grass and gorse and heather and rugged rocks and, of course, the high cliffs, which fell away to more rocks and golden sand and the sea below.

"Oh." She sounded awed. "It is so vast. How on earth am I going to learn to be mistress here? Even my father's house would look insignificant if it were set beside it. My cottage would look like a gardener's shed."

He set an arm about her shoulders. "I have a perfectly competent housekeeper, who has been with me forever," he told her. "I married you because I wanted a wife and a friend, not because I needed a mistress for Penderris."

She turned her face away from the window and regarded him with what he thought of as her practical, sensible look. It was laced now with a touch of exasperation.

"What an utterly foolish thing to say," she said. "As though one can marry a duke and expect to get away with being simply his wife and his friend. How all your servants would despise me! And they would speak to other servants and merchants, and they would speak with their employers and customers, and very soon everyone for miles around would look upon me with scorn and contempt. I am not just your wife, George. I am also, heaven help me, your duchess. And don't you dare grin at me like that, as though I were a mere amusement to you. I am going to have to learn to be mistress of this . . . this mansion, and don't try telling me anything to the contrary."

So much for her famous inner serenity. Poor Dora. While he had been looking forward to coming home with her, she had clearly been approaching it with growing agitation. Even though he had not imposed any expectations upon her, she had imposed them upon herself. He squeezed her shoulder and kissed her.

"Just keep in mind," he said, "that there are hearts fluttering with fright within that mansion. It is not because I am coming home. I am a known quantity. It is because you are coming, the new Duchess of Stanbrook. They would be quite mystified if they knew that you are frightened of them."

She sighed. "I told you about Miranda Corley a couple of days ago," she said. "She is tone deaf, to put it kindly, and there are ten thumbs attached to her hands instead of just two with eight fingers. She is also of an age at which she is experiencing all the sullen rebelliousness of oppressed youth. Yet her parents believe her to be a musical prodigy and employed me to nurture her genius. I tell you this so that you will understand what I mean when I say that I would rather at this moment be facing a triple lesson with Miranda than facing my arrival at Penderris."

He chuckled as the carriage rocked to a halt at the foot of the front steps, and withdrew his arm from about her shoulders.

"We are home."

Just keep in mind that there are hearts fluttering with fright within that mansion . . . because you are coming, the new Duchess of Stanbrook.

Dora kept those words firmly in mind for the rest of the day. She had adjusted to new circumstances before in her life, and she would do it again. Besides, she was not without experience at being mistress of a home. It was just that Penderris was on such a grand scale. *So much* grander than any other place she had lived.

At least she was spared here the formal welcome she had received at Stanbrook House on her wedding evening, perhaps because it had been impossible to predict exactly when they would arrive. However, by the time she sat down to a late luncheon with George, she had met the butler, who had greeted them at the front doors upon their arrival, and the housekeeper, a plump, matronly lady who had looked appraisingly at Dora but without any open disapproval. Dora had informed her that she looked forward to a lengthier meeting tomorrow and perhaps a tour of the kitchens.

She met Maisie, the maid who had been appointed her in London, in her dressing room, which was as large as her whole bedchamber in her cottage. She spent an hour or so alone in the duchess's bedchamber, presumably resting. Instead she sat on the window seat, her knees hugged to her bosom, gazing across the park to the cliffs and the sea in the distance beyond. The stark beauty of it all was going to take some getting used to. George took her for a short walk in the inner park afterward, and then it was time to dress for dinner, which was taken according to country hours, earlier than it had been in London. Dinner was served in a large dining room at a table that seemed to stretch almost its whole length. Fortunately her place had been set beside her husband's at the head of the table, and they were able to converse without having to yell at each other over a vast distance.

It was a bewildering but not an unhappy homecoming. Within a few days, she was sure, she would become familiar with her surroundings and her new duties and would be able to relax and feel at home.

Something had bothered her from the moment of her arrival, however. Or perhaps it was the absence of something. She had expected signs of the first duchess, however slight. She had not seen very much of the house yet, of course, for George had taken her outside for some air, at her request, when she might have asked for a quick tour of the house instead. But from what she had seen there was nothing to suggest that Penderris had ever been anything but the home of a bachelor until now.

Dora ought to have felt relieved, for she had felt some unease during the days in the carriage over the knowledge that she was the second duchess, that her predecessor had lived here and ruled here for almost twenty years. She had stepped inside the duchess's bedchamber, feeling a bit like an interloper, fearing that it would somehow bear the stamp of the other woman. What she found instead was a beautiful room decorated in varying shades of mossy green and gold, but one that was also quite impersonal, like a guest chamber or like a room waiting to take on the personality of its occupant.

There were no signs of a woman's touch anywhere else either—not in the drawing room, not in the dining room, not even in the gardens. There were also no signs that there had been a child here once, a boy, a young man, the son of the house. It all made Dora feel a little uneasy. Of course, both the first duchess and the son had been gone for more than ten years, and since then Penderris had been used as a hospital and convalescent home. Perhaps orders had been given recently that any remaining signs be stripped away out of deference to her. If that was so, then it had been a tactful move upon someone's part but quite unnecessary. No two people's lives should be so obliterated from the place that had been their home.

It was almost as though they had never been.

But Dora was tired after the long journey. Perhaps tomorrow when she toured the whole house she would see all sorts of evidence of George's first family—perhaps a nursery still filled with books and toys, perhaps a young man's room still kept as it had been, perhaps a portrait of the duchess. Dora had no idea what she had looked like.

After dinner George drew her hand through his arm and led her from the dining room. But instead of taking her to the drawing room, he took her upstairs to what he described as the duchess's sitting room. It was between their dressing rooms and the bedchambers beyond each. Dora had not looked into it earlier. It was a cozy room, she thought immediately, furnished with comfortable-looking upholstered furniture. A fire crackled in the hearth and the candles in the two candelabra gave a warm, cheerful light.

Dora's general impression of the room was a fleeting thing, though, for her attention focused almost immediately upon one familiar object—her pianoforte, looking old and battered, looking like home.

"Oh!" she exclaimed, and she withdrew her arm from George's and took a few hurried steps into the room before stopping again and swinging around to face him, her hands held prayer fashion against her lips.

He was smiling. "I hope," he said, "you were not congratulating yourself upon being rid of it at last."

She shook her head and bit her upper lip—and lost sight of him.

"Don't cry." He laughed softly, and she felt his hands clasp her shoulders. "Are you that unhappy to see it?"

"It is such an ugly old thing," she said, swiping at her tears with both hands. "I did not like to say anything about it. I said goodbye to it at the cottage and hoped whoever bought the place would have some use for it. What made you think of having it brought here?"

"Maybe a desire to please you," he said. "Or perhaps a memory of listening to you play it for a very short while the day after I asked you to marry me. Mainly a desire to please you—and myself. Are you pleased?"

"You know I am," she said. "Thank you, thank you, George. How very kind you are and how good to me."

"It is my pleasure to please you," he told her, his hands squeezing her shoulders. "Will you play it for me, Dora? After we have drunk our tea?"

"Of course I will," she said. "But before. I cannot wait."

She played for an hour. Neither of them spoke a word during that time, even between pieces. He did not applaud either or show any other sign of appreciation—or boredom. Dora played without looking at him even once, but she was aware of him at every moment. She played for him, because he had asked her to play, but even more because he had thought to have her pianoforte fetched from Inglebrook, because he had looked so pleased at her surprise, because he was *there,* listening. She felt more fully married during that hour than she had at any time before. She was consciously happy. Words, even looks, were unnecessary, and that was perhaps the happiest thought of all.

As they drank tea afterward and conversed comfortably on a variety of topics, Dora thought of how very, very sweet marriage was and how fortunate she was to be married at last.

"Time for bed?" he suggested after the tray had been removed.

"Yes," she agreed. "I am tired."

"Too tired?" he asked.

"Oh, no," she assured him. "Not too tired."

How could she ever be too tired for his lovemaking? Or for him? She was, of course, hopelessly, irrevocably in love with him. She had admitted that to herself long before now. It made no real difference to anything, however. They were just words—being in love, romantic love.

She did not need words when the reality was so very lovely.

13

George spent most of the next morning at home, first with his secretary, then with his steward. He had some catching up to do since he had been gone for a while, first for Imogen's wedding and then for his own. Dora, looking neat and trim in one of her new dresses and with her hair simply styled, had informed him at breakfast that she would spend the morning with Mrs. Lerner, the housekeeper, and that she intended to visit the kitchens too and make the acquaintance of the chef and some of the indoor servants. She intended to have all their names memorized within a few days and hoped they would make allowances for her until she did. She would be careful not to tread upon any toes, however, for she understood that some chefs guarded their domain quite jealously and resented interference even from the mistress of the house.

George had listened fondly and wondered what the servants would make of her. She had made no attempt to look like a duchess—she actually looked more like a provincial music teacher—or to behave like one.

Nevertheless, she intended to be the duchess and mistress of her new home. She would do it her way.

"Even Mrs. Henry, my housekeeper in Inglebrook, could get cross if she felt I was encroaching upon her duties," she had added.

George would wager that his servants would soon respect his wife and even come to love her. He doubted his first wife, Miriam, had known any but a very few of the servants by name. But he did not intend to be making comparisons.

He had planned to suggest a walk down on the beach during the afternoon, but the weather continued inclement. A cloudy, blustery morning gave way to a drizzly, windy afternoon, and he was forced to think of some indoor amusement instead. It was not difficult, for of course she had not yet seen a great deal of the house. He had learned during luncheon that her morning activities had taken her no farther than the morning room and the kitchens.

He took her on a tour of the rest.

First she wanted to see where everyone had stayed during the years when Penderris was a hospital. He showed her the rooms each of the Survivors had occupied, and time passed quickly as he reminisced with some stories about each of them—at her instigation.

"It may seem strange to you that I think back fondly on those years," he said as they stood at the window of what had been Vincent's room. It faced the sea, though he had been unable to appreciate the view. He had liked to listen to the sea, though, after his hearing returned, and he had kept his window open even on the most inclement of days so that he could smell the salty air. "There was a great deal of suffering, and sometimes it was almost unbearable to watch when there was so little I could do to ease it. But in many ways those were the happiest years of my life."

"I daresay you saw human suffering at its worst and human endurance and resilience at its best," she said. "I do not know all the wounded who spent time here, of course, only the six who became your friends. But they are extraordinary human beings, and I believe they must be such strong, vital, loving people at least partly because of all their suffering rather than despite it."

"I have been privileged to know them," he said as he led her to the room in which Imogen had stayed for three years. It overlooked the kitchen gardens at the back of the house.

"I believe you have," she said. "And they have been enormously privileged to know you."

She was perhaps a little biased.

"Why did you do it?" she asked.

"Open my home as a hospital?" he said as she gazed down upon the regimented beds of multicolored blooms in the back garden with which the urns and vases in the house were kept filled. "I really do not know where the idea originated. I have heard it said that some artists and writers do not know where their ideas come from. I do not put myself on a par with them, but I do understand what they mean. The house felt empty and oppressive. I felt empty and oppressed. My life was empty and meaningless, my future empty and unappealing. There was nothing but emptiness all about me and within, in fact. Why did it suddenly occur to me to fill my home and my life with horribly wounded soldiers? It might well have been seen as exactly the wrong solution for what ailed me. But sometimes, I believe, when one asks a question from one's deepest need and waits for an answer without straining too desperately to invent it, the answer comes, seemingly from nowhere. It is not so, of course. Everything comes from somewhere, even if that somewhere is beyond our conscious awareness. But I am getting tangled up in thought. I ought to have stopped after 'I really do not know' as an answer to your question."

"Perhaps," she said softly without turning from the window, "the idea came to you at least partly because your son was an officer and died. And because your wife could not bear her grief and shattered your already broken heart."

He felt as though she had planted a very heavy fist low to his abdomen. He felt robbed of breath and raw with sudden pain.

"Who knows?" he said abruptly after a silence it seemed neither of them would break. "Let me show you the room where Ben learned to walk again and Flavian learned to deal with his rages."

"I am sorry," she said, frowning as she turned from the window and took his offered arm.

"Don't be," he told her. He heard the curtness of his tone and made an effort to correct it. "You need not apologize for anything you choose to say to me, Dora. You are my wife." Now his voice sounded merely chilly. Not to mention stilted.

The room to which he took her next had been converted back into a salon that was rarely used since he never entertained on a large scale. At one time, though, there had been sturdy bars along the full length of it, one set fixed to the wall, the other a short distance from it and parallel to it, both at just the right height for Ben to hold on to on either side of his body as he forced weight onto his crushed legs and feet and learned to move them in a semblance of a walk. It had been a painful sight to behold. And very inspiring.

"I have never seen anyone more determined to do something that was apparently impossible," he told Dora after describing the contraption. "His face would pour sweat, the air was often blue with his language, and it is a wonder he did not grind his teeth to powder when he was not using his mouth for cursing. He was going to walk even if he had to traverse the coals of hell to do it."

"And indeed he does walk now with his two canes," she said.

"Out of sheer hellish stubbornness," he said with a smile. "We were all very happy when he finally convinced himself that using a wheeled chair was not an admission of defeat but actually just the opposite. That did not happen, though, until after he had met Samantha and gone to Wales. He also rides and swims."

"And Flavian?" she asked him.

"We had a stuffed leather bag suspended from the ceiling for the use of your brother-in-law," he said, "and leather gloves for him to wear while he pounded the stuffing out of it. He learned to come here when his thoughts were so hopelessly jumbled that he could not get any words out, even allowing for his stammer. His frustration had a way of releasing itself in violence and scared a number of people half to death. It was why I brought him here. His family did not know how to cope with him."

"Whose idea was the pounding bag?" she asked.

"The physician's?" he said. "Mine? I cannot remember."

"I think it was probably yours," she said.

"You are turning me into a hero, are you?" he asked her.

"Oh, no," she told him. "You are a hero. You do not need me to proclaim what already is so."

He laughed and bore her off to the family portrait gallery, which ran the whole width of the house on the west side of the upper floor, where the sun was less of a problem than it would have been on the east.

He might have taken her back to the drawing room instead, he thought later, when it was too late. They had already spent a good portion of the afternoon in the hospital rooms, and it was not too early for tea, especially when he had a surprise awaiting her afterward. But he was enjoying showing her their home and watching her genuine interest. He was loving her company and the knowledge that she belonged here now, that she was not a mere visitor who would leave sooner or later.

So he took her to the gallery.

The Crabbe family could be traced back in an unbroken line to the early thirteenth century, when the first of their recorded ancestors had been awarded a barony for some military exploit that had brought him to the attention of the king. The title had mutated to viscount and earl and eventually to duke. George was the fourth Duke of Stanbrook. There were portraits reaching back to the beginning, with very few omissions.

"I failed a history test on the Civil War when I was eight or thereabouts," George told Dora. "I could not muster up any enthusiasm for Cavaliers and Roundheads and would not have got a single answer right if I had not been gruesomely fascinated by the fact that King Charles I had had his head chopped off. My father punished me by sending me up here to learn the history of my own family. It was the dead of winter and my poor tutor was sent with me, perhaps as punishment for not having ignited my interest. On a test the very next day, set by my father, I got every answer correct and even exasperated my tutor by writing an essay for each when a single sentence would have sufficed. I have loved the gallery ever since when I suppose I might have come to see it as a sort of torture chamber."

She laughed. "Am I to be given the test tomorrow?" she asked him.

"I doubt you would have incentive enough to do well," he said. "It is not winter, and I do not keep a cane at the ready in my library as my father did, though to be fair he never actually used it on me—or my brother."

They moved slowly along the gallery while he identified the people in each portrait. He kept his commentary brief so as not to bore her, but she asked numerous questions and saw likenesses to him in several of the family members dating back to the last century or so despite elaborate powdered wigs and black facial patches and vast quantities of velvet and lace.

"Ah," she said with evident pleasure as they came to the large family portrait that had been painted not long before his mother's death when he was fourteen. He had thought himself very grown-up while it was being painted, he recalled, because neither the painter nor his father had had to tell him even once to sit still— unlike his brother, who had squirmed and yawned and scratched and complained through almost the whole tedious process. "You look very like your father, George. Your brother looks more like your mother— and Julian looks like him. Do you miss your brother dreadfully? And he was younger than you."

"Yes, I miss him," he admitted. "Unfortunately, he got himself into the clutches of alcohol and gambling when he was a very young man and never could seem to pull himself free even when most of his contemporaries had finished sowing their wild oats and were settling down to sober adulthood. If he had not died when he did, there would have been virtually nothing left of his property for my nephew to inherit. It seemed for a while that Julian would follow in his footsteps, but he was fortunate enough to meet Philippa, a mere schoolroom miss at the time. He waited for her to grow up, though her father very rightly sent him packing and he did not set eyes on her for a number of years. He used the time to make himself worthy of her and acceptable to her father. I was and am very proud of him—as well as very fond."

Dora had turned to look at him. "I could see when I met him in London that you love him dearly," she said, "and that he returns your regard. He will be a worthy successor to the title."

"But not too soon, I hope," he said.

"Oh." She laughed. "I hope not either. I rather like you right here with me."

"Do you?" He lowered his head and kissed her briefly on the lips.

She turned back to the wall, and for the first time it struck him that he ought not to have brought her. For she was looking at the blank wall beyond that family portrait and then glancing over her shoulder at him, her eyebrows raised.

"But that is the last one?" she asked him. "There are no more?"

"No," he said. "Not yet."

He had been fourteen when that picture was painted, three years before his father's death. He was forty-eight now. That made for a gap of thirty-four years. He had never had a family portrait done with Miriam and Brendan. And no official one of either of them alone.

He had not thought soon enough of how that blank wall would look to Dora.

"Perhaps," he said, his voice a little overhearty, "we will make it a project for next winter, Dora. It is a long and tedious business, I recall, sitting for a portrait, but it ought to be done. I would like to have it done. I will find a reputable portrait painter and bring him out here to stay. He can paint us on days when it is too cold and dreary to venture outdoors."

But she had turned to face him fully now, and her eyes were on his, a puzzled frown between her brows.

"There is no painting of you with your wife and your son?" she asked him. "You did not have it removed out of deference to my feelings, by any chance, did you? You really did not need to do that, George. You must have it put back. I do not resent the marriage you had for almost twenty years long before I even knew of your existence. I am not jealous. Did you think I would be? Besides, they are a part of all this family history you have displayed here."

Instead of answering, he turned on his heel and took several long strides along the gallery, his boots ringing on the polished wood floor. He stopped as abruptly as he had started, but he did not turn back to her.

"There is no portrait, Dora," he said. "There ought to have been, perhaps, but I never got around to arranging it. Nothing has been hidden away from your sight. They were a part of my life for many years, Miriam and Brendan, and then they died. Much has happened since—at Penderris, in my life. Now you are here, the wife of my present and of as much of the future as we will be granted. I prefer not to look back, not to talk about the past, not even to think about it. I want what I have with you. I want our friendship, our . . . marriage. I have been happy with it, and I have felt that you are happy too."

He had not heard her come up behind him. His arm jerked and then stiffened when she set a hand on it.

"I am sorry," she said.

He swung about. "*Don't* keep saying you are sorry."

Her hand went straight up, as though she had scalded it, and remained suspended above the level of her shoulder, palm out, fingers spread. For a moment there was a look of alarm on her face.

"I am sorry," she said again.

His shoulders sagged. He could not even remember the last time he had lost his temper. And now he had lost it with Dora.

"No," he said, "I am the one who needs to be sorry, Dora. I do indeed beg your pardon. Please forgive me. When I married you, I very much wanted life to be new and good for both of us, unencumbered by memories of the past. The past has no real existence, after all. It is gone. The present is the reality we have, and for that fact I am grateful. I like the present. Do you? Do you have any regrets?"

It bothered him that a moment passed before she shook her head and lowered her arm to her side.

"I have always dreamed of being married to a man I could like," she said, "even though I did not waste my life waiting for him to put in an appearance."

"And can you like me?" he asked. He found that he was holding his breath

"I can," she said gravely. And then she smiled, an expression that began in her eyes and spread to her mouth. "And I do."

"I think," he said, clasping his hands behind his back, "we ought to go down for tea."

Despite a certain amount of nervousness, Dora had quite enjoyed the morning. She had established a working relationship with both Mrs. Lerner and Mr. Humble, the chef, though she believed the latter must be grossly misnamed. She felt she had won their cautious approval. She had met several of the kitchen staff after

Mr. Humble had lined them up for her inspection and
scolded one bootboy for slouching and one maid for
having a stain on her apron even though it was still only
morning. Dora was confident that she would remember
each servant and even be able to attach the correct
name to the correct person.

She had fully enjoyed the afternoon despite the fact
that the rain had prevented the walk down on the beach
to which she had been looking forward. But there was
so much to discover in the house itself that she was not
greatly disappointed. And it was lovely indeed to be
shown about by George himself, who so clearly loved
the house and loved talking about it. She had thoroughly enjoyed his reminiscences about his fellow Survivors and the years when they had all stayed here. And
she had loved the visit to the gallery and listening to
him identify his ancestors in their portraits and describe
a little of their histories. He was not normally a talk-
ative man, she knew. He preferred to listen, and he was
very skilled at drawing others, including her, into talking about themselves. He had become absorbed in his
family history there in the gallery, though, and he had
looked relaxed and contented.

But now she wished they had not gone there at all.

There was something horribly wrong.

Any stranger who knew nothing about the family
would assume after being in the gallery that George
had been a bachelor until now, though even then the
stranger might expect that he would have had a portrait
of himself painted at some time during the past thirty

years. But in reality he had married a mere three years after that family painting. His son had been born the year after that. And though both the wife and the son were now gone, they had lived as a family for many years. Almost twenty. Right here. At Penderris Hall.

The truly puzzling part was that George loved his family history. That had been obvious this afternoon, as well as the fact that he was proud of those portraits, reaching back in an unbroken line for several centuries. Why, then, had he broken the chain by neglecting to commission a portrait of his own family?

They walked in silence to the drawing room, her hands clasped at her waist, his behind his back. Dora shivered inwardly when she thought of his reaction to her question about the absent portrait. He had turned on his heel and hurried away. Even though he had stopped almost immediately, he had not turned back toward her. And then his temper had snapped and he had blazed at her. For a moment he had seemed like a rather frightening stranger. Oh, he had recovered very quickly and apologized to her. But she had been left with the feeling that she had been told in no uncertain terms that his past was off limits to her. And to everyone else too. There did not seem to be any record of it, any sign, any trace of it.

He had, in so many words, told her that everything that had happened in his life between the ages of seventeen and thirty-five or thirty-six was none of her business. A huge, dark gap of years. And he was right, of course. His former marriage was none of her business. Except that he was her husband and there was supposed to be openness between marriage partners, was there not?

And except that he had somehow induced her to spill out her own life history with all its skeletons and demons before they even left London.

Dora walked beside her husband and realized that she knew him scarcely at all and perhaps never would. For how could one know a man if one experienced only the present with him and knew nothing of the past that had shaped him into the person he was? He had done almost *forty-eight* years of living before she married him.

Her mind touched unwillingly upon that episode in the church, when the first duchess's half brother had accused George of murdering his wife. Dora did not believe it, not even for a single moment. And yet . . . And yet something had provoked the Earl of Eastham into coming to their wedding to make such a public scene.

What had happened? What had *really* happened?

A fire awaited them in the drawing room despite the fact that it was well into June, and the tea tray was being carried in even as they arrived there. George thanked the two footmen and Dora smiled. She liked that about him. She liked that servants were not invisible to him as they seemed to be to so many people who had always been waited upon hand and foot.

"The weather has not been kind to you so far, Dora, has it?" he said as she poured their tea.

"But it will be," she said. "Imagine my wonder when

I wake up one morning to find the sun sparkling from a blue sky onto a blue sea."

"I hope to be there to witness it," he said.

They settled on either side of the fireplace and chatted comfortably. His manner was relaxed, pleasant, even affectionate. He smiled often at her, and even when he did not, his eyes were kindly. His irritability, his fury in the gallery seemed almost like a dream. But Dora did find herself wondering about his almost perpetual kindliness, his smiling eyes. Were they a sort of shield? To stop other people from seeing in? To see the world and other people as he wanted to see them despite whatever it was that was shut up deep within him?

Or was she imagining that there was deep darkness inside him?

"I have a wedding gift for you," he said after setting his empty cup and saucer back on the tray.

"George!" She spoke reproachfully. "You do not need to keep lavishing gifts on me. Your wedding gift was a diamond pendant and earrings, and they were more than enough. I have never owned anything half as precious."

"Jewels!" He made a dismissive gesture with one hand as though they were nothing of any real value. "This is something more personal, something I believe you will like."

"I like my diamonds," she assured him.

"You will like this more." He got to his feet and took her hand in his. "Come. Let me show you."

He looked like an eager boy, she thought.

He took her downstairs and past the door to the room she knew was the library, though she had not seen inside any of the ground-floor apartments yet. She might be exploring for the whole of the next week before she saw everything, or so it seemed. He stopped outside the door next to the library.

"It is the music room," he told her, his hand on the doorknob. "It overlooks the rose garden rather than the sea, and I have always thought that a particularly clever touch. There has always been just a grand pianoforte in here apart from the chairs awaiting an audience. It has an excellent tone, and you will enjoy playing it, I believe, whenever you can tear yourself away from your own pianoforte in your sitting room."

She tipped her head sideways and looked up at him. He was deliberately delaying opening the door.

"It is neither the rose garden nor the grand pianoforte that is your wedding gift, though," he said.

"The chairs, then?"

He smiled and opened the door, standing to one side so that she could precede him into the room.

The grand pianoforte, standing almost alone in the middle of a large, high-ceilinged chamber, was indeed a magnificent instrument. That was immediately apparent to Dora. It had elegant, pleasing lines, and its high gloss gleamed even in the dull light that came through the windows. It was reflected in the highly polished wooden floor. Roses were blooming outside. But it was upon none of those beautiful things that her eyes focused.

"Oh." She stood rooted to a spot just inside the doorway.

A full-sized harp, intricately and elegantly carved and looking as though it might well be made of solid gold, stood to one side of the pianoforte, a gilded chair drawn up to it. "Mine? It is *mine*?"

"Only on condition that you allow me to listen occasionally whenever you play it," he said from behind her shoulder. "No, correct that. There are no conditions. It is a gift, Dora—my wedding gift to you. Yes, it is yours."

Memories of last year and her first meeting with the Duke of Stanbrook came rushing back to her. When she had entertained Viscount Darleigh's guests at Middlebury Park, she had played the harp first before moving on to the pianoforte. Everyone had been kind and appreciative, but it was the duke—George—who had got to his feet when she had finished at the harp and drawn the stool back from the pianoforte for her. It was he who had led her upstairs to the drawing room for refreshments afterward and filled a plate for her and brought her a cup of tea before seating himself beside her and speaking in warm praise of her talent.

She had fallen a little in love with him that evening, foolish and presumptuous though it had seemed at the time.

"I have never seen anything more magnificent. It is a work of art," she said, crossing the room toward the harp and touching the solid beauty of its frame with reverence before running her fingers lightly across the strings. A mellow ripple of sound followed their movement. She dared not even hazard a guess at how much it had cost.

And it was hers.

"When I was a girl," she said, "I was enchanted by an old battered harp that no one ever played at the home of one of our neighbors. I could not stop running my hand over its strings just to hear the sound that came from them. More than anything in the world I wanted to coax real music from it. My mother arranged with those neighbors to allow my music teacher to accompany me there on certain days and teach me to play. Sometimes they allowed me to go there alone and practice. Mama persuaded Papa to buy me the little harp I still have, the one I used to take with me when I visited the sick and elderly at Inglebrook. I did not encounter a real harp again until Viscount Darleigh—Vincent—employed me to give him pianoforte lessons and I saw it there in the music room at Middlebury Park. Even in my dreams I did not imagine that I would ever own one."

"But now you do," he said.

She swung around. He was still standing just inside the door, his hands clasped behind his back, beaming with pleasure.

"What have I done to deserve this?" she asked him.

"Let me see." He looked up at the painted, gilded ceiling as though deep in thought. "Ah, yes." He looked back at her. "You agreed to marry me."

"As if any woman in her right mind would have refused," she said.

"Ah, but you are not any woman, Dora," he said as he crossed the room toward her, "and I believe you would have refused me if you had not liked me just a little. I purchased the harp for you because I thought it would make you happy. And also for selfish reasons. For if *you* are happy, then I am happy too."

Dora felt suddenly uneasy again. For the thought had

occurred to her yet again as she gazed into his smiling eyes that he was a terribly, terribly lonely man. Still. And it occurred to her that he could deal with his loneliness only by giving, by making other people happy. Not by receiving. He did not know how to receive.

Who had taken that ability away from him?

He had not needed to have her pianoforte brought here. He had not needed to spend a fortune on a harp for her. He had married her and was kind to her. That was sufficient. Oh, that was more than sufficient.

"You do not need to cry," he said softly. "It is only a harp, Dora, and you do not even know for sure yet that it is a good one."

She raised both arms and cupped his face in her hands.

"Oh, it is," she said with conviction. "Thank you, George. It is the most wonderful gift I have ever received. I shall treasure it all my life, mainly because you gave it to me. And you may listen to me play whenever you wish. You have only to ask—or to come when I am playing alone. I am your wife. I am also your friend."

She did what she had never done before. *She* kissed *him*. On the lips. He stood very still until she was finished, though his lips softened against her own.

"Play for me now?" he asked her.

"I am very rusty," she warned him. "It is well over a month since I last played the harp at Middlebury. But yes. I will play for you. Of course I will."

He adjusted the position of the chair for her and stood a little behind and to one side of it as she drew the harp against her shoulder until it felt comfortable. Then she spread her hands over the strings. *Of her harp*.

She closed her eyes and played the simple, haunting melody of an old folk song. Like most ancient folk songs it was beautiful, and tragic.

But life did not need to be tragic.

Did it?

14

George's life changed gradually but perceptibly over the next few weeks.

For one thing, he was marvelously contented. His life followed the old routine to a large extent—he spent a few hours most days out on his land, sometimes in company with his steward, sometimes alone. His crops had grown into a ripple of green promise and the lambs were becoming small sheep and the sheep were looking as though they would soon be in dire need of shearing. He spent time in the office at the back of the house too since he liked to know exactly what was going on with his farms despite the fact that he had a competent, trustworthy steward.

The difference was that all the time he was busy about his own business he knew that his wife was busy too in the performance of her duties as mistress of Penderris Hall, even though she admitted that the housekeeper and chef could function very well without her, not to mention the butler. Like him, though, she needed to know and understand the inner workings of her home, and she still maintained that the servants would despise her if she did not show an interest. And his favorite foods were surely served a little more frequently than before, George thought, though he had never had any complaint about anything his chef served up.

The real difference was that when he was not at work, the hours were no longer long and empty. For he had a constant companion, one with whom he could discuss the day's events and any other topic that occurred to either of them. He had a companion with whom he could sit quietly for hours at a time while they both read or while he read and she, more productive than he, embroidered or crocheted or tatted. Sometimes he read aloud to her. He had a companion who shared his pleasure in the letters that often appeared beside his breakfast plate—and now hers too. They fell into the habit of reading most of the letters aloud to each other.

Sophia and Vincent had had another children's book published—another adventure of Bertha and Blind Dan; Sophia's second pregnancy seemed to be proceeding well—as were Chloe's and Samantha's and Agnes's; Imogen and Percy had lingered in London for a while longer than they had planned since his numerous relatives, almost to a man and woman, assumed they would be delighted to be feted in their post-honeymoon bliss even though they were by now an old and staid married couple—Percy had written that particular letter; Melody Emes was cutting her first teeth and Hugo was wondering if he would ever again in this life know what it was to sleep—apparently he walked the floor with the baby at night so that the nurse who was paid to perform the task could rest; Samantha's Welsh grandfather had recovered from the chest cold that had dragged him down since before Christmas; Mrs. Henry, Dora's former housekeeper, had been offered temporary employment at Middlebury Park; Dora's mother was still basking in the wonder of that day when *both* her daughters had called on her, and had sent two letters so far. In both, she had expounded on how happy she had been to see that they had grown up to be such lovely ladies and that both had made happy, advantageous marriages.

Percy had reported in a postscript to his letter that George would have kept from Dora if she had not been the one reading it aloud that the Earl of Eastham, having recovered from his indisposition, had taken himself off home to Derbyshire. George wondered to himself if that would be the last he heard of from his former brother-in-law. Dora made no comment except to raise her eyebrows and ask a one-word question.

"Indisposition?"

"Apparently," George said vaguely, and, apart from a long, hard look, she was contented to leave it at that.

And there was the music that now filled his life. Scarcely a day passed in which she did not play the pianoforte in her sitting room or the harp in the music room—or both. Sometimes she played the grand pianoforte, though she soon pronounced it slightly out of tune, something that was not apparent to his own ear. He never read while she played. The music she produced was pleasurable in itself, but the soothing effect it had upon him was pure joy. And that had more to do with her than with the music itself. There was true talent in her fingers, but there was a deep beauty in her soul. He had never seen anyone so totally absorbed in her playing as his wife was as soon as she began. He doubted she had any idea how very graceful a figure she presented as she moved slightly to the music— or how beautiful her face as she played.

His nights were filled with pleasure and contentment. They did not always make love, and when they did it was not always with fierce passion. Indeed, it rarely was, though it always brought him unalloyed pleasure, as it did her, he was sure. But even when they did not make love, she was content to lie in his arms and to sleep all night curled into him. Sometimes he would hold back sleep just so that he could savor the warm feel of her, the smell of her hair and skin, the soft sound of her breathing. His own wife in his own bed— but not as impersonal as that. *Dora* in *their* bed.

And then there were the other changes in his life.

Apart from a small core of neighbors whom George had long considered friends, no one had called upon him uninvited for years, just as he had called upon no one except those friends. Now a large number of people came, as was only proper, to pay their respects to the new Duchess of Stanbrook. His friends came, as did those who were friendly acquaintances he met regularly at church or on the village street. People he scarcely knew came, and so did a few of those who were his enemies, though *enemy* was far too harsh a word in most cases. They were mostly ladies who had been Miriam's friends, though less friends, perhaps, than hangers-on, sycophants, women who had basked in her high rank and beauty and preened themselves before their neighbors because they were the special friends and confidantes of the dear duchess. They were the same ladies as those who had hung upon Eastham's words after Miriam's death—though he had been Meikle then, not having inherited from his father until later—and had looked upon George himself as a villainous murderer. Perhaps they still did.

All these people came, and according to Dora the calls needed to be returned. He questioned the point, but she insisted that being a duchess did not set her above the dictates of courteous social behavior.

"Besides," she explained to him, "neighbors are important, George. One should always cultivate their good opinion when one can do so without compromising one's principles. Sometimes neighbors can become friends, and friends are precious."

Her words gave him an insight into the loneliness she must have felt when she moved to Inglebrook, an unmarried female, at the age of thirty. Yet when he had met her years later, she had been well established and well respected in the community.

He did not accompany her on all the return visits, but he did on some. And though there was tedium in making polite conversation with people with whom he had little in common, he was touched by the gratification with which they were received almost everywhere. And he was proud of his wife, who behaved with the dignity of her new rank and yet with the warm accessibility of the Miss Debbins she had been until very recently. She was generally liked, he saw, and the realization warmed him.

Miriam had not been. As always, he shook off the unbidden comparisons.

And she made two real friends. One was Mrs. Newman, the vicar's wife, a slightly faded creature about her own age who somehow blossomed into warm animation when Dora spoke with her. The other was Ann Cox-Hampton, the wife of one of George's own friends. At their first meeting the two ladies discovered similar interests in books and music and needlework and chattered happily while seated side by side on a sofa while George and James Cox-Hampton, freed of the necessity of keeping the conversation general, talked about crops and cattle and markets and the horse races.

During those weeks of change and contentment following his return to Penderris, George pushed aside the memory of that first afternoon, when he had made the mistake of taking Dora to the portrait gallery. They had not been there since, and they had not referred to the past since. Perhaps, he sometimes thought, it really could be put behind him and forgotten, or, if that was impossible, at least consigned to a remote corner of his memory where it would have no impact upon his present.

The present was really very sweet.

On one particular afternoon Dora was paying an afternoon call alone. While she knew George had visited far more of his neighbors with her than he had ever done before, she also knew that it was something he did not really enjoy. She might not have come herself today since the sun was shining and the air was warm and the beach beckoned. But she had mentioned to Mrs. Yarby at church on Sunday that she would call today if it was convenient, and the lady had assured her that indeed it was and she would look forward to Her Grace's visit. Dora's first amused thought upon her arrival was that it was a very good thing George had not come with her, for clearly Mrs. Yarby, forewarned, had made an Event with a capital *E* out of the prospective visit.

The housekeeper, looking as though every inch of her uniform had been ruthlessly starched, led Dora to the sitting room, threw open the door, and announced her. Standing proudly in the middle of the room, as though she had been anticipating the moment for some time, was Mrs. Yarby, dressed in afternoon finery that would not have afforded a second glance in a London drawing room but certainly did in a country village. Seated about the room but rising to their feet almost as one with a rustle of silks and muslins were five other ladies, looking as though they were about to set off to a garden party with royalty.

Three of the five had called at Penderris Hall, but perhaps they had not realized that Dora intended eventually to return the call of each. Perhaps Mrs. Yarby had persuaded them that she had been singled out for special attention.

Dora accepted the rehearsed greetings of her hostess with a smile—Mr. Yarby, she guessed, had taken himself off somewhere else or had been banished since Dora had made it clear that the duke would not be with her. She smiled too at each of the other ladies and inclined her head as she was introduced to the two she had not met before. It still felt a bit strange to her to be addressed as "Your Grace" and to be treated as though she was a creature apart from them.

Yet George, without any conscious arrogance, took such deference for granted.

The greetings all finished with, Dora was ushered to the seat of honor close to the fireplace with its unlit coals, and the tea tray was carried in almost immediately—or, rather, the tea trays. A silver tea service gleamed on the first with what was surely the very best china. Sumptuous foods covered the other, including crustless sandwiches with several different fillings and cakes and pastries and apple tarts smelling of cinnamon and scones with clotted cream and strawberry jam. The Yarbys' cook must have been busy since Sunday, Dora thought.

The weather provided a topic of spirited conversation for all of ten minutes. Inquiries about the dear duke's health died at the end of another five. After that all the ladies addressed themselves to the food on their plates and smiled brightly as though perfectly at their ease.

I am just me, Dora wanted to say. But of course "just me" was now a duchess, and really, she could perfectly well understand how these ladies felt when she remembered how very awed she had been last year when she and Agnes were invited to dine at Middlebury Park with Viscount and Lady Darleigh and all their guests, every one of whom was titled and one of whom was a duke—the Duke of Stanbrook.

She set about making Mrs. Yarby and her guests more comfortable by asking questions—about them, about their children, about village life, about the pretty harbor below. It was something she could remember her mother teaching her when she was a shy young girl just beginning to be admitted to adult gatherings. In the main, her mother had explained, people like to talk about themselves. The secret of good conversation was to induce them to do just that and then to appear interested in what they had to say. But not just to appear interested, Dora had added for herself in later years. One needed actually to be interested.

People were almost invariably interesting when one really listened to them. Everyone was so very different from everyone else.

The stiff, awkward silence was soon replaced with animated talk and laughter, and inevitably the general conversation broke into smaller tête-à-têtes and Dora no longer felt that she was the focus of everyone's attention, rather as if she were a species apart.

"The duke, your husband, is a dear friend of mine," the lady beside her said.

"Oh?" Dora smiled politely and made an effort to recall the lady's name—she was one of the people she had not met before today. Ah, she was Mrs. Parkinson.

"Yes." Mrs. Parkinson smiled graciously. "I had the pleasure of introducing my very dearest friend to him and his illustrious houseguests at Penderris Hall a couple of years ago. She and I made our come-out together when we were girls and soon became inseparable. She married Viscount Muir. I might have married an even more impressive title had I so chosen—I had enough offers, heaven knows. But instead I married Mr.

Parkinson for love—he was a younger brother of Sir Roger Parkinson, you know. Mr. Parkinson died a few years ago and left me in a state of nervous collapse and heartbreak, and my dearest Gwen, who was also a widow by that time, though I do not suppose she felt her loss quite as I did, came to stay with me to lend her support. *'Anything in the world for you, my very dearest Vera,'* were her very first words the day she arrived in the carriage of her brother, the Earl of Kilbourne. While she was still with me I introduced her at Penderris Hall, and Baron Trentham took a fancy to her and married her— though I understand he was not born with the title. Nor did he inherit it from his father. Indeed, it is said that his father was in trade. My poor Gwen—I daresay he kept very quiet about that until after he married her. She took a severe drop in rank."

Oh, dear, Dora thought silently.

"You must be very pleased that you had a hand in their meeting," she said. "Lord Trentham was awarded his barony by the Prince of Wales, now the king, after he had led a successful forlorn hope attack in Portugal. He is one of our great war heroes."

"Yes, well, if you say so," Mrs. Parkinson said. "Though one does wonder how a man who is not even a gentleman born could have been an officer, and why he was allowed to lead a charge when there must have been a dozen gentlemen who would have been perfectly willing to do it themselves without demanding any reward. Gentlemen do not behave with such vulgarity, do they? Our world is not what it used to be, Your Grace, as I am sure you would agree. Mr. Parkinson was fond of saying that it would not be many years before we have riffraff in Parliament. I did not believe him at the time, but I am not so sure now that he was not right. I can only hope that Gwen is happy with her impulsive decision to marry below her, I am sure."

"I believe they are both exceedingly happy," Dora said, and considered asking a question about the late esteemed Mr. Parkinson that might turn the conversation onto a different path. But the lady spoke first.

"I was sorely distressed for you, Your Grace," she said her voice suddenly softer and more confiding, "when I heard about the interruption to your wedding."

Ah.

But it had been too much to hope, Dora supposed, that such a salacious tidbit of gossip would not have traveled from London even before they did. It was surely *not* too much, however, to have hoped that no one would be ill-bred enough to mention it in her hearing or George's.

"Thank you," she said, "but it was a very minor annoyance in an otherwise perfect day."

Mrs. Parkinson laid a hand upon her arm and leaned closer.

"I admire you for being able to put a brave face on it, Duchess," she said, "though I am confident you have nothing at all to fear."

Dora looked pointedly at the hand that rested on her arm and then just as pointedly up into Mrs. Parkinson's face.

"Fear?" she said, and she could hear the chill in her own voice.

Mrs. Parkinson removed her hand rather hastily

from Dora's arm. Color stained her cheeks, and her eyes registered first chagrin and then . . . malice? But her mouth smiled sweetly.

"She was a lady to inspire passion in all men who beheld her," she said. "Though she never deliberately set one against another. The first duchess, I mean. She was blond and blue-eyed and tall and slender and altogether more beautiful than any woman has a right to be. I might have been jealous of her if she had not also been the sweetest person I have ever met. The duke adored her and guarded her jealously. No one could so much as look at her without drawing his wrath. He even hated her own family because they loved her and wanted to visit her here and have her visit them at her girlhood home. He got to the point of forbidding her own brother to come to Penderris and of forbidding his own son to go and stay with his uncle and grandfather even though they doted on the boy. Yet he hated the boy himself because for the duchess the sun rose and set upon him. Never has a mother so loved a child, I declare. She was inconsolable when he died after the duke had insisted upon purchasing his commission and packing him off to the Peninsula and into the very teeth of danger. He had hardened his heart against all the piteous pleadings of the boy's poor mother. Even if he did not push her over that cliff, he nevertheless killed her. But I daresay the worst of his passions died with her. He has been a different man since. You are altogether a different sort of woman, of course."

Dora was trying desperately to think of a way of silencing the woman. She would have jumped to her feet and quelled her quite firmly if she had not been fully aware of the other ladies around them, all talking and laughing at once, it seemed. But fortunately Mrs. Yarby came to her rescue at last.

"Mrs. Parkinson," she said rather sharply, "you will be quite boring Her Grace by so monopolizing her attention."

Mrs. Parkinson turned a sweet smile upon her hostess. "I was telling Her Grace about the time when I played matchmaker at Penderris Hall for my dearest friend, who was still Viscountess Muir at the time," she said.

"As I heard it," Mrs. Eddingsley remarked, "the lady met Lord Trentham while she was out walking alone and twisted her ankle when inadvertently trespassing upon Penderris land. He came upon her and carried her up to the house. I have always thought it a particularly romantic story with a happy ending."

"You are quite right, Mrs. Eddingsley," Mrs. Parkinson said. "But my dear Gwen lost no time in summoning me and begging to be brought back to my house, so embarrassed was she to have been caught on the duke's land. I was quick-witted enough, however, to insist that she remain at Penderris while her ankle healed. It was very clear to me that true love needed a helping hand."

A few of the ladies tittered.

What an absolute horror of a woman, Dora thought. She wondered what on earth had induced Gwen to come and stay with her. It was a good thing she had, though, or she would probably never have met Hugo. How strange the twists of fate could be.

"The first time my husband took me down onto the

beach," Dora said, "he showed me the steep fall of stones where that accident happened and the sheltered rock where Lord Trentham was sitting when he witnessed it." She smiled about at all the ladies. "Is it not a marvel to live close to golden sands and the sea? I feel wondrously blessed, having lived all my life inland."

As she had hoped, a number of the ladies had something to say on the subject, and the conversation remained general until Dora rose to take her leave. Although she had been the last to arrive, she understood that no one would make any move to leave until she did. She thanked Mrs. Yarby for her hospitality, smiled as she bade everyone else a good afternoon, and made her escape.

It was unfortunate that she thought of her departure as escape, she thought while she was conveyed back home in the landau. Mrs. Yarby had gone to great trouble to entertain her in style, and the other ladies had been amiable and flatteringly respectful.

But that woman! Oh, gracious heaven, *that woman*. Mrs. Parkinson was a bore and an obsequious name dropper—and those were her good qualities. What on earth had she been trying to accomplish with those last things she had said? Vent spite? But why? Cause mischief? *But why?* If Dora could have stopped her ears, she would have done so. Like a child, she would have hummed loudly while doing it. But it had been impossible given where she was, and now she feared her thoughts and dreams would be haunted by all the nasty little details Mrs. Parkinson had quite masterfully compressed into that minute or two.

As the landau approached the house, Dora could see that George was standing at the bottom of the steps before the front doors, watching it come. He looked dearly familiar, his hands clasped behind him, his face beaming with pleasure.

He did not wait for the coachman to descend from the box but opened the door of the conveyance himself, set down the steps, and reached up both hands for hers.

"I have missed you," they said together as she got down, and they both laughed.

Dora lifted her face for his kiss. He hesitated for the briefest moment while she remembered that they were in the presence of servants and she really ought to be behaving with more decorum.

He kissed her softly on the lips.

"I am so happy to be home," she told him.

15

She told him during dinner about her visit to Mrs. Yarby.

"Anyone would think," she said, "that I am someone special."

"But you are," he assured her. "And furthermore, you are a duchess."

That made her think—and then laugh with delight.

"You are such a flatterer, George," she told him, wagging a finger in his direction.

He told her about his afternoon, which he had not spent on the beach as she had not been with him. He had walked along the headland instead and almost lost his hat in the wind.

"I am very glad I did not," he told her. "I would have looked mildly undignified chasing after it across the park. Dukes are never undignified, you know."

He loved her laugh.

And yet there was something . . . It was there all through dinner and it was there after they had retired to her sitting room. She chose to play something rather melancholy on her pianoforte. He did not recognize it, and he did not ask. That something was still there after she had seated herself across the hearth from him and he had lit the fire even though it was summer and the day had been a warm one. They read for a while. At least, that was what they were apparently doing. But he kept glancing across at her. He was almost certain she had not turned a single page.

She looked up and caught his eye and smiled. "A good book?" she asked him.

"Yes," he said. "And yours?"

"Yes."

He closed his own, keeping one finger in the page to mark his place. He did not say anything else. Experience had taught him that silence often drew confidences when the other person obviously had something on his or her mind. And Dora clearly had something on hers.

I am so happy to be home, she had told him on her return from the village. But there had been no real happiness in her tone—or even simple weariness after a busy afternoon. There had been something else, something bordering upon desperation. And she had invited his kiss while they were in full view on the terrace with servants about them. That was unlike her.

She turned a page for the first time but then shut the book with a decisive snap.

"I have it on the best authority," she said, "that you are a dear friend of Mrs. Parkinson."

"What?"

"Not her *dearest* friend, however," she added, raising one forefinger. "That place in her heart and esteem is reserved for Gwen. Mrs. Parkinson introduced her to you and your fellow Survivors here, I understand, and she played fond matchmaker for her and Hugo."

This was what had been on her mind? No, he did not believe it. But he was amused anyway.

"And your best authority was the lady herself, I presume?" he said. "There is at least some truth in what she told you. She did indeed make very sure that Gwen remained here after she sprained her ankle, much to the chagrin of Gwen herself, who was mortified at the prospect of imposing upon a private house party of strangers. I believe Mrs. Parkinson's motive was something other than matchmaking, however. She saw in Gwen's predicament a way of ingratiating herself with me and my guests, all of whom, except Imogen, were handsome men with titles and fortunes, and none of whom was married at the time. She was extremely attentive to her dearest friend in the world and came here every day and stayed for several hours. I do believe Flavian had the distinction of being her favorite. You were in sore danger of not having him for a brother-in-law, Dora."

"What entirely escapes my understanding," she said, shaking her head slowly, "is why Gwen was staying with such a dreadful woman in the first place."

"Apparently they were acquainted as girls making their debut in society," he said, "and continued some sort of a correspondence afterward. When Mrs. Parkinson lost her husband, my guess is that Gwen felt sorry enough for her to offer her company for a while. I believe she came to regret her kindheartedness very soon after her arrival, but she was ultimately rewarded when she twisted her already lame ankle on my land and a certain gentle giant stepped down from among the rocks to scoop her up and carry her here."

"There is no truth to Mrs. Parkinson's first claim?" she asked him. "She is not your dear friend?"

He shook his head. "Alas," he said.

She leaned back in her chair, crossed her arms over her stomach, and grasped her elbows. Her smile faded. And he knew that she was coming to it—whatever it was.

"She commiserated with me," she said, "on the interruption to our wedding."

"Ah." He removed his finger from his book and set the volume down on the table beside him. "I suppose it was inevitable that word of such a dramatic scene would arrive here. I hope she said nothing else to upset you."

But he knew that something else must have been said. The past just would not die and leave him alone, would it? They had not spoken of it since that ghastly day in the gallery, and they had been happy. Life had been good. But here it was again.

He could see her hesitate before she spoke.

"I believe," she said, "I was being consoled for being unable to inspire any great passion in you—because of my age and my looks, I suppose. It is not a bad thing to be middle-aged and plain and unattractive, however, for apparently you grow hot-tempered and jealously possessive and perhaps even violent when you do feel a passionate attachment to a woman. At least . . . I believe this is what Mrs. Parkinson was implying. I believe she stopped liking me when I would not agree with her insinuations that Hugo was a vulgar upstart and Gwen married beneath her."

She spoke softly and rather tonelessly, her eyes on the dying fire.

George stretched his fingers in his lap, curled them into his palms, and relaxed them again.

"You must not put any great credence in anything Mrs. Parkinson has to say, Dora," he said. "Even from what you have told me, I can see that her words were full of contradictions. I have not treated you to any grand romance or passion since our marriage, but I have a deep regard for you. Your age and your looks make you more dear to me than if you were a young girl of dazzling youth. You are beautiful to me and just exactly the right age to be my companion and friend. You are perfect in every way as my lover."

"I did not believe her," she assured him, turning her gaze on him, a frown between her brows. "She is a spiteful, nasty person, one of the most unpleasant people it has ever been my misfortune to meet. I am happy with our marriage just as it is, George. I cannot imagine you being jealous or possessive or violent. You are everything that is the opposite, in fact. You do not cling to what you love. You give it wings instead and let it fly. I have only to know and speak with your fellow Survivors to understand that."

He felt strangely like weeping. "And then I wish they had not flown away," he said.

"No, that is not true of you." She set her head back against the chair and looked at him with the softness of what could only be affection. Her frown had disappeared. "You miss your friends when they are far away. You even feel a bit lonely without them. But you absolutely do not wish you had made them so dependent upon you that they would need still to be here living at Penderris. You are happy in their independence and happiness. There is no point in denying it even if you feel so inclined. I have seen you with them. And you have given me wings with your gifts of my pianoforte and harp. I am even more than partly reconciled with my mother because you encouraged me to visit her and talk with her. I will not fly away, however. Not ever, for you have married me and are good to me. I will stay. That is a promise and a commitment—not just because I made vows during our wedding, but because I could never wish to leave you."

Her eyes remained on his as he gazed steadily back at her and knew with some amazement that she spoke the truth. But why amazement? He had married her so that he would have a lifelong companion, someone of his very own who would stay. But . . . she had said "because I could never wish to leave you." He had never been offered such a priceless gift. How could he dare accept it without clinging desperately to it?

"I hope," he said, "I never give you cause to regret that promise."

"The Earl of Eastham must have loved your wife very dearly," she said.

His fingers curled into his palms again. He felt a twinge of pain as one of his fingernails penetrated the skin. What—?

"His sister must have been very dear to him," she said.

"Only that would explain his going to London and interrupting our wedding as he did. He must have been very upset to learn that you were about to remarry. It was not at all well done of him to react as he did. Indeed, it was shockingly bad of him. But when emotion gets the best of us, we can all behave badly. Perhaps it would be best to give him the benefit of the doubt and forgive him. I daresay he deeply regrets what he did so impulsively. May I write to him? Or would that merely cause him more pain?"

He inhaled sharply and let the breath out more slowly. "I would very much prefer you did not, Dora," he said. "You may very well be right. He was fond of Miriam and she of him. He had a hard time believing she could have killed herself. It was easier, I suppose, to believe that I had pushed her, especially as he and I had never particularly liked each other."

"Did you forbid him to visit your wife here?" she asked, her frown returning, her voice troubled. "And did you refuse to allow your son to visit his grandfather and uncle at their home?"

Oh, Lord!

"Never the latter," he said, "and not always the former. When I did, there were reasons. We did not have a happy marriage, Dora, Miriam and I. We were forced into marrying when I was seventeen and she was twenty. My father was dying and for some insane reason wanted to see me married before he went, and her father thought it was high time she took a husband. I met her for the first time when I proposed marriage to her—in the presence of her father and mine. I met her for the second time at our wedding the following day—the marriage license had already been procured."

"She was beautiful," Dora said.

Ah, Mrs. Parkinson really had filled her ears. He wondered what the other ladies had been doing while the woman had been tête-à-tête with Dora. Surely Mrs. Yarby would not have allowed such talk to go on unchecked in her drawing room if she had heard it.

"Incredibly so," he said. "She was one of the most perfectly beautiful women I have ever set eyes upon." But not one-tenth as beautiful to him as his second wife. The words would have sounded forced and false if he had spoken them aloud, though.

"Did you purchase your son's commission and have him sent to the Peninsula against her wishes?" she asked.

He felt a sudden wish to have Mrs. Parkinson's neck between his two hands.

"Against hers, yes," he told her. "But not against his."

"I am so sorry," she said. "That he died, I mean."

He drew a deep breath and held it for a while before letting it go. "I sometimes think," he said, "that Brendan had neither the wish nor the intention of returning alive from the Peninsula. And *that* is the burden I must bear upon my soul for as long as I have breath in my body, Dora. Perhaps now your questions are at an end."

He got to his feet and left the room without looking back.

It was many hours later before he went to bed. Indeed, he had half expected dawn to be showing on the eastern horizon when he made his way back along the headland. But it was still dark after he had thrown off his clothes and made his way into his bedchamber. He expected to find the bed empty. But she was curled up in the center of it, fast asleep, one arm flung across his half.

He stood in the darkness, gazing at her for many moments before moving her arm carefully aside and lying down beside her. He gathered her into his arms and pulled the covers over them both as she snuggled up to him, grumbling incoherently in her sleep. He nestled his cheek against the top of her head, closed his eyes, breathed in the warm, comforting scent of her, and slept.

Dora had fallen asleep fearing that she had ruined her marriage with her inquisitiveness. George had made it very clear on several occasions that he would allow no intrusion into his memories of his first marriage, but she had pried anyway. And it was no consolation that she had done so not just out of curiosity but out of a conviction that he *needed* to talk about the past, to exorcise some of the demons she was sure lurked there. And oh, there had been evidence that she was right.

I sometimes think that Brendan had neither the wish nor the intention of returning alive from the Peninsula. And that *is the burden I must bear upon my soul for as long as I have breath in my body.*

Whatever had he meant?

But she would never know. He would never volunteer the information, and she would never ask again.

She fell asleep fearing for her marriage but woke up some time after dawn to find herself snuggled, as usual, in his arms. When had he come in? She knew he had gone outside, but she had made no move to follow him.

She had not heard him return, but she was so glad—so glad—he had come home.

"If it was not quite barbaric," he said softly against the top of her head, "I would be quite happy to boil Mrs. Parkinson in oil."

It was so unexpected that she exploded into laughter against his naked chest and raised her face to his.

"It is barbaric," she agreed. "Did you know, though, that I just adore barbarians?"

His eyes smiled into hers. His hair was disheveled, the silver all mingled with the dark. He needed a shave. He looked gorgeous.

"I am deeply sorry about last night," he said. "But never let that woman sow doubts in your mind, Dora. I chose you consciously, and I chose even more wisely than I knew at the time. You are beautiful to me, and you are attractive, and both qualities encompass your appearance and your character and mind, and your very soul. Not for one single moment have I regretted going into Gloucestershire to find you again and claim you for my own."

She smiled at him and bit her lip at the same time. His words made her want to cry. But he looked troubled despite his words, and she could see he had not finished.

"My first marriage was difficult and unhappy," he said. "I had my friends and Miriam had hers. Mrs. Parkinson was one of them, though she was a very young lady in those days. I purchased Brendan's commission not just because he begged it of me and certainly not because his mother was adamantly opposed, but because I thought it was right for him—the only right thing. His death will weigh heavily upon me for the rest of my life, as will his unhappiness before he died, but I am not weighed down by guilt."

She gazed into his face as he spoke. He was giving her facts, she thought, facts that throbbed with emotion, but he had a tight leash upon that. Ah, George. There was so much more he was not saying.

"And that something else you have wondered about," he continued. "That absence in the gallery of a painting of my own family. My life was unhappy for many years, Dora, miserably, irrevocably unhappy. I had no wish to have it immortalized in paint for future generations to gaze upon. Perhaps I was wrong. Perhaps all those other portraits hide secrets that only those pictured there knew of. Perhaps it was not my call to deprive future generations of thirty years of family history."

He closed his eyes, and she heard him swallow. She spread a hand over his chest, but what could she say? Bland words of comfort or reassurance would be worthless. All she could do was be here with him. He opened his eyes again and smiled at her.

"My life is happy now," he said, and she bit her lip again to hold back the tears, "and I am content that all the world see it, both now and in the future. There will be a portrait after all of my family. You are my family, Dora."

She rested her forehead against his chest.

"Have I answered your questions?" he asked. "Are you content?"

"Yes," she said.

Oh, there were a thousand more questions she could ask, for what he had told her was really like the tip of an iceberg, she suspected. Why had his marriage been such an unhappy one? Irrevocably unhappy, he had called it. But he was such a kind, accommodating man. She would ask no more, however. If he wanted her to know more, then he would tell her. In the meanwhile all she could do was try to make him less unhappy with his second marriage. And that would not be difficult. *My life is happy now,* he had said. She must trust that he meant it, that he felt it, that he would always feel it.

"I mentioned appearance, mind, character, and soul," he said. "Did I also mention that I find you sexually attractive?"

She tipped back her head, pursed her lips, and frowned in thought before shaking her head. "No, you did not."

"Ah," he said, "but I do. I find you sexually attractive, Dora."

"Do you?"

"You do not believe me?"

"Perhaps," she said, "you had better show me what you mean."

And they smiled slowly at each other and *oh, she loved him, loved him, loved him.*

He showed her, taking all of fifteen minutes to do it. She lay in his arms again afterward, warm, a bit sweaty, a little bit breathless, and tried to remember her impression of him last year, when they had met at Middlebury Park. He had been handsome certainly, though a bit austere, kindly and charming too, confident and self-assured, the consummate gentleman and aristocrat, a man without troubles or needs, a man upon whom the sun must always have shone. In her dreams she had made a sort of fairy-tale prince out of him.

The real man was very different, far more vulnerable.

Far more lovable.

He was sleeping again, she could tell from his breathing. Soon enough so was she.

"Ah," George said while they were looking through their letters at the breakfast table the following morning, "Imogen and Percy are back in Cornwall. It seems they hosted a grand ball themselves and invited every member of his family to the third and fourth generation—Percy's words—with the warning that it was their farewell to London until at least next spring and there would be no point in anyone's organizing any further parties in their post-honeymoon honor. One has to be firm with one's doting relatives, he declares."

"I do like Percy," Dora said.

"I was appalled when I first met him," George told her. "He seemed rude and blustering and bad-tempered and about as unsuited to Imogen as it was possible to be. It did not take me long to realize that in fact they are perfect for each other. Ah, I must read you this."

And he read a paragraph full of complaint over the fact that Lady Lavinia Hayes's menagerie of canine and feline scruffs had noticeably increased in size since he was last at Hardford even if she did try to keep them hidden in the second housekeeper's room—and still no one had been able to explain to Percy why that particular room was so named.

"Lady Lavinia," George explained, "is the elderly sister of the last earl and has lived at Hardford all her life. She takes in strays of both the animal and human variety. You have not seen Percy's dog, have you? Have I described it to you before? According to Percy, it was the ugliest and scrawniest of the lot when he first went to Hardford, and it attached itself to him like glue despite his horrified and vigorous discouragement. He professes still to be exasperated that it follows him everywhere, but it is perfectly obvious to anyone with half a brain that he adores it."

Dora laughed.

"You have another letter from Mrs. Henry?" he asked.

"She is back living in the cottage at Inglebrook," she told him. "She is working for Mr. and Mrs. Madison, the new music teacher and his wife, and is enjoying their children, though she misses me. She could hardly say otherwise, though, could she, when she is writing to me."

"But she would not write at all if she were not missing you," he said

"Oh, dear, listen to this, George," she said. "The Corleys are complaining about him to anyone who will listen. Mr. Madison has informed them that they are wasting their money and their daughter's time and trying his patience to the limit by insisting that she continue her lessons. Apparently I was far more appreciative of Miranda's superior talents, but—oh, goodness!—that was because I had a musical ear while 'some people' do not." She put the letter down with a shake of her head. "Oh, the brave, foolish man. I simply must hear Sophia's version of this. She will surely write to tell me."

She looked up and joined in George's laughter. He reached out and covered one of her hands with his own.

"Your other letter is from your mother?" he asked.

"Yes." She had been saving it for last. She always felt a turmoil of unexamined emotions when she saw the familiar handwriting on the outside of a letter and thought of her mother and remembered that visit in London. Dora broke the seal and read what was written in the careful hand within. "There is nothing very startling. They have been to a card party with a few friends. They went for a long walk in Richmond Park one afternoon and had a picnic there on the grass. They have been working in their garden, both of them. They have not been able to keep the wilderness at bay with only one gardener employed there, but that very fact makes their flower garden more precious to them. There are flowers to nurture and weeds to banish."

She stopped there and bit her upper lip hard. She bent her head forward over the letter.

"Dora?" George's hand was upon hers again. "What is it?"

"Nothing," she assured him, swiping at her tears and fumbling with the handkerchief he pressed into her hand. "How foolish of me! It is just that she says the weeds may bloom in the wilderness with her blessing, but not in her flower beds. It is just exactly what I always said of my garden at Inglebrook. I— Oh, forgive me. How silly." She dropped the letter to her plate and spread his handkerchief over her eyes.

He waited while she dried her eyes and blew her nose and lifted her head to give him a rather watery, red-eyed smile. Then her gaze turned to the windows.

"It looks as if today will be as lovely as yesterday," she said. "Today I am not going visiting. Perhaps we can go down onto the beach later. I have a yearning to take off my shoes and stockings and paddle in the water. Is it childish?"

"Yes," he said. "But children are wise, spontaneous creatures and we would do well to imitate them more often than we do." He was silent for a moment, gazing at her. "Dora, let us invite your mother and her husband here."

Her eyes widened in shock. "To *stay*?"

"Well, it would hardly be practical," he said, "to invite them for tea one afternoon, would it?"

She gazed mutely at him.

"Let us invite them for a couple of weeks," he said, "or a month. Or longer if you wish. I believe you long to know your mother again, and perhaps Sir Everard Havell is not quite the villain you have always supposed him to be. Let them come. Get to know them."

"You would not mind?" she asked him. "Perhaps they would not be well received here."

"Of course they would," he said. "They are the mother and stepfather of the Duchess of Stanbrook, are they not? The in-laws of the duke? I am sure you know by now that we can count on our neighbors to receive them accordingly. Write to your mother after breakfast, while I write to Imogen and Percy. Tell her I will send the carriage for them. We can do some entertaining while they are here. You would enjoy that, would you not, now that you have met most of our neighbors and exchanged courtesy calls with them?"

"You have never done much entertaining here?" she asked him.

"Not on any grand scale," he said, "and not much on a small scale either. But . . . times have changed and I am happy to change with them. Would you enjoy hosting dinners, perhaps a few parties?"

"A ball?" she said.

He looked surprised for a moment and then smiled at her. "Why not?" he said. "Poor Briggs will have an apoplexy. Or perhaps not. He is fond of complaining that he is underworked."

"Oh, but I will help him," she said, her hands clasped to her bosom.

"You have a world of experience at organizing grand balls, I suppose?" he said.

"How difficult can it be?" she asked him.

His grin persisted. "Perhaps I will be kind enough," he said, "not to remind you of that question at a later date."

She gazed earnestly at him then, remembering suddenly what had started all this.

"George," she said, "are you sure about inviting Mama and Sir Everard?"

"I am perfectly sure," he said, serious again. "But what about you, Dora? It must be as you wish."

"I am so afraid," she said.

He raised his eyebrows.

"Since I called on her," she explained, "I have dreamed that something I thought irrevocably broken could perhaps be mended again—slowly and cautiously. At a distance. What if she comes here and I discover that it is impossible? It will be like losing her all over again."

He got to his feet, reached out a hand for hers, and drew her up into his arms.

"I truly do not believe that will happen," he said. "But if you wish to let matters remain as they are, then that is how they will be. Do you want to think about it for a day or two?"

"No," she said after a mere moment's hesitation. "I shall write this morning. And George? May I say your carriage will already be on the way by the time she reads my letter? So that she will know that we mean it? So that she will not say no? So that I will not have to wait too long?"

He laughed softly against the top of her head.

"We had better move," he said, "or the carriage will be arriving for them even before your letter is written."

He was very, very good, Dora thought a short while later as they sat in the library together, writing their letters, at persuading other people to solve their problems and be happy. But what of himself? He had told her enough last night to make it seem that he had told her everything. But she knew that was not so.

He was, she feared, fathoms deep in pain and grief, but for some reason preferred to bear them alone. *Why* would he not share with her? He had encouraged her to share her pain over her mother's defection, and some good had come of it—oh, perhaps a great deal of good. Pain, even pain from long ago, could heal. But repressing it, refusing to talk about it even with one's spouse, would not do that. Perhaps the difference was that her mother was still alive, while his wife and son were dead. Perhaps there seemed no way to heal the wounds of the past.

But oh, she wished she knew at least what the wounds were. They were not *just* grief, were they?

The realization that it was indeed more than grief that burdened her husband and caused his pain was almost more than Dora could bear. But did she really want to know? The answer was surely no. But . . .

She *needed* to know.

If their marriage was ever to be a truly happy one, then she *needed to know.*

And yet she also needed to respect his right to privacy.

She shook her head and returned her attention to her letter.

16

*D*ora was excited by the prospect of being hostess at her very own ball. She also experienced a bit of panic at the realization that she had no experience at organizing such a grand event. Perhaps she ought to have started with a dinner or a small, select party, and expanded from there. But it could not be *that* difficult, could it? And indeed it could not, she soon discovered, for her own part in planning the ball was to be a very small one.

She made her way to Mr. Briggs's office that same afternoon after her walk on the beach with George. But almost before she could mention the word *ball* to her husband's secretary, he slid across his desk toward her an impressively long guest list he had prepared for her perusal. He also had the tentative draft of an invitation card. A short while after, she summoned Mrs. Lerner to her sitting room, but her announcement of the coming event drew no exclamation of surprise from the house-keeper. Instead, she produced a written list of plans and details that Her Grace might wish to look over.

When Dora went belowstairs the following morning in the hope that she was not interrupting the chef at a particularly busy time, she discovered that indeed she was. But Mr. Humble ushered her over to one end of the long wooden kitchen table, sat her down with a steaming cup of tea and two large oatmeal and raisin biscuits fresh from the oven, and set before her a lengthy list of suggested delicacies for the refreshment room at the ball and a prospective menu for the sit-down supper at eleven. By that time Dora was not even unduly surprised. The servants of a large house, she was learning, knew everything almost before their master and mistress did. Mr. Humble even informed her that he knew of a number of people within five miles of the hall who would be delighted to provide the extra help he and the butler and housekeeper would need from a day or two before the ball until a day or so after. Her Grace must not worry her head about it.

Dora was quite unsurprised to discover when she ran the head gardener to earth in one of the greenhouses beyond the kitchen garden behind the house that he already had ideas about what flowers would be blooming and what greenery would be ready for filling the urns and vases that would decorate the ballroom and the main hall and staircase and other rooms that would be used on the evening of the ball. And she was almost expecting when she went to the stables to consult the head groom that he had plans already well in place for the handling of a large number of carriages and horses. Her expectations proved quite correct—Her Grace need not worry her head over it.

Mr. Briggs had informed her earlier that he was in the process of discovering and engaging the best orchestra available—subject, of course, to Her Grace's approval. He had also begun to draw up a suggested program of dances suitable for a ball in the country, though he did need to know whether Her Grace wished to include any waltzes. Although the waltz was by now widely danced in London, even at Almack's, he explained, there were people in the more rural parts of England who still considered it a somewhat scandalous invention. Dora instructed him to include two sets of waltzes, one before supper and one after.

The invitations had not yet been written when Dora called upon Barbara Newman at the vicarage one morning. Barbara was teaching her youngest daughters, aged eight and nine, to knit. They sat side by side on a sofa, as neat as two pins, wielding fat needles and thick wool, with identical looks of frowning concentration upon their faces. Dora already loved them dearly, as she did their mother. It was difficult sometimes to understand what drew one to some people as friends, above the level of friendly acquaintance. It had not happened often to her, but it had happened twice already at Penderris. She was very well blessed.

"Everyone is as excited as can be about your ball," Barbara said as soon as the initial greetings had been dispensed with. "There has not been one or indeed any sort of grand entertainment at the hall in living memory. How delightful that it is to happen now when the duke is a happy man at last."

Dora stared at her in surprise. "But how did you know?" she asked.

Barbara laughed. "Do you really imagine that there is a person left within five miles of here who does not know?" she said.

Dora laughed too. But her friend's attention was taken by the silent tears of the younger of the two girls, who had dropped a stitch and thought her work had been ruined. Barbara picked up the stitch, worked it through the loops down which it had run, and handed the needles back to the little girl with smiles and words of encouragement.

The ball, then, Dora thought as she made her way home later, would happen of itself, almost without her assistance. There was certainly no going back now, was there?

"I could easily grow accustomed to having an army of servants," she observed to George when he found her sitting in the flower garden before luncheon with a book open on her lap. She laughed when he raised his eyebrows and looked amused. "Not only do they have every detail of the ball well in hand already, but also they have left me not a single weed in any of the flower beds to pull."

In one way, she thought as the days passed, it was a pity there was so little for her to do as she waited in an agony of mingled excitement and trepidation for her mother's arrival—or for the return of the empty carriage. But gradually, during those days, something else happened to nag at her thoughts when she was idle. Or, rather, something did not happen, something that always happened with dependable regularity every month but had failed to materialize two weeks ago or on any of the days since.

She accompanied George on a tour of the farm one day and listened to explanations of crop rotation and drainage and lambing and pasture and shearing. She was able to assure him in perfect truth that she was not bored. On another day she went with him and his steward to look at a few of the laborers' cottages that the steward thought needed repairs and that George thought needed replacing altogether. While they discussed the matter and circled the buildings and climbed ladders and talked with a few of the men who lived in the houses concerned, Dora called upon their wives and exchanged recipes and knitting patterns with a couple of them while she observed from the inside the dilapidated condition of their cottages.

She returned alone the following morning with some baked goods for the families and sweetmeats for the children, all of which she had made herself the evening before after assuring a wary, somewhat shocked Mr. Humble that she would neither burn the kitchen down nor leave a mess behind her. She took her small harp with her and played for some of the elderly and the children. More important, she was able to take the news— with George's blessing—that the cottages would be replaced before winter came on.

On another day Dora accompanied George on the longish drive to visit Julian and Philippa. She found them as delightful as she had when she met them in London. She had feared they might resent her and even see her, perhaps, as a fortune hunter. But she saw no evidence of any such thing. Of course they did not yet know . . . If there was anything to know, that was.

"Uncle George is so clearly happy," Philippa told Dora while they were strolling together across a lawn to the lily pond. "Just look at him."

They both turned to look back to where Julian and George stood talking on the terrace outside the morning room. George held young Belinda on one arm, and the child was bouncing up and down. It felt to Dora as though her stomach performed a somersault.

Was he happy? she wondered as they drove home in the carriage later and she gazed at his profile next to her. Both Philippa and Barbara had used that word to describe him. But if he was, it was surely a fragile thing, easily destroyed. If she— But perhaps it was not so.

He turned his face toward her and took her hand in his.

"What is it?" he asked her.

She shook her head. "Oh, nothing," she said. "I am anxious about my mother's coming. And I am fearful that she will not come."

His eyes searched hers. "That is all?" he asked.

"All?" she said. "I have not known her for twenty-two years, George, a longer time than I knew her. And Sir Everard Havell is the man who took her away from us, though I have come to understand that perhaps it was a sense of honor more than villainy that motivated him. I do not know what to expect of either of them—or of myself. Sometimes it may be wiser to let sleeping dogs lie."

"But only sometimes?" he asked.

"It is an academic question anyway," she said with a sigh. "They have been invited and the carriage has been sent."

He was content to leave it at that. Perhaps she ought

to have answered his original questions truthfully since she had not actually been thinking of her mother at the time. But she had not done so, and it was too late now.

They rode the rest of the way home in what might have been a companionable silence if she had not been trying to convince herself with every passing mile that it was the uneven surface of the road and the resulting jolting of the carriage that was making her feel slightly bilious.

It had been good to have a lovely summer's day on which to visit his nephew, George thought, but it was a shame much of it had had to be spent cooped up inside the carriage. And Dora looked slightly peaked, though she claimed it was only nervousness over her mother's anticipated visit that was causing it.

The evening was as lovely as the day had been, only cooler. It was perfect for a stroll. He suggested one after dinner, and took her walking along a country lane behind the house instead of along the headland or down on the beach. Ripening crops waved in the slight breeze to either side of them, sheep baaed in the distance, a lone gull called overhead. The sky was turning pink in the west. The air was warm and slightly salty.

"Perfect," he said, drawing a deep breath of it into his lungs.

"And this is all your land," she said, gesturing to left and right. "What a dizzying thought."

"I try not to take it for granted," he said, "even though it has been either my father's or mine all my life. I have always tried to count my blessings, even at the darkest moments of my life—and we all have those. I have always tried to see to it that those who live and work on my land share some of its bounty. I am rather ashamed that those cottages grew so dilapidated before I realized that repairs upon repairs were no longer either feasible or fair."

He drew her to a halt a few steps farther on.

"Stand just here, Dora," he said, "where these lanes cross, and look back. It has always been one of my favorite spots on the estate or anywhere else for that matter."

They had been walking slightly uphill, though the slope was not really apparent until one stopped and turned to look back. There were the fields, separated by stone walls and hedgerows bordering the narrow lanes. Below them was the house, square and solid, and the cultivated lawns and gardens surrounding it. Beyond them, and in total contrast to them, were the cliffs and the sea stretching to infinity, it seemed. The water was deep blue this evening, with the sky above it a slightly lighter shade blending into pink and red-orange and gold on the western horizon. It was the best of all times for this view—though actually almost any time of day and any weather was the best of all times to be standing just here.

"Sometimes beauty goes deeper than words, does it not?" she said after a lengthy silence.

Ah, she understood. She felt it too—the heart of home pulsing here.

He set one hand on her shoulder and squeezed slightly. Miriam had hated the sea. She had hated Penderris. God help him, she had hated him. He moved his hand to the nape of Dora's neck and moved his fingers in a circle over the soft flesh there.

"You come here often?" she asked him. "Alone?"

"Not always alone," he said. "I believe each of my friends came here with me at least once while they were convalescent at Penderris. There is something soothing about the lanes and fields and about the sheep and lambs. Even Ben managed to walk this far with his canes, though I remember his temper becoming frayed on the way back when it was obvious he was exhausted and in pain. But of course he would not allow Hugo and Ralph to make a chair of their hands for him." He chuckled softly at the memory. "Most of my walks here—and elsewhere—have been solitary ones, though. I suppose I am a solitary sort of man. Or perhaps it is that I just did not find the perfect walking companion until very recently."

"Me?" She leaned slightly back into his hand.

"I am entirely comfortable with you, Dora," he told her, "and I still marvel at the lovely surprise of it. You are all I need—all I have ever needed or will ever need. Just you."

He was very close, he realized, to using the word *love*. And he might have done so in full truth, for of course he loved her. But the word was so polluted by youthful connotations of heavy-breathing passion and starry-eyed romance that it seemed an inappropriate word for him to use, for he was a forty-eight-year-old man and the love he felt for his wife was a quiet thing of contentment and adoration.

Yes, adoration. It was a better word than *love* to describe his feelings for her. But perhaps no specific word needed to be uttered aloud. That was the truly comfortable thing about Dora. Words were not always necessary.

He became suddenly aware, however, that the silence between them now had taken on a different quality and that there was a certain tension in the neck muscles beneath his hand.

"Are you not comfortable?" he asked her.

Her hesitation took him by surprise and alarmed him.

"Not at this precise moment," she said.

He stepped around her to stand between her and the view. The evening light slanted across her face and made it look pale and unhappy. Her gaze had come to rest somewhere in the region of his neckcloth.

The seagull above them sounded suddenly mournful. The slight breeze felt chilly.

"We have been married longer than a month," she said.

About six weeks, he believed. He dipped his head a little closer to hers.

"Nothing has happened," she said. When he said nothing, she cleared her throat and continued. "Something ought to have happened by now. More than two weeks ago, in fact. I have been hoping, but . . . Well, two weeks is a long time. I am so dreadfully sorry." She was looking at her hands now, spread palms-up between them.

Comprehension dawned like a club to the back of his head. "Are you speaking of your courses?" he asked her.

"Yes," she said. "I have never— I thought it might be because of the . . . the change in the circumstances of my life, but I do not believe it can be that. And it is possible that it is the . . . the change of life. I do not know. But I very much fear . . . I have been feeling—oh, not exactly bilious, but a little unsteady of digestion. I hope it is the change. I very much hope it. But . . . well, I do not think it is. I am so very, very sorry. I know it will ruin everything if I am right. I ought to have been more careful, though I really would not know how except not to— I ought—" She stopped altogether and spread her hands over her face.

By that time he had her shoulders gripped in his hands.

"Dora?" he said. "You are *increasing*?"

"I fear I must be," she said. "I think it is too much to hope it is the change of life."

He tried to look into her face, but her head was lowered and in the shade of his arm. His forehead almost touched hers.

"You are going to have a *baby*?" he said. "*We* are going to have a child? Dora?" Something strange had happened to his voice. He scarcely recognized it.

"I fear so," she said. "Indeed, in my heart I know so."

"I am going to be a father?" He was still speaking oddly. And then, still gripping her by the shoulders, he threw back his head, his eyes tightly closed. "I am going to be a *father*?"

"I am so sorry."

And finally he heard the terrible misery in her voice. He opened his eyes and lowered his head.

"Why?" His eyes met hers as she raised her own head. "Are you afraid, Dora? Because of your age, perhaps? Is this something you really did not want? Then

I am the one who ought to be apologizing. But . . . Do you not want to be a mother? At long last?"

Her hands grasped his elbows. "I do." The admission came out sounding almost like a wail. "Oh, I *do*. I have always wanted it, though for a long time I have thought it was something that would never happen. I put it out of my mind and my dreams a long time ago. Then, when I married after all, I assumed it was too late even though . . . Well, even though I ought to have known it was still possible. And now it has happened. But I know *you* do not want any more children. You made that very clear to me when you offered me marriage. You chose me because I was older, because it was impossible, because all you wanted was a companion and friend. And you just said that I am all you want. I am so sorry."

He felt like a brute. Had he really given that impression? Actually said it? And was she expecting that he would now blame her, even though he was the one who had impregnated her?

Lord God in heaven, was it possible? *He had impregnated her.* She was going to bear a child. He was going to be a father. They were going to be parents together.

He continued to gaze into her face for a few moments before gathering her into his arms.

"Dora," he said, "I chose you because you were *you*, regardless of age or ability to bear children. First and foremost I wanted you as my wife, as my friend, as my lover. But to be blessed with a child on top of all those things? To be a father?" He moved one hand beneath her chin and raised her face close to his own. "To have a child *with you*? Can there be so much happiness in the world? And you thought I would be upset, even angry? You thought I would blame you when you could not possibly have got yourself into your present condition without considerable help from me? Ah, Dora. How little you know me."

She raised one hand and ran the backs of her fingers over his jaw. She looked suddenly wistful.

"We are old enough to be grandparents," she said.

"But not too old, apparently, to be parents." He smiled at her. "Can you be happy now that you know that I am?"

"Yes," she said. "Deep inside I have been happy anyway, but I have been upset to think that perhaps you would not be "

She was shrieking suddenly then, for he had bent down like the young blade he was not and scooped her up into his arms and was twirling her about while her own arms tightened about his neck. He set her feet back down on the path and straightened up, pleased to note that he was scarcely winded.

"I am going to be a *father*," he said again, grinning like an idiot. "You were made for motherhood, Dora. I am so glad I have made it possible for you, that it is *my* child you will bear. I am honored."

She looked at him in the growing dusk, and he saw joy in her smile.

He felt it in his own.

He was going to be a father! He felt the childish urge to shout it out to the world as though no one else in the history of the universe had ever been so clever.

*   *   *

Life was the oddest experience ever invented, George decided later that night. He had woken up abruptly, remembered, and realized that euphoria had been replaced by panic.

Women died all the time in childbirth. And Dora was thirty-nine years old. She would be forty when the baby was born, and it was her first.

He slid his arm from beneath her head, eased his way off the bed so as not to wake her, and went to stand at the open window, where the air felt blessedly cool against his naked body.

He would summon the local physician tomorrow. Dr. Dodd had probably delivered several hundred babies during his long career.

How many of those babies had been stillborn? How many of the mothers—

He braced himself on the windowsill with his fisted hands, hung his head, and slowly inhaled the slightly salty air. How could he so carelessly, so irresponsibly have endangered her? But how could he not once he had married her?

Abstained?

And yet, all mingled up with his terror, more than half swallowed by it, was a euphoria of joy that threatened to burst from him at any moment, as it had last evening when he had picked her up and twirled her about.

He was going to be a *father*. It was like a great miracle. If, that was, she survived the dangers of childbirth. And *if* the child did.

That was two too many *if*s!

But . . . fatherhood. For the first time he wondered if the baby would be a boy or a girl. He did not mind which it was. He had his heir in Julian. He would be over the moon with happiness if it was a daughter. Oh, Lord God, a daughter, a little girl all his own. Or a son. He would love a s—

And suddenly, seemingly from nowhere, displacing both panic and euphoria, grief slammed into him, a grief so painful and so all-encompassing that he wondered for a few moments if he could survive it, or if he wanted to.

Brendan.

He closed his eyes tightly and pressed his knuckles against the sill to the point of pain.

Brendan. Ah, Brendan.

It did not lessen with time, the agony of grief. The intensity of it spaced itself out a bit more, it was true, but when it came—and it always did—it catapulted him as deep into hell as it ever had.

"Goodbye, Pa— Goodbye, sir." The very last words Brendan had spoken to him when he left to join his regiment. George had not seen him again before they went off to the Peninsula and the boy's death.

"Goodbye, sir." Not Papa, but "sir."

George did not know what the boy had said to his mother.

"George?" The sound came from behind him and he turned. "You must be cold. Can you not sleep?"

He straightened up. "It is not every day," he said, "that a man learns he has been clever enough to beget a child on his wife."

"I ought not to have said I was sorry so many times last evening," she said. "Or at all, in fact. It must have sounded as though I were sorry about the baby and I could never be that—*never,* George. And it probably sounded abject, as though I was cringing before your expected anger. That was not what I meant. I meant that I was sorry that your dream of a happy second marriage was to be shattered by something so unexpected, something you had said specifically you did not want. I meant I was sorry there would be a wedge driven between us. I feared you would not want the child or love it. The fear of that was breaking my heart. But I am not sorry about the baby and would not be even if you had been unhappy about it. I would just have been saddened—for you, for us."

He wrapped his arms about her and drew her against him.

"I have been standing here fighting my terror over the ordeal ahead of you," he said, "and feeling my joy." He added something he had had no intention of saying aloud. "And feeling grief over Brendan."

He lowered his forehead to the top of her head and fought the soreness in his throat that threatened tears.

"Would you like me to play the pianoforte in the sitting room for a while?" she asked softly after a few silent moments had passed. "And maybe go down to the kitchen first to make a pot of tea? It is how I used to coax Agnes to sleep when she had something on her mind."

It was tempting. A stealthy visit to the kitchen to make tea and maybe find some leftover biscuits, just like a couple of naughty children? And music?

"I think I'll settle for holding you instead," he said, "in bed, where it is warm. Did I wake you?"

"It was your absence that woke me," she said as they got back into bed and she snuggled up to him while he drew the covers over them. "Your presence lulls me."

"I am to be flattered, am I," he asked her, "to be told that my presence puts you to sleep?"

She chuckled softly, her breath warm against his chest.

His next conscious thought was that he really ought to have closed the curtains so that all this sunlight would not be shining directly onto his face.

And then he realized his wife was already gone from the bed.

17

It was not the change of life.

Her Grace, Dr. Dodd confirmed the following morning, was approximately one month and a half into her confinement, and if there was anything wrong with her health, he could certainly not detect what it might be, and why should her age have anything to say to the matter? Twenty-nine-year-old ladies were giving birth all the time with no trouble at all. What was that? Her Grace had said *thirty*-nine? A man did start to have some trouble with his hearing after the age of sixty, he was discovering. Well, *only* thirty-nine? There was still time, then, to have brothers and sisters as companions for this first one. Only last year he had delivered Mrs. Hancock of her fifteenth child at the age of forty-seven, and it would not surprise him if he were to be summoned for the sixteenth before she was done.

Dora wondered in some amusement if he talked non-stop even through the delivery of a baby and guessed that he probably did. It was, she realized, his way of relaxing a woman while he performed intimate procedures on her body.

One result of his visit was that well before the day was out—probably even before the morning was out—it was perfectly obvious that every servant in the house, and doubtless out of it too, knew that she was in an interesting condition, though no official or even unofficial announcement had been made and Maisie, Dora's maid, had assured her from the start that she was no tattler. Before another day was out, every servant for miles around would know too, and once the servants knew then so would everyone else.

Her suspicions were confirmed even sooner than she expected. Ann and James Cox-Hampton came to call the following afternoon, and Dora strolled in the rose garden outside the music room with her friend while George remained inside with his.

"Dora," Ann said, linking an arm through hers and coming to the point without preamble, "what is this we have been hearing about you?"

"What *have* you been hearing?" Dora asked her while noting that at last she had caught the gardeners out in being neglectful. There were at least two roses that were past their best.

"That you are in what they call a delicate state of health," Ann said. "Though how one would cope with nine months of discomfort and tribulation if one were delicate, I do not know. Are you in a delicate state?"

"Not at all," Dora told her. "But I am with child. I suppose everyone knows?"

"Everyone and his dog," Ann said. "Are you pleased?"

"Pleased?" Dora laughed. "I am ecstatic. You cannot know, Ann. You had all your children when you were young. You cannot know what it is like to watch all your contemporaries marry and have families and—"

"And live happily ever after?" Ann laughed too. "Just wait. James declares that our boys are sometimes more trouble than they are worth even though they are away at school for much of the year, and he grumbles that he will have to sharpen his sword soon to hold at bay all the men who will be eyeing our girls with lascivious intent. He attributes every one of his gray hairs to our offspring. And of course, he loves them all to distraction. I am delighted for you, Dora. We both are. George has always been such a melancholy figure—until recently. The transformation in him has been quite remarkable. Is he pleased?"

"He declares that he would shout the news from the ramparts," Dora told her, "if it were not an undignified thing to do—and if Penderris Hall had ramparts. Shall we stroll out to the headland?"

Ann Cox-Hampton was her own age, perhaps a year or two older. She had five children, two boys and three girls, all past the age of ten. And, as with Barbara Newman, Dora had felt an immediate affinity with her, perhaps because she was an accomplished lady and they had a great deal in common. Ann was a reader. She also tried her hand at writing poetry and at miniature portrait painting. She played the pianoforte and sang, though her real interest lay in the ten-stringed mandolin her grandfather had brought back from Italy after his grand tour almost a century ago. Ann had inherited it and learned to play it.

It felt lovely, Dora thought, to have two particular friends, and ones who lived close by. And to have a husband she liked so well—and loved so dearly. And to be with child. Oh, she could never in her wildest dreams have predicted any of this just three months ago.

No happiness was ever unalloyed, however.

Parenthood was a new and wonderful prospect for her, but for George, joy was mingled with grief, for parenthood was not new to him. He had had a son—Brendan—and his joy in anticipating the arrival of a new baby must be tempered by guilt at rejoicing when his first child was dead.

And of course, for Dora there was all the anxiety over her mother. She had still not come. But neither had the carriage returned without her.

Sir Everard and Lady Havell arrived late in the afternoon two days later. Both of them looked weary, George thought as he stood on the steps outside the front doors with Dora, waiting to greet them. Lady Havell also looked apprehensive, as her daughter had been looking ever since she had sent the invitation on its way and he had sent the carriage. They looked remarkably alike, despite the older lady's somewhat larger girth and silver hair. Dora gripped his arm tightly as the footman who had ridden up on the box with his coachman jumped down to open the door and set down the steps.

"Dora," Lady Havell said as she stepped down onto the terrace. "Your Grace."

She looked as though she was about to curtsy to them. Dora must have seen it too, for she released his arm and hurried down the steps.

"Mother!" she cried, and launched herself into Lady Havell's arms. "You came! I am so glad. The days have been interminable, not knowing if you would come or when you would arrive. Oh, Mother, I am going to have a baby."

And then she stepped back in sudden embarrassment, a feeling George shared, though he was also amused. He would wager Dora had not planned *that* particular greeting. But Lady Havell's face was lighting up with a warm smile, and Sir Everard was descending from the carriage behind her.

"But that is wonderful, Dora," she was saying as George held out a hand to shake Havell's.

"Welcome to Penderris," he said.

"This is a beautiful place, Stanbrook," Sir Everard said, looking about appreciatively.

The weather had been kind for their arrival. It was a sunny, warm day, and even the almost omnipresent wind had reduced itself to a gentle breeze. The sea was sparkling off in the distance.

"Ma'am." George turned his attention to Lady Havell and offered his hand. "I am honored that you came. I trust you had a pleasant journey, though I know from experience that it is also a long and tedious one."

Dora meanwhile was greeting Sir Everard, who was bowing to her and addressing her as "*Your Grace.*" She had reprimanded him, George remembered, for making free with her name and Agnes's on an earlier occasion. She probably remembered it too.

"Sir Everard," she said, extending her right hand to him. "I would be happy to have you call me Dora."

"Dora," he said. "The sea air must agree with you. You look remarkably well."

"Did you hear what she said, Everard?" Lady Havell asked. "She is with child. She and Agnes both. How very happy I am."

Dora linked an arm through hers and led her up the steps to the house. "Let us take you up to your rooms," she said. "You must be weary."

George exchanged a slightly sheepish look with Havell and followed them inside. All was going to be well, he thought. One never knew for sure when one encouraged people to take a course of action they were reluctant to take on their own—even when it seemed the right thing to do.

"Congratulations are in order, then," Havell said.

"Thank you," George said. "I am indeed feeling rather proud of myself."

There was no real decision to make, Dora discovered after that remarkable scene on her mother's arrival. She had not planned anything like it. She had even wondered beforehand whether she would shake her mother's hand or merely incline her head in a polite greeting. She had certainly not thought she would be so overwhelmed with emotion at seeing her mother again and then so disconcerted at the realization that she was about to curtsy to them that she would rush down the steps to hug her and blurt whatever chose to come out of her mouth without first being filtered through her brain. She had even told her mother that she was expecting a baby.

She was a little embarrassed to have behaved without

any of the refined dignity one might expect of a duchess, and she apologized to George afterward for having embarrassed him. He laughed and assured her that he actually took great delight in having the world informed that he was to be a father at the age of forty-eight.

But it was impossible to go back and greet her mother and Sir Everard any other way, and on the whole Dora was glad of it. Why decide if she ought to forgive her mother or not? One could not change the past anyway. Why let it blight the present and the future?

Her mother was clearly happy to be here, and Sir Everard did not seem unhappy. He appeared to enjoy tramping about the estate with George while Dora went over the plans for the ball with her mother and showed her the ballroom and the other state rooms and took her to meet Barbara Newman at the vicarage. Her mother and Sir Everard were introduced to a number of other people after church the Sunday following their arrival, and if anyone knew their story—Dora did not doubt that everyone did—no one either made reference to it or showed any reluctance to curtsy to them or shake their hands. Sir Everard, of course, Dora remembered from long ago, was capable of great charm, as was her mother.

Sir Everard went with them when they called upon Mr. and Mrs. Clark one afternoon—George had some business with his steward to attend to. The Clarks had been early visitors at Penderris, but it was only now that Dora was returning their call, having promised after church that she would do so.

She had not warmed to Mrs. Clark during her visit to

Penderris. She had found her manner just a little too obsequious, especially to George, though Dora did concede that the poor woman had perhaps simply been awed. Today both she and her husband made a great effort to please. Mr. Clark drew Sir Everard into a discussion of the relative merits of town living versus country living, while Mrs. Clark and her daughter were all that was amiable as they talked with Dora and her mother about fashions and bonnets and the weather and their health. Dora might have felt comfortable after all had Mrs. Parkinson not also been present and had it not been clear that the two ladies were friends and that the latter had been invited.

Dora had been able to avoid all but a nodding acquaintance with Mrs. Parkinson since that dreadful afternoon at Mrs. Yarby's. She sat at some distance from the lady this afternoon and drew her mother to sit down beside her. She was certainly not going to allow another such tête-à-tête as the one she had suffered on that occasion.

There was another surprise in store, however, before the socially acceptable half hour of their visit was at an end. It came with the arrival of another guest, whose appearance so took both Mrs. Clark and Mrs. Parkinson by surprise that Dora did not believe for one moment that it was unexpected.

"*My lord!*" Mrs. Clark exclaimed, leaping to her feet and smiling and curtsying as the Earl of Eastham was announced. "I could be knocked right off my feet with a feather, I do declare."

"Well, this is a delightful surprise, I must say," Mrs.

Parkinson said, rising and curtsying more deeply than her hostess. "You did not tell me, my dear Isabella, that you were expecting his lordship."

"But how could I, Vera," Mrs. Clark asked, all amazement, "when I did not know he was even in Cornwall?"

Her daughter was curtsying, her eyes fixed upon the floor.

"How d'ye do, Eastham?" Mr. Clark said, shaking his guest by the hand. "In the neighborhood for a while, are you?"

"I am on a tour of the West Country," the Earl of Eastham explained, "and am currently staying at an inn a mere three miles away from here. I thought I would call in upon the friends who were so kind to me many years ago when my sister died. But . . . the Duchess of Stanbrook?" He started with surprise.

Dora had been regarding him in some dismay. She had seen him only once before in her life—when he was accusing her bridegroom of murder and trying to put a stop to their nuptials. She had tried since then to view his actions in the most sympathetic light possible, but it was really quite ghastly to find herself in a room with him without any decent chance of escape.

"Oh, do allow me to present you," Mrs. Clark said. "But . . . oh, dear me, I had quite forgot. You have met the duchess, have you not? In London a couple of months ago. Oh, this is *very* distressing."

"Pray do not upset yourself, ma'am," the earl said, making his bow to Dora and looking at her, concern in his face. "Duchess, allow me to apologize now for any pain I caused you during our last encounter. I do assure you I meant you no harm whatsoever. Indeed, the whole of my behavior on that occasion was ill-considered. I am your servant to command. I will immediately withdraw from this house and from this neighborhood if it is your wish."

Dora thought him sincere, though it was hard to believe that all this had not been deliberate. She inclined her head slightly.

"Your call is being made upon Mr. and Mrs. Clark in their own home, Lord Eastham," she said. "You must not withdraw upon my account."

"My lord," Mrs. Clark said, "do allow me to present Lord Everard and Lady Havell. Lady Havell is Her Grace's mother."

Dora had felt her mother stiffen beside her as soon as the earl was announced by name and knew that she had made the connection with what she must have heard had happened at Dora's wedding.

After acknowledging the introductions, the earl first made brief conversation with the gentlemen and then, after Mrs. Clark had set a cup of tea in his hand, came to sit on a stool close to both Dora and her mother. He then proceeded to make himself agreeable to them with details of his travels and questions about their own impressions of Cornwall.

It was perhaps one of the most uncomfortable half hours of Dora's life, though she did admit to herself afterward that she was not altogether sorry it had happened. The Earl of Eastham had appeared to her as a complete monster at her wedding, and even as she made excuses for him afterward, she had not quite been able to believe in his humanity. Now she did. He was older than George by a number of years and looked it. Even so, he possessed the remnants of the good looks he must have enjoyed as a young man, his manners were engaging, and his conversation was amiable. He left the Clarks' house at the same time as they did, and he handed her mother into the barouche with great courtesy before Sir Everard did the like for Dora.

He made his bow after they were all seated and addressed himself to Dora.

"I thank you most sincerely, Duchess," he said, "for permitting me to remain at the home of my . . . sister's erstwhile friends and my own. It was good to see them again after so long. I will remember your kindness and hope the time will come when you can forgive me for my impulsive and offensive behavior on your wedding day. Your servant, Lady Havell. Yours, Havell."

Her mother's hand sought Dora's as the barouche moved away. "How dreadfully unfortunate that was," she said. "I am inclined to believe, though, that he does indeed regret spoiling your wedding day, Dora. I daresay it is hard for a man to see his sister's widower marry someone else. Love of a sibling is different from love of a spouse. In some ways it is more enduring because of the bond of the blood relationship. A wife can be replaced; a sister cannot."

"She was his half sister," Dora said. "Do you think Mrs. Clark and Mrs. Parkinson were really surprised. Was he?"

"It did not occur to me," her mother said, "that perhaps they were not. Do you mean you believe he wanted to meet you and enlisted their aid? But even if that is so, Dora, it would not be a bad thing. It would suggest even more that he has been suffering remorse and wished to apologize to you in person. What do you think, Everard?"

Sir Everard, thus appealed to, looked thoughtful. "If the man wished to make his apology to Dora," he said, "he might have written to her. Or he might have presented himself at Penderris Hall and asked to speak with her. Though I daresay Stanbrook would have had something to say to either of those approaches."

"Meeting her thus was . . . clandestine, then?" Dora's mother asked him.

"Or merely accidental," he said with a shrug. "You will tell Stanbrook, Dora?"

"But of course," she said. It would not occur to her not to tell George. Though she did not look forward to it. She felt almost guilty. Perhaps when the Earl of Eastham had offered to leave the house, she should have left instead. But it would have been very ill-mannered to her hosts, and word of it would have been around the neighborhood in no time.

It would be around the neighborhood anyway. But at least it would be reported that she and the Earl of Eastham had been civil to each other.

There was a tap upon the door of George's dressing room just before dinner, and Dora answered his summons to enter. His valet had just finished knotting his neckcloth with his usual flair for elegant artistry without any added ostentation. George waved him away before he could add the diamond pin that lay waiting on the dresser. Something was bothering Dora and had been ever since her return home this afternoon, though she had denied it and merely smiled brightly when he had asked her.

"You are ready to go down?" He got to his feet.

"There is something you ought to know," she said. "You will probably be . . . upset about it, though I do not believe you need to worry."

He raised his eyebrows and clasped his hands at his back. "You are not feeling unwell, I hope," he said.

"Oh, nothing like that," she assured him. "Mother and Sir Everard and I called upon the Clarks this afternoon. Mrs. Parkinson was there too."

"Ah," he said. Both ladies had been Miriam's friends. "Was the visit a severe trial to you, then, Dora? I hope there was no repetition of what happened at the Yarbys'."

"Not at all," she assured him. "Mr. Clark drew Sir Everard into conversation, and the ladies were perfectly amiable to Mother and me. But . . . another guest arrived while we were there. Mrs. Clark reacted with great surprise when he was announced, as did Mrs. Parkinson, but I had the feeling they had been expecting him. He was the Earl of Eastham."

What the devil? George felt rather as though his head had been plunged into an ice bucket.

"He is traveling in Cornwall," she told him, "and staying at an inn a few miles from the village. He called upon the Clarks because they were kind to him after . . . after his sister's death. They were delighted to see him, as was

Mrs. Parkinson. But it did seem to me that his visit was not the surprise they pretended it was. Mr. Clark did not look surprised at all, and Miss Clark looked merely embarrassed. And then he—the earl—was shocked to see me."

"Good God, Dora." George exploded into wrath. "The impertinence of it. Did you leave immediately? I hope Havell—"

But she was holding up both hands, palms out.

"I was given the impression that the meeting was contrived," she said, "but I believe the earl's motive was a sound one. He apologized to me most handsomely for what happened on our wedding day. He admitted that he behaved very badly on that occasion and begged my pardon in everyone's hearing when he might have taken me aside to speak privately and so saved himself some embarrassment. Are you very annoyed that I stayed and listened?"

Annoyed? He was almost vibrating with fury. He was also curiously . . . afraid.

"I daresay," he said, "it was those kind friends in the village who wrote to inform him of my upcoming wedding."

"Oh, yes," she said. "I had not thought of that. And of course everyone here knows what happened at the church. Perhaps he felt he really ought to make his apologies for all to hear, for the Clarks were surely dismayed to hear of his misuse of the information with which they had provided him."

"Dora," he said, stepping forward and taking both her hands in his, "stay away from him."

"I am quite sure I will be able to do so without any effort," she said. "I doubt I will see him again. He will be continuing his travels. But he made himself very agreeable to both Sir Everard and Mother during tea—and to me. I do believe he really is sorry for what happened. And if he did know I was to be at the Clarks', then it was even more commendable that he came there to speak with me. It must not have been easy and could very well have been avoided. "

"Dora." He squeezed her hands more tightly. "Mrs. Clark and Mrs. Parkinson were at the forefront of the vicious, baseless accusations that were bandied about after Miriam's death. They, together with Eastham himself. The man wrecked your wedding day."

"Oh, not quite," she protested. "And he certainly has not wrecked my marriage, has he? This afternoon could not have had any malicious motive behind it. What could they have hoped to accomplish beyond my embarrassment? That would have been very little reward for a malevolent conspiracy. It seems far more likely that they all wanted to mend some fences, and I appreciate it even if I cannot feel any great liking for those ladies. As for the Earl of Eastham—George, he was once your brother-in-law, and he was clearly very fond of his sister. He was upset by the news of your upcoming marriage to me and behaved badly. It happens. He has apologized. That happens too. I suppose in a sense he still is part of your family. People do not stop being your in-laws just because the person who formed the link between them has died, do they? Agnes would still be your sister-in-law if I were to die."

"Don't," he said, raising both her hands to his lips. "Don't die before me, Dora. In fact, I expressly forbid it."

She tipped her head to one side and smiled at him. "I shall try to obey," she said, "since you have not commanded my obedience much since our marriage. George, I think it would be a wonderful gesture if we invited him to our ball. The whole neighborhood would see that all that unpleasant business is over and done with. And then I daresay he would go on his way and we would never see him again."

"No!" His head had turned icy again. "Eastham will *not* be invited to the ball or to this house, Dora. Ever. He might once have been my brother-in-law, but there was never an ounce of love lost between the two of us. *Never.* Quite the opposite, in fact, and it grew worse toward the end. I am not much given to hatred, but I can say without hesitation and without apology that I loathe Anthony Meikle, Earl of Eastham. And I can assure you beyond the shadow of any doubt that he has always returned the sentiment with interest. Stay away from him."

She gazed at him, an inscrutable expression on her face. "Is that a command?" she asked.

He released her hands and turned jerkily to pick up his diamond pin, which he proceeded to secure in place among the folds of his neckcloth.

"No," he said. "I hope I will never try to command you, Dora. It is a request. But we must be keeping your mother and Sir Everard waiting in the drawing room and—worse—the chef in the kitchen."

She continued to gaze at him for a few moments longer

before stepping forward and batting away his hands to adjust the pin more to her liking.

"Shall we go to the music room after dinner?" she suggested.

"If you were willing always to play the harp," he said, "I would *live* in the music room."

She laughed. "Mother used to have a beautiful voice," she said. "Perhaps we can persuade her to sing to the harp's accompaniment. Or to play the pianoforte while I play the harp."

He leaned forward and kissed her lips.

"You are glad we invited her?" he asked.

She lifted her eyes to his. "I am glad," she said. "*Very* glad. But them, not just her. I believe I like Sir Everard."

18

For the week before the ball Dora was unable to concentrate upon much else, though there was remarkably little for her to do beyond occasionally flitting about looking busy. A few times she felt guilty over her idleness, but it was a very good thing to know that one had such a good and efficient staff. She had told George once that she could easily grow accustomed to having so many servants, and indeed it had happened. However had she managed in her little cottage with only Mrs. Henry for help? The answer was obvious of course. It had been a little cottage, and she had never tried to host a grand ball there.

The servants at Penderris were being even more solicitous of her than usual, she came to realize, because of the delicate state of her health. She always smiled to herself at the memory of what Ann Cox-Hampton had had to say about that word *delicate*. Dora had never felt in better health in her life.

By the day of the ball the whole vast house gleamed with cleanliness; the ballroom floor had been polished to such a high gloss that it resembled a mirror; all the chandeliers had been lowered onto large sheets spread over the floor and had been cleaned until the crystal drops that were suspended from them sparkled, and each holder had been fitted with a new candle, dozens in all; the ballroom and the balcony outside the French windows had been decked with large pots of purple and fuchsia and white flowers and leaves and ferns; so had the sides of the staircase; a red carpet was rolled up at one side of the hall ready to be fitted down the outside steps late in the afternoon; the kitchens and the pantry were so laden with food it was a wonder anyone could move around without knocking some of it off surfaces onto the floor, which was almost as spotlessly clean as the tabletops; a number of the guest rooms had been aired and the beds made up and a vase of flowers, a bowl of fruit, and a bottle of wine with a tray of crystal glasses arranged in each.

There was really nothing for Dora to do after an early luncheon but await the arrival of those guests who would stay the night, though it was doubtful any of them would come for hours yet. Julian and Philippa had arrived before luncheon, but they were family and had come for a visit as well as to attend the ball. They had come early so that there would be plenty of time to settle Belinda in the old nursery with her nurse. Dora had mentioned to Mrs. Lerner that she intended to find some toys and books for the child's amusement, but even in that she was thwarted. One of the attic rooms was filled with suitable items, moved there after they were no longer needed by any children of the house. A couple of footmen were sent to fetch them down and make sure they were clean. They included an old rocking horse, which George remembered as a great favorite when he was a child.

George took Julian and Sir Everard out riding with him after luncheon, using as an excuse that they would be out of the servants' way if they made themselves scarce. Soon after they left Belinda settled down for an afternoon nap and Dora's mother went into the village with Philippa, who wanted to see if the shop had a length of ribbon in just the shade of pink she had been searching for to trim the bonnet she had purchased in London. Dora did not go with them. She stayed to receive any of the guests who might by chance arrive early. She had also promised both George and her mother that she would retire to her room at some point during the afternoon to rest.

She did spend half an hour in her room, but she could not sleep, and there was no point in lying on her bed staring at the canopy over her head. Her brain and her stomach were too busy churning with mingled excitement and apprehension about her coming duties as hostess of her very own ball. She so very much wanted every moment of the evening to be perfectly happy and memorable.

Her mother and Philippa found her upon their return in a salon that had been set up for card playing—it was too much to expect, of course, that everyone would wish to dance. She was moving a table an inch here, a chair half an inch there, just as though the furniture were not perfectly arranged as it was. Philippa waggled her reticule triumphantly from the doorway before hurrying off to the nursery.

"I found a whole roll of satin ribbon in just the shade I wanted," she announced, "and just the right width too. What a miracle!" She paused and looked again into the room. "Whatever are you doing, Aunt Dora? Uncle George would have fits if he saw you moving that table."

"I was putting it back where it was originally," Dora said apologetically. "Sometimes I almost wish our servants were not quite so efficient."

"I am off to see if Belinda is up," Philippa said before disappearing.

"Oh, Dora," her mother said as the door closed. "I am so glad to find you alone. When we were coming out of the shop, we ran almost headlong into the Earl of Eastham, who happened to be passing along the street. He insisted upon escorting us to the alehouse and ordering us a glass of lemonade. He had called at Mr. and Mrs. Clark's, he told us, but when he discovered that they were busy preparing for a ball here this evening, he cut short his visit despite their protests. He had been intending to have a glass of ale alone before returning to his inn and resuming his travels tomorrow."

"Oh, dear," Dora said, "I thought he would have been on his way long before now. George was not willing that he be invited to the ball, but it does seem unmannerly not to have done so. He and George have always had something of an antagonistic relationship, though I do not know why. And then, of course, it grew worse and culminated in the earl's not only blaming George for not preventing the duchess's suicide but even suggesting that he had pushed her to her death. It is not surprising that he would not allow me to invite the earl, is it? But it is all very unfortunate that he chose today of all days to come to the village again and so discovered that we are having a ball here but have excluded him. I daresay he may feel hurt."

"But he perfectly understands," her mother assured her. "He said so. He did write to His Grace, you know, directly after he spoke to you at Mrs. Clark's that afternoon. He felt he ought to so that it would not be thought he had approached you behind your husband's back. George returned his letter unopened."

"Oh, dear."

Her mother moved closer and patted her hand. "He does not wish to upset you," she said. "He is truly sorry that on your wedding day you were caught in the middle of a foolish quarrel that in no way concerned you. He would like to explain a few things to you, however, so that you may conceive a more informed and perhaps a more kindly opinion of him than you have now."

"I do not believe George would like me exchanging any correspondence with him, Mother," Dora said. "And I do not feel so inclined anyway, though it probably was just a foolish quarrel. Most are, are they not? Though they can cause years of unnecessary estrangement and pain."

She might have been describing herself and her mother, she thought, except that they had never actually quarreled. Her mother had just disappeared. And what had happened to cause their estrangement had been no foolish squabble.

"He will be leaving tomorrow morning to continue his travels," her mother said. "He understands that you must be very busy today. However, he did ask me if I would inform you that he will be walking near the headland above the harbor just beyond the Penderris park limits for the next hour or so and would be honored if you would grant him a few minutes of your time there."

It sounded a little clandestine to Dora and really quite unnecessary. She did not wish any harm to the Earl of Eastham, and apparently he wished her none. But George was adamantly opposed to her having anything more to do with him. He even professed to loathe him, an admission that had somewhat startled her as she had not imagined that her husband could hate anyone. And George was not even at home this afternoon to consult. But the Earl of Eastham could hardly know that, could he? And having lived through long years of a separation from her mother and only now having found her again, Dora was saddened to think of all the lost years family quarrels brought about. The earl had reached out to her to apologize for spoiling her wedding day. He had even written to George. And now he was requesting a few minutes of her day in which to explain himself a little more fully. She still felt a bit guilty about not inviting him to the ball. The least she could do, surely, was listen to what he had to say.

Perhaps there was still a chance that she might persuade George that people often hurt themselves more than anyone else when they cling to old hatreds and resentments even after an olive branch had been extended. Perhaps it was an olive branch the earl was extending today.

Her mother was looking at her in some concern. "Perhaps I ought not to have said anything," she said. "He seems a pleasant, sincere man to me, but Everard was not quite so sure after we met him. Stay here, Dora. I do not suppose he is really expecting you anyway."

Dora frowned and then laughed. "I suppose," she said, "that if I do not go, I shall feel guilty all evening and unable to enjoy the ball fully. I shall go."

"Then let me come with you," her mother said.

"You have just walked all the way to the village and back," Dora said, "on a warm day. Go and rest, or go to the drawing room and order up a pot of tea. Keep it warm for me. I will not be long."

But this was foolishness, she thought a few minutes later as she strode along the driveway in the direction of the eastern gate. The Earl of Eastham ought not to have asked it of her, and George would be annoyed, to say the least. She would, of course, tell him even if the earl had changed his mind and gone back to his inn without waiting for her—which she hoped he had done.

Before she reached the gate, she had almost made up her mind to turn and go back to the house. But then she saw him off to her right, standing motionless on the headland, gazing out to sea. He looked lonely and rather forlorn, and it struck her that it must be the first time he had been back here since his sister died. And he had been very close to his sister.

She noticed then that he was actually on Penderris land, not beyond its limits as he had said he would be. However, he was not trespassing by very much, and he was outside the cultivated part of the park.

Dora hesitated only briefly before turning off the path and making her way toward him. He turned when she approached closer, and he watched her come with a warm and welcoming smile. He bowed when she was close, took her right hand in his, and raised it to his lips, a curiously courtly gesture for such surroundings.

"You came despite the fact that you must be very busy today," he said. "I did not really expect it, Duchess. I am touched by your kindness."

She repossessed herself of her hand. "I am expecting guests soon," she said, "and must not be from home very long. My mother informed me that you had something particular to say to me, and I came. It was kind of you to take her and Mrs. Crabbe for a glass of lemonade. I know they appreciated it on such a warm afternoon."

"It was my pleasure," he said. "Lady Havell is a charming lady. So is young Julian's wife."

But she had not come here to exchange pleasantries with him. She looked questioningly at him and waited.

"I wish you to understand," he said, gazing earnestly into her face, "that I have no quarrel whatsoever with you, Duchess. I wonder how much your husband has explained to you."

Dora hesitated. "I do not pry into my husband's affairs, Lord Eastham," she said, "any more than he does into mine. I have always understood that your disruption of our wedding had nothing to do with me. You do not even know me, after all, or I you. I bear no lingering grudge, if that is what concerns you. You doubtless had your reasons for feeling deeply offended when you heard that your late sister's husband was about to marry again.

I do not fully understand why, though I can make some guesses. It does not matter, though. What was between you and my husband concerns the two of you, not me. I do appreciate the fact, though, that you made the effort to apologize to me in person at the home of people who were your sister's friends and even in the presence of my mother."

He nodded, his expression serious.

"Shall we walk?" he suggested, gesturing to the path that ran parallel to the headland and led farther onto Penderris property. "You are quite right, Duchess—you do not understand, though it makes perfect sense to me that Stanbrook would say nothing to enlighten you."

"As is his right," she said firmly as she fell into step beside him. "I really do not need to know anything about the past, Lord Eastham, that he chooses not to tell me."

"You are too good, Duchess," he said. "He was always cold toward the boy, and in the end, cruel."

"To his *son*?" She turned her head toward him, startled. His face was grave now and looked lined with age.

"He desperately wanted to send the boy off to school," he said, "even though Brendan was a sensitive child of delicate health and his mother doted on him and would have been brokenhearted if he had been sent away. Stanbrook gave in to her pleadings, but he hired tutors who were harsh and humorless and frequently chastised the boy and kept him from his mother for long hours of every day. And then, finally, when he was little more than a child, Stanbrook forced a military commission upon him and sent him off to his death in the Peninsula."

Dora really did not want to be hearing this. It felt

deceitful, as though she were deliberately going behind George's back to gather more information than he was willing to give her himself.

"I believe it is usual for boys of his class to be sent to boarding school at a certain age," she said. "If there was a disagreement between your nephew's parents over the matter, then it would appear that the duke deferred to the duchess's wishes. The hiring of tutors as an alternative plan was surely understandable. One would hardly wish the heir to a dukedom to grow up without any sort of education. Sometimes it is a tutor's job to be strict and even to impose punishment. And a commission was what your nephew actually did want after growing up at home, presumably without much experience of the outside world."

And with what sounded like an overprotective mother. But, Dora thought, she did not want to involve herself in a conversation like this. She would not have come if she had known this was what he wanted to talk to her about.

"Really, Lord Eastham," she said, "I must be—"

"It was done to punish my sister," he said as they walked past the gap in the cliff face where it had collapsed at some time in the distant past and provided a steep way down over stones and pebbles to the beach below. They would be in sight of the house soon. Dora really did not want to be seen with the earl before she could tell George about this meeting. At the next gap in the gorse bushes she really must be firm and make her way through it and back to the house. Clearly he had nothing to share with her except stories that reflected badly upon George.

"With respect, I really do not wish to listen to any of this, Lord Eastham," she said, stopping a little farther along the path, just where it curved outward to follow the contour of the cliff top. The house was in sight from here. "I can understand the concern you must have felt for your sister and nephew if you believed them unhappy, but I would suggest that perhaps you did not know all the facts, or, if you did, you knew them only from your sister's point of view and not also from your brother-in-law's. What went into the decisions that were made within that family group really concerned them alone, not you, and certainly not me."

He had stopped beside her and regarded her with a peculiar half smile on his lips. The path was narrow here, she noticed, and it was impossible to put more of an acceptable distance between them. Prickly gorse would be snagging the muslin of her dress if she took so much as a half step back.

"One essential fact was indisputable, Duchess," he said. "Brendan was not Stanbrook's son."

She stared at him in incomprehension.

"He was mine," he added.

Her confusion grew. "But the duchess was your sister."

"Half sister," he said. "Do you think a man and a woman cannot love in that way just because there is a forbidden degree of relationship between them, Duchess? You would be wrong if you do. I had been away from home a number of years, doing what a young man does while sowing wild oats. When I returned, I saw the changes those years had wrought in the daughter of my father's second wife. She had grown up, and she was breathtakingly lovely. Did you know that of her? She blushed and smiled when she saw me for the first time in almost five years, and—we fell in love. It was entirely mutual and quite total. We never fell out of love. Never. Ours was that rare sort of passion that holds firm and immovable for a lifetime and beyond. Our father tried to tear us asunder by marrying her off to an insipid young pup of a duke's son, but he succeeded only in the sense that he gave *my love* into the hands of a coldhearted boy—he could hardly be described as a man—and *my son* into the hands of a man who eventually found a way of killing him without having to wield the weapon himself. And in so doing he found a way too of ridding himself of the wife he had finished punishing."

They had been standing still too long, Dora thought, and her body had been held at an unnatural angle, bent back slightly from the waist to gain some distance from him. She thought she might well faint. There was a sort of buzzing in her ears. Full comprehension had not quite caught up yet to what she was hearing.

"This has *nothing* to do with me. I do not even wish to hear it." Her voice sounded fuzzy to her ears, as though it were coming from a long way off. But it was too late *not* to hear it.

"But, Duchess," he said, and he was frowning now, "it has *everything* to do with you."

She had had enough—more than enough. She would listen to no more. She turned sharply about and took a step forward, desperately hoping she could forge a way through the gorse bushes without proceeding even another step along the path with him. But two things happened simultaneously. The earl caught hold of her arm above the elbow, none too gently. And in the distance, close to the house, she saw three men, one of them George. It was obvious too in that brief moment that he saw her. But she was spun back to face the Earl of Eastham before she could see more.

"Release me, sir," she said indignantly, and was almost surprised when he did so.

"Why, Duchess," the earl asked her, his face close to hers, "should Stanbrook be allowed to have a child of his own when he took mine away from me? And why should he be allowed to have a woman to comfort him when he deprived me of mine?"

Her head turned cold. He knew of her pregnancy?

"If all you have told me is true, Lord Eastham," she said, "the Duke of Stanbrook was tricked into taking a child who was not his own and the woman who was bearing him. If you are telling the truth, it was your father who did the tricking, though perhaps he did not know there was to be a child or even that the two of you were lovers. In either case, my husband was a victim at least as much as the two of you were. But *however it was,* it is none of my concern. I came at your request and I have listened to you against my will. Now I must bid you farewell. I have business to attend to at the house."

She tried to turn from him again—but with even less success this time. He caught both her arms so that she could not turn at all. And it suddenly occurred to her that perhaps she had something to fear. She heard his last words like an echo in her brain—*Why, Duchess, should Stanbrook be allowed to have a child of his own when he took mine away from me? And why should he be allowed to have a woman to comfort him when he deprived me of mine?*

She looked at him, coldness in her eyes and in her body. "Unhand me," she said.

This time he did not comply with her demand. "Has anyone ever pointed out to you, Duchess," he asked her, "where exactly on the cliff top my sister was standing when she was pushed to her death?"

No one had. But she could guess the answer.

He pointed downward with one finger.

"Here," he said. "Or actually a little closer to the edge. Let me show you."

"No, thank you," she said.

But he still had her by one arm, and he was moving her off the path onto the coarse grass, which ended suddenly no more than seven or eight feet away.

But even as she saw that distance closing, she heard a distant voice. It was George's. "*Eastham!*"

"*Keep your distance, Stanbrook. You have no business here,*" the earl shouted back without taking his eyes off Dora. He lowered his voice again. "It is in the nature of an eye for an eye, you see, Duchess. A woman and a child for a woman and a child—and in almost the exact same manner, though I cannot, alas, arrange for the child to become fodder for enemy guns."

"And you cannot arrange for me to jump unassisted as your sister did," Dora said, amazed to hear the calmness of her voice. She seemed suddenly to have turned to icy calmness all over, in fact, a strange thing when she ought to be incoherent with panic and terror.

"He has you hoodwinked, Duchess," he said. "But I daresay that as an aging spinster you were ripe for the picking and did not much care what sort of a man you married. However, I do not mean to insult you. I do not dislike you. I meant what I said when I told you I have no grudge whatsoever against you. It is just unfortunate for you that you have become the perfect instrument of revenge."

Poor George, a dispassionate part of Dora's mind thought. He was going to have to go through this nightmare for the second time in his life.

"My husband can see everything," she said. "So, presumably, can the two gentlemen with him. It would be more than foolish for you to do what it is in your mind to do, Lord Eastham. Do you imagine that you will feel better after you have taken the life of an innocent woman and her unborn child? Do you imagine that you will be able to escape and to continue living as a free man?"

He smiled at her. "I will know the answer to your first question for only a moment, Duchess," he said. "And yes, I will escape—into the freedom of eternity, which I will share, it is to be hoped, with Miriam and Brendan. It is life on this human plane, you see, that is hell to me."

"*Eastham.*" The voice came from somewhere farther along the path they had been walking. It was not George's voice this time.

The earl looked up, the smile still on his face. "Oh, yes," he called out, "I know you are there, creeping up on me, the three of you. It is too bad you cannot get me completely surrounded, is it not? And unfortunately for you, it is by the fourth, unguardable side by which the duch—"

As he spoke, his hand had loosened infinitesimally on Dora's arm. His attention had been very slightly distracted. It was now or never, Dora knew as she wrenched her arm free, caught up her skirts with the other hand, and dashed back onto the path and along it the way they had come. There was no time to break through the thick barrier of the gorse bushes. There was no time to escape, no time for George to run to her rescue. The earl would be upon her in a moment.

"Behind you, Eastham!"

She half heard George's voice, but she could already sense the earl just behind her, his hand reaching out to grab her. She was back to the fault in the cliff face. If she stayed on the path, which bent around it, he would catch her long before she was halfway to the other side. If she went straight forward . . .

She did just that and found herself on the fall of boulders and rocks, all of them loose to varying degrees, all of them different sizes and positioned differently on the steep slope, which was a treacherous descent even when one had the leisure to make one's way carefully downward and had a steady male hand to help one every step of the way. Dora had no such luxury. She went hurtling downward and heard the earl shout out just behind her. She heard the sound of his boots on the loose stones. And then another shout. And now she was blind with terror, her icy calm having deserted her. She expected every moment to lose her balance, and she expected every moment to feel a hand grab at her back or her arm. In her panic, she realized, she had turned away from safety rather than toward it.

But the second shout turned almost instantly to a long scream, at the same time she heard a shout of warning from another voice that caused her to twist away to one side in order to claw at some coarse grass growing there and a rock that jutted from the cliff face. The rock held, and she came to a jarring halt and watched in horror as the Earl of Eastham went sliding and somersaulting past and down the steep fall of rocks, until he came to a stop against one particularly large boulder close to the bottom and lay still and spread-eagled on its face. He looked curiously broken.

"DORA!"

She was aware of someone else coming down the rocks behind her at an incautious speed, and then, before she could turn, she was gathered up into someone's arms and pressed to his chest, his head against the side of hers.

"Dora!" There was a universe of pain in his voice.

There was a buzzing in her head, a coldness in her nostrils as she went limp in his arms and slid down a different kind of slope.

"What kept you, George?" she heard herself say.

But there was no chance to hear his answer or to revel in any sudden sense of safety. She kept sliding until everything went suddenly cold and dark.

19

George had been walking back from the stables to the house with Julian and Sir Everard Havell after a pleasant ride they had all enjoyed. He hoped Dora had found time to rest or that her mother had insisted upon it. She was endearingly excited about the upcoming festivities, but the servants had all the preparations well in hand and really did not need her assistance. Some of the guests would be staying overnight, though, and would therefore be arriving earlier than the rest, in time for dinner, at least. Dora would no doubt wish to be the perfect hostess and greet them at the door and see them settled in their rooms. For a moment George felt a twinge of guilt about not remaining to do it for her while she rested.

It was Havell who drew his attention to the two figures standing on the cliff top away off in the distance.

"I hope they are not as close to the edge as they look to be," he had said, nodding in their direction. "I have never had much of a head for heights."

George looked, and his first reaction was a fond sort

of exasperation, for if one of those persons was not Dora, he was much mistaken. Whatever was she doing out walking, though, today of all days when the sun was rather hot and she ought to be resting for the busy evening ahead? He did not immediately recognize the man with her, but he assumed it was one of the early arrivals. Could he not have explored on his own if he had felt so inclined?

His stomach lurched with discomfort then, for he realized that by unhappy chance they were standing just where Miriam had stood when . . . And with that realization came sudden recognition—and a certainty of understanding. By God, it was Eastham! At the same moment he realized this, Dora took a step away from the earl and turned toward the house—but only for a moment. George was not even sure she had seen him.

"Dear God!" he said, stopping in his tracks.

"Is that not Aunt Miriam's brother with Aunt Dora?" Julian asked at the same moment, shading his eyes with one hand. "What the devil is he doing here after the ass he made of himself at your wedding? You have not invited him to the ball tonight, have you?"

But George had already turned and begun to hurry across the south lawn toward the wilder land above the cliffs. The lawn seemed a mile wide. But the exact distance did not signify anyway, for he knew with a desperate hope that he was wrong that he would not get there in time. Eastham was facing toward the house. He must be able to see the three of them.

The other two were now running along either side of him.

"Is that the man who almost ruined Dora's wedding day?" Havell asked. "What in thunder—"

"He is going to push her over," George said. "He is going to kill her. Eastham!" He yelled the last word, but of course it was hopeless. The man was not going to take fright just because George was hurrying to the rescue. Indeed, he would revel in just this situation.

"Keep your distance, Stanbrook," he yelled back.

"What in thunder—" Havell said again.

"It is just the spot where Aunt Miriam jumped," Julian said. "But . . . he must just be showing Aunt Dora where it happened. He surely wouldn't push her over. It would be madness. He has three witnesses."

"That will not deter him," George said. He had stopped, but his mind was racing. If he moved any closer, he would merely provoke Eastham into pushing her over sooner. But if he stayed and did nothing, Eastham would do it anyway. He had already drawn her off the path closer to the edge of the cliff. "God!" He plummeted off a cliff of his own into the sheer hell of terror, panic, and despair. There was nothing—

That was when Sir Everard Havell took charge of the situation.

"Crabbe," he had said crisply, addressing Julian, "go to your right. I will go left. Get through all that gorse and then call his name. I will do the same directly after you. Perhaps we can distract him long enough to give Dora a chance to break free. Get ready to dash in to help, but only if she has managed to get back a bit from the edge. George, stay here and keep his attention focused on you."

George stayed there because he could do nothing else. It was all hopeless. Just as it had been the last time, though this situation was different. There was no course of action that would prevent catastrophe. Yet inaction would not prevent it either. He was scarcely aware of the other two moving away to the sides. What should he do? Move forward? Utter threats? Beg and plead? None of those options would do any good whatsoever. Miriam had jumped, and Eastham would push. But he took a few steps forward anyway and drew breath to say something.

"Eastham!" It was Julian's voice, not his own, coming from down on the path to the right.

Eastham answered him, his voice raised in mockery.

But miraculously, terrifyingly, Dora jerked away from him and fled in the opposite direction. Eastham recovered his focus almost instantly. She could not possibly escape.

"Behind you, Eastham," George yelled, and Eastham's pursuit was slowed while he turned his head to look in the direction from which Julian's voice had come. But only for the briefest of moments.

He was after Dora again in a flash. Within moments he would have her in his grasp once more. But those moments offered a slim sliver of hope, and George sprang into action. He never afterward knew how he got past the gorse bushes, but get through them he did, leaving deep scratches in his boots and tearing his breeches and drawing blood from his knees and thighs and hands. The path bent around the steep fall of rocks that they used as an access to the beach, but Dora did not go around. She kept on going forward instead, and, even as Eastham's hands reached for her, she disappeared over the edge, moving at a full run.

George felt that nightmare sensation of trying to run at full speed through air grown thick and gummy. But this was reality, not nightmare. He had failed to reach her in time, and Havell was on the other side of the gap in the cliff and too far away to grab her and haul her to safety. Havell was not too far away, however, to raise one booted foot as Eastham turned downward in pursuit. The foot caught Eastham at one ankle, and he tripped and lost his balance.

There were shouting voices—one of them may have been George's—and then a scream.

George arrived at the top of the slope as Havell, teetering on the edge, regained his balance and called a warning down the slope. But George saw only one thing. He saw Dora partway down, her body spread across a jagged, jutting rock.

He was quite unaware of going down to her. He was just *there,* and he was gathering her to him, calling her name, knowing that she could not hear him, that she was dead.

"Dora!" he said again, and he felt his heart shatter and sanity slip from him. He held her for what seemed an eternity before he heard a sound.

"What kept you, George?" she asked, her voice faint and slurred.

He jerked his head back and stared down at her. Her eyelids fluttered for a moment, and then she was gone, her face as white as parchment.

"Ah, Dora," he whispered against her lips. "My belovèd. My *only* belovèd."

"Is she hurt?" It was Julian's voice, and he was crouched beside George and pressing two fingers to the side of her neck. "A strong beat, thank God. She has just fainted."

George looked at him in incomprehension. "She is alive?"

Julian clapped a hand on his shoulder and squeezed hard.

"You look as though you are going to be the next one to faint," he said. "She is alive, Uncle George. Can you hear me? I do not even see any wounds. I believe the only blood is coming from the scratches on your hands. I have some on mine too. Those damned gorse bushes. But she is *alive*." He squeezed George's shoulder again.

"He is dead," a voice called up from below—Sir Everard Havell's. "I have killed him, and by Jove I am glad. Is Dora hurt?"

Dora woke up wondering if it was time to get up yet. But there was something about the angle of the light coming through the window of the bedchamber that was not quite right. It brought her eyes snapping open. What time was it? *When was the ball?*

She would have thrown back the bedcovers if her hand had not been imprisoned between two larger hands.

"George?"

He was sitting on the side of the bed, looking as pale as a ghost. "Thank God," he said. "You recognize me."

"Recognize—?" She frowned, and remembered.

"Oh." Her eyes widened. "How did I get here?"

"I carried you," he said. "You fainted. More than fainted actually. We could not bring you around. You have been unconscious for more than an hour."

She stared fixedly at him. "He was going to kill me. An eye for an eye, he said. A woman and child for a woman and child. He had no personal grudge against me, he assured me. It was revenge against you."

"And a very effective one, had it worked," he said. "A thousand times more effective than killing me."

"What happened to him?" She tried to sit up, but he coaxed her back against the pillows with one hand on her shoulder.

"Sir Everard tripped him as he turned to follow you down the slope," he said. "He fell almost to the bottom. He is dead."

"Dead," she repeated. "He meant to kill himself too, you know. That was why he was unconcerned about you and the others witnessing what he did. I think he actually wanted to be seen, especially by you. But what did you say? Sir Everard tripped him?"

A stifled sob drew Dora's attention to the foot of the bed. Her mother was standing there, clinging to the bedpost on the other side, just as pale as George.

"It was all my fault, Dora," she said. "I sent you to talk to him. You almost *died*."

"But I did not," Dora said. "And I did not have to go out there to him. It was my decision, remember?" She closed her eyes again for a moment and licked dry lips.

"Sir Everard saved your life, Dora," George said.

"He arranged the diversion with Julian to distract East-ham to give you a chance to break away, and then he stopped Eastham before he could pursue you down the slope."

Dora's eyes filled with tears as she looked at her mother.

"He fears heights," her mother said.

Dora smiled wanly. How could it be that they had come full circle now? That the very man who she had always believed had ruined her life by stealing her mother away had now saved her life? And then her eyes widened in sudden panic. "But what time is it? There must be guests arriving. It must be almost time to—"

The hand that had pressed her shoulder back down to the bed was still there.

"It is time to lie where you are," George said. "There are other people to show the guests to their rooms. Dodd ought to be here soon. Julian went dashing off to fetch him."

"But I do not need a doctor," she protested. "I need to get ready for dinner and the ball. What time *is* it?"

"It is still only late afternoon," he assured her. "Listen to me, Dora. You have suffered a severe shock. I do not suppose you have felt the full effects of it yet. And there is the added complication that you are with child. You will lie there until Dodd has examined you, and you will lie there even after that if he feels you ought. And that is a command. Dinner and the ball will proceed without you if they must, though everyone will regret your absence, no one more so than I. Philippa has agreed to host the evening's events if necessary, and she is perfectly capable of doing so."

"I will stay here with you, Dora, if the doctor advises rest," her mother said. "You will not be alone. And no one will blame you for not putting in an appearance. Word of what has happened has no doubt spread through the village and beyond by now. And your condition is common knowledge. Indeed, I would think everyone would be more surprised if you did appear tonight."

Dora looked in dismay from one to the other of them. "But this is our first grand entertainment together," she said to George. She turned back to her mother. "And we deliberately planned it for the time you and Sir Everard would be here."

"There will be other balls and parties and concerts, Dora," George said. "But there is only one of you."

"It is enough that we are here," her mother told her. "Everyone has been most kind. You and His Grace especially."

Dora clutched a handful of the bedcovers with her free hand. "I am not going to lose the baby, am I?" she asked.

Her mother shook her head, but it was George who answered.

"It is to be sincerely hoped you will not," he said, "but you must listen to the doctor, Dora, and do as he says. I would not risk our child or—and, frankly, far more important at this stage—you for the sake of a mere ball, important as I know it is to you. My God, I almost lost you today. I almost *lost* you and would have had it not been for Sir Everard and Julian."

His eyes glittered down into hers, and she realized that he was on the verge of tears. She relaxed back against the pillows.

And the image came suddenly and vividly to mind of the vast emptiness of space that had yawned a mere foot or two in front of her with the Earl of Eastham's hand gripping her arm and propelling her forward. She thought of the desperate flight when she had somehow managed to wrench her arm free and of her split-second decision to take the slope down rather than the path around—and the almost simultaneous realization that she was never going to make it to the bottom alive. She remembered a tumbling, screaming body hurtling past her. She remembered arms holding her tight and a voice from the encroaching darkness as she lost consciousness, calling her name. She remembered a voice from the depths—*Ah, Dora. My belovèd. My* only *belovèd.*

George's voice.

"I ought to have heeded you when you begged me to have nothing more to do with him," she said. "But I thought I knew better than you. I thought there might be a way of reconciling the two of you."

"It was not your fault," he said. "I ought to have given you a reason. But let us all stop assuming blame for what happened this afternoon. There was only one man to blame, and he will never hurt you again."

"He is dead." She closed her eyes and drew a slow breath. "How dreadful that I cannot feel sorry."

"Neither can I," her mother said with some spirit. "I am only sorry it was Everard's foot that tripped him, not mine."

Dora smiled at her. "I am glad it was Sir Everard," she said.

Her mother looked back in some surprise.

"I am only glad someone did," George said fervently, and Dora turned her gaze on him. And remembered . . . Ah, and remembered.

George's son had not been his but the Earl of Eastham's. The earl and the duchess had harbored an illicit passion for each other for many years. Their father had forced her into marriage with George in order to separate them. Had he known about her pregnancy? Perhaps. Probably, in fact. When had George discovered that the child was not his? Had he always known? Dear God, he had been only a boy at the time. What sort of permanent effect had that knowledge had upon him? But she was looking upon those effects, had been looking upon them for as long as she had known him. The almost perpetual kindness in his eyes also held a tinge of sadness. She had never quite identified that sadness until now. And there was his very private loneliness she had sensed but never been able to penetrate.

His hand tightened about hers, and two tears spilled over and trickled down his cheeks.

"I almost lost you," he said.

"Oh," she said, "I am not so easily misplaced."

Her mother went to open the door to whoever had just tapped on it and stepped aside to admit Dr. Dodd.

The physician was unable to detect any physical sign of the ordeal Dora had endured during the afternoon. There was no indication that a miscarriage might be imminent. She had suffered a dreadful shock, of course, and he could not predict how that might manifest itself in the hours and days ahead. But at present her pulse was steady and her color healthy and her mind clear. He strongly advised a few hours of bed rest. It was up to the duchess herself to decide if she would put in an appearance before her guests during the evening, but if she did, he advised that she not exert herself unduly and that she not participate in any vigorous dancing.

Dora reluctantly agreed to remain in her apartments during dinner. She would decide later what to do about the ball.

"Though I do hate to miss even the dinner," she told George with a sigh. "And really, I feel fine and quite fraudulent lying here."

She was not willing for her mother to stay with her.

"Though I do appreciate your concern, Mother," she assured her, "I would not be able to sleep if you were in the room. I would want to talk so that you would not be bored."

Fourteen persons sat down to dinner an hour later. It was all a severe trial to George. The guests were polite, of course, but it was clear they were bursting with curiosity to know exactly what had happened during the afternoon that had somehow sent a dead man to the village to await an inquest and the duchess to her private apartments, where a physician had attended her. There was no point in being overly evasive, George had decided in consultation with Julian and Sir Everard and the ladies. Everyone already knew that the Earl of Eastham had once accused his brother-in-law of pushing the first duchess to her death and had more recently renewed that accusation at the duke's wedding to the second duchess. He had been silenced on that occasion, but clearly he had been obsessed and perhaps even deranged by his conviction that his sister did not take her own life—even though it had been clear to all who knew her that she was beside herself with grief over the recent death of her only son. So George and Julian had agreed that the rest of the story should be explained, that Eastham had come to Cornwall, tricked the new duchess into walking with him along the headland at Penderris, and tried to push her and her unborn child to their death in the exact place where his sister had died. They did, however, refrain from mentioning Havell's specific role.

The story was exclaimed over and discussed among the guests almost to the exclusion of any other conversational topic. George was very glad Dora was not present to hear it. He hoped he could dissuade her from coming down later, though he would not forbid it. Everyone who came for the ball would be agog with whatever facts and rumors had reached their ears and would want to know the truth and to hear it from those who had been personally involved. Dora would be the star attraction if she were present.

What had Eastham told Dora out there on the headland? A great deal that she had not known before, no doubt. A great deal that *he* ought to have told her himself. But there was little time for introspection or shock or self-blame. He was hosting a dinner. He smiled, answered questions from those seated closest to him, changed the subject, answered more questions, changed the subject again, and ate his dinner without tasting a thing or even noticing what was being served. His chef would weep if he knew.

At last he was able to go back upstairs to see if Dora had slept and to try persuading her to stay in bed. She was in the private sitting room, he realized as soon as he entered the bedchamber. He could hear music coming from that direction. He went through his dressing room to find her.

She was seated at her old pianoforte, playing something soft and sweet and totally absorbed in it. And she was dressed magnificently in a shimmering gown of fuchsia pink expertly styled to show the elegant, slim curves of her body. She was wearing his diamonds at her neck and in her ears. Her dark hair had been piled high in elegant curls with waved tendrils trailing over her neck and ears. And she was wearing the duchess's diamond tiara that had been his grandmother's and his mother's but never Miriam's. A pair of long silver gloves was draped along the top of the pianoforte. One soft silver slipper was wielding one of the pedals.

She looked her age, George thought, but the very best a woman of her age could look. She was surely more beautiful now than she could possibly have been as a young girl. Every line of her body professed maturity, womanhood in its fullest bloom. And growing within her womb was their child. For a moment his knees threatened to give out from beneath him when he thought of that scene out on the cliffs earlier.

She finished what she was playing and looked up with a smile. She must have sensed his presence in the doorway.

"Are you going to a ball by any chance?" he asked her.

"Indeed I am," she said. "I am looking for an escort."

"Allow me the honor." He made her an exaggeratedly courtly bow after proceeding a few steps into the room.

She turned on the stool. "How was dinner?" she asked him.

"It was probably delicious," he said. "I might have noticed if I had been paying attention to it. Our guests seemed well satisfied, though. Philippa took your place without fuss and with a quiet charm. She is a real gem, Dora. The tale of what happened this afternoon was told and retold. Nothing was withheld. Nothing was either exaggerated or dismissed. I wish I could say that now everyone is satisfied and prepared to enjoy the evening without further reference to what occurred, but of course most of the ball guests were not even at dinner. The story will have to be told again and yet again. I wish you would stay here."

She got to her feet and came toward him to make some minor adjustment to the folds of his neckcloth.

"And waste this gown and these jewels and Maisie's very best hairdressing effort?" she said. "Everyone will be agog to see me, knowing what almost happened this afternoon. It is human nature, George. If they do not see me tonight, then it will happen on another occasion, at church on Sunday, perhaps. I cannot hide away all my life. I would rather it be now. They would rather it be now. Besides, I have been looking forward to our ball immensely and am likely to have a tantrum if I am forced to miss it."

He gazed into her eyes and saw fathomless depths there. The story that had been told at dinner was a true and accurate one but not a complete one. Only she knew the rest of it. But she would never refer to it, he realized. She would never confront him with whatever Eastham had told her. She would leave him his privacy and the illusion of his secrets.

It was perhaps at that moment that he realized fully how much he cared for her. How much he loved her. He loved her more than the air he breathed. He loved her with all the youthful passion he had packed away in some hidden inner vault immediately after his first marriage. He had long since thought he had lost the key. But somehow she had found it and fitted it into the lock and turned it.

"We will talk," he told her, taking her hands in his and raising them one at a time to kiss the base of each palm.

"If you wish," she said. He could see that she understood what he meant.

"I wish."

He went to fetch her gloves from the pianoforte, waited while she drew them on, and offered his arm.

Their ball guests would be starting to arrive very soon—and he doubted anyone would be late tonight.

20

*D*ora did not believe she had ever smiled so much in her life. And the strange thing was that much of the time it was with genuine happiness. And why not? She might have been dead, but was alive and unharmed—except, she suspected, emotionally. She had been saved by the combined efforts of her husband, her husband's nephew, and her mother's husband, whom she had despised for years and had only very recently grown to respect and even like.

What was *not* to be happy about?

And the evening she had dreamed about for weeks was happening all about her. She had missed the formal dinner, it was true, but the hours of the ball stretched ahead, and she could scarcely contain the excitement she felt at the sight of the flower-decked staircase and ballroom, of the chandeliers raised back to their place below the ceiling and blazing with candles and crystals, of the floor gleaming with polish, and—oh, and everything. The orchestra had arrived. Their instruments were propped on the dais at one end of the long ballroom. A violinist was tuning his strings at the pianoforte. Long tables in the adjoining salon were spread with crisp white tablecloths and adorned with vases of flowers and china and crystal glasses and silverware. The food and beverages would be carried out as soon as the guests began to arrive. The few who were already present, strolling about the perimeter of the room or seated on velvet-backed chairs, were gorgeously clad and coiffed for the occasion.

And this was all her doing—though she smiled with genuine amusement when she thought of how little she had had to exert herself to bring it all about. She and George must have the world's best servants.

Oh, what was there *not* to be happy about?

Well, for one thing there was her knowledge of the terrible unhappiness of much of George's life, most of it still locked up inside himself. And then there was the knowledge that the Earl of Eastham had wanted to kill her this afternoon and had very nearly succeeded. He had assured her that it was nothing personal, but it had felt very personal. It was a dreadful thing to have encountered a murderous hatred like that. And there was the fact that he had died. It lay heavy upon her spirits to know that someone with whom she had walked and talked a mere few hours ago was now dead. She knew she would remember the sight of him tumbling past her and the sound of his scream for a long, long time. She wondered what had happened to him, or, rather, to his body.

The first thing Dora did after stopping in the doorway to admire the ballroom was slip her arm free of George's in order to make her way about the room, greeting the guests who were staying for the night and apologizing to them for not having been present to show them to their rooms earlier or to entertain them at dinner. It felt very good, she thought, to be able to do this alone without expiring from terror. Terror? There was nothing so very terrible about shaking hands with people who seemed kindly disposed toward her, about acknowledging curtsies and bows and hearing herself called "Your Grace" and making conversation. After this afternoon surely nothing could ever make her afraid again.

She had come a long way in a few short months.

Everyone, of course, assured her that there was nothing for which to apologize, and expressed their concern for her well-being, as well as commiserated with her on her dreadful ordeal. She must expect more of the same when the outside guests arrived, she realized. At least no one this evening would lack for a topic of conversation.

But there were two other specific things she wished to do before the guests did arrive—and the earliest of them would surely be here any minute. She spotted Julian and Philippa over by the orchestra dais, just turning away from talking with the violinist.

Dora held her hands out to Philippa and kissed her on both cheeks.

"I have it on the best authority," she said, "that you are a real gem, Philippa, and acquitted your duties as hostess during dinner with your usual quiet charm. But I did not need to be told. Thank you, my dear."

"I cannot believe," Philippa said, "that I allowed that man to buy lemonade for me this afternoon and that I would have told you of his request to speak with you myself if Lady Havell had not assured me that she would tell you so that I could run on up to the nursery. I am so very sorry, Aunt Dora."

"Don't be," Dora said. "As George observed earlier, we must all stop blaming ourselves. There was only one man to blame." She turned to Julian, set both hands on his shoulders, and kissed him too on both cheeks. "It was you who distracted him sufficiently to allow me to break free. Thank you, Julian."

He grinned at her and patted her hands on his shoulders. "I had to do something to protect the future heir," he said, "since Philippa and I have decided that it would be far better that he be Uncle George's son rather than his nephew."

"Well," Dora said, "the heir may still be the nephew, you know, if this child should turn out to be a daughter. George and I will be equally happy either way."

They all chuckled, and the laughter felt good. But Dora had spotted her mother just coming through the French windows with Sir Everard. They must have stepped outside onto the balcony for some air.

"Oh, do excuse me, if you will," she said, and hurried toward them.

Her mother's face lit up with pleasure. "How beautiful you look, Dora," she said. "Pink always was a good color for you, though you used to protest that it was better for blondes. But are you sure you should be down here? You will not overexert yourself?"

"I promise I will not," Dora assured her. "I have already had the lecture from George."

Her mother too looked rather magnificent in a silver-blue gown that was of classic rather than fashionable design and that Dora suspected she had made herself. Her mother had always been a skilled needlewoman. Her silver hair was elegantly styled. The extra weight she had gained since her youth actually suited her, Dora thought, as did the soft smile that brought back so many memories of the mama she had adored.

"I approve of His Grace," her mother said.

"Oh, so do I." Dora laughed and turned to Sir Everard. She held out her hands to him, but when he took them, she drew them free impulsively, wrapped her arms about his neck, and kissed his cheek. She blinked back tears. "I owe you my life, Sir Everard. And really, I do not believe there is anyone to whom I would rather owe it. You have been good to Mama. You stood by her when you might easily have abandoned her. I am sorry I snubbed you when we called on you in Kensington. I did not understand then how good you had been or how good you are. And I thank you for my life."

"My dear Dora." He possessed himself of her hands again and looked rather embarrassed, though Dora's mother was gazing at him with a beaming smile. "I was there this afternoon and had to do something vaguely heroic. I am only glad that somehow you survived intact. And as for your mother—well, I suppose I loved her even before she was unjustly shamed and forced to flee her home. I would never have admitted it, even to myself, if circumstances had not presented me with the greatest gift of my life. I love her, my dear. Remaining at her side has never been any sacrifice. Quite the contrary."

Oh, she *liked* him, Dora thought. For of course he had sacrificed a great deal when he had stood by an older woman with whom he had been enjoying what had probably been no more than a light flirtation. She had been ostracized by society when she had left Papa and he had divorced her. And though the man in such situations usually fared rather better, nevertheless his own social life must have been severely curtailed and his chances of making a more advantageous marriage totally lost. It was clear that although he was not impoverished, neither was he a wealthy man.

But he was a loyal and affectionate man. And a dignified man. He was, she thought disloyally, more worthy of her regard than her own father was.

"I believe the guests are arriving," she said. "I must join George."

The Penderris ball would not have qualified for that prized appellation of "sad squeeze" if it had been taking place in London, Dora thought over the next half hour or so. Even before some of the guests, mostly the older ones, drifted off to the card room and a number of others wandered into the salon to look over the refreshments, there was room to breathe in the ballroom. Nevertheless, to her eyes it seemed a dazzlingly crowded event, for everyone who had been invited had come.

Even the Clarks came, both of them looking stiff and rather drawn. They came, Dora guessed, partly out of curiosity, and partly so that their absence would not suggest they had somehow conspired with the Earl of Eastham in a murder plot. George smiled and bowed politely to them. Dora smiled too and assured Mr. Clark when he asked that she was feeling quite well after resting for a couple of hours on the physician's advice.

Mrs. Parkinson came a little later with Mr. and Mrs. Yarby, smiling and gracious and eager to inform Dora that she had received a letter that very morning from her dearest Gwen and could only feel sorry that dear Lady Trentham was less loyal to an old friendship than she was and wrote only one short letter for every three long ones Mrs. Parkinson herself wrote.

"Though I do make allowances, Your Grace," she added, "for the fact that she has a young child and I am not at all sure Lord Trentham has hired a superior nurse to assume the full care of it—or that he understands a lady's obligation to spend her mornings dealing with her correspondence. His father was in business, you know. My poor, dearest Gwen."

She must remember to share that little tidbit, Dora thought, the next time she wrote to Gwen.

Ann and James Cox-Hampton arrived with their two eldest daughters, who would not have been deemed old enough for a London ball but were very welcome at this one. James wrung George's hand wordlessly while Ann hugged Dora for several seconds.

"You look beautiful," she said, "and very poised after your dreadful ordeal. If it were only genteel for a lady to make a wager, I would have just won a fortune from James. He bet you would not make an appearance tonight."

"But then, my love," James said, "I would have had to live off my wife's fortune for the rest of my days, and you would have lost all respect for me. I am glad you are keeping a stiff upper lip, Dora."

Barbara Newman also hugged Dora tightly when she arrived with the vicar.

"I very rarely pay much credence to gossip," she said. "It is almost always either grossly exaggerated or entirely untrue. But the Earl of Eastham is dead, so I suppose your life really was in grave danger."

"But I have survived," Dora said. "Do enjoy the ball, Barbara. I shall find some time later to tell you all about it, when you are not dancing."

And finally it seemed that everyone had arrived. Since country entertainments tended to end earlier than London ones, there were never many latecomers. The phrase *fashionably late* was scarcely known in the country.

And now George was drawing her arm through his and looking closely at her. "You are glowing," he said, "and I am dazzled. But are the smiles and the sparkling eyes hiding fatigue, Dora?"

"They are not," she assured him. "But I will keep my promise not to dance even though Dr. Dodd mentioned only the more strenuous ones. It will be enough to watch and enjoy the fruits of everyone's labors except my own."

He laughed. "But the ball was your idea," he said, "and that is what counts. Allow me to take you to Ann. She has been busy seeing to it that her girls have respectable partners for the opening set and seems to have no intention of dancing herself."

He did not need to take her anywhere. She was the Duchess of Stanbrook. Goodness, she was even wearing her tiara. And she was hostess of the ball. But she allowed him to lead her to her friend's side before going to open the dancing with Philippa. During that set of vigorous country dances she told Ann everything that had happened—omitting only some of the details the earl had revealed to her. It was, she discovered, a relief to unburden herself to someone who had not been involved. She would probably do the same with Barbara later, but not with anyone else. Let other people tell the story.

More than anything else tonight, Dora wanted to enjoy herself. There was so much to celebrate—her marriage, her pregnancy, her reconciliation with her mother, friendship.

Life itself.

She spent the evening circulating among her guests, as she had always intended to do. She had never meant to do much dancing. She spoke with everyone, occasionally answering questions about the afternoon but talking on a number of other topics too. She found partners for all the younger people who clearly did want to dance but were too shy to make themselves noticed—and that applied to young gentlemen as well as to young ladies. Indeed it applied more so to them, for the girls had mothers to help them find partners while the boys were expected to fend for themselves. She fetched plates of food for a few elderly people who could not move easily among crowds, although there were servants constantly circulating with trays. She deliberately stood with Mr. and Mrs. Clark between two sets and made them laugh with stories from her music-teaching days. She went up to the high gallery that ran along one end of the ballroom when she spotted the two young children of a couple of her houseguests up there with their nurse. And she delighted them by fetching them a plate of sweetmeats from the refreshment room after obtaining the nurse's permission.

Oh, yes, she did indeed enjoy herself. How could she not? For the ball was clearly a success. She had been a little afraid that the fact of a man's having died on Penderris land earlier today might put a damper upon the festivities, but it had not done so. George spent much of the evening dancing and the rest moving among the guests, as Dora was doing. He looked happy and at ease.

But oh, she thought treacherously a couple of times during the course of the evening, how she wished she could dance at least once. Not all the dances were strenuous ones. But she had promised . . .

The second of the two waltzes planned for the evening was after supper. George had danced the first with her mother, who was as light on her feet as she had been when Dora was a girl. Dora had watched rather wistfully until she had spotted those children up in the gallery and distracted herself by going up to them.

Now the guests were instructed to take their partners for the second waltz. Dora, standing with Barbara, whose attention had been taken for a moment by someone on her other side, cooled her face with her fan until it was taken from her hand.

"You are overwarm?" George asked, continuing to ply the fan. "You have been exerting yourself too much?"

"I have not exerted myself at all," she assured him. "But is it not the loveliest ball you have ever attended, George? And do feel free to lie."

"Ah, but I can speak only the truth," he said. "It is by far the loveliest ball I have ever attended, perhaps because the loveliest lady I have ever known is here."

"I will not ask who she is," she said. "I might be mortified by your answer."

"But I can speak only the truth, remember," he said. "She is you."

She laughed and his smile deepened. It had surprised and delighted her since their wedding to discover that they could occasionally exchange silly banter and share laughter.

"I am speaking the truth," he assured her. "I remember your telling me soon after you agreed to marry me at St. George's that you had always dreamed of waltzing at a London ball. We will do it one day, but will our own ball here at Penderris serve the purpose for now? Will you waltz with me?"

Oh. She felt a great surge of yearning. "But I promised a certain tyrant that I would not dance at all."

"The certain tyrant recalls, though, that only strenuous dancing was prohibited," he said. "He also had a word with the orchestra leader after supper and specifically asked for a slower, more sedate version of the waltz than the one that was played earlier." He looked deeply into her eyes. "Will you waltz with me, Dora?"

She took her fan from his hand and closed it. "It would make the evening perfect," she said.

He offered his arm, and she placed her hand on his cuff.

She had waltzed once, at a local assembly in Inglebrook, with a gentleman farmer who must have practiced the steps while prancing away from a frisky bull. It had not been a particularly enjoyable experience, though she had always felt that it could be. It was surely the most romantic dance ever invented—when danced with the right partner.

She was sure she had the right partner tonight.

He set a hand at the back of her waist and took her hand in a warm clasp. She rested her other hand on his shoulder—so warm and firm and dependable. She had time only to notice a few of the other couples who had taken the floor about them—her mother with Sir Everard, Ann and James, Philippa and Julian. And then the music began.

Any fear she might have had that she would not know the steps well enough was soon dispelled. They moved about the ballroom as though one, and it felt, Dora thought, like being right inside the music and creating it with one's whole body instead of just with one's fingers upon a keyboard. It felt like a creation of all the senses instead of just sound. There were the crystal chandeliers and the candlelight to see overhead and the flowers and greenery below. There were the perfumes of the plants and of various colognes—and even of coffee. There were the sounds of music and feet moving rhythmically on the floor and voices and laughter. There was the aftertaste of wine and cake. And there was the feel of an evening coat beneath her one hand, of a larger hand in her other, of body heat. There were people enjoying themselves. And nothing was static, as nothing ever was with music—or life. Everything swirled about her with light and color, and she swirled in its midst.

All was life and joy.

But there was the one constant at the center of it

all—the man who held her and waltzed with her. Sturdy and elegant, stoic and kind, aristocratic and very human, complex and vulnerable—her companion and friend, her husband, her lover. Creating the music of life with her.

It was strange how such an uplift of euphoria could follow so closely upon life-threatening terror. The two extremes of life. Or perhaps not so strange.

She remembered his saying that he had carried her up to the house from partway down that rock face. The reality of that fact had not impressed itself fully upon her consciousness until now. He had *carried* her.

But thought drifted away as they waltzed and only sensation remained.

She felt a trifle bereft when the music finally drew to a close. But George held her a little longer while the other dancers moved off the floor.

"I would like you to go up to bed now," he said. "Will you? I will make your excuses, and everyone will understand. There is to be one more set, I believe. And then there will be all the bustle of everyone's leaving."

She was suddenly weary and nodded.

"Come," he said. "I will escort you up."

He left her outside her dressing room, having given instructions downstairs that Maisie was to be sent up without delay. He took both her hands in his and kissed the backs of them.

"Good night, Dora," he said, and for a brief moment she thought she saw something unguarded in his eyes—some unhappiness, some deep-seated suffering. But the light was dim and she might have been mistaken. He had not brought a branch of candles up with them. There were only the candles flickering in the wall sconces.

He turned away and strode back along the corridor.

We will talk, he had said earlier. But she wondered if they ever would.

George was glad he had persuaded Dora to go to bed. He had never hosted a grand ball, though of course this was a country affair and therefore not quite the squeeze he might have expected in London. Nevertheless, he knew something about all the chaos of the ending of a ball, when people suddenly wished to talk with one another as though they had not had a chance to do so all evening, and when carriages jostled for position at the door and then, when successful, had to wait for their owners to take a protracted leave of their hosts and every friend and acquaintance they had ever had. Even when the final carriage had disappeared along the driveway, there were still the houseguests, who wished to talk about how wonderful the evening had been before going off to bed.

Well over an hour had passed since the ending of the ball before George let himself quietly into his dressing room so as not to wake Dora in the adjoining bedchamber. But, just as had happened earlier, like déjà vu, he could hear soft music coming from the sitting room.

Why had he expected that she would be asleep, exhausted as she must be?

He undressed without the assistance of his valet, whom he had instructed to go to bed, and donned a nightshirt and dressing gown before letting himself into the sitting room.

She stopped playing and looked up at him with a smile. She too was dressed for bed. Her hair was loose and had been brushed to a shine. She looked very weary.

"I take it," she said, "no one left early."

"No one even left late," he said. "Everyone left *very* late. A sign of the great success of your ball. It will be talked about for a decade."

"We must entertain more often," she said, "even if not always on such a large scale."

"We must," he agreed, walking closer to her. "But not tomorrow, if you do not mind, Dora, or the day after. You could not sleep?"

She shook her head. "I was afraid to try."

"Afraid of nightmares?"

She turned on the stool so that her knees touched his own. She nodded, and he rested one hand against the top of her head and smoothed it over her hair.

"There were only maybe two more steps between me and a vast emptiness," she said. "And I knew that nothing was going to change his mind. Nothing I said, nothing you said."

They were both silent for a while until she leaned forward to wrap her arms about his waist and bury her face against his chest. And she wept with great heaving sobs.

He held her, his eyes shut tight, and wondered what the insanity would have felt like afterward if . . .

She wept until the front of his dressing gown and the nightshirt beneath it were soggy, and then she raised her face to his so that he could dry it with his handkerchief. She took it from his hand and blew her nose.

"I want to go there tomorrow," she told him, setting

the handkerchief down on the bench behind her. "I want to walk along the headland path, and I want to go down onto the beach. This is my home, and if I do not do it tomorrow, I never will. Come with me?"

He was horrified.

"Of course." And it struck him, even as his knees felt weak beneath him, that she was quite right—and incredibly brave. "But it is very late and we must sleep. I will hold you against the nightmares, Dora. I will not let anyone or anything harm you." Foolish words in light of his utter helplessness this afternoon. One could not always protect what was one's own. "We will talk, I assure you, but not tonight." He hesitated a moment. "Allow me to show you something tonight, though."

She got to her feet and set her hand in his. He took her into their bedchamber and opened the top drawer of the rarely used bureau there. He took out an object wrapped in a soft cloth and unwrapped it. He picked up the nearest candle and held it aloft while he handed her the framed painting.

"It was originally a sketch that Ann made at a picnic one day," he said. "I asked for it, and she offered to make a proper oil portrait out of it. She made it a little bigger than a miniature. It is a good likeness."

She gazed at it for a long time. "Brendan?"

"My son, yes," he said. "I loved him."

She lifted her eyes to his. "Of course you did," she said. "He was your son."

He could see from her eyes that she knew the truth. But she spoke the truth too. Brendan was his son.

"Did you keep it displayed," she asked him, "before you married me?"

"No." He shook his head. "It is not for the gallery, though it will probably end up there eventually. It is not for the sight of any servant who steps in here. It is for my eyes alone. And now yours."

"Thank you," she said softly.

He wrapped the portrait carefully and put it away.

"Come and sleep," he said.

"Yes."

21

*D*ora woke up to the sound of rain lashing against the window. It was full daylight. George was sitting at the bureau in his shirtsleeves, writing. Amazingly, she had slept deeply and apparently dreamlessly.

She turned quietly onto her side and gazed at him. He did not usually write his letters up here. Indeed, she had never before seen the bureau actually being put to use. But she guessed that he had not wanted to leave her to awaken alone. He dipped his quill pen in the inkpot and continued to write, his head bent over his work.

Her eyes strayed to the top drawer, and she felt tears prick them though she blinked firmly. She had been enough of a watering pot yesterday. There would be no more of that today.

There had been such tenderness in his hands as he had folded back the linen that covered the picture, and such tenderness in his eyes as he had looked briefly at the painting before handing it to her. And tenderness had been in his voice when he spoke. *My son, yes. I loved him.*

The boy must have been about fourteen or fifteen when the sketch was made and then painted in oils, a plain-faced, plumpish boy, his fair hair somewhat tousled by the outdoors, the shy suggestion of a smile lending him both vulnerability and charm. He looked as unlike George as it was possible for a boy to be.

It is a good likeness.

I loved him.

It is for my eyes only. And now yours.

There was no family portrait in the gallery. But there was this, a very private, prized possession. A portrait of a boy who had not been his own flesh.

My son, yes.

She must have made some sound. Or perhaps he was just keeping an eye on her every few minutes. He turned his head and then smiled and—oh, she loved him.

"Good morning," he said softly.

"Good morning." She had thought yesterday only of herself, of the fact that she might have died. This morning she thought of him. What would it have been like for him now, at this moment, if she *had* died? She did not believe he felt any great romantic passion for her, but she did know he was dearly fond of her and content with his marriage.

Ah, Dora. My belovèd. My only belovèd.

Had she really heard those words? Or had it been part of some dream into which she had sunk when she lost consciousness?

"No nightmares?" he asked.

"None," she said. "You?"

But she knew the answer even before he shook his

head. He had not slept at all. There were dark smudges beneath his eyes, and the creases that extended from his nostrils past his mouth to his chin were more pronounced than usual. There was little color in his face.

"There was a letter from Imogen this morning addressed to both of us," he said, "and one for you from your sister." He tapped an unopened letter on the surface beside him.

"What does Imogen have to say?" she asked.

"You must read it for yourself," he said, "but I will play spoiler and tell you her main item of news. We Survivors are all being admirably prolific in ensuring the survival of the human race."

"She is with child?" Dora sat up abruptly and threw back the bedcovers. "I thought she was barren."

"So did she," he said. "Apparently you were both wrong."

"Oh, goodness." She began counting on her fingers. "Agnes, Imogen, Chloe, Sophia, Samantha. Me."

"One wonders, does one not," he said, "what is wrong with Hugo? I shall have to write and ask him. Though they do have young Melody."

"Imogen and Percy must be ecstatic. Oh, I must write. It is to them you are writing?" Dora crossed the room barefoot to look briefly over his shoulder—he was writing to them—and to pick up Agnes's letter. It felt fatter than usual. But that, she soon discovered, was because there was another letter folded within it addressed to their mother. It was the first of its kind, Dora was almost sure, though she remembered Agnes's saying she would inform her mother when the baby was born. She looked quickly at her own letter. But Agnes had not delivered early. She was still feeling large and ungainly and breathless and generally cross whenever Flavian patted her largeness and looked pleased with himself. She was also feeling excited and a bit apprehensive, and since she could not steal Dora herself, then she was going to try to steal their mother away from Penderris instead. She hoped Dora would not mind too terribly much, and she hoped her mother would be willing to come.

"I must have buried memories from early childhood," she had written. "Although I cannot bring any specific details to mind, I have a general feeling of safety and calm and comfort whenever I think of our mother. Was she like that, Dora? Or is it just you I am remembering?"

"Agnes has written to Mother," Dora said, holding up the folded letter. "She wants her to go to Candlebury Abbey for her confinement."

"Oh, she will go," George said. "But you will miss her."

"Yes," she agreed. "But they intended returning home within the next week anyway. They have been happy here, I believe, but they have their own lives, as we all do."

"There will be no walk today," he said, nodding toward the window. "It is a good thing Philippa and Julian are to stay longer. The roads will be muddy. It is to be hoped our other guests will be able to get safely home."

It was still raining heavily, and blowing too, judging by the rattle of the window. It was a reminder that autumn was upon them and that winter was not far off.

"Perhaps it will ease up later," she said. She still desperately wanted to take that walk she has spoken of last night, and the sooner the better, before she lost her nerve. For the very thought of it made her knees turn weak and her heart start thumping. Then she caught sight of the clock on the mantelpiece. She had forgotten about those overnight guests. "I must get dressed and go downstairs. Whatever will everyone think of me?"

"What your husband thinks," he said, "is that you look rather delicious."

She shook her head at him and clucked her tongue as she made her way to her dressing room.

The rain eased after luncheon and then stopped. But only just. Dark clouds hung low and the wind still blew in gusts. It was, in fact, a thoroughly unpleasant afternoon, cold and damp and cheerless and best spent indoors. Nevertheless, a group of people left the warmth and shelter of Penderris Hall for the outdoors early in the afternoon, all of them bundled up against the chill as though it were January already. George and Dora led the way, and then came Sir Everard and Lady Havell, Philippa and Julian, and Ann and James Cox-Hampton. All of them had been assured that they must not feel obliged to come, especially the Cox-Hamptons, who had merely called to inquire into Dora's health. All had come anyway, as grim and purposeful as the weather itself.

They might, George thought, have waited for a more auspicious day on which to expose themselves to the cliffs and the beach, but then this outing was not about pleasure. Quite the contrary. Dora had hovered close to the south-facing windows all morning when she was not seeing overnight guests on their way, fretting over the rain, imagining it had stopped long before it actually did, and considering going out even if it did not stop.

"What are boots and rain capes for, after all," she had asked at one point of no one in particular, "if one never goes outside in the rain?"

No one had been able to think of a decent answer. Or, if anyone had, no one had said what it was.

Dora had wanted to come out—or needed to, rather—and so all of them had come. She was, George thought, that precious to everyone. She had almost been murdered yesterday, and no one was willing to leave her far out of their sight today. Everyone was ready to pamper her every wish.

They strode first along the driveway Ann and James had driven over half an hour or so ago, their feet crunching on wet gravel. It seemed safe enough, as though they were all on a stroll to the village. The wind buffeted them from behind, though it would cut into them as though to rob them of breath as soon as they turned in the opposite direction. And turn they would, for they were not going to the village, of course. Dora was retracing the route she had taken yesterday. Before they reached the park gates they veered off to their right, toward the cliffs, and then turned right again to walk along the path that ran roughly parallel to the edge for a few miles until it descended a gentle slope to provide an easy access to the beach a couple of miles or so west of the house.

They would not walk that far, though.

George drew Dora's arm firmly through his own and clamped it to his side. He held her hand with his free one. Julian moved up on her other side while Sir Everard offered his free arm to Philippa. Julian would have taken Dora's other arm, but she would have none of it.

"Philippa needs your arm," she told him, "and Sir Everard does not need two strings to his bow. It might make him conceited."

Even now she could make a joke that set them all to laughing, though none of them, George guessed, were feeling very amused. Yesterday's events were still much too raw in all their minds. Julian and Havell had been out here with him yesterday afternoon, and their wives had doubtless heard all the details. Dora had told Ann, he believed. He had told James. This was madness.

But it was a necessary madness, it seemed. Necessary to his wife. Dora would not even allow him to take the outside of the path, which would have been the gentlemanly thing to do even under ordinary circumstances. She insisted on taking it herself. He was feeling a terror to rival yesterday's even before they reached the part of the path that skirted the fall and the slight promontory beyond it. She stopped when they reached that and drew her arm free of his. She stepped off the path and onto the grass, which must be slippery from all the rain. George clasped his hands behind his back and fought the almost overwhelming urge to grab her and haul her back to safety. Though she was not unsafe. She was nine or ten feet from the edge.

Everyone else had come to a stop on the path and

stood in an unnatural silence. George wondered if they were all holding their breath, as he was doing.

"It is beautiful," Dora said. The wind blew her words back to them. "Nature can seem very malevolent at times, even cruel, but really it is devoid of feeling or intent. It just *is*. And it is always beautiful."

After which strange little speech she turned and stepped back onto the path and took George's arm again. She smiled with what looked like genuine amusement.

"Everyone is so very silent," she said.

"If the wind were not so noisy, Dora," James told her, "you would hear all our knees knocking."

"And our teeth chattering," Julian added.

"Poor Everard is afraid of heights," Dora's mother said.

"I do not suppose," Philippa said, "any one of us is actually in love with heights. It would be foolhardy. But you are quite right, Aunt Dora. This is beautiful—the scenery and the weather. Wild but beautiful."

"And safe," Havell said. "It really is safe. The path is not really muddy, is it? I thought it might be slippery, but there are too many small stones. And it is not as close to the edge as I remembered."

"If you all keep on talking now that you have finally started," Dora said, "you may even convince yourselves that you would rather be out here enjoying the walk than drinking tea by a cozy fire in the house."

"Tea?" James said. "Not brandy?"

"I am going down onto the beach," Dora told them. "But no one must feel obliged to come with me."

Everyone did, of course.

George had used this particular descent all his life. So had everyone else at the house. Why go two miles to the easy access when this was so much closer to the house? All his fellow Survivors with the exception of Ben with his crushed legs had used it regularly. It was steep and needed to be treated with respect, but it had never been considered dangerous. However, Dora had almost died here yesterday, and Eastham actually had. Today they all picked their way down with more than usual caution until they were standing safely on the beach.

It was not difficult to choose a direction, since to their left stones and rocks and pebbles jutted out into the water and offered a rough passage around a bend to the harbor below the village, invisible from where they stood. That was the route by which the body had been taken yesterday. To their right was a beach of golden sand, bordered on one side by tall cliffs and on the other by the sea stretching apparently to infinity. The tide was on the rise, though it was still some distance away. It was rough today. Waves were breaking into foam well before they encountered the beach, and were tumbling in, one after the other, each one climbing a little higher up the sand before subsiding beneath the next. Farther out, the water was slate gray and foam flecked.

They walked along the beach a short way, all of them silent again, but Dora did not stop below the small promontory upon which she had stood yesterday, nor did she look up. None of them did. Some distance away from it she stopped and turned toward the sea, drawing her arm from his as she did so and lifting her face to the wind.

It was a signal for them all to relax.

"I will bet, Julian," Philippa cried suddenly, grabbing up her skirts and breaking into a run, "that I can race you to the water's edge."

Julian looked at the rest of them as she streaked away. "I have to go in pursuit," he said. "She did not say what she was betting."

And he was off after her at an easy lope. She looked back to see if he was following, shrieked when she saw that he was, and flew onward.

"Children, children," James said, laughing and shaking his head.

"I wish, Dora," Ann said, "that I had my sketchbook with me, though it would probably blow away in the wind, would it not? I would love to capture you as you are right at this moment. 'Woman Triumphant,' or something like that but not so pretentious."

"I will not suggest that you try to race me, my love," Havell was saying to his wife. "But shall we?"

They began a sedate stroll toward the incoming sea.

Dora smiled at Ann. "With red, shining nose and windblown hair beneath windblown bonnet?" she said. "'Woman Cold and Windblown'?"

Ann laughed. "I shall sketch you from memory and show you when I see you next," she said. "Or I shall hide it from you and swear I never did it. Some of my efforts are not for sharing."

"But very few," James said loyally.

Dora took George's arm again. "Let's go closer," she said.

"Have some ghosts been blown away?" he asked her when they were out of earshot of anyone else.

She nodded. "Events come and go," she said, "but this remains." She indicated the landscape about them with a sweep of her free arm. "And it is beautiful, George. After my cozy little cottage in its picturesque village, I wondered if I would regret having to live in starker surroundings close to the sea. And when I first came to Penderris, I wondered even more. Everything—the house, the park, this—was on such a vast scale. But I have grown to love it, and I will not allow an . . . event to spoil it all for me. It is an event that is in the past. Though not quite, is it? There will be an inquest?"

"Tomorrow," he said. "In the village. You will not be expected to testify, Dora. Neither will I, I suppose, but I will."

"Sir Everard and Julian will?" she asked.

"Yes," he said. "And your mother wishes to testify."

"Ought I?" she asked.

"No," he said firmly.

"Will Sir Everard admit to having tripped the earl?" she asked.

"I did suggest that he need not do so," he said. "It would be quite credible that the man lost his footing and fell unassisted. But Havell insisted upon telling the truth last night and he will repeat it tomorrow."

"George," she said, "he is a good man."

"Yes."

"But I do not want to be talking about this," she said.

Julian and Philippa were dashing along close to the edge of the water, shrieking and laughing like a couple of children. Julian had just stooped down and scooped up a handful of water and flung it in her direction. Lady

Havell was selecting some seashells and brushing the sand off with her glove before placing them gently in one of Havell's capacious pockets. He was grinning at her. Ann was standing with her back to the water, looking back at the cliffs. She was pointing out something to James, using both her arms in great sweeping gestures.

"Like a party of staid elders, standing here while the children frolic," Dora murmured. And then a little louder, "I am not ready to be a staid elder yet."

She kicked off one of her shoes, used his shoulder for balance while she pulled off her silk stocking, and then moved to the other foot.

"What exactly do you have planned?" he asked her, though actually it was rather obvious.

But she only laughed, gathered up her skirts with both hands, and dashed the few remaining feet to the water. George, torn between amusement and dismay—but he was not a staid elder either, was he?—went after her.

She splashed into the water until it was above her ankles. That was all well and good since she was holding her skirts up closer to her knees, but did she not know anything about the nature of waves, especially when the tide was incoming and especially on a rough day? Apparently not. A wave broke over her knees and splashed her to the chin. She gasped and laughed with what sounded like sheer delight.

"Oh, goodness," she said, sounding again for a moment like the spinster music teacher she had been, "it is cold."

"I am not sure you are telling me anything I had not already guessed," he said, glancing down ruefully at his boots and then wading in after her—only ankle deep, it was true, but there were other waves heading relentlessly their way. "You are going to lose your footing if you are not very careful. You are mad."

He looked at her and laughed just as foam and water broke over her upheld hems again and over the tops of his boots.

"I am not," she protested. "I am *alive. You* are alive."

She looked at him with eager, sparkling eyes. Her cheeks were shining red. So was her nose. The brim of her bonnet was flapping out of shape in the wind. Tangled tendrils of dark hair were blowing about her face and down her neck. The hems of her dress and cloak were dark with wetness and the rest of her had not fared much better. He had never seen her more vibrant or beautiful, George thought as he noticed a particularly strong wave rise beyond her. He snatched her up into his arms, but the wave broke over them both, soaking them from the waist down and splashing their faces and making them both gasp with the chill of it. For a moment he staggered, but he managed to regain his footing.

"Alive, yes, and mad too," he said, laughing and tempting fate by twirling about with her while she clung to his neck and—giggled.

"Oh." She shrieked as another wave attacked them and he beat a hasty retreat to the shore.

But he did not immediately set her down on her feet. He gazed into her face, and she gazed back.

"It is good to feel youthful again," he said, "and alive."

"And cold and wet and lacking all dignity," she said, smiling fondly at him.

He could almost see his reflection in the tip of her nose.

He set her down on her feet and noticed that Ann and James were no longer gazing back at the cliffs and the Havells were no longer picking shells. Julian and Philippa were standing a short distance away, hand in hand. All of them were staring at him and Dora.

"Yes, we are mad," George said in his best ducal tone, "and wet."

"And alive," Dora said, bending to pick up her shoes and stockings. "Most of all, we are alive. And cold. Whose foolish suggestion was it that we come outside this afternoon?"

"When we could be drinking . . . tea in the drawing room," James said mournfully.

Dora smiled dazzlingly at him.

Dora did not attend the inquest at the village inn the following morning. However, she had sat down the evening before and written a brief statement of what had happened, both at Penderris and at her wedding. She had omitted some details of what the Earl of Eastham had said to her, of course, but she had included enough to leave no doubt in anyone's mind that he had intended to kill her and her unborn child in revenge for what he imagined had happened to his sister, the first Duchess of Stanbrook, when she had thrown herself over the cliff.

Philippa did not go either since she had nothing to add to what Dora's mother would say regarding their meeting with the earl in the village and really did not want to go. She remained at Penderris with Dora and

Belinda. Dora's mother did not want to go either, of course, but she was determined to make it clear to all that her daughter's meeting with the earl had been entirely at his suggestion.

It was an event, Dora told herself, just as the scene out on the cliffs had been. It was an event that would soon be in the past, never to be forgotten but to be put firmly aside. She would not allow the Earl of Eastham to exert any power over her, even from the grave. Perhaps in time she would even be able to find it within herself to pity him.

But not yet.

The carriage returned from the village soon after noon. The inn had apparently been bursting at the seams with the interested and curious—Julian's words. The earl's death had been ruled an act of justified defense of the life of his stepdaughter, the Duchess of Stanbrook, by Sir Everard Havell.

His body, Julian explained, was to be taken back to his home in Derbyshire for burial. A cousin of his would succeed him to the title. And there was an end of the matter.

An end of the matter.

Dora looked across the room at George, who was looking gravely back at her.

An end of something, yes, but not of everything.

We will talk, he had told her, but she wondered if they ever would.

22

Sir Everard and Lady Havell left after breakfast the following morning, bound for Candlebury Abbey in Sussex.

"I only hope we get there in time," Dora's mother said as the two of them strolled a little way along the terrace while the bags were being loaded into the carriage. "This is one thing I can do for Agnes after so many years of neglect, and she has asked for me, bless her heart."

"There are a few weeks to go yet before her time," Dora said.

Her mother stopped walking. "I cannot thank you enough, Dora," she said, "for inviting us here and being so kind. I can never ask your forgiveness for the past because it is not forgivable, but—"

"Mama!" Dora caught up her mother's hands in her own. "This is an altogether new phase of all our lives. Let it be new, unshadowed by the past. If the past had been different, everything would be different now. I would not be married to George, and you would not be married to Sir Everard. Either would be a pity, would it not?"

Her mother sighed. "You are generous, Dora," she said. "I do love him, you know. And it is very clear that yours is a love match."

Was it? Dora loved George with all her heart, but did he love her with all his? Sometimes she believed it. Oh, most of the time she did. Surely he did. She smiled.

"I have adored having you here," Dora said. "And Sir Everard too, even apart from the fact that I owe him my life."

A teary-eyed farewell followed before George's traveling carriage was finally bowling along the driveway. Seeing Philippa and Julian and Belinda on their way an hour or so later was altogether more cheerful, for they lived not very far away.

George set a hand on Dora's shoulder as the carriage disappeared from sight. "Alone at last," he said.

She laughed. "Is it not strange, that feeling?" she said. "I can remember when I used to have visitors at the cottage. I enjoyed most of those visits immensely, but when I shut the door behind the last of the callers, there was always a huge feeling of almost guilty relief that I was alone again. This is even better, however, because we are alone together."

He squeezed her shoulder and they went inside.

The house felt very quiet for the rest of the day with all the guests gone and all signs of the ball cleared away. George went off somewhere with his steward, and Dora spent some time with Mrs. Lerner in the morning room and Mr. Humble in the kitchen. She wrote long letters to her father and to Oliver and Louisa. She briefly considered returning a book she had borrowed from

Barbara, but even the prospect of a cheerful conversation with her particular friend was more than she could cope with today. She wanted peace.

George found her later in the music room, playing the harp. She spread her hands over the strings to stop their vibrations and smiled at him.

"It will always be the most wonderful gift ever," she said.

His eyes smiled. The rest of his face did not. It looked austere, she thought, thinner and paler than it had looked even just a few days ago. If she were meeting him now for the first time, she would be far more awed than she had been last year.

"Summer is playing us a swan song," he said. "It is really quite warm outside. Would you care to sit in the flower garden?"

She stood the harp upright and got to her feet. He stood too and looked at her for a few moments before offering his arm and leading her outside. They sat on the wooden seat beneath the window of the morning room in the small flower garden that was her favorite part of the cultivated park. It was always sheltered from the wind and it had a special rural appeal because it was out of sight of the headland and the sea. Multicolored daisies grew in the stone urn that stood at the center of the plot. Late in the year though it was getting to be, there were still chrysanthemums about them and asters and snapdragons among other late-blooming flowers.

"But never a weed," she said aloud. "I have never been able to find a single one."

"It would be more than a gardener's job would be

worth," he said. "He would be cast into outer darkness, without notice and without a reference."

She laughed, and they subsided into a silence that must have lasted for several minutes before he broke it.

"I was the greenest of boys," he said at last, "when my father summoned me home from my regiment and expected me to sell out only a few months after he had purchased my commission. It did not occur to me to fight him though I was bitterly disappointed. I was also grief-stricken to learn that he was dying and overwhelmed at what lay ahead for myself. Why he got it into his head that I should marry before he died when I was only seventeen years old, I do not know. I do know that my brother and he were always at loggerheads over something or other. They were too similar in nature, perhaps. My father wanted to make sure I would get to my duty early, I suppose, and produce an heir so that my brother and his descendants would be safely distanced from the succession. However it was, I did not fight him on that issue either. I was young, but I had a growing boy's appetites. When I saw Miriam for the first time, I could not believe my good fortune, even though I was also consumed with embarrassment, for I was being forced to make her an offer in the presence of both our fathers. She was extraordinarily beautiful and remained so all the rest of her life."

He stopped talking as abruptly as he had started. He was sitting, apparently relaxed, on the seat beside Dora, but he was turned very slightly away from her.

"I was hideously nervous on our wedding night," he said. "But I need not have worried. She refused me admittance to her room. I did not actually try the door, but she told me the next day that she had locked it. She also told me it would remain locked against me for the rest of our lives. I have no idea if it did. I never put the matter to the test."

Dora turned her head sharply to stare at his profile. She could feel her pulse drumming in her ears and her temples. Did that mean . . . ?

"She also told me," he said, "that she was passionately in love with someone else, that she always would be, that she was with child by him, and that her father had married her to me with instructions to be very sure to have marital relations with me at the earliest possible moment so that the child would appear to be mine. She even told me, when I asked, who the father was. I suppose he told you?"

"Yes." Dora was almost surprised to hear her own voice sounding normal.

"She defied me to turn her out," he said, "to refuse to acknowledge the baby as mine, especially if it should turn out to be a boy. It was apparent that she utterly despised me, an impression she gave for the rest of her life. She was three years older than I. I must have seemed like a gangling boy to her, especially when her lover was ten years older."

Dora lifted one hand to set against his back, closed it in on itself, and returned it to her lap.

"I have been inclined to condemn myself as spineless," he said. "But really I was just young. My father died three weeks after my wedding, and while he still lived he was in no condition to share my burden and give advice. Perhaps I would not have consulted him anyway. I was too ashamed. I said nothing to anyone. I believe that for a few months I was full of inward bravado and the determination not to remain a victim of such deceit. But when the baby was born—a son—and I saw him for the first time, I saw that he was puny and ugly and crying and my mind hated him while my heart felt his helplessness and his innocence. I was eighteen. I had been dazzled at my first sight of Miriam. But I fell in love at my first sight of her son."

He spread his hands before him, closed them into fists, and relaxed them.

"I do not know what Miriam hoped for," he said. "That I would accept the child as my own so that she could remain respectable and her son would be heir to a dukedom? Or that I would repudiate him so that she would be irrevocably ruined and beyond the power of Eastham, her father, and could be set up somewhere in a cozy love nest by Meikle, her half brother? She never said which she would have preferred, and I did not ask. Brendan was my son from the moment I saw him. Though I was probably not motivated entirely by love. I probably felt a certain satisfaction in keeping Miriam from the other alternative, which was obviously what Meikle hoped for."

He examined his palms for a few moments.

"I was a mere boy," he said. "Such a green boy. She doted on Brendan and kept him from me as much as she could. She used to go off to visit her father for weeks at a time, and I did not forbid it. Meikle used to come here to visit her—and it was years and years before I had backbone enough to show him the door and tell him never to return. I like to believe I would have matured far faster than I did if my father had lived and my life had continued as it was. But life is as it is. We never know what twists and turns it will take or what hand we will be dealt. It is what we do with the unexpected and with that hand that shows our mettle. I did not lose my virginity until I was twenty-five. Pardon me, I should not mention this, I suppose. But even then I felt guilty because I was married and had vowed to be faithful. I may not have lost it even then if Miriam had not told me she was with child again. She miscarried after three months. I was a cuckold and a weakling, Dora, and ultimately, an adulterer."

This time she did set a hand on his back. He was leaning slightly forward, his arms draped over his thighs, his hands hanging between them. His head was lowered.

"I was *twenty-five*," he said.

"George." She circled her hand over his back and patted it.

"Whenever I felt rage against the two of them and felt I must at last *say* something and *do* something," he said, "I thought of Brendan and what any scandal would do to him. He was not an attractive child. He was overweight and petulant. Miriam was overprotective of him. She always fancied he was of a delicate constitution and would not allow him to mingle with any of the neighborhood children or do anything she deemed dangerous or anything at all with me. She gave in to his tantrums and gave him whatever he wanted. The servants disliked him. So did the neighbors. Miriam loved him. So did I. It was perhaps the only thing we ever had in common. And she hated me for it."

Dora patted his back again.

"Self-pity," he murmured. "I have always fought against it. It is not an admirable trait. She would not allow me to send him to school when he was old enough, and she fought against the hiring of a tutor. It was one thing over which I did assert myself, though. I did not want my son to grow up both ignorant and detestable. I chose the man with care. And then one day, when Brendan was twelve, I caught a look on his face when he heard that I was about to go to London for a month or so. He looked—wistful. I asked if he would like to go with me. He had never particularly liked me, perhaps because I would never take notice of his sulks, but he brightened when I asked him that. And he said yes before sneering and adding that of course I would not take him. I had to fight Miriam over it, but he was legally my son and she could not stop me. We were in London for three weeks, my boy and I, and they were three of the most precious weeks of my life. Of his too, I believe. He blossomed before my eyes, and we saw everything there was to be seen. Only once did he try sulking and having a tantrum. I observed that he was being a prize ass, and we looked at each other and both—laughed."

He paused to smile and then sigh.

"He was my son indeed after that," he said. "Oh, I will not say that life changed and became suddenly perfect. It did not, and Brendan often returned to his old self, especially in his mother's presence. But we did things together. We went fishing and shooting targets.

We went riding. He had never been allowed to ride before then for fear he would fall and kill himself. He lost some of his weight and his sulky looks. I took him over to my brother's a number of times and he and Julian established something of a friendship, certainly more than I had seen Brendan establish with any other boy. I had great hopes for his future."

He inhaled, lifted his head, and looked around him as though he had forgotten where he was.

"And all that," he said, "was the good part of my married life, Dora." He turned his head to look over his shoulder at her. "Perhaps you can see why I have kept it all to myself until now. I have never told even my fellow Survivors, all of whom have bared their souls to me and one another. I have kept it to myself, however, only partly because it reflects badly upon me. That does not matter *that* much." He snapped two fingers together. "I have kept it to myself out of respect for my dead son. He was *my son,* and no one knew differently except Miriam and her father and her half brother and me. Now I am the only one left and I have told you. I did not intend to do even that, as you are well aware. Brendan must live in memory as my son. But I owe you all of myself, past, present, and future. I would trust you with my life. I can trust you with my son's memory."

Dora blinked and bit her upper lip.

And all that was the good part of my married life.

What, then, was the bad part?

"Thank you," she said. There seemed nothing else to say.

He looked up at the sky. The afternoon was growing

late, and the air was cooler. But neither made a move to go back indoors.

"Meikle came for a visit the year Brendan turned seventeen," he said. "His father was still alive at the time so he had not yet inherited the Eastham title. And I had not yet forbidden him the house, though I had made it clear for the previous few years that he was unwelcome here. He liked to spend time with Brendan, but Brendan did not particularly enjoy his company. I do not know why. Actually, I do. I cannot remember the context, but I do recall Brendan's saying to me in clear resentment one day when he was fifteen or so, '*sometimes he acts as if he is my father.*'" On this occasion, Miriam wanted to go back home with Meikle for a while, and she wanted Brendan to go with them. He refused and she got upset. Brendan dug his heels in. Meikle tried to wheedle and persuade, and when that failed, he lost his temper and told Brendan everything. The full truth. I was away from the house at the time."

Dora closed her eyes and clenched her hands in her lap. There was a silence that seemed to go on forever. But he broke it eventually.

"I came home," he said, "to find Miriam distraught, Brendan locked inside his room and refusing to come out, and Meikle roaring with rage against me for corrupting his son and turning him against his mother and father. I soon understood what had happened. That was when I told him he had half an hour to leave Penderris land and never return. Interestingly enough—sometimes I forget—Miriam was shrieking the same thing at him. She was beside herself."

Dora noticed that her knuckles were white and uncurled her fingers.

"The damage was done, of course," he said, "and there was no mending it. I finally got inside Brendan's room, but I could not persuade him to accept that he was my son in every way that mattered, and that I loved him. All he would say, in a horribly flat sort of voice, was that he was his mother's bastard, that if he ever set eyes upon his *father* again, he would kill him, and that I was not his father and he would never be the Duke of Stanbrook after me even if he had to kill himself to prevent it. He would not look at me. All I could do over and over again was tell him I loved him. Love has never felt more inadequate. The next day he came to me, and he looked me in the eye and told me that if I loved him, as I claimed to do, I would purchase a military commission for him with a regiment that was active in the Peninsula. I held out against him for two days, but I could not prevail. If I did not do it, he told me, then he would go off and enlist as a private soldier—and I believed him. I did as he asked even though Miriam did not cease weeping over him and raging against me. He went away, Dora, to fight a war against every imaginable enemy a boy could ever have. A young officer who was with him out in Portugal came and told me afterward that he was skilled and brave and daring and happy and well liked by his men and his fellow officers. I cling to that image of him, true or false."

"George—" Dora said. Her chest felt tight with pain. She could scarcely breathe.

"Miriam was inconsolable afterward," he said. "So

was I, but I held to sanity better than she did. She blamed me; she blamed Meikle. He came. I do not know where he stayed, but it was not here. She would not see him. And then one day she could bear it no longer and did what she did. I saw her when I was returning to the house from somewhere. I tried to reach her in time—I never for one moment doubted what she was about to do. But although in all my nightmares since I come close enough almost to touch her, almost to think of the right thing to say to persuade her to step back, in reality I was still some distance away and yelling incoherently into the wind when she threw herself over."

"George," Dora said, wrapping her arms about his waist from behind and resting one cheek against his shoulder blade. "Oh, my dearest."

"After a few years," he said, "I conceived the idea of turning Penderris into a hospital for wounded officers. I thought perhaps that way I could atone somewhat. I felt oppressed by guilt—at how I had mismanaged my life and those of all who had been my own to protect. I blamed myself for two deaths, one of them of the person most dear to me in this world. And the scheme was largely successful. My money was able to purchase the services of an excellent physician and good nurses, and my home was able to provide a spacious, quiet environment for healing. And I was able to give time and patience and empathy and even love to everyone who came here. I received abundantly in return. Six of the patients at that hospital are now the dearest friends anyone could dream of having. And then a short while ago, after Imogen married, I conceived the idea of marrying again, but a real marriage this time. I thought perhaps I could allow myself some contentment and perhaps even real happiness at last. I thought perhaps I could forgive myself."

"Oh, George!" Dora turned her face to bury it against his shoulder.

"I did not ever intend to pull you into the darkness that will never quite leave me," he said. "I am sorry, Dora. I am sorry that I did not take Eastham seriously enough at our wedding to protect you against future harm. I am sorry for the terror to which my carelessness exposed you even though I knew he was lurking in the neighborhood. And I am sorry he told you what he did."

"George," she said, "I am your *wife*. And I *love* you. I needed to know what you have told me. You do not need to push it all deep inside any longer. Perhaps after our baby is born, we can ask Ann to paint a portrait to match the one of Brendan, and they can hang side by side in the gallery—two brothers or a brother and sister. Brendan *was* your son, and no one is now going to snatch that from you."

He moved then, turning to set an arm about her so that her head nestled on his shoulder beneath his chin.

"George," she said after a brief hesitation, "when you came to me out at the cliffs and held me and I fainted, did you say something to me?"

His brow furrowed in thought. "I believe I said something profound to the effect that I had you and you were safe," he said. "You asked me what had kept me."

Oh, goodness. Had she really?

"After that," she said.

She felt him swallow. "I told you that I loved you," he said.

"'*Ah, Dora. My belovèd. My* only *belovèd,*'" she said. "That is what I thought you said."

"It is an old-fashioned word, is it not?" he said. "A beautiful one, though. Sometimes one feels the need of a word more powerful than love, or at least one more exclusive to the love of one's heart."

"Is that what I am?" she asked.

"Oh, yes," he said. "You are everything I hoped you would be to me, Dora—companion, friend, lover. I can remember telling you that I did not have the passion of romantic love to offer, only a quieter sort of affection. I was wrong about that. The word may sound a bit ostentatious, but it perfectly describes what you are to me—*my* only *belovèd.*"

She nestled her head closer and sighed. "I wish I had thought of it first," she said. "I always have loved you, you know, with far more than a sedate, middle-aged affection. I fell in love with you that first evening at Middlebury Park, when I was awed by you but you were so kind to me. I loved you when you walked home with me a few afternoons later. I loved you all through the year that followed when I did not see you and did not expect to see you ever again, and I loved you when you walked in on me at my cottage and asked if I would be obliging enough to marry you. Except that all that time I had no idea that after marrying you I would come to the point of . . . oh, of brimming over with love. You have made me very happy. It is your greatest gift, you know. You make people happy."

He turned his head to rest his forehead against the top of her head and sighed deeply.

"It is what he said, you know," he told her, "just the day before everything came tumbling down. He was telling me that his uncle and his mother wanted him to go to his grandfather's with them, but that he was determined to remain at Penderris with me. *'You make me happy, Papa,'* he said. Poor Brendan. Ah, poor Brendan."

He did not weep. But for several minutes his breathing was ragged. Dora stayed relaxed and still, her arms about his waist. And finally he lowered his head, found her mouth with his own, and kissed her warmly and gently.

23

or the first time since they had all left Penderris Hall after their long convalescence there, the seven members of the Survivors' Club had agreed to postpone their annual reunion from March until the summer. It was a bit of a pity it had been necessary, George had thought just yesterday. They were having a spell of perfect spring weather for March, with blue skies and gentle breezes. When he had strolled up the country lane behind the house with Dora, they had feasted their eyes upon primroses and daffodils blooming wild in the grass to either side of the lane. They had stopped to admire a few very white lambs frolicking close to their mothers upon long, spindly legs.

Yesterday they had reveled in the springtime all about them, and yesterday they had thought it a pity that this year of all years their friends were not here with them. Today, however, George was unaware of sunshine and spring flowers and lambs and absent friends. Today he was in the library pacing. So was Sir Everard Havell.

At least, he was present in the library. He was not doing much pacing, though he was looking every bit as restless and anxious and helpless as George did.

Dora was into her confinement and had been since sometime last night, when she had woken George, all apologies, to inform him that she had had a series of pains in a row and was rather sure the baby must be coming. Right on time.

The baby was still coming an indeterminate number of hours later. George, if confronted, would not have been able to say whether it was morning or afternoon, night or day. It was actually early afternoon. Dora had been laboring for thirteen hours or perhaps longer if one included the earlier pains she had not been sure of.

Her mother was with her. So was her maid. And so was Dr. Dodd. George had been banished about breakfast time, when his mother-in-law had informed him that he was behaving like a caged bear except that bears did not constantly call down recriminations upon their own heads. But how could he not? His wife was suffering and it was his fault. Moreover, she was suffering quietly when, in her place, he would have been bellowing with agony and wrath.

"George," his mother-in-law had said eventually, a firm hand on his arm, "you really must leave, my dear. You are distressing Dora."

Humiliation upon humiliation. He had left and not tried to return.

He had been pacing ever since. He had no idea if he had had breakfast. He did not even know that lunchtime had come and gone or that it was too early for dinner. After a few hours it had occurred to him that he could pace farther if he opened the door into the music room. But then the idle harp accused him and he returned to the library and shut the door.

"At least," Sir Everard said, "you are not sawing the air with one hand, George, and cursing it blue with a stammer as Flavian was doing back in the autumn when Frances was born."

George stopped his pacing. "You mean I am not the only man who has ever gone through this?" he asked. "Have a brandy."

"No, thank you," Sir Everard said. "As you observed earlier when I offered you one, one would not wish to be a staggering drunk when the announcement is finally made."

"I'll never forgive myself if anything happens to Dora," George said.

"Nothing will happen to her," Havell said, and George stood and stared at him, wishing he could believe it.

Good God, she was forty years old. She had had her birthday last month.

The door opened behind him. Lady Havell stood there, her cheeks flushed, her silver hair slightly disheveled.

"You have a son, George," she said. "A perfect little boy."

"And *Dora*?" George held his breath.

"Perfect too," she said. "My daughter is perfect."

It was all George needed to hear. The rest of her

announcement scarcely registered on his consciousness as he pushed past her and took the stairs two at a time, watched by a footman who let down his guard sufficiently to smirk at His Grace's back.

The maid, Maisie, was in the room. So was the physician, talking. George did not see or hear either of them. He saw only his wife on the bed, her cheeks flushed, her eyes weary, her lips smiling, her hair damp and twisted into a knot on top of her head. She was alive. She was also holding a blanket-bound bundle in the crook of one arm, and it was squawking softly.

It was only then that his mother-in-law's words registered belatedly on his hearing. *You have a son. A perfect little boy.*

He leaned over the bed. The room had fallen silent except for the soft squawking.

"Dora?" He blinked back tears.

"We have a son," she told him. She laughed and bit her lip. "We have a *son,* George."

Only then did he lower his eyes to the bundle. He could see a little hand with five perfect little fingers and fingernails. And he could see the top of a head with a mop of wet, dark hair. He reached for the bundle and lifted it into his arms. It weighed nothing at all, but it was soft and warm and alive. The face was red and wrinkled, the head slightly misshapen. Two unfocused eyes peered out of slitted eyelids. The little mouth was making the sounds he had heard.

For the third time in his life, George fell deeply and irrevocably in love.

"Christopher," he said—the name they had chosen

for a boy. "Marquess of Ailsford. Welcome to the world, little one. Welcome to our family."

And then he was laughing softly—with tears running down his cheeks.

He transferred his gaze to his wife.

"Thank you, Dora," he said. He smiled. "My belovèd."

He leaned over her and kissed her and laid their son back in the crook of her arm. The little fussing noises had ceased.

EPILOGUE

Three years later

*I*t might have been hard to keep an eye upon seventeen children, the oldest of whom was six, as they frolicked on the beach, the sea not far in front of them, climbable rocks and cliffs not far behind, an endless stretch of sand all about. Fortunately, there were seven sets of parents to do the watching, and two of the children—Arthur Emes and Geoffrey Arnott—were too young to do anything but sit, Arthur trying to eat the sand beyond his blanket despite his father's attempts to dissuade him, and Geoffrey banging upon an upturned pail with a spoon and laughing as his father winced horribly at the racket he was making.

They had started as seven wounded warriors, George mused as he gazed fondly about him, six men and one woman who had dubbed themselves, only half in humor, the Survivors' Club. Now, with spouses and children, they were thirty-one. Survivors indeed!

Three years ago, when Christopher was born in March, the annual reunion, usually held in that month, had been postponed to the summer. The summer gathering had been so successful that they had decided to make the change permanent. The fact that they were all producing children at an exuberant rate made sense of the change.

Today, after three days of rain and lowering clouds, the sun was shining, the sky was a clear blue, and it was hot without being oppressive. It was the perfect day for the picnic they had all been hoping for. The picnic fare had been brought the long way around by a few servants. Ben and Samantha had come that way too, since Ben could not walk too far, especially over steep terrain. They had taken their young son Anthony with them, though Gwyn, his older brother, had come with everyone else down the steep descent closer to the house. Even Vincent had come that way, blind though he was.

There was not much Vince would not do. At present he was offering horsey rides on his back to a succession of infants. Eleanor and Max, two of his own, had started it, but they had been followed by Abigail Stockwood, Ralph and Chloe's child, and by Bella and Anna Hayes, Imogen and Percy's twins. Thomas, Vince's eldest, kept him on a more or less straight path, as did Shep, his guide dog. Even as George watched, Vince whinnied and half reared, reaching back with one hand so that he did not quite unseat a shrieking Anna.

Dora and Agnes were unpacking the food hamper

and arranging the feast on a large blanket. Ben and Chloe, whose rounded abdomen proclaimed the fact that by next year there would be another child of the group, were organizing the drinks. Gwyn Harper and Frances Arnott were scrambling among the rocks at the base of the cliffs, watched closely by Samantha, Gwyn's mother. Pamela Emes, aged two, and Rosamond Crabbe, George's daughter, aged one and a half, were running in a straight line toward the water, but Gwen was in hot pursuit despite her permanent limp, so George relaxed. George Hayes, his little namesake, Imogen and Percy's youngest, was toddling along the beach, his hands flapping at his sides, in the hope of outpacing his father in a race for the far horizon. Imogen was explaining something to Bella, who was wailing out a complaint about her twin's ride upon Uncle Vince's back being longer than hers had been.

No scene was ever without its discordant note.

Melody Emes, age four, came striding purposefully along the sand to take up a stand before George and address him in her very precise way.

"Uncle George," she said, frowning, "this is the most best day I can ever remember."

"Well, thank you, Melody," he said. "And we have not even had tea yet."

She moved on to her father, whom she informed that if he would only lift Arthur onto his lap, the baby would not be able to eat sand.

"You are quite right, Mel," Hugo admitted. "But he would be having far less fun."

She plumped down onto the blanket to tickle her brother's stomach and rub her nose across his. Young Arthur grabbed her hair, pulled, and laughed.

"No one ever m-mentioned," Flavian said, "that fatherhood would bring with it the severe risk of d-deafness. Geoffrey, you would be doing your poor papa a great favor if you would cease and desist."

His son turned his head to give him a smile wide enough to display his two lower teeth—his only teeth—and brought the spoon down upon the pail.

"Quite so," Flavian said. "Good boy."

Ralph was tossing a ball to Lucas, his three-year-old, and showing a great deal of patience since the child was catching maybe one in five throws, and even that only when his father practically placed the ball in his hands. Christopher and Eleanor Hunt soon joined the game and tried Ralph's patience even further.

Sophia, Vince's wife, was doing a charcoal sketch, doubtless a caricature, watched by Anthony Harper—with his thumb in his mouth.

After tea they would all go down and splash around in the water before returning to the house, doubtless taking half the beach with them. One hamper—the one that was still closed—was full of towels and a change of clothes for each of the children, even the babies, whose bottoms would no doubt be lowered into the water so that they would not feel neglected. Ben had even expressed his intention of going for a swim, something he could do well and actually did often although his crushed legs would not enable him to walk properly even with the aid of his two canes.

Percy had returned with the runaway George and was tossing him skyward and catching him. Percy's shaggy dog, his almost constant shadow, pranced about them, yipping excitedly.

"He thinks he is one of the children," Percy said. "It would be most embarrassing for him if he ever discovered the truth. Down, Hector."

Percy seldom had a good word to say for the dog but clearly adored him. So did his children.

"Could we have imagined any of this twelve years ago?" Imogen asked from just behind George. She had not spoken loudly but she had caught the attention of a number of them.

It was roughly twelve years ago that the six of them had been brought to Penderris, terribly wounded even if some of the wounds had not been physical.

"Or even nine years ago," Flavian said.

Nine years ago they had all left Penderris to pick up the threads of their lives as best they could.

"It was six years ago," Hugo said, watching his daughter amuse the baby on the blanket beside him, "when I was sitting in a nook beside that fall of rocks back there, minding my own business, when a certain lady in a red cloak decided to climb up and ended by slipping and spraining her lame ankle. Eh, but she weighed a ton when I was carrying her up to the house."

"Gwen is out of earshot and cannot p-protest on her own account," Flavian said. "But when you carried her into the hall, Hugo, you were not even out of breath. She could not have weighed more than a feather."

"She did not sound as if she weighed more than that,

Hugo," Vincent said with a grin, getting to his feet and flexing his back before taking the leash of his dog from Thomas's hand.

"It was the beginning of it all," Hugo said. "I married her and you were all jealous and within two years you had all copied me."

"It was Vince who led the way in reproducing, though, Hugo," Ben said.

"Well, I can't always lead," Hugo said with a chuckle.

Curiously that silenced them all with the memory of Hugo's being brought to Penderris raving and in a straitjacket even though—or probably because—he had no physical injury. The forlorn hope attack he had led in Spain, the one that had left so many of his men dead, had caused madness in him.

No, he did not always have to lead.

"Melody just told me," George said, "that this is the most best day she can ever remember. We can look back far farther than she. Can anyone recall a better day than this?"

"I can think of a few that might match it," Ben said. "But any that were better? No, it would be impossible."

It was at that moment that they all heard a screech from the direction of the water and then loud wails as Gwen scooped up a child and came limping quickly up the beach.

"Rosamond lost her balance and sat down in the water, even though I was holding her hand," Gwen called as she came. "She was just at the edge, but she is soaked anyway, poor thing."

At least, that was what George thought she was saying, though her voice was more than half drowned out by the indignant bawling of his little girl.

He scrambled to his feet and reached out his arms for her while Dora bent over the towel hamper.

Two mornings later, while the adults were still at breakfast, a letter was brought into the room and delivered into George's hand. The butler explained when Dora looked at him in some surprise that Mr. Briggs had thought it ought not to wait with the rest of the day's post for His Grace to peruse at his leisure since it had been personally delivered.

"It is from Julian," George said as he broke the seal. He read quickly and smiled.

"Philippa has been delivered of a healthy boy," he said.

"Oh." Dora's hands flew to her cheeks. "But I promised to be with her."

"The child could not wait for you," he said. "He was born three weeks earlier than the physician had predicted and with less than three hours' warning."

"A boy," Dora said. "After the two girls. Oh, how delightful. They will be very happy. Philippa is well?"

"She is," he said, and looked around the table at all their friends. "The one misgiving I had when I married Dora and we discovered that she was increasing was that for years Julian had been my heir. I thought it might be a bit of a disappointment to him if our child was a boy, as indeed he was. But both he and Philippa assured us that they could not be happier for us, that they were perfectly contented with what they have and what they will be able to leave their own children. Now they have a son."

"And I am quite sure, George," Ben said, "that today the very last thing they are thinking of is that he might one day have been a duke. I have met Julian a few times, and I have the greatest respect for both him and his wife."

"Julian was quite grief-stricken, you know, when word was brought that Brendan had been killed," George said.

All his friends gazed at him in silence, and Dora guessed that he had rarely if ever spoken to them about his first son.

"Has everyone seen the gallery?" she asked.

"I believe everyone has," Vincent said, "except me, of course. But I have listened to the history lesson. George tells it well."

"There are two new portraits there," Dora said. "They were hung a few months ago, on Christopher's third birthday. Shall we show them, George?"

He folded the letter and set it down beside his plate. "Of course," he said. "Has everyone finished eating?"

Half an hour later they were all up in the gallery, even Vincent. And even Ben, walking with his two canes rather than have someone carry up his wheeled chair. They walked along the length of the room, George and Dora leading the way, not stopping at any of the paintings before the last two. They were a matched pair, just a little larger than miniatures, painted in oils, displayed one above the other.

"George's two sons," Dora said. "Brendan and Christopher. Brothers, born thirty years apart, but together contributing to the long history of the family."

"Ann Cox-Hampton, one of our neighbors and friends, painted them," George added. "She is working on one of Rosamond. It will be added when it is complete."

"I did not know there was a portrait of Brendan in existence," Imogen said.

"I kept it for my eyes only until I shared it with Dora," George said. "But his memory is not for me alone. It is for my family, present and future, and all who come here. My living son and daughter will learn all there is to know about their brother."

"I wish I could paint portraits like that," Sophia said, "instead of just caricatures. The one of Christopher is very like, so I suppose the one of Brendan is too. He is fair-haired, Vincent, and just turning from boyhood toward manhood. He looks very sweet and a little uncertain of himself, as boys of that age do. You must have loved him very dearly, George."

"Oh, I did," he assured her. "Correction, I *do*, just as dearly I love my other two children. Not that I am unique in that."

He smiled about him as he wound an arm about Dora's waist and drew her closer to his side.

"Something has occurred to me," he said. "We have

not had any of our late-night sessions this year, the seven of us. Other years we have scarcely missed a night, though we did miss several last year, I seem to recall."

Those informal meetings, from which the spouses had always absented themselves though they had never been asked to, had characterized their reunions. It was during the late evenings, George had explained to Dora, that they discussed their progress—physical, mental, and emotional—their setbacks, their triumphs, all that was deep inside themselves and needed to be shared. It was really quite startling to realize that they had not met privately even once yet this year. She had not even noticed until now.

"Has anyone missed our meetings?" George asked.

"Perhaps," Hugo said, "we do not need them any longer."

"I believe you are right, Hugo," Imogen said. "Perhaps all we need now when we are together is to celebrate friendship and love."

"And life," Ralph added.

"And memories." George's arm tightened about Dora's waist. "We must never forget any of the people and events and emotions that have made us who we are today. Not that it is likely we ever will."

He smiled rather sadly at the upper portrait of Brendan and then a little more happily at the lower one of a chubby-cheeked Christopher as he had still been a year ago before he changed from infancy to little boyhood.

Everyone looked a bit dewy-eyed, Dora thought as she gazed about and then up at George to smile at him.

"I am going to go over to see Philippa and the new baby," she said. "Would anyone care to accompany me?"

An hour later a cavalcade of carriages set off from Penderris Hall to celebrate a new life.

Read on for a sneak peek at the first title
in Mary Balogh's new Westcott Series,

SOMEONE TO LOVE

Available in November 2016
from the Berkley Group.

*D*espite the fact that the late Earl of Riverdale had died without having made a will, Josiah Brumford, his solicitor, had found enough business to discuss with his son and successor to be granted a face-to-face meeting at Westcott House, the earl's London residence on South Audley Street. Having arrived promptly and bowed his way through effusive and obsequious greetings, Brumford proceeded to find a great deal of nothing in particular to impart at tedious length and with pompous verbosity.

Which would have been all very well, Avery Archer, Duke of Netherby, thought a trifle peevishly as he stood before the library window and took snuff in an effort to ward off the urge to yawn, if he had not been compelled to be here too to endure the tedium. If Harry had only been a year older—he had turned twenty just before his father's death—then Avery need not be here at all and Brumford could prose on forever and a day as far as he was concerned. By some bizarre and thoroughly irritating twist of fate, however, His Grace had found himself joint guardian of the new earl with the countess, the boy's mother.

It was all remarkably ridiculous in light of Avery's notoriety for indolence and the studied avoidance of anything that might be dubbed work or the performance of duty. He had a secretary and numerous other servants to deal with all the tedious business of life for him. And there was also the fact that he was a mere eleven years older than his ward. When one heard the word *guardian,* one conjured a mental image of a gravely dignified gray-beard. However, it seemed he had inherited the guard-ianship to which his father had apparently agreed—in writing—at some time in the dim, distant past when the late Riverdale had mistakenly thought himself to be at death's door. By the time he did die a few weeks ago, the old Duke of Netherby had been sleeping peacefully in his own grave for more than two years and was thus unable to be guardian to anyone. Avery might, he sup-posed, have repudiated the obligation since he was not the Netherby mentioned in that letter of agreement, which had never been made into a legal document any-way. He had not done so, however. He did not dislike Harry, and really it had seemed like too much bother to take a stand and refuse such a slight and temporary inconvenience.

It felt more than slight at the moment. Had he known Brumford was such a crashing bore, he might have made the effort.

"There really was no need for Father to make a will," Harry was saying in the sort of rallying tone one used when repeating oneself in order to wrap up a lengthy discussion that had been moving in unending circles. "I have no brothers. My father trusted that I would provide handsomely for my mother and sisters according to his known wishes, and of course I will not fail that trust. I will certainly see to it too that most of the servants and retainers on all my properties are kept on and that those who leave my employ for whatever reason—Father's valet, for example—are properly compensated. And you may rest assured that my mother and Netherby will see that I do not stray from these obligations before I arrive at my majority."

He was standing by the fireplace beside his mother's chair, in a relaxed posture, one shoulder propped against the mantel, his arms crossed over his chest, one booted foot on the hearth. He was a tall lad and a bit gangly, though a few more years would take care of that deficiency. He was fair-haired and blue-eyed with a good-humored countenance that very young ladies no doubt found impossibly handsome. He was also almost indecently rich. He was amiable and charming and had been running wild during the past several months, first while his father was too ill to take much notice and again during the couple of weeks since the funeral. He had probably never lacked for friends, but now they abounded and would have filled a sizable city, perhaps even a small county, to overflowing. Though perhaps *friends* was too kind a word to use for most of them. *Sycophants* and *hangers-on* would be better.

Avery had not tried intervening, and he doubted he would. The boy seemed of sound enough character and would doubtless settle to a bland and blameless adulthood if left to his own devices. And if in the meanwhile he sowed a wide swath of wild oats and squandered a small fortune, well, there were probably oats to spare in the world and there would still be a vast fortune remaining for the bland adulthood. It would take just too much effort to intervene, anyway, and the Duke of Netherby rarely made the effort to do what was inessential or what was not conducive to his personal comfort.

"I do not doubt it for a moment, my lord." Brumford bowed from his chair in a manner that suggested he might as last be conceding that everything he had come to say had been said and perhaps it was time to take his leave. "I trust Brumford, Brumford and Sons may continue to represent your interests, as we did your dear departed father's and his father's before him. I trust His Grace and Her Ladyship will so advise you."

Avery wondered idly what the other Brumford was like and just how many young Brumfords were included in the *"and Sons."* The mind boggled.

Harry pushed himself away from the mantel, looking hopeful. "I see no reason why I would not," he said. "But I will not keep you any longer. You are a very busy man, I daresay."

"I will, however, beg for a few minutes more of your time, Mr. Brumford," the countess said unexpectedly. "But it is a matter that does not concern you, Harry. You may go and join your sisters in the drawing room. They will be eager to hear details of this meeting. Perhaps you would be good enough to remain, Avery."

Harry directed a quick grin Avery's way, and His Grace, opening his snuffbox again before changing his mind and snapping it shut, almost wished that he too were being sent off to report to the countess's two daughters. He must be very bored indeed. Lady Camille Westcott, age twenty-two, was the managing sort, a forthright female who did not suffer fools gladly, though she was handsome enough, it was true. Lady Abigail, at eighteen, was a sweet, smiling, pretty young thing who might or might not possess a personality. To do her justice, Avery had not spent enough time in her company to find out. She was his half sister's favorite cousin and dearest friend in the world, however—her words—and he occasionally heard them talking and giggling together behind closed doors that he was very careful never to open.

Harry, all eager to be gone, bowed to his mother, nodded politely to Brumford, came very close to winking at Avery, and made his escape from the library. Lucky devil. Avery strolled closer to the fireplace, where the countess and Brumford were still seated. What the deuce could be important enough that she had voluntarily prolonged this excruciatingly dreary meeting?

"And how may I be of service to you, my lady?" the solicitor asked.

The countess, Avery noticed, was sitting very upright, her spine arched slightly inward. Were ladies taught to sit that way, as though the backs of chairs had been created merely to be decorative? She was, he estimated, about forty years old. She was also quite perfectly beautiful in a mature, dignified sort of way. She surely could not have been happy with Riverdale—who could?—yet to Avery's knowledge she had never indulged herself with lovers. She was tall, shapely, and blond with no sign yet, as far as he could see, of any gray hairs. She was also one of those rare women who looked striking rather than dowdy in deep mourning.

"There is a girl," she said, "or, rather, a woman. In Bath, I believe. My late husband's . . . daughter."

Avery guessed she had been about to say *bastard,* but had changed her mind for the sake of gentility. He raised both his eyebrows and his quizzing glass.

Brumford for once had been silenced.

"She was at an orphanage there," the countess continued. "I do not know where she is now. She is hardly still there since she must be in her middle twenties. But Riverdale supported her from a very young age and continued to do so until his death. We never discussed the matter. It is altogether probable he did not know I was aware of her existence. I do not know any details, nor have I ever wanted to. I still do not. I assume it was not through you that the support payments were made?"

Brumford's already florid complexion took on a distinctly purplish hue. "It was not, my lady," he assured her. "But might I suggest that since this . . . person is now an adult, you—"

"No," she said, cutting him off. "I am not in need of any suggestion. I have no wish whatsoever to know anything about this woman, even her name. I certainly have no wish for my son to know of her. However, it seems only just that if she has been supported all her life by her . . . father, she be informed of his death if that has not already happened, and be compensated with a final settlement. A handsome one, Mr. Brumford. It would need to be made perfectly clear to her at the same time that there is to be no more—ever, under any circumstances. May I leave the matter in your hands?"

"My lady." Brumford seemed almost to be squirming in his chair. He licked his lips and darted a glance at Avery, of whom—if His Grace was reading him correctly—he stood in considerable awe.

Avery raised his glass all the way to his eye. "Well?" he said. "*May* her ladyship leave the matter in your hands, Brumford? Are you or the other Brumford or one of the sons willing and able to hunt down the bastard daughter, name unknown, of the late earl in order to make her the happiest of orphans by settling a modest fortune upon her?"

"Your Grace." Brumford's chest puffed out. "My lady. It will be a difficult task, but not an insurmountable one, especially for the skilled investigators whose services we engage in the interests of our most valued clients. If the . . . person indeed grew up in Bath, we will identify her. If she is still there, we will find her. If she is no longer there—"

"I believe," Avery said, sounding pained, "her ladyship and I get your meaning. You will report to me when the woman has been found. Is that agreeable to you, Aunt?"

The Countess of Riverdale was not, strictly speaking, his aunt. His stepmother, the duchess, was the late Earl of Riverdale's sister, and thus the countess and all the others were his honorary relatives.

"That will be satisfactory," she said. "Thank you, Avery. When you report to His Grace that you have found her, Mr. Brumford, he will discuss with you what sum is to be settled upon her and what legal papers she will need to sign to confirm that she is no longer a dependent of my late husband's estate."

"That will be all," Avery said as the solicitor drew breath to deliver himself of some doubtless unnecessary and unwanted monologue. "The butler will see you out."

He took snuff and made a mental note that the blend needed to be one half-note less floral in order to be perfect.

"That was remarkably generous of you," he said when he was alone with the countess.

"Not really, Avery," she said, getting to her feet. "I am being generous, if you will, with Harry's money. But he will neither know of the matter nor miss the sum. And taking action now will ensure that he never discover the existence of his father's by-blow. It will ensure that Camille and Abigail not discover it either. I care not the snap of my fingers for the woman in Bath. I *do* care for my children. Will you stay for luncheon?"

"I will not impose upon you," he said with a sigh. "I have . . . things to attend to. I am quite sure I must have. Everyone has things to do, or so everyone is in the habit of claiming."

The corners of her mouth lifted slightly. "I really do not blame you, Avery, for being eager to escape," she said. "The man is a mighty bore, is he not? But his request for this meeting saved me from summoning him and you on this other matter. You are released. You may run off and busy yourself with . . . things."

He possessed himself of her hand—white, long-fingered, perfectly manicured—and bowed gracefully over it as he raised it to his lips. "You may safely leave the matter in my hands," he said—or in the hands of his secretary, anyway.

"Thank you," she said. "But you will inform me when it is accomplished?"

"I will," he promised before sauntering from the room and taking his hat and cane from the butler's hands.

The revelation that the countess had a conscience had surprised him. How many ladies in similar circumstances would voluntarily seek out their husbands' bastards in order to shower riches upon them, even if they did convince themselves that they did so in the interests of their own, very legitimate children?